Praise for *77 North*

'Epic action, mind-twisting mystery and relentless fun. The tension ratchets up page by page until it feels like the book is going to explode in your hands' Tim Glister, author of *A Loyal Traitor*

'An absolute masterclass in how to write an action thriller. Every scene oozes adrenaline. You're in for one hell of a ride'
    Robert Scragg, author of *End of the Line*

'Titanically enjoyable and monstrously exciting, *77 North* is an electric blitzkrieg of masterfully written thrills'
    Rob Parker, author of *And Your Enemies Closer*

'John Tyler is back, and *77 North* gives fans of the series everything they want and more! It starts at breakneck pace and keeps it up until the final page. There are car chases, gunfights, exotic locations and enough snow to chill you to the bone. John Tyler is at his best – like Jason Bourne on steroids – only wittier and from Yorkshire! This is D. L. Marshall at his very best'
    Chris McDonald, author of *Roses for the Dead*

'Gritty, witty and explosive – adventure fiction at its absolute best'
    Marion Todd, author of *What They Knew*

'Another relentlessly pulse-pounding John Tyler thriller from D. L. Marshall, this time giving us Tyler's origin story alongside the usual non-stop action, scarily atmospheric settings, another of Marshall's signature locked roo⟨...⟩ ⟨...⟩ts and turns than Tyler's driving' Alex ⟨...⟩

'The end of John T⟨...⟩ ⟨...⟩ing, as ghosts, both literal and figu⟨...⟩ ⟨...⟩vealing how a sharp-tongued green ⟨...⟩ ⟨...⟩icient black ops scalphunter. Riotously thrilling and deftly intelligent, turning the mayhem up to eleven whilst surgically exploring ideas of duty and honour and betrayal and revenge. Paints a mural in blood of the deadly psychic hinterlands in which intelligence agents operate'
    Dominic Nolan, author of *Past Life*

D. L. Marshall was born and raised in Halifax, West Yorkshire. Influenced by the dark industrial architecture, steep wooded valleys, and bleak Pennine moors, he writes thrillers tinged with horror, exploring the impact of geography and isolation. In 2016 he pitched at Bloody Scotland. In 2018 he won a Northern Writers' Award for his thriller *Anthrax Island*.

Also by D. L. Marshall

The John Tyler series

Anthrax Island
Black Run
77 North

77 NORTH
D.L. MARSHALL

CANELO

First published in the United Kingdom in 2023 by

Canelo
Unit 9, 5th Floor
Cargo Works, 1–2 Hatfields
London SE1 9PG
United Kingdom

A CIP catalogue record for this book is available from the British Library.

Print ISBN 978 1 80436 431 4
Ebook ISBN 978 1 80436 432 1

Cover design by The Red Dress

Look for more great books at www.canelo.co

Printed and bound in Great Britain by Clays Ltd, Elcograf S.p.A.

1

Chapter One

The corpse gazed at me from behind the windscreen of an ASBO-green '71 Plymouth 'Cuda.

I knew the car was a rare '71 thanks to the distinctive headlights and grille.

I knew the guy was a corpse because it was me who'd put him in there to die.

He'd spluttered, eyes bulging, all the way through 'Walk Like an Egyptian' on the radio. Three minutes twenty seconds. I'd wanted to switch it off, it seemed disrespectful. Not of him – he was a scumbag who deserved everything he got. But it was disrespectful of the process.

But I couldn't switch off the radio up in the car dealership's mezzanine-level office. I wanted to touch as little as possible. I was a ghost: tread light, leave no trace. If he always had the radio on at this volume and tuned to this station, well then, that's how it'd have to stay.

This meant I'd had to watch his breathing become more laboured, his body slumping lower and lower in the tobacco leather seats all the way through 'Edge of Seventeen' by Stevie Nicks. It's a long song, five and a half minutes. Then *Upbeat '80s*, as the cheesy jingles had constantly reminded me was blaring out, had played 'Welcome to the Jungle' by Guns N' Roses. That's another long song, so rather than sit there watching him gasp like a fish I'd wandered around the showroom.

The radio in the office drowned out his slurred pleading as I peered at the immaculate interiors of old Porsches, Lamborghinis, Ferraris. Most looked like they'd just rolled off the production line. These were cars built to be driven hard, but the perfect seats and low odometers all suggested they'd been owned by rich Americans and mollycoddled in centrally heated garages even in this northern Californian town.

Finally I'd walked back to the lurid green Plymouth by the closed roller shutters, and slid up onto the bonnet of a glorious De Tomaso Pantera next to it.

At last his chest stopped moving during the dying bars of a Tears for Fears song – which was fitting, because while it was Eighties, it was anything but upbeat.

I have some proficiency in this field, and in my experience killing doesn't get easier. Even offing scumbags isn't particularly pleasant, at least not if you're anywhere vaguely this side of normal. Especially sitting, watching, waiting for them to die, their eyes burning right into the back of your skull while Men at Work sing about Vegemite sandwiches. Knowing full well they're thinking, *I'm about to go, this is it, it can't be, surely someone will stop this.* Knowing deep down there's nothing anyone can do about it but still holding out hope to the last twitch.

I *could* have done something about it, I just didn't *want* to. I slid off the bonnet. Now it was done.

The rumble of the idling 7.0 litre Hemi V8 was muted through reams of duct tape securing both tailpipes onto plastic hoses, jammed and taped into the top of the almost-closed passenger window. Clouds wafted as I opened the driver's door. I held my breath as I reached into the stinking interior to unlock the heavily padded handcuffs from the steering wheel.

As I removed them from his wrists, I checked him over. No marks, no worries. I knelt to avoid the worst of the fumes still flooding the car and reached around the back of the seat, releasing the cargo straps holding him in place. The sponges underneath the straps had held his head nicely, preventing him thrashing around and doing himself a mischief.

Thirty seconds later he was untied with not a mark on him, slumped in the seat, door shut, fumes filling the interior again. I had a sudden thought and reached back in to remove his glasses. Pressing his fingers against the lenses for fresh prints, I folded them and placed them on the dash.

I'd read somewhere that suicides always take off their glasses.

By the time he was found there'd be no question that's what it was. Especially when they found the receipts for the hoses in the footwell of his blue Carrera S out front, oil-smudged and ripped to obscure the transaction details. But since the smudged fingerprint was his, it could hardly be considered suss. Likewise the fact he wasn't long since divorced and liked young women, horses, and coke, not necessarily in that order. Plenty of reasons an enterprising detective could find for why he'd topped himself, even before they delved back into his extremely chequered past.

A clattering sound shattered the peace between tracks on the radio. I spun to see movement, an empty Pringles tube rolling across the concrete floor. I traced it back to the door at the side of the showroom. The handle moved again, slowly, all the way down, then just as slowly back up. Even with a key no one could get in, not without a fair bit of force. I'd screwed the door into the frame before sliding the empty Pringles tube over the handle as an early warning system.

I checked my watch: only eight a.m. Customers wouldn't be arriving to browse yet, and an hour ago I'd forced the owner to drop a text to his three employees telling them to take the day off.

Perhaps it was one of them checking up on him.

I opened the car door again and reached into the footwell where I'd left the owner's phone, still unlocked and open on his texts, as if he'd been about to type a message to those left behind but hadn't found the words before passing out. There were no other messages, nothing to suggest anyone was expected. I pocketed his phone and closed the door softly.

The roller shutters were all down over the big glass windows at the front, with their fuses flicked off so we couldn't be disturbed. I wondered if there was another way in that I'd somehow missed.

I jogged across to a staircase, jumping three steps at a time up to the office. There were more windows up here but the blinds were drawn, so I vaulted a desk, landing at the nearest window, sliding against the wall. I moved the blind a crack with my finger. Down below, on the weed-strewn strip of gravel between the back of the

3

building and the high steel fencing, was a man in a dark suit which was far too warm for a day like this. I darted back. An unusual sight round the back of a classic car dealership on an unseasonably sunny Saturday morning, but even more so, the man was crouching, and from his manner and expressions, he wasn't alone.

I peered round again. He gestured beyond the railings. I followed his hand signals and saw another suit pressed into the corner of the DIY warehouse behind. I ducked back, mind racing, forming conclusions in milliseconds.

Suits on a Saturday morning screamed authority. Two round the back suggested more elsewhere. Crouching and hand signals suggested covert. Conclusion: for some reason the law were about to force an entry into a classic car dealership to find me standing here with a dead guy.

Which would be inconvenient.

I dropped to the floor and pulled out my phone, swiping to the camera. Pushing it up like a periscope, I watched the screen as it edged above the window sill and automatically focused on its new view. I tilted it until I could see the railings and there, at the corner of the building opposite, was one of the mysterious men. I zoomed in. He inclined his head slightly, looked like he was talking into a radio. I turned the phone around slowly. I couldn't spot anyone else but did see two distinctly government-issue-looking SUVs pulled up side by side on the path out back. FBI, or one of the worse acronyms?

Time to leave.

I was about to run for the stairs when I had a brainwave. On the wall was a widescreen TV, but on a filing cabinet behind the desk sat a second, smaller TV. I scanned the desk and spotted a remote that matched the brand, and turned it on.

Bingo.

The screen was split between four CCTV cameras, three quadrants showing a different view of the exterior and the last covering the showroom floor and gleaming cars.

Further down the street, at the extent of a camera's view, four more SUVs were pulled up in a row. A group of suited men were standing next to the first car and looked like they were in a heated conversation. The thing that really grabbed my attention was the guys in the parking lot out front, because they weren't wearing suits. These guys were dressed in dark body armour, clutching submachine guns.

Someone wasn't fucking around. There was no way to know if they were here for me, the dead guy, or something else entirely. No matter; a clean getaway had slipped further down my priority list. Now I was only interested in the getaway part.

I brought up the map on my phone, switching to satellite view. Zooming around with my fingers, I quickly oriented myself. I'd studied the layout but it always pays to recap. Directly opposite the loading door, that big steel shutter on the side of the building, was a parking lot. After that was a side alley, then a backstreet behind a row of restaurants and shops that dead-ended not ten metres from where I'd parked my rental car.

I glanced down at the showroom below, and the car nearest that exit. With bulging wheel arches, an exhaust note that sounded like the world was ending, and a spoiler your family could eat around at Christmas, the De Tomaso Pantera was hardly inconspicuous – but it only had to get me a couple of blocks before the goons outside latched on.

I grabbed a stained coffee cup from the desk and placed it in front of the TV, pulled out my phone and dialled a number. The dead guy's phone started vibrating in my pocket. I pulled it out and stuck it upright in the cup.

The car keys in the locker were all handily labelled and in less than a minute I was downstairs and at the shutters flicking up fuses. I leaned into the car, stuck the keys in the ignition and twisted them. Thankfully, the electrics came on. Someone had obviously driven this Eighties girl recently. I looked at my phone, still open on a video call to the dead guy's phone upstairs in the office. Its camera was pointing at the CCTV screen, which meant it was now relaying the CCTV video to me down here. I could see figures had begun to swarm around the main entrance at the other side of the showroom, readying for the breach. One camera pointed along the side of the building; there was no one covering this side exit and the roller shutters yet, but they would. It was time.

I opened the padlock, kicked it away, then pushed a switch on the wall. I was already in the driver's seat and slamming the door when the roller shutter lifted from the floor. I jabbed the starter button: the motor whined, coughed and died. There was a shout outside, a shape moved in the widening gap. I pressed the button again, holding it down for what seemed like ages as the starter spun. Finally, the big V8 hacked up and blasted into life, blowing black shit across an E-type Jag behind.

Legs appeared in the slowly opening shutter and a suit crouched to peer under. I reckoned the door was just over a metre off the ground, so I gave the accelerator a couple of blips then floored it. My calculations were only a smidge off. I winced as the rising door took a stripe of paint off the roof, but then I was out into the Californian sunshine before the guy could pull his weapon. I glanced at my phone. The throng of agents at the front were moving, some round the side, some back to the SUVs. My attention returned to the windscreen. I was into the alley and up into second gear.

Engine screaming through the narrow strip of gravel, I looked through the flashing steel fencing to my right, along the backstreet. Just a few hundred metres and I'd be away, jump out, over a wall, into my rental car before anyone could get close.

Crunch.

It happened in slow motion. First, a shadow fell across the end of the alley, swiftly followed by a long bonnet. It ended with a huge wheel directly in front of me. I was pressing the brakes before I knew what was happening. Then my brain caught up and told me the Mack truck that'd pulled across the alley wasn't going to come off worse than a forty-odd-year-old supercar. As the bonnet began to fold up in front of me and the steering wheel came up fast, it flashed through my mind that they'd obviously left that side exit clear for a reason.

They'd planned it.

Chapter Two

The room was uncomfortably bright. Presumably it was designed that way, but the mild concussion, like a hangover gnawing behind my eyeballs, made it worse. That was probably intentional as well. Bare concrete walls vibrated in the glare of the buzzing strip lights, making me squint, but I forced my eyes open to take in the room.

There wasn't much to see. The cliché of a featureless table, an empty plastic chair behind it facing me, and another underneath my arse. A blank wooden door, most likely locked, was the only way in or out.

I didn't have much time to take any more in before the door opened and a man strode in carrying a paper bag in one hand. He took off a pair of Oakleys and tucked them into an inside pocket of his grey suit.

He looked my age-ish, with fuzzy greying hair that he was keeping hold of at the expense of his waistline; his suit was fighting a rearguard action and slowly losing. He left the door open, leather-soled shoes clicking on the concrete as he walked.

Whatever was in the bag was bulky and heavy; it thudded and tipped as he placed it on the table.

'Who are you then?' I asked.

'That's irrelevant,' he said with a smirk, 'but I know you're the mysterious John Tyler.' He pointed at the zip ties on my wrists. 'I was told you get angry when you're cornered.'

'My name's Kaplan,' I said.

'Sure. George Kaplan. Just like it was Michael Armstrong a couple of weeks ago, and John Ferguson in May.' He took a large penknife from his pocket and placed it on the table next to the bag and papers. 'In March it was Ben McKenna. I'm not a Hitchcock fan by the way.'

'I don't know those people.'

'Lemme see, you've lost some weight in the last few months. Long hair now, but I think we've got the right guy. Forty-three-year-old male? Tick. Wiseass Brit? Tick. Shabby lookin' motherfucker with a bad attitude? Tick, tick. Then, of course, there's this.' He pulled a pistol from the bag. 'A Heckler and Koch VP70, modified to accept a suppressor and able to maintain burst mode without the stock. No professional killer on Earth is stupid enough to carry around this antique piece of shit.'

I leaned back in the chair and grinned. 'I found that in a bin.'

The man flicked the gun across the table. He reached into the bag again, out came a thin cardboard file. He stepped back, opening it, and tossed a piece of paper on the desk. I glanced down. A photo of a badly bloated corpse on golden sand.

'Two years ago, a Scot named David Fraser, ex-Army, washed up on a beach in Brittany, France.'

'The currents there can be murder.'

'Yeah, so can a knife in the chest. Fast forward to a few months ago.' He dropped another photo, this time a fresher corpse in a rock pool. 'Saxon, Rob. Another Brit, ex-special forces, this time sunbathing on his yacht off the coast of Croatia. Fell overboard and drowned.'

'Poor fella.'

'Yeah, thing is, this guy was in your Special Boat Service. I always thought those guys could swim?'

I shrugged and blew out my cheeks.

Another photo dropped on the table.

'McDonald, Mark. Irishman. Overdosed in a brothel in Rio a month back.'

I shook my head. 'Don't do drugs, kids.'

'Strange, none of his buddies knew he was using. And this guy.' Another photo. 'Meryl, Russ. Hanged himself from a wardrobe door in Amsterdam. Pants round his ankles, looks like it was accidental.'

'Next you'll be telling me he wasn't a wanker.'

'Thing is, these guys were all ex-forces before joining a European private military outfit. Cresswell Security. And they worked together for years, would you believe it? Real close-knit team. And now they've all died within months of each other.'

'If coincidences didn't exist there wouldn't be a word for it.'

'And this morning we have a car dealer named Watson, ex-SAS. Retired now, but would you believe Watson also happened to be a member of that very same squad? Gassed himself right while you were browsing for a new sports car.' He stood up straight, dropping the file on the table. 'So quit fuckin' around.'

'You're the one fucking around.' I leaned forward in the chair, wrists straining on the ties. He flinched just slightly.

'You know,' he said, stepping forward to mask the flinching, 'I was told you were a smart guy. Not that smart, eh?'

'Yeah, okay, I'll give you that one. Still smarter than you, though.'

'Oh yeah?' He leaned in close. 'I'm not the one tied to a chair by fuck-knows-who in a basement fuck-knows-where.'

'I know who you are. And where I am.'

He stood back and glared at me.

'I'm not in a basement for a start. You took off your shades when you came in; doubt you'd have walked up or down stairs in them, so we're near the door, at ground level. The door looks wooden but the hinges are hidden and when you opened it I could see it's too thick. It's reinforced steel and there's no handle on the inside. The table and chairs are bolted to the floor. That all adds up to a purpose-built room. That in turn suggests law enforcement, but no, there's no two-way mirror, no recording device, no CCTV. So… it's something else.'

'They said you were a cocky bastard.'

'I can't have been out for long.' I twisted my head to look down at my shoulder. 'Presume my head went through the side window of that poor Pantera. Did you know there were only a couple hundred of those made, and you just killed one?'

'One less rich bastard's mid-life crisis.'

'No accounting for taste. Anyway, it's only a small cut, it didn't bleed a lot. Blood on my cheek is still wet though.' I gave an exaggerated wink with my left eye and felt it sticky. 'So we're what, ten minutes max from the car dealership in San Anselmo. West through San Rafael is all prime real estate, but no, I heard a ship a minute ago

9

when you opened the door. Is it the ferry terminal? Some industrial unit near San Quentin Prison? This place is off the books, for when you don't wanna take people to a Federal facility, but you've got the prison nearby if you need it. I'm guessing this is one of your low-key holding locations for undesirables before they get shipped off to Guantanamo?'

He was just standing there, staring at me. He crossed his arms, so I used it as a signal to continue.

'There's no tell-tale bulge under your well-fitting jacket. That's a nice shirt, and your suit is far too expensive for a regular lawman. That and those black SUVs back at the dealership mean you're a shady acronym of some kind, but the suit's too expensive for an FBI salary. Slightly short on the cuff though, the suit's not tailored, it's from a rack. A very expensive rack. You make good money and dress well, but you're still a government stooge. Sadly, if you were one of the bad guys you'd be paid more. Anyway, like I said, I'm not the one fucking around.'

'You can make smart remarks all day, buddy. Won't change the outcome.'

'Go get the organ grinder or you'll get twice fuck-all from me.'

He sniffed and walked closer, leaning in until his face was inches from mine. 'I'm the organ grinder, and you better shut this attitude down or you'll find out just what kind of place this really is.' The guy's face was set in stone, the creases deepening around his narrowed eyes.

'Now I'm gonna take a wild stab here,' I said. 'And you gotta be honest if I'm right. Those nice Italian shoes are the kind of thing my old CIA buddy Mason wears. And that tweed tie, that's him all over. That, along with the nice suit – I think you're one of his bag-carriers. And that's how I know I'm not talking to the organ grinder. And I can afford to be cocky because whatever this is,' I rolled my head around at the room, 'I don't know if it's supposed to scare me or impress me or something, but Mason and I go way back, we were chasing bad guys across deserts while you were still in an academy somewhere...'

A noise from the doorway cut me off. In walked another man, this one wearing very similar shoes. But his was a nicely tailored suit.

'Mason,' I said, grinning. 'I knew you—'

'Hit him.' The first guy didn't need telling twice. He swung a palm into the side of my head immediately.

With my arms fastened to the chair and the chair bolted to the floor, there was nowhere for me to go. It hurt like hell. When I opened my eyes, Mason was sitting on the other side of the table, arms folded. My ear throbbed.

'Again,' said Mason. 'Hurt him this time.'

I was ready for it but he went low, a fist whipping up below my ribs. There was hardly any power to it but I felt sick, writhing against the ties, breathless. I screwed my eyes up, gritting my teeth. Through the rush of blood I could vaguely hear Mason telling the other guy to leave the room. It was a good thirty seconds or so before the pain subsided enough for me to open my eyes.

Mason narrowed his. 'That's just so you understand we're not buddies any more.'

I was all out of quips so just concentrated on getting my breathing back to normal.

'You're getting sloppy,' he continued.

'I'm retired,' I wheezed, 'and the wrong side of forty, and it *still* took five carloads of your agents.'

'The five carloads of agents were there to bait you into leaving by the side door, thereby stopping millions of dollars of fancy cars getting shot up. It's the fact you did exactly that which means you're sloppy.'

'If I'm that sloppy, why do you need me for a job?'

'Who says I do?'

'You let me kill him.'

'What's that?'

'You were staking the place out. Or tracking me. Maybe both. Either way, you had a team there at the showroom. You knew what I was gonna do, and yet you still let me.'

'No.'

'Yes. You know what that means? It means you want leverage. You need something from me. It means there's an agenda.'

'You already owe me.'

I presumed he was talking about the deal we'd made a couple of years ago on a rainy hillside in Scotland: four million dollars for a vial brimming with a unique strain of bioweapon.

'Look, how was I to know that anthrax was worthless?' A lie. I'd disposed of the real stuff rather than hand it over to anyone, even him.

He waved a hand dismissively. 'I don't give a shit about anthrax. What I do give a shit about is Uncle Sam picking up a hefty tab for your medical bills and having nothing to show for it.'

Arranging my treatment following an assassination attempt which had failed by a whisker, and then helping me stay dead in the eyes of the world, were marks in his favour. But I've always made a point of being a free agent – I'm not a fan of being owned.

'I've repaid you several times over.'

'Not by my accounts.'

'El Salvador? That job in Berlin? Ukraine should have evened it up. You'd have been in serious shit there.'

'And you'd be a long-dead corpse in a car park in Yorkshire if it wasn't for me. I got people asking me questions. It wasn't just money I paid for that anthrax in Scotland, I gave you information.' He wagged a finger, face glowing red. 'The name didn't come easy, so I did not expect his corpse to wash up on a French beach.' He threw his hands in the air. 'Stabbed through the heart and thrown overboard. Very discreet.'

'I didn't do that.'

'And I don't give a shit. I gave you the name, people know I gave you the name, now he's dead. You were careless. And now this? No sooner do you abscond than there's four more dead bodies – that I know of – who were all part of the same team in Afghanistan that killed your brother.'

'I'm sorry, abscond?'

'You've been executing everyone you hold responsible. Did you think no one would notice? And yes, I do mean abscond: you came out of hospital on a short leash. I told you what'd happen if you slipped it.'

'I don't belong to you, or anyone else.'

'Even your Colonel Holderness is still sat in his cosy office in Whitehall, mourning the death of his protégé. You want me to call him up and let him know where his favourite mercenary has really been these last two years?' He saw my face set hard, his voice changed. 'Shit, four dead within a few months, that's not the Tyler I know.'

'We're all products of our environment.'

'You know why you're good at your job? It's because you can do this *and* retain a conscience. Once you lose that...' He shook his head.

'Can we skip to the bit where you tell me what you want? I need to be in Santa Cruz by tea time.'

He swept the pictures out of the way and leaned across the table. 'You can play the tough guy act all you like.'

I stared back at him.

He sighed and leaned back in the chair. 'Saxon, the guy you drowned in Croatia, he was on the payroll, that's why alarms went off. So far, I don't think it's been linked to you or what happened in Afghanistan, but I've got evidence that puts you at the scene of three *accidents* and a *suicide*, and one of those *accidents*,' he made the air-quote fingers, 'was a CIA operative.'

'We both know I'll never be allowed inside a courtroom, so it's up to you what you do with that information.'

He pushed the chair back and stood, hands on hips. 'I overlooked that affair in Scotland a coupla years ago because I thought to myself, no way would John Tyler double-cross me. Not *me*, not after twenty years.' He jabbed a finger. 'I arranged your treatment at Menwith Hill after you were shot, your recuperation over here in the States, the new identity. I didn't do it because we're friends. I did it because you're useful. An asset that the world thinks is dead. A ghost. Win-win.' He flicked open the knife on the table and came closer. 'But if you're no longer useful, then...'

'Skip to the good stuff.'

'Here's the deal. You do one last thing for me, and I let you take one of those new identities and disappear for good.'

'And if I refuse?'

He slid the knife under the ties one by one. 'We can help each other out here.'

I massaged my wrists. 'I don't need help, and I don't feel like giving any.'

'Fine, you don't need my help.' He stood back and held his hands up. 'You don't wanna hear me out first?'

'Nope.'

'Have it your way. But there's someone in Siberia knows you're not dead.'

Chapter Three

Mason perched on the edge of the table. 'Two weeks ago we were contacted by a Professor Balakin from Novosibirsk University.'

'Should I have heard of the guy?'

He shrugged. 'Informant, small-fry. He's been passing fairly useless information to the embassy for years, hoping to get in our good books. This time was different. Long story short, his message landed on my desk.' He waved a hand in the air. 'People know I'm always interested in these kinds of things.'

'What things?'

'An arms deal, mostly low-level stuff, crates of Kalashnikovs and RPGs, obsolete vehicles. Being hosted by a guy named Golubev, Viktor Golubev.'

'Now *that* name rings a bell, but I don't know where from.'

'An enigma. Usual ex-KGB type with all the right connections. Millionaire, and I mean like in the high numbers, but not so high that he's firmly on the radar. Word is he practically has his own private army up there. I wouldn't normally be interested but there's one thing caught my eye: Golubev's got his hands on small amounts of bioweapons. Selling off old Soviet stock to the highest bidders. There's a sort of inspection going on prior to bidding. Might be some anthrax, if you're lucky.'

'Cocktails, canapés and Novichok,' I clapped my hands together. 'It's just like Gatsby. I know Siberia's a big place but why doesn't Golubev get shut down?'

'Where do you think he gets his supplies? Officially, they have to destroy old stock. In reality, what's the point in destroying it when Golubev can generate pocket money for the people at the top?'

'But why are you interested in obsolete Soviet weapons?'

'I'm not, I'm interested in who's buying and where it's going. I pick it up once it crosses a border, get it out of terrorists' hands, everyone's happy.'

'Very noble.'

He shrugged. 'Whatever works. Problem is, the dealers don't like it. If word gets around, it puts buyers off. We have to be discreet, turn a blind eye, let fish swim away now and again.' He raised an eyebrow. 'You understand discreet, yes?'

'My middle name.'

'That'd be a first,' he mumbled. 'Anyway, this kind of thing still doesn't give me a hard-on. What I'm really excited about is their bioweapons expert.'

'Strange fetish, but okay.' He sighed, so I filled in the blank he'd left open. 'Let me guess, Professor Balakin of Novosibirsk University?'

'Bingo. He's responsible for handling the nasty stuff.'

'Which brings us to that message that ended up on your desk?'

Mason made a finger gun. 'Boom, you're on fire. Balakin is looking for a change of career. Unfortunately, he's closely watched, so he needs our help with his relocation arrangements.'

'So you want to get a Russian bioweapons expert across to the States. That's standard stuff, why me?'

'Here's the money shot. He asked for you.'

I did a little double-take. 'Me?'

'Did I stutter? I presume he doesn't know what an asshole you are. Point is, my guy over there met with him and apparently Balakin asked for you specifically. He knows you're alive and living in the States, and he wants you to get him out. In return for a white picket fence, he has some honey.'

'What flavour?'

'Information. A Russian double-agent well-placed within NATO, who's been involved in these arms deals.'

'How the hell does he know I'm alive? And why me anyway?'

Mason shrugged.

I shook my head. 'I don't know why you think I can help.'

'You're in tight with General Kayembe.'

Of course, he was referring to the benevolent (when it suited him) central African dictator I'd known for some twenty years or so.

'Nambutu is a long way from Siberia, in more ways than one.'

I started to rant about the CIA's involvement in countless republics and coups around the world, but he waved a hand dismissively. 'These slush funds don't spend themselves.' He shook his head to ward off further protest. 'I don't care, I don't care. Kayembe buys from Golubev, so it was the perfect cover for us.'

'You just used the past tense.'

'We sent a couple of agents to Golubev's private island two days ago. They went in undercover of buying on behalf of General Kayembe. In reality, they were there for Balakin, and that intel.'

'And what's Kayembe getting out of this?'

'There's a kickback in it for him, but anyway, don't you see, it all fits like Legos. Kayembe loves you. You'll go there undercover as his man on the ground.'

'It may fit like Lego to you, but Siberia's bloody cold.'

'Imagine how pissed Balakin will be if you don't show. He might spread it around. Lots of people out there might want a piece of John Tyler if they know he's not six feet under.'

'So let me get this right. You want me to fly out to literally the middle of nowhere, undercover, to meet some of the worst people on Earth.'

'A normal day for you.'

'You then want me to somehow smuggle a well-guarded scientist out of Siberia, under the eyes of a reclusive arms dealer and his private army, and transport him thousands of miles around the planet? In secret?'

'Shit no, why would you think that? Fuck Balakin, I'm only interested in the intel.'

'You're a real people-person.'

'Wise up, he's looking to move to the States because he wants to drive a Mustang down to the strip club.'

'You've got plenty of decent agents you could send if that's all you want.'

'I already told you, we sent two, they flew in on Thursday. Burton—'

'I know Burton, good guy. And a hard guy. Arctic expert, right?'

Mason clicked his fingers at me. 'Hey, it's like we know what we're doing. Burton also knew Professor Balakin from some job way back, so he was the perfect guy for the job. It's the real wild west out there, no contact, no backup, so Burton was also there to protect my tame nerd.'

'And who's that?'

'Dr Carr, a legit bioweapons expert who can talk the talk, while Burton walks the walk. On the face of it, Dr Carr was sent there by General Kayembe to check over the goods pre-sale. Obviously, in reality the mission was to cosy up to Professor Balakin and obtain my intel.'

'Go on then, I'll bite. If you've already sent two agents, why is Balakin asking for me?'

'Somehow he managed to access a radio to get a message out. He thinks we screwed him, sending Burton, now he's refusing to cooperate until you get there. That was last night, no more messages since.'

'And your agent, Dr Carr?'

'No word. We're presuming Carr's still in place but no way to verify.'

'I noticed you said Burton's role "was" to obtain the intel.'

'Well that's the kicker. Burton's dead.'

'No. Absolutely not. No way.'

Chapter Four

Black sea-ice stretched in every direction below, making it impossible to tell which direction we were flying in. I assumed north-east still, but for how much longer? It had been an hour since we'd left behind the dark, undulating Kara Sea, and over twice that long since we'd left the twilight of Dikson Airport in Siberia. Thanks to the time gained flying west – fast jets island-hopping the Pacific from California to South Korea, and charter flights via Yakutsk to Dikson – by local clocks, it was still the evening of the same day I'd been coerced into this shit by Mason.

I shuffled, stretching out across the seats. Adjusting the cold-weather jacket that I'd laid across my legs as a blanket, I picked up a map from the floor.

One of the world's most isolated and northerly settlements, the tiny port of Dikson clings to a headland at the top of civilisation and barely gets above freezing. I'd seen enough of it through a Tupolev's window as we'd come in, and doubted it was somewhere I needed to revisit.

I traced our route north-east from there. On this modified ex-military Mil helicopter, we were flying further still, skimming moon-light reflecting off the frozen sea. The map was fairly useless this far north, given the featureless views. We'd already burned up the precious few hours of dingy twilight, and now we penetrated deeper into night, the heart of the darkness.

Northern Siberia is a lonely, desolate region in the sunlight, and at this time of year the black would be almost endless. All real daylight ended before October did, and the sun wouldn't rise above the horizon again until the middle of February. Even then, it'd only be for an hour or so.

Up here hadn't seen a day, as we know it back in Britain, for over a month. As it was now, in late November, a dirty dusk swept the barren landscape for just a few hours each day before throwing in the towel.

Another clunk echoed throughout the helicopter. I instinctively looked back towards the doors at the rear of the cavernous cargo hold, wondering what had fallen off. I'd been terrified of flying all my life; strange how dying puts things in perspective. There were no other passengers to share my discomfort, just the two pilots in the cockpit up front and empty rows of uncomfortable metal-framed seats behind me.

'Five, yes?'

I turned to the front. One of the pilots was leaning backwards, giving me a thumbs up through the stinking cigarette haze drifting through the bulkhead. He grinned while chewing gum with his mouth open, then turned back to the controls.

Neither of them spoke more than a few words of English, and my own Russian was terrible, so I focused on the chair opposite, doing my best to ignore the noises and instead thinking about this suicide mission.

Because that's what it was, and Mason knew it. Intel and prep: non-existent. Gear: some clothes hastily bought from the nearest stores in California, and US Marines cold-weather equipment. My own pistol and a box of fifty rounds of ammo. Backup: none. Working for the CIA was just as bad as working for the British under Colonel Holderness.

Apparently, all the information I needed would be found with Mason's remaining agent, his "tame scientist", Dr Carr. Mason had made it clear Carr was in charge and would keep me on a tight leash, and that further instructions would be relayed one-way directly to Carr from Mason.

The only thing I did have was a goal. Professor Yaroslav Balakin. 52. Male. PhD in Biochemistry from St Petersburg. Candidate of Science in Molecular Biophysics from Moscow State. Lecturer at Novosibirsk University. Bioweapons expert. Terrorist supplier. CIA Informant.

And on that last point, Balakin would in turn be giving me a name. I still wasn't sure what would happen after that, but I hoped Mason's agent on the ground knew what they were doing because it'd likely involve us rapidly getting the fuck out of Russia.

I'd never heard of Balakin, so was curious how he knew of me. How he knew I was alive was an even bigger mystery, topped only by the reason he'd asked for me. Here I was, nonetheless, on a helicopter flying ever deeper into the Arctic Circle, towards Severnaya Zemlya. One of the last great wildernesses of the planet.

Most people know more about the moon than the Arctic. The island chain of Severnaya Zemlya was only charted a hundred years ago, the last archipelago to be explored on Earth.

I leaned back against the window and stared at a suspicious stain on the seat across the aisle. Rusty brown streaks on the metal frame showed where something had dripped down, forming a puddle on the cabin floor. A corresponding hole in the seat gave a clue as to what had dripped out of someone.

I glanced down at the map again, where I'd circled our destination. The small island of Barensky was much closer to the mainland than the larger islands – not that it made much of a difference with the sea solidified. A barren rock that had once been a Soviet store and refuelling station on the way up to their Polar research stations. Now all that was left, beyond the crumbling pier, grounded old torpedo boats, and discarded junk I'd seen on the sat images, was a large, incongruous hotel.

Not much is known about Barensky; nothing more than rumours. It'd been run by the military before they suddenly abandoned it in the late Seventies, and had been in private hands since the fall of the wall. Now it was the last refuge of a reclusive arms dealer, used to host parties for terrorists.

'Now!' came a shout from the front.

The co-pilot started unfastening his safety harness. Still nothing out of the window, nothing to suggest we were approaching our destination. I couldn't even tell if we were over sea or solid ground. No lights. I stood and walked to the other side of the cabin, but the view was almost identical. I went backwards and sat in another seat, cupping a hand on the glass as my eyes readjusted to the darkness. The full moon glowed on the ice, flecks of snow whirled in the wind from the rotors. Utter emptiness.

'Are we on the island?'

'You go fast.'

I turned. The co-pilot was standing at the front, one hand resting on the handle of the sliding side door. I glanced back out of the window and realised we weren't landing; we were hovering.

'Fast,' the man repeated.

I shook my head. 'No chance, mate.'

'Ice.' The man made a motion with his hands, holding one out then pushing the other down onto it. It clicked. We were above the sea, and the pilot didn't want to put ten tonnes onto the frozen surface.

I grabbed my thick parka from the seat and shrugged it on.

'Go now.' He turned to slide open the door. 'Low fuel.'

A blast of Arctic air instantly filled the compartment, sucking the air from my lungs. I breathed shallow to avoid freezing them up, pulling a mask up over my mouth and nose. The man secured the hatch open, then stood, head cocked to one side. We stared at each other through swirling snow for a moment before he broke the stalemate by pulling my rucksack off the chair.

'You go,' he shouted, barely audible above the whirling maelstrom.

I lurched forward but it was too late. He dragged the heavy bag to the door and shoved it out. I went to the side window and looked down but couldn't see anything. I clenched a fist but when I looked up, the barrel of a pistol was pointing at me from the cockpit behind him, held in the fist of the not-too-happy-looking second pilot.

'Go!' he mouthed, flicking the pistol towards the opening and narrowing his eyes.

The co-pilot took a step back into the cockpit, pulling out a pistol of his own.

I staggered to the door and leaned out. Impossible to tell distance and I couldn't spot my bag.

I turned back to them. 'This isn't Barensky, is it?'

The co-pilot shrugged, leaning on the bulkhead, still chewing his gum.

'You've messed with the wrong people, you know?' I tried to inject some bravado into my voice but it's difficult when you're facing down two guns held by pilots who don't give a shit, doubly so considering they probably couldn't even hear me and didn't speak much English. 'What is this, a racket? You take money for ferrying people then throw them out in the middle of nowhere? Well, my people won't—'

A shot echoed in the cabin.

I flinched, the two pilots burst out laughing. The nearer one had fired through the open doorway.

He waved the gun.

I zipped up my parka. With one last look back, I sat, dangling my boots over the edge. Still impossible to judge the drop but the feeling of cold metal suddenly pressing into the back of my head sped up my decision-making process. I pulled my gloves from my pocket and slipped them on, then reached for a grab handle below the doorway and swung down into the wind. Again, the cold air froze inside my throat. My boots hung over nothing; I didn't know how long I could hold on in the gloves. Above me the co-pilot was still chewing, still grinning. He pulled on the door, sliding it shut behind me.

Well, I was now outside the helicopter and it wasn't going to get any lower. Any second now they'd pull up and leave me dangling here until I froze and fell to my death anyway. I opened my hands, possibly my least elegant disembarkation from an aircraft.

Chapter Five

The Peoples' Democratic Republic of Nambutu / French Equatorial Africa

1999

My shoes hit the ground, my body in shock at the temperature change. The moment I stepped off the stairs, I knew I'd made a mistake. The baking sun reflected off my box-fresh shoes, sweat instantly stuck my shirt to my back and my shoulder-length hair to my face. I shrugged my arms around inside my dark suit jacket as it shrink-wrapped around me.

I looked back up at the tiny Air France prop plane and briefly considered running up the stairs into the cabin, until a side glance from a soldier at the edge of the tarmac forced my eyes down to my feet. I shuffled forward with the few other passengers, cursing the heat, cursing my brother, but mostly cursing myself for agreeing to his get-rich-quick scheme.

When I looked up, the soldiers had multiplied, all of their eyes seemed to be fixed on me. I looked dead ahead, eyes on the small terminal building shimmering in the midday heat.

The big metal letters spelling the city's name lay rusting slowly in the weeds where they'd fallen off the front of the building. The following 'International Airport' lettering remained in place, and while not strictly a misnomer, was certainly aggrandising what wasn't much more than a large corrugated metal shed, brightly coloured in green, red and more rust. Beneath the broken sign, blue plastic sheeting flapped in the breeze, gaffer taped over a large hole. The burnt-out shell of a Peugeot 4X4 suggested an explosion of some kind had blown the location off the building.

I was wondering what could have caused an explosion near an airport terminal when a distant thud pulsed through the air. I flinched, half ducking as the sound rolled away. In the distance, a column of smoke began to drift up from the ocean of green bordering the runway. I looked round but nobody had given it so much as a glance. I pulled the straps of my big rucksack tight and hustled forward quicker.

The ratatat of machine-gun fire came from somewhere in the distance behind. I ducked and looked round but all I saw were soldiers pointing at me and laughing. I squinted at the tall treeline beyond the chain-link fence but the sun burned my eyes, reminding me of what I'd forgotten: sunglasses.

If that was all I'd left at home I'd be okay.

Any hopes that the airport building was air conditioned evaporated quicker than the sweat pouring out of me. It took a few seconds for my eyes to adjust to the relative gloom, and in that time over half the passengers had been waved through a wooden fence funnelling everyone towards three passport checkpoints. Two of them were empty, and why the sole border guard had chosen to use the third, which leaned drunkenly to one side under the weight of a huge old PC, was beyond me.

The last of the passengers bustled past me towards the desk, where they were waved through with barely a glance from the bored-looking man behind it. I shuffled forward and fumbled inside my jacket pocket for my passport, all too aware that the soldiers from outside had followed me in. Another soldier, clearly in charge because he wasn't carrying a gun, stepped up behind the immigration desk. He removed a pair of gold-rimmed Ray-Ban aviators and stuck the temple between his teeth, leaning in to whisper something in the border guard's ear.

I looked around. The place was almost empty now, but even if it wasn't, I'd have stood out like a hammered thumb. Barely nineteen, I'd only been abroad three times and it'd been nowt like this. Spain twice on family holidays, and a school trip to France. It was the memory of the latter that I brought forward as I flexed my language skills, French being the only subject in which I'd excelled.

'You,' said the man behind the desk.

'Good afternoon,' I said in perfect French. 'How are you today?'

The man behind the desk stared at me for a long moment, then thrust his hand out. I handed him my passport, trying to avoid the gaze of the officer behind him. As the guard opened it, the soldier behind him leaned forward to look.

'Nice weather today,' I said, still in French. 'Warmer than I thought it would be.'

The border guard looked up at me, raising his eyebrows. 'You are English?'

I swept my sweaty hair behind my ears. 'Yes?'

'Then why are you trying to speak French?'

I hadn't thought it possible for my face to go any redder but I think it managed it.

'Why are you here?' the man continued.

'I'm on business,' I said, sticking to English, trying to sound self-important. The idea of flying 4,000 miles for business had seemed exciting back in Yorkshire. Now, wearing my Burtons interview suit in thirty-degree heat with the humidity of a swimming pool, surrounded by angry-looking dudes carrying rifles, I realised I was so out of my depth that I couldn't see the bottom or the sides.

'What business?'

The man behind the guard folded his arms. The rolled sleeves of his khaki shirt stretched around his biceps. I looked back at the mildly less intimidating border guard.

'Wood.'

The officer behind him finally spoke. 'We have enough wood, thank you.'

'Jungle's full of it,' added the border guard.

I smiled. 'Mahogany. I work for a furniture company.'

'We have the best mahogany.'

'Yes, that's why I'm here.' I glanced at the officer behind but he seemed to be losing interest.

'And you think it is fair to take the best wood from our land to make your fancy English beds?' said the border guard, voice rising.

'I'm not... I mean, we pay...'

'And where are you staying in Nambutu?'

'At a hotel, the erm...' I reached into my pocket. There was a rustle behind me, and I turned to see one of the soldiers had raised his AK-47. I slowly removed my hand. 'The Montmartre.'

'You are not staying at The Montmartre.'

'I have a reservation, my brother has...'

The guard turned to the officer behind him, who whispered something. The guard nodded and glared at me as the officer strode away into an office at the side.

The soldiers who'd followed me into the building shouldered their weapons and strolled through the barriers and out of the glass doors at the front, leaving us alone. Obviously I'd said something right.

The guard picked up a stamp and rolled it around on an ink pad. 'There are taxis outside that will take you where you want to go.'

'I want to go to The Montmartre.'

'The Montmartre no longer exists.'

'Has it changed its name?'

He slammed the stamp down on my passport and snapped it shut. I held a hand out for it, he stared hard at me. I reached further and took it, pushing it into my pocket.

'The Montmartre was destroyed this morning by a car bomb. You want pussy, I recommend the Hotel le Dauphin.'

'I'm just here for a business meeting.'

'No one at The Montmartre is here for business.' This time he smiled broadly.

I stared a moment longer, trying to think of an appropriate comeback before deciding to just shift my arse. I picked up my rucksack, tried to peel my shirt off my skin, and gave him a smile. He was looking down at the computer. Evidently that was that.

I hoisted my rucksack and walked towards the dusty glass doors. The burning sunlight hit my retinas hard as I pushed through. I squinted and threw a hand up. First thing I needed to do was buy a pair of bloody sunglasses.

Here, on the other side of the building, sounds drifted up from the city. Horns, sirens, screaming mopeds. The doors had led me straight into a dirt car park, mostly empty, save for a few 4x4s and a couple of shabby-looking Citroëns. The group of soldiers that had followed me through from disembarkation were standing under a sign for the baggage claim. Most were smoking and chatting, rifles slung across their backs, but two of them were eyeing me. I quickly looked away.

The passengers from my flight seemed to have disappeared already.

Beyond the chain-link fence, a hard-packed orange dirt road ran in one direction, curving through the tall, thick trees. In the distance the column of smoke was still growing. I guessed that marked downtown. Beneath it, at the far end of the car park, an old Seventies Citroën in a shade somewhere between hearing-aid beige and nicotine-stained ceiling idled noisily. The Dulux-white driver took a pull on a cig, blew smoke out of the window, and flashed his headlights twice.

I looked back at the baggage claim. Behind the soldiers was a golf cart hitched with a small trailer. On the dirt next to it, open and upside down, sat my suitcase. I sighed and started to walk towards it, reaching into my pocket to take out a pack of Embassy No.1, fishing in the other pocket for my lighter.

As I got halfway to it, one of the soldiers stepped forward, swinging his rifle round and into his hands in one fluid movement. 'Stop.'

Obviously I obliged, see-through pink plastic lighter halfway to my mouth.

'The *Capitaine* wants to talk to you.'

'Me?' I looked round; clearly there was no one else.

The other soldiers were still chatting and laughing, occasionally looking over with bored indifference. No security threat from me. What the hell did it mean?

I heard the door behind me swing open, then turned to see the officer from inside, beckoning. With a glance at the idling Citroën at the far end of the car park, I jammed the cig into my pocket and followed him back into the building.

He strode through the door into the side office. The border guard at the immigration desk didn't even look up. I followed, finding myself in a small room just as stuffy as the rest of the building but with the added benefit of roasting wind from a fan rocking precariously on top of a filing cabinet.

The Captain walked round a dented wooden desk and looked out of a dusty window at the plane I'd just got off.

'Shut the door!' he said in English.

I did what he asked and stood waiting to find out what this was about.

He spun to face me. 'You think you are better than us, is that what you think?'

I shook my head.

He took off his Ray-Bans and threw them on the table.

'When did you land in Nambutu?'

'You know I just—'

'I asked when, I did not ask for a biographical account of your life history.'

'Well, about,' I looked at my faithful Casio, 'ten minutes ago.'

He leaned back against the windowsill and folded his muscular arms. 'And already you have broken the law.'

'I'm sorry, I didn't... what did I do?'

'You think I am stupid? You think I do not know a smuggler when I see one?'

'Sorry, I think there's been a mistake.'

He pushed off the window and leaned over the desk. 'No mistake. You're going to jail, my friend. This is a very serious offence.'

'Look, I don't know what you think I've done...'

'I saw you with my own eyes.' He marched round the desk and stood with his face inches from mine, so close the sweat from his brow dripped on my shoe.

I did my best not to back away but all I could think about was what the inside of their cells must be like. He reached into my pocket and came out with my cigs and lighter, holding them up to my face.

I narrowed my eyes. 'You think I smuggled cigarettes?'

'You did not buy these in the airport, did you?'

I shook my head again.

'You admit to bringing contraband into the country?'

'I didn't know they were forbidden.'

'Cigarettes must be purchased in Nambutu.'

'But wait...' I realised it was bullshit, a setup, and relaxed a little. My brother had warned me there might be something like this.

I switched down the tone of my voice. 'I'm very sorry. It was my mistake. I assume you'll be confiscating them?'

He threw the pack and lighter on the table and nodded, then opened a desk drawer and pulled out a form. He hunted a little more and came out with a ballpoint pen.

'Sit,' he commanded.

I did. He spun the paper round and scribbled on the top with the pen. It left an indentation but no ink. He scribbled some more then threw the pen across the room.

Scooping the lighter and cigs into the drawer, he pushed his chair back and stood. 'Wait here.'

He marched from the room, closing the door behind him. I spun the form round and started reading. From what I could gather it was some kind of lost baggage claim form. Speckled trails of sunlight flashed as the plane outside taxied past, the light caught in the reflection of his Ray-Ban sunglasses on the desk.

No sunglasses and now no cigs. I was ill-prepared for this.

I was still leaning over the desk when the footsteps returned. I quickly sat back down, slumping back in the chair just as the door opened. The Captain slammed a pen on the desk and pulled the paper across in front of me.

'This document lists the penalty for smuggling items into Nambutu. You will sign this, and the police will be here shortly to take you into the prison.'

'I'm really sorry. It was an honest mistake, is there anything else I can do?'

He inhaled, making a sort of low growling noise, then sat down on the edge of the desk. When he spoke, his voice had softened. 'Usually tourists are fined, but you are not a tourist, you are a businessman. Businesses do not pay the fines, so,' he held up his hands, 'I can do nothing.'

'And what if I was a tourist? What if I pay the fine myself? Would that work?'

'No, if I receive a fine then I must give you a receipt, and I need to make a note of it. If I do this they will know you are not a tourist.' He held up a finger. 'This is a discrepancy.'

'Right, so what if I say I don't need a receipt?' I reached into my pocket and pulled out my wallet. 'What if I pay the fine in cash so that you don't have to make a note of it?'

'The fine is very large.'

'How large?'

'The fine is thirty dollars. Plus another ten dollars administration fee for not issuing a receipt.'

I pulled out two twenty dollar bills and reached across the table. He snatched them and narrowed his eyes.

'It is also another ten dollars fee to destroy the contraband.'

I pulled out another twenty dollar bill and held it out. 'I'm very sorry. I won't break any more laws while I'm here.'

He grabbed the twenty. 'Very well, Mr Tyler, you may go.' He folded the notes, then stood. 'Do not think you can come to my country and do what you please. We have had enough of that from people like you.'

I nodded and stood, giving him a smile as I backed towards the door. 'I'm sorry, again. Have a great day.'

He grinned. 'I hope you find everything you came for.'

As I walked towards the frosted glass doors for the second time, I could see a shape on the other side. I shoved through to be met by the beige Citroën, now pulled up right outside the doors. The driver leaned out, flicking a spent cig at me.

'Are you Walshe?' I asked.

He pushed a grubby baseball cap up on his head to wipe the sheen of sweat from his brow. 'What took you?' he asked, faint accent coming through that I couldn't place.

'Landing taxes,' I winked.

'Get in.' He ran an oily hand across his grimy stubble and repositioned his hat. 'We need to haul arse.'

I glanced at the soldiers who were ignoring us, and beyond them, my spilled suitcase.

'Leave it,' Walshe said. 'We'll get you some more clothes.'

An engine sounded on the highway outside, I could just about make out a car approaching through the trees. One of the soldiers had started watching us with interest, and tapped the man next to him.

Walshe put a hand to his hat and smiled at them as he reached across and opened the glovebox. Inside was a pistol.

I walked round the car and climbed in, shutting the glovebox. 'Absolutely not.'

Walshe looked across at me as he put the car in gear. 'Never tell me what to do.'

His breath stank of alcohol, the car of stale sweat and rotten meat. I couldn't decide if his accent was South African or Kiwi. He gunned the engine and pulled the wheel, heading for the exit. Out on the road a big old Eighties Chevy Suburban kicked up dust as it sped alongside the chain-link fence.

'Get down,' said Walshe. I ducked as he slowed to let the Chevy 4X4 roar past into the car park, and slid back up in my seat in time to see it in the wing mirror. It pulled across the front of the doors under the watchful eyes of the soldiers, then we were out onto the road and driving along what constituted the main highway into the city.

I looked back through the trees at the brightly painted corrugated shed, then settled into my seat, starting to crank the window open.

'Don't do that,' Walshe shouted. 'It'll ruin the air conditioning.'

'Smells like something died in the air con. Who was that dude in the car?'

'Someone you don't wanna meet. We need to get off the highway.' He reached in the door compartment and pulled out a strip of chewy-looking dried meat, sticking it in his mouth. 'We'll take the long way round.'

'How long is long? Is there anywhere to get a brew? I'm gasping.'

'Are you always this annoying?' Flecks of meat spattered the dash as he spoke. He pushed the cap up again and wiped his forehead with the back of his hand, leaving a smear of black. 'There's water in back.'

I turned and grabbed a bottle from a cool box belted on the back seat, then reached into my pocket and pulled out my slightly crumpled pack of Embassy No. 1 and pink plastic lighter, liberated from the security officer's desk drawer.

'Open the window if you must do that,' Walshe said, taking another bite of dried meat.

'Dude, it'll play havoc with your air con.' I clamped the cig between my lips and flicked the lighter.

'It's a disgusting habit,' he said, spraying more meat at the windscreen.

'Not half as disgusting as this car,' I muttered.

'Just keep your mouth shut and we'll get there happy, okay?'

I cranked the window. 'Suits me.' I reached into my other pocket and pulled out my new gold-rimmed Ray-Ban aviators. I put them on and reclined the seat, putting my feet on the dashboard, gazing into the mirror, and taking a long drag on the cigarette. 'Suits me just fine. But you know we're being followed, right?'

Chapter Six

Severnaya Zemlya, Siberia
Present day

I landed heavily on the rough sea-ice, rolling onto my side and coughing violently, caught in a vicious cycle of Arctic air freezing my throat and lungs. I put my hands over my face, warming the air and forcing my breathing to steady.

The sound of the helicopter disappeared quickly, swallowed by the wind and its constant low-frequency moan over the ice. I slowly got to my feet, pulled up the hood of my parka, and watched the little flashing star until moments later that too was swallowed by the driving snow.

I've worked in plenty of cold places, but Siberia is no ski resort. Real burrow-into-your-soul cold, it quite literally takes your breath away. I've only done a couple of jobs near the top of the world, and was grateful for the cold weather warfare training in Norway that Colonel Holderness had swung for me. Maybe I wasn't a fully fledged Arctic Commando, but I at least had a handle on the basics. The first thought is always panic, but that's fleeting. Logic tells you it does no good and wastes energy, but really for me it's the nauseating feeling of *same shit, different day*, a mixture of incredulity and rage that simply leaves no room for mad panic.

The wind was already eating through the down of the parka. I pulled open my rucksack and took out the Wintergreen wind-proof shell anorak I'd hastily bought, and threw it over the top. I zipped it up and clicked into survival mode.

The Arctic Circle wants you dead, and will try at any opportunity. If you do nothing about this it wins even faster. Shelter takes priority, but all I could see was grey ice and then black. I opened the front pocket of my bag and brought out my torch and ski goggles.

A million tiny diamonds whipped through the beam, crystals and drift pulled off the hummocks and flung around. To describe my surroundings as featureless wouldn't be entirely correct; this wasn't a flat blanket of snow. The topography was all over the place, undulating in the bright white beam, spikes of ice jutting here and there. There were small hills where bergs had collided before the sea had frozen, forced upwards to be covered in snow, ice boulders carved by the unending wind, drifts ten feet tall. For a flat sea, it was surprisingly three dimensional.

I pulled the goggles on, hoisted the big pack onto my back, and jogged sideways to the wind, heading for one of the hills. In its shadow, the wind skipped over the top, offering some respite. I dropped to my knees and started trying to scoop out snow to create a shelter, but after the top few centimetres it was pack ice.

I unslung my bag and pressed myself back into a crack between two ice boulders out of the biting wind, then pulled my pack in front of me.

I tugged my hood down lower, pulled the ski mask right up over my goggles and thought about my options.

I had a few bottles of water and some snack food, so dying of thirst or hunger wasn't an immediate issue – as long as I put a bottle under my jacket to stop it freezing. My clothing was good and I had more I could pull on if I got desperate, so freezing wasn't an immediate issue, as long as I wasn't stupid.

The main issue was probably being miles from anywhere, with no idea where I was. I had a phone that wouldn't pick up a signal for a thousand miles, and a torch but nothing to see. Navigation by starlight was impossible with the clouds. With my watch and a good shadow, I could fashion a rudimentary compass, but that would mean sitting and waiting for hours and, worse, it wouldn't actually help me since there were no features to orientate myself by. Best case scenario, I could head in a specific direction. But which one?

I huddled down further, tucking my head down, and tried to work up a plan.

That lasted all of ten seconds as a voice drifted on the wind. I pulled open my hood and listened. It was faint, but thankfully I hadn't imagined it. I pulled down my mask. Definitely a voice, and it sounded like it was shouting my name.

At least, the name I was currently going by on this job.

I pulled my pistol from my pocket, cocked it, and pushed my bulky gloved fingers into it. I moved my bag out of the way and stood, immediately spotting a light off to my left, round the corner of the snow hill.

I threw the bag onto my back and crept forward, pistol ready. Heading into the wind, within seconds my goggles were coated in ice. Wiping them and holding an arm up against the onslaught, I could see the lights were casting a bright beam through the swirling flakes. I couldn't see what they were connected to, but it was clearly a vehicle of some sort. A chugging engine pulsed, fading then louder as the sound was pulled around by the wind.

Sticking behind the vehicle, I jogged through the shadows. Movement flashed, a figure entered the bright pool of light.

'Chambers!' it shouted, voice faint and torn off by the savage wind. Their hood looked around in every direction.

The lights were attached to a van, an old military UAZ painted up in Arctic camo and covered in thick, padded panels to insulate the engine and running gear. The bright spotlights pointed front and sides from a rack on the roof.

I crept round the rear and dropped my bag by the chugging exhaust.

'Chambers!' the figure called again.

I grabbed the rear door handle and yanked it open, gun up, sweeping the interior. It was empty, benches down each side and the front seats lit in the dim, sickly glow of the interior light. With my gun still ready I stepped up, pulling my bag behind me, and quietly closing the door. I pushed my goggles up and shuffled forward, lifting my head above the seats to watch the figure outside stumbling around in the glare of the headlamps. It turned and the hood blew down in the gusts, its ice-rimed fur lining framing a softer face than I'd expected. It was a woman, scrabbling at her hood as her hair and most of her face was instantly coated in a layer of ice.

Running back to the van, she opened the driver's door, climbed up, and slammed it shut. She tried to shake the ice from her long dark hair and blew in her hands, holding them up to the heater vents, then muttered under her breath as she pulled a cig from a crumpled pack on the dash and sparked it up.

'What's an Australian doing all the way up here?' I jabbed my gun into her back.

'Fuck me dead!' she jumped, spitting out the cig, then frantically scrabbling for it on her lap. She turned, face red-raw from the few seconds' exposure. 'You'll be Chambers, then?'

For the purposes of this job, I was. 'Who wants to know?'

'Your bloody Uber driver, mate, that's who.' She retrieved the cigarette and clamped it between her blue lips, speaking out the side. 'You tryin' to get lost out here or what?'

I jabbed her again. 'What's going on?'

'Whaddaya mean? I'm the airport transfer.'

'What's with the theatrics?'

She blew smoke across the windscreen. 'Sorry I was late, normally I'm waiting for the chopper.'

'I could have died.'

'Well, that'll happen if you wander round the Arctic like a silly bugger. Listen, mate, we've only got half a tank of petty. If you wanna sit and chat that's fine, but I'll have to turn the bastard off, and it's only getting colder out here.'

'Turn it off then.'

'Nah, you don't want me to do that, mate.' She flicked ash down into the footwell and took another drag. 'She's a moody old bitch and if she doesn't start again we've got a long, cold walk.'

'We're not going anywhere until you tell me what's going on.'

'You know what this is?' She jerked her head to the side.

I followed the motion and saw she'd somehow produced a grenade from below the dash, *sans* pin, and was clutching the lever in.

'You shoot me,' the cig jerked between her lips as she continued to speak out the side of her mouth, 'I drop this down here in the footwell. You reckon you can find it before it blows?'

Chapter Seven

Severnaya Zemlya, Siberia

Present day

I looked at the grenade clamped between her fingers and smiled grimly. 'I guess that's checkmate then.'

'Nah, not really mate,' she said, ash dropping from the cig dangling between her lips. 'Cos if you make me get out, I'll freeze to death; if you make me sit here for too long, we'll run out of petty and freeze to death; and if you shoot me, I'll die. I reckon that makes your threats irrelevant, and I also reckon you're not the kinda guy who tortures poor lonely chicks in vans. The best thing we can do is make friends, drive to the hotel, and get some bevvies in.'

I pressed the safety on and slipped my pistol into my pocket. 'I like you.'

'Abi.' She tossed the grenade into the passenger footwell, leaning back to offer her hand.

I looked at the grenade then back at her as I shook it.

She smiled and turned to blow smoke at the side window. It fogged as the smoke rolled across the cold glass. 'It's a dud. Shits up the tourists though, eh?' She wiggled the gearstick into first, and we lurched off over the rough ice.

I climbed over onto the passenger seat. 'So why did I get dropped off way out here, why not land on the island?'

'They pull the old jump routine on ya? Silly bastards are superstitious. The pilots won't fly any closer to the island. No one goes there, no one who's heard about the place anyway. So they drop guests off here.'

I noticed we were following the flashing digits on a GPS unit stuck to the dash. There were no tracks on the ice; all snow was blown and reblown instantly.

'And yet you're happy to go there?'

'Mate, I'm just hired help. I go where the money is. Just like you I guess, right? So what was it, The Regiment or...'

'No.' I shook my head, transferring my pistol onto my lap.

She made a face, looking back at the windscreen in silence, concentrating on the oncoming snow. I relaxed into the seat, but after a couple of minutes I was starting to get hot in the tiny van. I threw my goggles onto the dash, pushed my gloves into my pockets, and ran my cold hands through my thawing hair.

'So why won't pilots fly in?' I asked.

'Oh, now you want me to play tour guide? Righto.' Abi steered around an ice boulder. The rear broke traction but she skilfully brought us around sideways while flicking ash onto the floor, steering us back on track. 'Some of these pilots, they're a mad bunch. They won't come closer on account of what happened there. Haunted, ya know? Soviet *Shining*, thanks to experiments they did there back in the day. Bugger, what's this?'

I followed her gaze as she braked slowly. Something was reflecting at the edge of the spotlights' white pool.

'What is it, a building?'

'We're still a mile or so out to sea. Didn't think anyone else was out tonight.'

We crawled forward and pulled to a halt fifty metres or so from a Jeep parked up facing us in the middle of the worn ice trail. I looked at Abi.

She cracked her window a centimetre and flicked the tab end into the wind. Her face was lined, mouth set straight. She flashed the lights several times and beeped the horn. Nothing moved out in the swirling blizzard.

She wound the window back up. 'That's Stevo's Jeep. Security. No reason for him to be out here though.' She grabbed a handset from a CB set bolted under the dash and turned the volume up. Static burst from a speaker. 'Stevo, you there, mate?'

Static replied.

'Mate, you there? Pick up.'

More static. She switched frequency and tried again. 'Taxi to base, you there?'

The static got louder, she adjusted a dial but nothing came through.

'It's Abi, I've got Stevo's Jeep out here, what's going on?'

A voice drifted somewhere behind the static but it was impossible to make out the words. Music crackled and faded in and out, then Russian voices; sounded like they were issuing commands.

'Mate, I'm not fucking around, what's the deal?'

She hung up the handset but left the static jabbering to itself. Eyes glued to the Jeep, she reached behind her and came out with two AK-12 rifles.

'You expecting trouble, all the way out here?' I asked.

'Always,' she grunted, and handed one to me, then cocked the other. I pulled the magazine, checked it was loaded, then cocked it.

Still nothing moved in the Jeep.

'Go on then,' she said.

'We both go.'

'Thinking's not your forte, eh? You fancy driving through this, you know the way?'

I looked at the tracks already disappearing in the snow and shook my head.

'You might be some hot-shit hard man but I'm guessing you're not the Arctic expert here. Listen, we can't turn off the engine, cos if it doesn't start again we're buggered. So I'll wait in the van.'

Her argument did make sense.

She caught the expression on my face and shrugged. 'If I wanted to kill you I'd have just not picked you up. You'd be an ice pole by now.' She pulled the van forward, swinging it round to hold the Jeep in the bright spotlight beams. 'I'll watch your back.'

I flicked up my hood, opened the door, and climbed out into the wind. She gave me a grin of encouragement and a thumbs up, then pulled it shut behind me.

I zipped up the outer jacket and held the rifle into my shoulder, advancing slowly, careful to stay out of the spreading beam of the van's lights. My fingers burned with cold but I didn't move them from alongside that trigger-guard. Likewise my ears and forehead stung, my eyes were forced almost shut by the ice needles, but I'd rather that than muffle my senses.

I glanced back at the van, squinting against the spotlights, and could just about make out Abi in the driver's seat.

The Jeep was brightly lit, so I could see the interior. Looked empty. I paused to look beyond the Jeep, to the sides. There didn't look to be anywhere anyone could be. With one last glance at the van, I stepped into the pool of light and braced myself.

I don't know what I'd been expecting, but nothing happened. I stepped forward, rifle still trained on the Jeep, until I reached the driver's door. I pulled it open.

Blood had soaked into the seat base. I kicked the door open fully, swinging the rifle to cover the rear, but it was empty.

A tangle of torn wires hung from under the dash. It clearly wasn't going anywhere. Then my attention was caught by a rifle propped in the passenger footwell, smeared with more blood. It'd dripped onto the bare metal floor where a black pool had gathered, already congealing in the minus temperatures. I crouched on the ice and put my hand up behind the front wheel, feeling the underside of the engine. Lukewarm, but out here that meant it'd been driven very recently.

I looked back at the van, shook my head, and walked around the rear of the Jeep. I pulled my gloves from my pocket and was fastening one when a scream cut across the ice, torn off abruptly by the wind. Hot on its heels came a muffled gunshot from somewhere up ahead. I looked back at Abi. She hadn't moved, probably hadn't heard it.

Another gunshot ripped across the ice. I set off at a sprint, rifle pushed against my shoulder. The wind whipped my hood down as I squinted along the rifle. In the corner of my eye, I spotted a streak of red on the ice. Another scream, a man shouting *no*. This time it was close.

A third scream died as I approached a mound of ice, piled with driven snowdrifts. There was a sound, a soft rush of air, a flash of orange. Another scream choked away to nothing as the ice grew brighter, lit by something behind the mound. I slowed, creeping forward. The unmistakable splutter of flames licked out as I rounded the edge of the ice.

The sight was not a pretty one.

A man – that was my best guess, based on the screams – was slumped with his back against the mound of ice, facing into the driving wind. The snow wasn't getting a chance to settle on what was clearly now a corpse, on account of the fierce flames engulfing him. His clothes were already mostly gone, flesh spitting and crackling, so intense was the mini inferno.

I kicked mounds of snow up at the flames, but it was so fine it sprayed everywhere in the whirling wind. I dropped to my knees, scooping up armfuls of snow and throwing it, sizzling, onto him, but it had zero effect.

I stood and looked down at the poor guy. Pools of blood had congealed around him. The flesh on his head and hand was already almost gone, revealing pink bones turning black, yellow fat sputtering and fizzing. In his blackened right claw, he held a radio handset, already melting into the ice. In his almost-intact left hand, he clutched a pistol, aimed somewhere into the distance. I swung the rifle around, but couldn't see a thing in the swirling snow.

Then a shape moved. I swung the rifle onto it but too late, it disappeared. I ran forward, lurching over the ice, coughing with every breath. I stopped to look around, wishing I'd grabbed my goggles, when I saw it again. Right on the edge of vision in the swirling snow, a figure hunched over, arms in the air. I crouched and raised the rifle. Abi had said no one should be out here, and the guy burning up behind me suggested that whoever this was, they were unlikely to be friendly. I took the risk and squeezed the trigger.

The figure turned to look straight at me, though it felt more like they were looking into me. The fur-lined hood was pulled up tight around a hollow dark hole, moonlight caught on the filthy white

42

jacket. They darted into the blizzard, so I set off after them but quickly stopped, holding a hand up against the snow and turning through 360 degrees. I'd got disorientated, could no longer see which way I'd come. I looked at my tracks and realised they, too, ended just behind me, so fine was the snow on top of the solid sheet ice, and so fierce was the wind whipping it about.

A dim glow was just about visible to my left. With the rifle still ready, I walked back cautiously, thankfully with the wind behind me. I found the corpse still burning intensely.

The clatter of automatic gunfire tore through the wind. Another burst of gunfire, glass shattered. I came back round to the Jeep and slid to one knee, rifle on the cab of the truck. Orange flashes popped inside. It was Abi shooting, but at what?

With the exertion, shallow breaths were all but impossible. I doubled over, racked with coughing as freezing air clawed my throat. I pushed back across the ice, round the Jeep, and steadied my breathing. Abi wasn't shooting at me, that was clear. A quick glance down the side of the Jeep, along the rifle's sights, but I couldn't see anyone. A shout rolled across the ice. I held a hand up against the glare from the van's spotlights but couldn't see much beyond them. Getting out of their beam was a priority. I ran towards the nearest hillock and pressed in, rifle swinging around in all directions. The ice was as empty as before, nothing moved. I quickly pulled on my other glove and yanked my mask up over my mouth and nose, tugging the hood pulls tighter.

I turned and ran around the ice mound, coming up in the deep shadows on the far side. The van's spotlights abruptly shut off, the rumbling engine died, making the screaming wind seem louder. From this angle I couldn't see inside it. The driver's door swung in the wind, clattering noisily.

Suddenly the interior lit up bright yellow.

I ran towards the van. The only sound was the driving wind, the banging door, and distant rumble of shifting ice. I reached the driver's side, moving the door and flexing my finger on the trigger.

Wires spilled from under the dashboard. The ignition had been torn out. Flames licked up the back of the passenger seat. An unmistakable smell tickled my nostrils: the petrol tank had ruptured. I turned and ran.

The light hit first, searing white, then a whump that lifted me off my feet. Before my body had registered what had happened, I was lying in the snow looking back at the burning skeleton of a UAZ van. Flaming debris rained down, hissing through the snow.

The clatter of gunfire opened up again. I rolled over and spotted a set of tracks rapidly vanishing in the wind. I leapt to my feet, grabbing the rifle, then looped the strap around my arm and set off after them before they were blown away completely.

The boot prints were toes only, long stride, looked like Abi was running full pelt. From something, or towards it?

A single gunshot cracked and died on the wind. It'd been close.

I rounded a mound of ice, rifle at my shoulder, and saw the change in the tracks. The boots stopped in a mess of churned snow, but it was what followed that got my attention. A streak of red, the furrows of something – or someone – being dragged.

Chapter Eight

Severnaya Zemlya, Siberia

Present day

The trail was short. I followed it into the blizzard for a few seconds before I spotted Abi in the whirling snow. She was laid on her back, one hand clutching her leg. Her jacket and trousers were torn open, dark blood spilling onto the ice.

I scanned the blurred horizon and dropped to a knee. She shoved me away and rolled over, grabbing her weapon.

'He's gone.'

'Who?'

'Fucker just appeared out of nowhere.' She reloaded and shouldered her weapon, squinting into the wind. 'Turned round and he was right there in the back of the van.' She sat up, clutching her leg. Blood was still running onto the snow.

'What did he look like?'

'Cold weather gear, couldn't see his face.'

'I think I found your security guard.'

'Is he okay?'

'He's dead, I'm sorry.'

'Don't be, he was a wanker.'

'Well, on the plus side, he's warm.'

She screwed up her face. 'Fire?'

'And lots of it.'

'Pozharnyy,' she muttered.

'What's that?'

'Nothing, help me up.'

45

'We need to stop that bleeding.'

'It'll stop right enough in this temperature,' she said grimly.

Something caught the corner of my eye. I spun and saw a shape creeping along the ice just at the edge of my vision.

I squeezed the trigger as I set off running towards it. He continued to crawl away, so I must have hit him this time, or Abi had. That should slow the fucker down. I fired again just to be sure but I'd been wrong, as he took off at a sprint, galloping across the snow on hands and knees like a dog. He was fast, inhumanly so, I couldn't keep pace. He darted around an ice mound up ahead. I fired again as he disappeared, then the rifle clicked on an empty chamber. I swung it round onto my back and drew my pistol in one motion, arm flitting between either end of the mound. I glanced behind: only swirling snow, Abi hadn't followed me, I was alone. With the pistol outstretched, I stepped around the ice.

A dark shape huddled in the shadows. I moved forward and gave it a kick, almost losing my balance as the shape unfurled and flapped against the ice. This is what had caught in the wind, dancing on the gusts with the snow, a discarded parka. Discarded to distract us while the owner made a swift exit? I looked round then crouched and turned it over. It was old, filthy. The hammer and sickle badge on the chest and red CCCP lettering told me it was a cold war relic. The inside was covered in blood, which I presume meant Abi or I *had* hit the wearer. I picked it up and something rolled out of the sleeve: an empty water bottle and a few snack wrappers, also covered in blood. Had someone been staking out the Jeep?

I jogged back to Abi, still sat on the snow.

'Has he gone?' she asked.

'Fucked if I know.' I helped her up, still looking around in all directions at the swirling white. 'What was that word you said earlier?'

'It's nothing, just legends.'

'If it's relevant, then…'

'Look, we're gonna die out here if we don't get back to the van.'

'Bad news,' I said, shifting my weight and holding her up on one leg. 'There is no van.'

'What do you mean?'

'Looks like your legend torched it before scarpering.'

The wind howled, a banshee cry that rolled slowly across the dismal landscape. We both looked round nervously, eyes landing on each other. Abi put an arm across my shoulders as we limped back to the fire.

'You need to tell me what's going on here,' I said.

'Was Stevo really burning? Did you speak to him, did you…'

I shook my head. 'I got there too late.'

We found the van groaning and tilting as it melted into the ice. We gave it a wide berth and headed back to the Jeep. I let her down and crouched beside her in the shelter from the howling wind.

'How far is the hotel?' I shouted.

'Only a mile or so, but in this…'

'Get in.' I stood and pulled open the Jeep's door.

She climbed into the passenger seat, grunting at the blood-covered rifle and looking over at the torn wires. 'We're not getting there in this.'

'No, but at least you'll have shelter while I get help.' I took off my outer layer and handed it to her.

'No way.' She pushed it back at me. 'I agree I'll hold you up, but you need this if you're walking out. If you go now, you have a chance.'

I removed the magazine from the rifle. Brass glinted back at me as I reloaded my own rifle and handed it to her. 'I'll be moving, you'll freeze if you sit here.'

'Not if he comes back.'

'Look, this is someone flesh and blood, and if they do come back, you empty this magazine into them.'

She didn't look convinced. 'You need to get going.' She put the rifle on the driver's seat. 'I'll be dead before you get back, whether I've got your jacket or not.' She looked into my eyes and grabbed my arm. 'Go quickly. And if you see anyone, *anyone*, don't stop running.'

I thrust my jacket back at her and slammed the door, heading in the direction of the roadway cut through the ice.

The ruts of the track disappeared into the darkness. With a glance back at Abi shivering in the Jeep, I started running, pistol held up

47

in front, but quickly abandoned that when my hands went numb. I stopped to look back again. The Jeep was lost behind me in the blizzard and the fire had almost gone out.

I realised I was shivering uncontrollably. How much more exposed it was here, in a flatter area of sea ice, with nothing to stop the wind whipping straight into me. It groaned over the hummocks, a deep writhing sound like a tormented animal that vibrated up through my boots. The snow it carried wasn't like the stuff of snowmen; these were tiny ice needles that stung any exposed skin, like rubbing fibreglass insulation on my face.

I turned my back to the wind, squinting at the pinprick of burning van. My bag had been in it, as well as my goggles. I pulled my hood tighter and tugged the mask right up to my eyes.

The cold was already well into the down of the jacket and numbing my arms. A gust dragged my hood from my head. I pulled it back up and tugged the cords as tight as they went, so I was looking through a narrow slit.

I had a pistol in my pocket with 18 rounds. My cold-weather gear was no longer adequate, I had no goggles, no hat, no provisions, and no shelter. In the last half hour or so, my chances of survival out here had first skyrocketed, then plummeted.

The fire went out, leaving me alone, black in every direction. I turned to face back into the wind and started walking again, following the meagre tracks cut down through the ice. After a few minutes, I realised they were getting fainter. The fine snow was driven hard, whipped into a frenzy by the wind. Below it, the pack ice was crusted with frozen rime as hard as steel and almost as dense. I tripped and stumbled, putting my hands out and crashing face first onto the ice.

It felt good to take a break from walking. I closed my eyes, just for a moment.

–

I don't know how long I'd been lying there. My eyes sprang open, the moaning and howling was back. I struggled to my knees and looked at my hands. They looked dark. I panicked, thinking they were frostbitten, until I realised I had my gloves on and they were just numb.

I fumbled with my pocket to try to get my torch, but couldn't get the zip open. I stood, pulling my arms up inside the sleeves and hugging them around my body to try to get a little more warmth into my fingers. Somewhere in the distance something howled, a long, low moan that swept across from the tundra and sea ice.

I started to walk again and realised I wasn't following the scant track any more. I turned to look in every direction. Nothing. I backtracked and could see a couple of boot prints leading off a few metres or so until they were blown away. How long had I been lying on the ground?

Something howled again, closer this time. Didn't sound like an animal. Or was it my imagination?

I turned again, but everywhere was a flat field, no tracks, not even my own boot prints any more. Grunts and snarls came from every direction, stalking me, just out of sight, filling my head with macabre visions, faceless hoods and burning skeletons with melting flesh searing into my mind.

There were no sounds, I told myself. It was all in my head. I angled my head down and stumbled onward into the wind.

Almost immediately I tripped over and collided with the snow again. This time I forced myself up onto my knees straightaway.

At least I thought I did, but when I looked behind, I realised I'd actually been lying on the ground for a while again, as my prints had completely disappeared. I couldn't feel my hands. I was tempted to remove my gloves to see if I had frostbite but there was no point – if I did then there was nothing I could do, and if I didn't, then I'd speed the process along by taking the gloves off.

The wind howled long and low again. I knew I wouldn't survive long sat on the ice in the pitch black of an Arctic blizzard. I stood, took a bearing on where I thought I'd come from, and staggered in what I reckoned *might* be the right direction.

Chapter Nine

The Peoples' Democratic Republic of Nambutu / French Equatorial Africa

1999

I blew smoke out of the speeding Citroën's window and watched in the side mirror the Chevy 4X4 that was tailing us, visible just for a second before we turned a corner.

'He's still following,' I said. 'You need to go faster.'

'Don't tell me how to drive, kid,' said Walshe, fumbling a gear change as the Citroën juddered around a corner.

We'd meandered through bustling streets with the 4X4 never more than a few cars behind. Now, on the dirt roads at the far edge of the city, it was even harder to lose it.

'He's gaining.'

'This car might be old and French, but it does have a mirror.'

Now I decided the dude's accent was Dutch.

He yanked the wheel, sliding the big car gracefully around a wide corner until the rear wheel clunked through a rut, sending us back the other way. Walshe fought with the wheel and accelerated hard away from the treeline.

'Pull over and let me drive,' I said.

'You're not old enough. And stop looking behind.'

'Who is it?' I asked, leaning round in my seat. The Chevy was dropping back again as Walshe threw the old car hard along the road.

'Hang on,' he said, slamming the brakes and spinning the wheel. The heavy car slewed to the left, avoiding a fallen branch, and darted down an even smaller track, thickly canopied and densely packed with overhanging bushes that smacked against the roof and glass.

'There's a tractor,' I said, pointing out of the window.

'I know,' said Walshe, pressing the accelerator harder.

I reached and grabbed the handle above the window. 'There's a tractor!'

'I FUCKING KNOW!'

He wrenched the wheel, stood on the brakes, pulling the car into a layby. Walshe forgot to take the car out of gear and it juddered and stalled. The tractor thundered along without missing a beat, driver staring at us as he passed. A long, rusted trailer loaded up with logs rolled past the window, one of its wheels seized and scoring a deep furrow in the dirt.

For a brief moment the air was thick with birdsong and overdue rain, then Walshe was twisting the key and the old engine clattered back into life. I leaned round and saw the Chevy had skidded to a halt, flashing its lights at the oncoming tractor which steadfastly refused to slow.

Walshe put the car in gear and flew out of the layby as a horn blared behind.

'Ha!' he shouted, pumping his fist out of the window. 'I'll get you later!'

We sped through the trees, bouncing through ruts and over fallen branches, not slowing for corners or for the group of workers jumping out of the road in front of us.

After ten minutes we came to a junction with a paved road. He skidded out onto the asphalt and turned right. I looked behind but there was no sign of the 4X4.

I took another swig from the water bottle and leaned back again. 'How far?'

'Nearly there.'

We drove in silence for another ten minutes or so before Walshe slowed and turned onto another track. As the leafy canopy reached in overhead, the skies darkened. The distant rumble of thunder rolled through the trees. Walshe wound his window up. I copied him just in time, as fat raindrops began to pelt the roof. Walshe slowed, pushing the car through rapidly filling ruts that were turning the road into a river.

Fortunately, we turned a corner and climbed out of the mire, into a small clearing in the trees. Walshe pulled up at the edge and killed the motor.

'We walk from here.'

'In this?'

As if on cue, the rain stopped. By the time I'd opened the door the sun was beating down through a gap in the high canopy just as ferociously as before. I took off my suit jacket and slung it over my shoulder, turning through 360 degrees to survey the steaming forest. Tall trees and dense trunks filled every direction, with the narrow dirt track the only navigational aid. Animal calls filled the air, birds or monkeys or something, maybe both. The clearing was bad enough, all knee-high weeds and ferns, I dreaded to think what insects awaited me in those dark trees. As if to taunt me, a butterfly the size of a small helicopter fluttered past my head.

'Get a wriggle on,' Walshe shouted.

Definitely not Dutch.

I turned and hauled my rucksack out of the car and kicked the mud-spattered door shut, following him into the trees.

'Where are we going?'

'Got a camp going up here.' He stopped and waited for me. 'Few rules: if it has more legs than you, avoid it. If it has more legs than a dog, squash it. If it has no legs, run away.' He held his hand out, gesturing for me to continue.

I looked at the undergrowth and shuddered, then swept a hanging vine out of the way and pressed on into the dense, noisy green hell.

'What if it only has two legs?' I asked.

'The white demons are worst of all,' said Walshe.

I felt a sharp pain at the back of my head, which quickly dulled as my vision dimmed, fading to black.

Chapter Ten

Severnaya Zemlya, Siberia
Present day

For the second time in as many days I woke in a bright room. The saving grace was that it was somewhat warmer than the frozen Kara Sea, which was all I could remember, and at that moment that's what mattered. I screwed my eyes up and breathed deeply, the lights burning through my eyelids for a few seconds until gradually my senses adjusted. When I reopened them, the lights had toned down somewhat, and my head wasn't splitting like it had been when I'd woken in that interrogation room.

The other difference was that I wasn't tied down. I was lying in a bed, not the most comfortable but it was warm and soft – a welcome contrast to the ice and howling wind.

I was staring at the ceiling trying to piece together the walk, wondering how long I'd been out, when a noise spun my head. A young man quickly stood and opened the door, nearly knocking over his chair. He bustled out, closing the door behind him, leaving me alone.

The chair rocked, my sweater and overtrousers that'd been hung on it tipping it against a desk in the corner of a room which looked like a budget motel from the Seventies, emphasis on the budget. Other than the fact the mustard-yellow wallpaper was peeling around the door frame and the laminate desk was chipped, the room was a time capsule, right down to the beige faceless telephone and bile green glass ashtray.

I pulled the duvet back and found I was still wearing my thermal layer. It wasn't cold, considering the outside temperature, but it wasn't particularly toasty either. Golubev was stingy with the thermostat. The rich don't stay rich by spending money.

I swung my legs round and tested everything. Aching, but working. I'd been worried about frostbite, but my fingers and toes were the right colour. I stood, holding the bed for a second to get my balance, and walked to the chair. The pockets of my trousers were empty. No sign of my jacket or boots, or even my socks come to think of it.

I looked at the bare desk then yanked open the drawer. It pulled out too far and came away in my hand, spilling my watch onto the floor. It stank like the inside of a school desk, musty and stale. I pushed the drawer back in, and after a quick check of the room, I concluded my gun wasn't here.

I picked up the watch. Only 8 p.m. As far as I was concerned I needed to locate this scientist, get my intel, and find a way off this island. I didn't fancy hanging around any longer than strictly necessary. A gun would make all of that easier, but that was something I'd have to tackle on the fly.

I threw my watch on the desk and rested my hands on the old radiator for a few moments, then walked back to the small window.

Beyond the steamed triple-glazing it was pitch black, but a cluster of moving lights flickered a short distance away. I leaned my forehead on the cold glass and looked down to the ground, what I reckoned was several storeys below. It was difficult to make out any details, but the building I was in looked huge, a solid block that stretched in both directions. The massive entrance was a few bays away down to my right, marked by a big blocky porte-cochère and what would probably look like a large turning circle and car park were it not for the churned dirty snow covering it. A few light military trucks and Land Rovers stood around, some blanketed in snow, others not so much, which showed they'd recently been used.

The flickering lights in the middle of the car park were the torches of people swarming around a big truck. Behind it was the stricken Jeep, dragged all the way back. So a search party *had* come after us.

'It's awake!'

I turned to see a very different Abi in the doorway. No longer snow-encrusted, wearing just jeans and a sweater, she looked entirely different. Her wet hair was pulled back into a ponytail, face fresh red from a shower rather than windburn. She limped across the room and gave me a quick, awkward hug.

'You made it back!' I said, glad of a friendly face. 'How's the leg?'

'Thanks to you.' She pulled away, looking me up and down properly. 'Leg's fine, a few stitches. How are you?' She limped to the window, resting against the sill. 'Everything still attached?'

'I think so, not tested it all yet. Who do I thank for saving my life?'

She thumbed at herself. 'Me.' She turned and pointed down outside. 'Greggy in the guard station heard me on the radio and came out after us. Picked me up not ten minutes after you left me.'

'What about the guy who attacked us?'

She sniffed and dabbed a tissue at her nose. 'Not a trace of anyone, not even the jacket. Nothing.'

'And the security guard I found?'

'Same. You sure that's what you saw?'

'Hard to mistake it.'

'Shits you up, being alone out there in the never-ending night. Different in here with the lights on, I can tell you.'

'An overactive imagination didn't burn a guy alive. We didn't chase our imaginations across the ice.'

'Fuckin' oath! First Goddamn week of winter… Probably one of the guests a sandwich short, mate. On the plus side, no one's come back in – so by now…' she made a throat-cutting motion. 'Anyone still out there is an ice pole.'

'Well, thank God you found me.'

'It was an accident.' She sat on the bed, swinging her legs up and lying back on the pillow. 'I got Greggy to circle on the way back, you were way off-course. If you'd been stronger, or a better walker, you'd have kept going all the way to the North Pole. But hey, good job you're not.'

She'd said it with a twinkle in her eye, but I knew it was true.

'Didn't do a great job of getting help, did I?'

She sat up and pulled her legs in. 'If you hadn't carried me back and put me in the Jeep with your jacket, I reckon I'd be dead. I guess you're not the heartless mercenary they said you were.'

'Who said that?'

She shrugged. 'You think they let just anyone come here?'

'Can't say I've ever been to an arms deal before.'

'You do surprise me, Mr Christopher Chambers,' she winked, 'if that is your real name.'

'Pretty sure there are no angels here, including you.'

'*Moi*?' she made a face. 'I'm ex RAEME.' She pronounced it ray-mee, the Royal Australian Electrical and Mechanical Engineers – an Army mechanic, then. 'I just look after the vehicles.'

'For an arms dealer.'

'Mate, at least I'm just a dumb mechanic. You're here to buy biological weapons, you don't have much of a moral high ground.'

'Fair enough.' I leaned back against the wall and cleared my throat. 'Listen, on the ice earlier, what was it you said? Pash…'

'They call him Pozharnyy.' She pronounced it Pajarny.

'Pozharnyy?'

'Means Fire Man, it's just a nickname.'

'Terrifying.'

'The pilots, the military guys, sometimes call him the White Demon.' She saw my face and continued. 'Right, hang on…' She got off the bed and limped to the door, checking the corridor, then lowered her voice. 'So, back in the Cold War, the CIA had those men who stared at goats, right?'

'The Stargate project.'

'Righto, well, here in the Seventies they had the crazy commie psycho brigade.'

'Someone's been watching too much Netflix.'

'I've just heard the stories, right? Mad shit went down, mind control and shit, ya know? They were trying to make fuckin' super-soldiers. I mean, I'm not saying *I* believe in this stuff, I'm saying *they* did.'

'Tech was advancing faster than ever then, nothing was off-limits.'

'Well, during the experiments there was an accident, a big fire. Half the building burned down, heaps of people died. Apparently, they were researching telekinesis… teleportation… I don't know. Soldiers who can pop up anywhere. Light fires, kill people. They're the facts.'

I arched an eyebrow.

'It's real, all right? Maybe not the super-powers bit, but they did all sorts of experiments. Anyway, what I do know is weird stuff still goes down here now and again.'

'Like what?'

'Well, that's where the ghost stories come in. They say this Pozharnyy white demon appears when someone's gonna die, a prophet-of-doom kinda scenario. A few people have seen him over the years.'

'Have you seen him?'

'Until tonight – no. Whenever people *do* see him there are unexplained fires all over the building. I've seen *those*, and the results, plenty of times. It's never pretty.'

'Anything else odd happened this week?' I wanted to steer the conversation away from ghosts and onto Burton, my predecessor. Finding his killer was priority one. Fortunately, Abi delivered straight away.

'Apart from your guy winding up dead yesterday?'

'You mean Burton? Did you drive him in like me?'

'Yup. Couple of hours later, bam, killed. My advice, watch your back.'

Like that was advice I needed. 'I thought his death was an accident?'

'Sure.' She shuddered. 'Same time as Pozharnyy shows up.'

'What the hell does this demon, these ghost stories, have to do with Burton's death?'

'Well, what's your explanation?'

'Well, it was either natural circumstances or an accident, but I don't believe in coincidences, or obviously someone killed him. Someone in this hotel.'

'You really don't know how he died, do you?'

I shook my head. 'I know nothing.'

'It was horrible. He was found alone in his room on the floor below.'

'Right?'

'He'd burned to death.'

57

I didn't have chance to reply as a cough came from the doorway.

'Leave us.' A tall, ruler-straight man stepped into the room, Savile Row's finest clinging to his equally well-cut physique.

Abi's eyes went wide, she shot me a look and bustled out of the room.

'I'll see you later,' I said, as she disappeared out the door.

'That is unlikely,' said the man.

His clean-shaven face had the pallor of the dirty snow outside, unmarked but for a faint scar across one of his angular cheekbones. Under the sickly lightbulb, his black hair glistened like the diamonds in his watch, his emerald eyes shone the colour of the ashtray on the desk. The accent was southern Russian, but only a trace of it poked out from behind his perfect English.

I rose from the bed and offered my hand. 'Thank you for not leaving me in the snow. Mr...?'

He ignored my hand and looked around the room with an upturned nose. 'You are here by invitation of my employer, it is our duty to see you are taken care of.' He smiled with all the care of a shark, the pale skin stretching like clingfilm across his sharp cheekbones.

I jerked a thumb over my shoulder at the window. 'You towed the Jeep back. Any news on your man?'

The corner of his lip began to curl. 'Not a trace of him, which is, well, convenient.' He sat on the bed with a creak and glared at me. 'So Mr Chambers, why don't you tell me what happened out there?'

'I don't normally chat to strangers, Mr...?'

'My name is Volkov, I am Mr Golubev's chief of security.'

'Okay, Mr Volkov. First off, fuck your theatrics and your shit pilots and your looming sense of dread. You can tell Mr Golubev that I brought my best suit and it's currently at the bottom of the Kara Sea along with the rest of my gear. Secondly, I need to get on with my job, like right fucking now—'

'Mr Chambers!' he snarled. 'I need not remind you that you are a guest in this hotel, and that invitation can be revoked at any time, *very* permanently. It would be better if you stay in your room until it is time to leave. We have adequate security to keep all attendees safe during

58

tomorrow's negotiations. Meals will be provided here, and then you can escort your ward back to Africa.'

'With respect, Mr Golubev can fuck himself. I work for General Kayembe and, since I gather my predecessor suffered an accident, my job is to keep his representative safe. I can't do that from this room, and if anything happens to Dr Carr, General Kayembe will no longer be doing business with Mr Golubev. So first you're going to go and fetch my gun. Then you're going to bring me some fresh clothes and fuck off to leave me to do my job.'

Volkov's face had been turning from pasty to red, and was now practically burning.

'Mr Chambers,' he said, his voice a guttural growl, 'why don't you tell me why you're really here?'

'You know why I'm here. It's my job to keep Dr Carr safe, and from the looks of things so far I've arrived not a moment too soon.'

'Really?' He picked up my scratched Bremont watch from the desk, turning it over in his hands. 'And tell me, what is your connection to Professor Balakin?' He sat back on the bed, red face now radiating smug. His voice dropped to barely a whisper. 'You know you will never get to him.'

So that was it then: there was a leak. Five minutes here, and I was blown.

'I've never heard of Professor Balakin and I couldn't give a flying fuck if I never meet the guy. But I need to find Dr Carr.'

He held the watch up. 'So be it.' He slipped my watch onto his wrist and held it out admiringly, watching it catch the light. I was so fixated I didn't notice his other hand, and before I knew what was happening, he'd snapped a set of cuffs around my left wrist.

I pulled back as he yanked me forward with the cuffs, at the same time sweeping a leg out to catch my ankles. I overbalanced, reaching to the desk behind me as I leaned to counteract. No doubt of it: he was bigger, stronger, faster, and with a firm grip on the cuffs, he had me. I couldn't let the guy pin me. 'Fuck this,' I muttered, as I whipped my right hand round off the desk and into the side of his head.

There was a dull thud. He instantly went limp, letting go of me and slumping onto the bed.

I wiped the big glass ashtray on his suit then put it back on the desk.

A tiny bead of blood ran down his temple from his perfect hairline. I quickly ran my hands up and down him. In a slim holster in the side of his trousers was a nice compact Glock 29 and a spare 10-round magazine, which solved my first problem. I slipped both into my pockets and shoved a hand into the inside of his jacket. A few bits of paper, some chuddy, and a handcuff key.

I unfastened the cuffs, took my watch from his wrist, then wrapped his body in a blanket from the bed and stuffed it into the wardrobe.

Chapter Eleven

Severnaya Zemlya, Siberia
Present day

The long corridor outside the room stretched in both directions, a blue Seventies floral print untouched by either redecorators or time. The matching carpet felt deep underfoot, unbothered by a vacuum cleaner. There was a wide opening down to the left, which seemed likely to lead to some kind of main staircase or lifts in line with the entrance.

I set off right instead, towards the wall at the far end. My socked feet made no sound on the carpet. Numbered doors counted upwards from mine at 425, so with Russia following a similar system to the States, I reckoned I was on the third floor and getting closer to the outer wall.

I needed a plan to find my scientist as soon as possible, but before I could come up with something, a more pressing plan was required – I was up to room 431 when voices drifted from the stairwell.

I pressed an ear to the room door, which told me it was probably empty – or at least, no one was doing anything noisily. The voices were getting closer. A quiet knock got no answer, so with one eye on the corridor, I pulled out the pistol. Holding it down low, I pressed my shoulder against the door and shoved. It gave easily, fifty-year-old chipboard and screws tearing the lock from the surround with hardly a sound.

I pushed it back closed and looked around. The same floral pattern covered the walls but this time in an insipid yellow and green. The room was mercifully empty, though a bag on the unmade bed told me it was occupied. My luck held when I opened the wardrobe and found it was a man's room, or at least someone who wore a bigger size than me. I quickly swapped my underclothes for a stiff pair of Levi's that didn't fall down but were slightly too long in the leg, and a slim-fit white shirt that was probably made to cling to the muscles of the room's owner but fair drowned me.

I tucked the pistol into the waistband at my back and rolled up the shirtsleeves, then rooted in the bottom for something for my feet. The guy had come prepared for all eventualities, with some beige loafers two sizes too small. Ordinarily I'd have died before putting them on, but I had a hunch wandering round in bare feet would look a tad suspicious.

I squeezed into them and waited by the door. There were no sounds now; whoever it was had gone. I waited a few more seconds then slowly opened the door and looked out to find the corridor empty. Closing the door behind me, I continued along to the end, figuring there must be another staircase here somewhere. Then I noticed the end room wasn't numbered. Instead, the plaque on the door said something in Cyrillic. I gave the handle a pull.

It didn't budge, so I rammed against it with my shoulder. It still didn't give, so I applied some heel and finally the surround splintered. I pushed it the rest of the way to reveal a bare concrete stairwell. Bingo.

Closing this door behind me plunged the stairs into pitch black. It was freezing, and it wasn't just my psychological reaction. I shivered and reached for the handrail, it stung to the touch. I grabbed it firmly anyway and tentatively made my way forward. I couldn't see a thing, the cold was already eating its way through the thin clothes.

I hit a landing, the handrail bending through 180 degrees, which I took to be halfway down the flight of stairs. I carried on, shuffling down, counting the landings until I figured I'd gone far enough to reach the ground floor. The handrail turned on its way to the basement but I felt for the door.

Music carried through it, weird Euro dance music, but not at a volume suitable for a party. I pulled the handle, but no give. Since the door opened inward it'd be harder to bust open, but, like the door above, it was only internal, with what was likely a tiny latch. I turned round, feeling behind me for the handle, then aimed a donkey kick backwards with my heel. There was a crack and a give in the wood, I pulled the handle again and this time after a few jerks it pulled inward, turning up the volume on the music.

The stairwell opened into a musty room rather than a corridor like the floors above. A cold-looking service area with shelves full of grubby linen, presumably folded there since the place closed down decades ago. Several fridges stood along one wall, the bottles racked up along a shelf nearby hinting at the contents.

But it wasn't any of that which had frozen me, it was the open doorway across the room. Specifically, the people gathered in the dim room beyond.

I'd call it a ballroom, being in a hotel, but I honestly couldn't picture Cold War Soviet generals and politicians holding a ball in a concrete box at the end of the Earth.

I slid inside the storeroom, sticking to the shadows as I crossed to the fridges. I sidestepped to the door and peered through the crack between it and the frame.

Various besuited men stood in huddled groups, though not as many guests as I'd hoped to blend in with. It was less a party, more a get-together of a select few clients and their retinues. Hushed murmurs sounded under the background music, glasses glinted in the dim lights, but the room exuded all the joy of a wake.

On a long table across the opposite wall, gleaming rifles and ammunition were laid out. Amongst the standard stuff I could see brand-new AK-19s and AK-308s, a couple of high-powered Havoc sniper rifles. Even RPGs and small missiles were stacked in a pyramid down the far end of the room.

It was easy to differentiate the clients here to make deals on these weapons, from those here to protect them. Half the people in the room seemed carefree, drinking and laughing; the others' eyes darted between doors, windows and other groups of people. The guys – because they were mostly men – with the darting eyes were generally big, muscle-bound fellas, but it was the smaller guys I thought looked more threatening. Anyone can choose a giant of a bodyguard based on muscle mass, but to choose a regular-looking bodyguard? Well, I figured they must be good at something.

I could see a couple of Middle Eastern and African terrorist groups represented (or freedom fighters, depending on your leaning), ex-Soviet-state militias, drug cartels, and probably just a few shady fuckers who wanted big guns. The nearest fell into that category; I recognised the guy from the minimal briefing mainly because his double-denim Texas Tuxedo stood out against the well-groomed men and the odd few women in dresses that glided across the parquet floor. All the style and panache of a Rustler's microwave burger.

He was a redneck dickhead, leader of a bunch of right-wing survivalists. One of my favourite things is the mental gymnastics some of these guys do to justify buying Soviet weapons and lining the pockets of Russian government officials, while proclaiming to be the proudest patriots.

A shadow flashed across the gap as a man stepped into the storeroom, speaking rapidly in Russian to a second man who was clearly his subordinate. The bigger man pointed at the fridges then turned, pausing as he saw me.

I found myself face-to-face with a man I somehow instantly knew. Expensive suit, powerful build, slightly older than me. His chiselled features were fringed with a beard that was both better groomed than mine and somehow less grey. I put it down to money but his close-cropped side parting was just as dark, with the grey at the temples saying it wasn't due to hair dye. The debonair rogue looked like a fashion marketeer's idea of what a fisherman at a wedding would look like. This was the top man.

'Good evening,' I said, pulling an arm from behind me, holding a bottle of red from the shelf. 'Couldn't find the beer.'

Viktor Golubev paused, looking me up and down with large watery eyes the colour of the ice outside. 'We haven't been introduced, Mr...' His granite face cracked then split into a wide crevasse of a grin as he wagged a finger and narrowed his eyes. '... Chambers, I think? Dr Carr's new escort? Welcome to Barensky.'

His teeth gleamed as he barked instructions to the other man, a small weasel clearly functioning as some kind of waiter, then waved him away. He picked at an imaginary piece of fluff on his sleeve, then tugged it down over the crisp white cuff of his shirt. 'You certainly look warmer now.'

I nodded. 'Much better, thanks. Now if you'll excuse me, I have a job to do.'

He put an arm across my chest. 'Your ward, Dr Carr, is quite safe, I assure you.'

'I think I'll stick close if you don't mind, given what happened to the last guy.'

'Ah,' he opened the door wider. 'Well, yes, I see Dr Carr may indeed be in need of rescuing.'

I followed his eyes to a woman with her back to me, in conversation with the redneck patriot whose face had lit up now he was talking to one of the few women in the place. She looked familiar, though I couldn't place her from the view I had of her back. The short dark hair pulled back in a no-nonsense ponytail and the long black cocktail dress gave nothing away, but there was something about the way she stood, the way her fringe bounced as she talked. *Something* was nagging at me.

This was my contact, the American scientist sent here by the CIA, the woman who was going to help me get the intel I needed to complete my mission. While Mason hadn't mentioned anything, I was sure I knew her.

Golubev called over one of the generic larger men with earpieces in, speaking rapidly in Russian. The man rushed away just as quickly.

'Sorry, Mr Chambers.' Golubev turned back to me. 'I don't suppose you have seen my head of security, Mr Volkov?'

I shook my head.

'He is new, very efficient, but sadly tends to get lost. He was on his way to speak to you.'

'Well, I haven't seen many people since I woke up.'

'Of course, there was some excitement, I think. One of my men got himself lost on the ice. A peril to life, up here. It is not for everyone.'

'If by lost you mean killed by someone...'

'It seems he was new, too. Coming out to escort you back in when his Jeep broke down. Hypothermia can set in so quickly.'

65

'Hypothermia doesn't set people on fire, or chase people through a blizzard.'

'Unfortunately, it can do all those things. And I think all you chased was his jacket?' His teeth shone again as he grinned. 'It is called paradoxical undressing. As cold affects the nervous system the victim feels like they are burning, and undresses – thus worsening their situation. As they become more confused, they can do anything. Likely he set himself alight trying to start a fire.' He waved a hand dismissively. 'But let's talk of more interesting things, Mr Chambers. You work for General Kayembe, tell me, how is his car collection?'

'A work in progress, as always.'

'Like his country. Do you know, I found him a very nice Zil limousine a few years ago, a Politburo model with armour plating. He didn't take it, but I gather he has need of it now, with the situation in Nambutu.'

'It wouldn't drive as well as his De Gaulle Citroën DS. Mr Golubev—'

'Please, call me Viktor.'

'I'm struggling to place your face, have we met before?'

'Very possibly. General Kayembe is a good client. Among other things...' he waved a hand, as if talking about guns was beneath him, '...he asks me to always be on the lookout for unique cars.'

'It must be where we've met. Did you broker the deal for his Porsche 64 that was thought destroyed in the war?'

'I did.' Golubev rocked on his feet, chest swelling. 'In fact, I thought I had found him an unknown Zil-112 Sports in a barn outside Volgograd last year,' he pointed a finger as he thought about it, 'but no, it was a replica. You have just reminded me, I may have an ex-Antarctic Kharkovchanka for sale soon. You are a fan of cars?'

'Among other things. I just tested a De Tomaso Pantera for him, actually.'

'This is a passion of mine. You know, I always have need of men like you. And my rates are much better than the general's.' He opened the nearest fridge, reached in, and handed me a bottle of Bud.

'Ah, but I get a tan when I visit Kayembe. Look, this is all nice but if you don't mind...'

'Of course.' Golubev looked over his shoulder. 'Come, let's save your Dr Carr together.' He strode out of the door into the ballroom. I opened the bottle and threw the opener on a table, then followed as he weaved his way across the room, smiling and tipping his glass at people.

He was intercepted by a man dressed almost as immaculately as himself, like a Middle-Eastern version of the Russian, were it not for an extra inch of height. Another difference was that he held a cup of tea instead of a glass. He ran a hand through his quiffed hair.

'Golubev, I must speak to you about these Verbas.'

He was referring, of course, to the latest Russian surface-to-air missiles, their version of a Stinger.

'Mr Abid, tomorrow is for business. Tonight we—'

'Do I know you?' The man named Abid cocked his head and squinted at me. It seemed everyone here knew everyone.

'This is Mr Chambers, representing our friend General Kayembe.' He turned to me. 'Mr Abid is a friend of mine.'

'Have you ever been to Afghanistan?' he asked me.

'Haven't we all, at some point?'

'You are English?' he narrowed his eyes. 'You seem familiar.'

It clicked. He hadn't been so immaculately dressed last time I'd seen the guy, in his fatigues and baggy shirt, with a wiry beard beneath his turban. No point telling him the last time I'd seen his face it'd been down the magnified lens of a rifle while staking out an enemy position.

'I don't think we've met.' I smiled.

Across the room an argument erupted between a burly security guard and a couple of women serving canapes.

Golubev's smile dipped briefly. 'Mr Abid, control your man.'

Abid left us, shaking his head.

Golubev grinned. 'You are not squeamish, Mr Chambers?'

'It doesn't bother you that you're taking opium profits to prop up a horrific regime? Not to mention those rockets could be used to shoot down airliners.'

'Does it bother you that your taxes pay for the torture and execution of innocent people around the world to prop up your country's regime?'

'You're assuming I pay taxes.'

'You are here to buy biological weapons for a Central African dictator, let's not fall out.'

He tapped my scientist on the shoulder, she turned to look at him and smiled warmly. Then she saw me and the smile melted away. Despite me trying desperately to hold it together, I think mine must have done the same, as Golubev did a double-take and cocked his head, watching us both intently.

I'd been right, there *was* a reason my CIA contact had seemed familiar. Dr Susan Carr was, like me, travelling under a pseudonym. But she was someone I'd never thought I'd see again and, like Clark Griswold, if I'd woken up with my head sewn to the carpet I wouldn't have been more surprised.

Mason's tame nerd, as he'd called her, was a legitimate top-flight biological weapons expert with plenty of first-hand experience, forged at Porton Down in England. I knew this. I also knew from a job a couple of years ago that she was a traitor, a murderer, and she'd tried to kill me. The last time I'd seen her she'd been pulling the trigger of a gun, pointed at me, on a Royal Navy destroyer off an anthrax-infested island in north-western Scotland.

'Good evening, Dr Carr,' I hissed. It took every ounce of restraint not to call her by her real name of Dr Alice String.

Chapter Twelve

The rainforest at night is a hot, sticky mess for the senses. Whoops and hisses, crackles and drips. Stagnant water, rotten flesh, damp earth and sweet pollen. I coughed and inhaled sharply as that afternoon came swimming back into focus all at once. I wasn't sure if the bastard had stuck me with something or belted me, but either way I didn't like it.

My head was killing, my joints ached, my muscles were stiff and frozen. I tried to lift a hand but it wouldn't move. I pulled my arms and realised they were bound behind my back. A wiggle of my feet told me my ankles were tied, too. My back was resting against something hard. When I stretched my fingers, I felt the rough bark of a young tree.

I could feel blood matting my hair, too, and as I squinted, dried blood on my cheeks cracked and pulled my skin. The high-pitched whine of a mosquito buzzed next to my ear. I shook my head to swish my hair, which hurt like hell.

Crackles of a fire came from behind, the orange glow flicking shadows across the dark tree trunks as if spirits were dancing through the undergrowth. Through the coppery tang of blood, I smelled the smoke. I leaned back and arched my neck. Sparks drifted upwards. I followed them through clouds of insects to see stars in a dusky blue sky way above, a circle of light surrounded by a dark canopy like the iris of an evil eye.

The bushes behind me rustled. I turned, but got a slap around the face for my efforts.

'He'll pay good money for you, son. Yep yep yep.'

I waited until the sting had subsided then tried to keep my voice steady. 'What's going on, Walshe?'

'Horror has a face,' he cackled. 'Befriend horror. If you don't, horror becomes your enemy.'

He was babbling, crouching in front of me, then started singing quietly in a language I didn't understand. He was so close I could smell alcohol, coffee, and stale sweat. He pulled out a knife and grinned broadly, turning it over so the campfire light flashed on his teeth. Strings of meat were stuck between them. He took off his cap and ran the knife across his hair like a comb, then wiped the blade on his shorts.

He disappeared behind me, making a crashing noise in the brush as he stamped away, leaving me alone with the crackling fire and the ominous animal sounds coming from the treeline. I tried to think about the animals that lived in the equatorial rainforests. Jaguars? Were they South American? Leopards? Zoology was not my strong subject, although I suspected the insects were probably more dangerous. I just hoped the fire would keep anything away.

I pulled at the ropes on my wrists, straining as I watched the undergrowth. Something moved in the trees in front of me. I froze, eyes on stalks. It didn't move again. I pulled at the ropes with renewed vigour, scanning the trees. Then I saw it.

A dark shape, almost imperceptible in the orange glow, but definitely a pair of eyes flashing in the firelight. The figure was staring at me intently. I shuffled back against the tree and held my breath.

It was a man, head and shoulders slowly rising above the bushes. As he continued to stand up I saw he carried a rifle that looked like an AK-47 in the dim glow. He looked around then quietly stepped into the clearing, rifle up at his shoulder.

It was another out-of-towner: shaved hair, big moustache, tight dark T-shirt and combat trousers over heavy-looking boots. He didn't look at me as he stalked closer, scanning the clearing until he reached me. He crouched, eyes still on the bushes.

He kept the rifle up, finger hovering near the trigger, and brought up his left hand, putting a finger to his lips. I stared at the thick hair across the back of his hand. He reached down to his belt and came up with a knife, flicking it and slicing the ropes between my ankles then reaching behind and cutting the ropes on my wrists, nicking my skin.

I grimaced as he sheathed the knife and held the rifle solidly, before he walked backwards into the bushes.

Finally he gave me an exasperated look, gesturing for me to follow him. I did, walking as quickly and quietly as I could. There was a noise from the other side of the clearing. In the light of the fire, I saw my rucksack. The new guy was waving his arm but I ran to the fire, grabbed my rucksack, then pelted towards the trees.

The man turned and walked quickly, somehow moving at speed through the dense undergrowth without disturbing it, as I seemed to crash in his wake. After a couple of minutes, we stopped.

He turned and crouched, pulling a water bottle from his hip and offering me some.

'You bloody wetwipe,' he said in broadest Cockney. 'You're just like your brother.'

'Who are you?'

'I'm Walshe, but people call me Triple-F.'

'*You're* Walshe?'

'That's what I said, prick. People call me Triple-F, or Eff for short.'

'Why?'

He grinned. 'Cos I was put on this Earth to feed, fight and fuck, and I don't do nuthin' else.'

'I'll just call you Walshe.'

The grin slipped. 'Mummy never tell you not to get into strangers' cars?'

'Who is that guy?'

'Bad news. Keep bloody moving.'

He pushed through tight ferns and crept forward. I followed, but we'd gone no more than a few paces when a roar rolled through the trees behind us. Walshe picked up the pace, I followed suit.

'I'll get you, boy!' came a shout from somewhere behind.

Walshe crouched at the edge of the trees, I came up next to him. We'd come to a road. He motioned further down, where a big old brown Chevy Suburban was pulled into the bushes.

'You were the one following us?'

'Go,' he whispered.

'Boy!' came another shout, closer this time.

'Go!' hissed Walshe, more insistently.

We ran down the dirt road, he flung open the door and turned the key as I jumped up into the passenger seat.

'You know how to use this?' he asked, thrusting the rifle into my hands.

'Yes, I use them all the time at home,' I said.

He must have missed the sarcasm as he said simply, 'Well, shoot, then.'

He shoved the Chevy into drive and took off down the road. I wound the window down and pointed the gun out, just as a figure darted into the road ahead of us. I pulled the trigger but nothing happened. I tried again.

'Safety! Give it here, you fucking pansy.'

Too late, we were past the guy. Walshe slammed on the brakes, I smacked my head on the brown plastic dashboard as he put the truck in reverse. He snatched the rifle off me, and with one hand on the wheel he reversed up the track at high speed, holding the rifle steady on the top of the door.

The figure darted back into the trees. Walshe skidded to a halt across the road and pulled the trigger, raking the bushes with a deafening burst of automatic fire.

'Fucker,' he shouted. 'Come back!'

'I'll get you, boy,' drifted the reply.

'Creepy bastard,' said Walshe. 'No chance of getting him in the jungle.' He threw the rifle on the back seat, slammed into drive, and pulled away again. 'You see him again, you run to mommy, yeah?'

'Run. Yeah.'

The trees flashed in the yellow beams of the headlights. Soon they thinned, the dirt gave way to concrete road. A brick shanty up ahead was smoking; as we passed I saw it was on fire. The flames licked out of the corrugated tin roof as a bunch of people stood around staring at it. We carried on, slowing for a street dog with a death wish, another small fire up ahead, a burning oil drum surrounded by a small crowd of people. Walshe slowed, then at the last moment sped up.

'Ten points for a native!' he laughed, swerving towards the crowds as they darted to the verge.

I grabbed the door. 'Bloody hell, what are you doing?'

He beeped the horn, still laughing. 'Silly bastards shouldn't be in the road.'

'Jesus fucking Christ!' I slammed my hands against the window, turning and arching my neck to look back. 'That wasn't a bin fire.'

'Woo hooo.' Walshe whistled. 'Smells good, right?'

'It was a man.'

Walshe grinned and put on an accent. 'Smells like KFC.'

I turned and stared through the back window as Walshe accelerated. 'Why… why would someone do that?'

'Traitors to the revolution. *Père Lebrun*, it's called, they stand you up straight and pull a tyre filled with petrol over you, pinning your arms. One match, whumpf.'

'That's fucking brutal.'

'It's a brutal fucking country.' Walshe slowed for a corner. 'Don't fuck with the PVN if you don't have the skills to back it up.'

'The who?' I turned to face the front as we came around a curve in a rocky pass, starting down a long snaking hill.

'The militia, something something Nambutu, Christ only knows.'

I caught myself nodding, as if this were an entirely normal concept. I brushed my hair behind my ears and gazed out of the window. Everyone gets what they want eventually. I'd wanted adventure, and for my sins, I'd got it.

Chapter Thirteen

Severnaya Zemlya, Siberia

Present day

Dr Alice String of Porton Down – for that's how I knew her despite her current alias of Susan Carr – quickly turned back to the redneck, face aglow. I could see my presence was as much a surprise to her – and an equally unwelcome one. Mason had known full well what he'd been doing, and had screwed both of us. I swore if I got out of this he was bumped to the top of my list.

Alice downed her champagne and handed her glass to the bemused redneck, who'd gone quieter now in the big man's presence.

'I'm afraid I'm going to have to borrow Dr Carr,' I said.

'I'm not going anywhere with *you*,' she hissed out the side of her mouth.

'Dr Carr, we *need* to discuss—'

Redneck found his voice. 'Lady said she ain't goin' with you, buddy.'

'Wind your neck in, sunshine.' I grabbed her arm but she shrugged me off.

The skin under the redneck's combover went as red as Alice's face but he didn't know what to do about it.

Golubev looked amused. 'Mr Chambers, have you met Mr Peterson of the Fifty Rifles group?' The way he said it made it clear what he thought of them.

'All white?' I said.

'We got a problem, buddy?'

'*All right*,' I smiled. 'I said, are you *all right*? Enjoying the party?'

74

Alice gave me shit-eye then looked at Golubev. 'You'll have to excuse me,' she said. 'I said I'd call in on Professor Balakin.'

'Ah yes,' Golubev glanced round for a waiter to take his empty glass. 'Has the professor emerged from his room?'

'Not yet, but I thought I'd try.' Alice was doing a fantastic job of avoiding looking at me.

Golubev turned to me. 'Of course, you will meet Professor Balakin. A great man, he is facilitating the sale of some of our products, but unfortunately he seems to have been taken ill.'

'Ill?' More like scared shitless because they'd sent the wrong man to extract him, who'd wound up dead for his troubles.

Golubev said something but I wasn't listening. I noticed redneck Mr Peterson was still staring at me, now more puzzled than angry.

'Dr Carr, we have matters to discuss first,' I said, ignoring the redneck's gaze. 'Then perhaps we can go and see Professor Balakin *together*?'

She still didn't look at me, and Golubev had picked up on it, watching us with a mixture of amusement and interest.

Alice gave me more side-eye, then said, 'I'm fine here.' She made a grabbing motion to the redneck, who passed her another glass of champagne from the side table. She downed it in one and finally looked at me. 'I don't need a chaperone, thank you.'

'I'm sorry, Dr Carr, but your safety is my responsibility.' I took her arm to steer her towards the door. 'And we have a *lot* of detail to go over.'

She snatched her arm away. 'Mr *Chambers*,' the venom dripped from the syllables, 'General Kayembe entrusted me to advise on this deal, and this is not my first rodeo.'

'General Kayembe entrusted me with your life, just like he entrusted my predecessor, who...' I lowered my voice, '...it seems was probably murdered yesterday, surprise, surprise. For all we know, *you* could be next.'

Golubev was still observing our exchange amusedly when one of his men walked over, leaning in close to whisper something into his ear. They moved away towards the wide door, which I presumed led to the lobby.

Watching Golubev out of the corner of my eye, I tried to take Alice's arm again. 'We're here to do a *job*,' I reminded her, hoping she got the inflection as I lowered my voice. 'So we're going to get on nicely, and we're going to do that job, then we're going to go home.'

Redneck moved to intercept but Alice handed him her empty glass. 'Mr Peterson, I'll no doubt see you tomorrow.'

More security guards were materialising at the doorway like wasps at a picnic bench. A towering, suited woman glared at me as she spoke to Golubev; from the way she carried herself, she obviously held some authority.

I started pulling Alice towards the door, keen to get out of here before the swarm increased. This time she relented.

'What the fuck are *you* doing here?' she hissed.

'Honestly, I have no idea,' I whispered back.

'But... you're dead.'

'Then you're stuck in Hell with me.'

Alice's face twisted into a snarl. 'This is my job, and I'm fucked if I'm letting you—'

'Look, this guy Balakin managed to get a message out on the radio.'

'So you're Burton's replacement?' She stopped, hands on hips. 'They're blaming me for his death, aren't they? What are you, divine punishment?'

'Keep your voice down.' I looked round, satisfied no one could overhear us. 'Now's not the time.'

'But Mason never mentioned—'

'Mason screwed us both,' I snapped back. 'Balakin asked for me. I don't know why, and believe me if I'd known you were here I'd still be in California right now. Don't forget it was *you* tried to kill *me*!'

'And it was you who ruined my life!'

I led her forward. 'We're in a ton of shite here and we're neck deep together, understand?'

She nodded. I looked straight ahead as we neared the doors. The tall woman motioned towards me, Golubev said something to her and she pulled out a Makarov pistol in response. As we reached the doors, Golubev put a hand up.

'Dr Carr, I'm afraid I'm going to have to borrow Mr Chambers for a short while.'

The woman next to Golubev waved her pistol.

Alice looked between us, unsure of what to do for the best.

'Pascha, please escort Dr Carr to her room and see she is safe,' Golubev continued.

Alice gave me a nervous smile, then let go of me as one of the other guards stepped forward. He took her arm and led her along the corridor to where it widened out, presumably the lobby and lifts. She looked back over her shoulder.

I gave her a terse smile and turned back to Golubev, glancing at the pistol in the woman's fist.

'If anything happens to Dr Carr…' I said.

Golubev held up his hand. 'Anya here will ensure she is quite safe.'

Shouts erupted in the lobby; suddenly people were running in all directions. Security guards, some in suits, others more like Arctic commandoes togged out in cold-weather gear, were slung with submachine guns.

The woman Golubev had called Anya spoke rapidly in Russian. Golubev replied, ignoring me entirely, then turned to shout commands to the other security personnel, who buzzed away again. A team looked to be gathering at the end of the corridor, zipping up white parkas and slamming magazines home into submachine guns. Shit was obviously going down, but what kind?

Finally Golubev turned to me.

'My apologies, Mr Chambers. I need your help with something.' A smile cracked his face but made it nowhere near his eyes. 'Come with me.'

'Where are we going?'

Anya waved her pistol, and I took the hint; wherever we were going was no business of mine. I followed Golubev to the front of the two-storey lobby, past a long walnut reception desk. I turned to walk backwards, taking in an enormous tiled wall mosaic stretching the full height of the space. It was the Earth, as seen from above the North Pole. Russia and most of the Pole was coloured red, completely dominating the globe from this angle and harking right back to Stalin's *Red Arctic* propaganda. The gold hammer and sickle of the Soviet Union sprouted leaves, cradling the planet, with a shining star marking the North Pole.

Bright lights flashed, reflecting off the mosaic. I spun to the doorway to see headlights turning outside.

'Put these on,' Golubev said.

One of the guards was holding out a white Parka and overtrousers. Golubev himself was being helped into one while waving commands at a group of guards by the stairs.

I took the coat. Evidently we were going outside.

'It's minus thirty out there and I'm wearing loafers with no socks,' I said.

Anya shouted to one of the security team on the reception desk, who jogged over and knelt down, untying his laces.

'Put his boots on,' said Golubev.

I bent to pull on the disgustingly warm boots.

'Don't worry, you won't have time to feel the cold.'

'Always with foreboding menace,' I muttered, but Golubev was already marching away towards the back of the lobby. I looked at the main doors and headlights outside, then back at Golubev, now speaking with the small group of heavily armed soldiers that'd been gearing up.

I pulled the laces tight then followed Anya's waving pistol to Golubev.

'Where are we going?' I asked.

She grunted and pushed me forward.

'Mr Chambers,' Golubev called out. 'Please, this way.'

Flanked by his guards, he led me across the back of the lobby, underneath a huge floating staircase that rose through the central tower all the way up several stories. Music and voices drifted from the ballroom but back here, with the temperature and the sense of abandonment, of isolation, the place felt dead.

'You seem to get on well with Dr Carr,' he said, with a crease of an almost-smile. 'You know each other?'

I just nodded.

He pushed open a door, holding it for me. 'When hosting events such as these, we like to accommodate guests in, if not luxury, then at least in safety and as friends. We are, after all, working towards the same goal.'

'What goal is that?'

He overtook me, holding an arm out to herd me along. 'Well, we each get what we want. In my case, it is money. In your case, it is weapons for General Kayembe, who pays you for doing so. Which makes your goal money, exactly the same as mine. This makes us friends.'

The music from the ballroom had disappeared. I turned to see Anya locking the door behind us before striding to catch up.

I nodded at Golubev. 'I'm glad to hear that.'

'But friends do not have secrets.' He raised his eyebrows. 'Please bear that in mind.'

'I'm only here because Burton – Dr Carr's previous escort – was killed. I think it's *you* who owes *me* answers.'

'Mr Burton's death was not suspicious.'

'So how did he die?' I stopped. 'I gather there was a fire?' He carried on walking so I grabbed his arm, there was a shuffling of weapons from the security guys behind me.

He shook his head at them then shrugged me off. 'Drunk as a fish and smoking in bed. There is nothing to suggest it was anything other than a tragic accident.'

'Just like that security guard burning out there on the ice was an accident?'

He stopped and spun. 'You have no doubt heard the rumours,' he lowered his voice. 'You know strange things are said to happen here…' He looked at the ceiling for the right word. 'Certain… *phenomena*. But that's all they are: rumours.'

'Until the next person turns up burned to death?'

He grunted and led me onwards in silence, the only sound being our footsteps and the eerie moan of the wind assaulting the walls outside. We were in the other wing of the hotel, where the tiled floor was grimy, with decades of uncleaned muck clinging to yellowed plastic signs on the wall. Golubev paused at yet another door. Its newer sign said, *No Entry,* in English. I presumed that's what the older Russian sign above it said, too.

He rested his hand on the wall. 'You *have* heard the stories about the hotel, I take it? The reason the pilots will not land here. The older pilots, the ones who remember what happened.'

'All I've been told are children's ghost stories,' I replied.

'Oh, they're not stories, Mr Chambers. These things happened.' He grabbed the handle and opened the door, the temperature plummeted. Beyond was a corridor decorated exactly the same, but all life had been sucked from it, the saturation and warmth dialled right down. He took a torch from a hook on the wall and clicked it on, illuminating dust that swirled as we walked in. More torches clicked on as the guards shuffled through behind us, the cold LED beams giving off all the warmth of the blizzard outside. The door closed behind us, the harsh blue-white light bleaching whatever colour there'd been. I looked at Anya, still gripping the pistol, still in her suit, but appearing not to feel the cold.

'The hotel was completed in the early 1970s, a shining example of what I think you would call Brutalist architecture,' said Golubev, striding into the gloom. 'But the architecture was seldom seen, given its latitude.' He waved a hand around the corridor. 'I used the word "hotel" loosely, you understand. *Barensky Hotel*, it is a joke people made. But it was an important position. There was at the time a large Naval base just north of here, a resupply station for the Northern Surface Fleet and scientific vessels, as well as submarines, obviously. There is a large space defence program about thirty miles away, and several ballistic missile silos. The Severny atomic bomb testing ranges are west of us. All abandoned now. There were also large mines on the islands. Copper, lead and zinc. And oil, lots of petroleum offshore.

'The hotel was built to house visiting military officers, business owners, executives and politicians.'

'I can just see the who's who of Moscow clamouring to visit.'

He stopped at a corner and shone the torch back towards the door we'd come through. The guards had unslung their submachine guns and were stood either side of the corridor warily. Anya pushed through them, fishing in her pocket.

'She is a Yakuts, she doesn't feel the cold like we do,' Golubev chuckled. 'Yes, this was not a popular destination, but busier than you might think. Until it was shut down, of course.' He turned and shone the torch the other way as Anya passed me. The corridor here hadn't been touched in decades. Wallpaper was peeling, the paint was bubbled and discoloured, bare light fittings hung from the drooping ceiling. It ended in a huge steel door, the kind you'd see on a ship or submarine. 'In 1975 the building was turned over to the KGB. A couple of years later there was an… incident.'

'What kind of incident?'

Anya inserted a large key into the steel door. There was a thunk as bolts withdrew, the temperature dropped again as she swung the door open. It groaned on its hinges, yawning into a black chasm.

I zipped the jacket tight and pulled the hood up. 'Where are we going?' I asked, my breath fogging in the air.

Golubev motioned the guards forward, who surrounded us as we walked into the darkness. He looked at me and smiled, as cold as the steel door.

'We are going to see my head of security, Mr Volkov.'

My stomach dropped, my blood instantly as cold as the ice crusting the concrete.

Chapter Fourteen

Severnaya Zemlya, Siberia
Present day

I shifted around in the jacket, feeling the pressure of the pistol at my spine and weighing up my options. There was nowhere to go. Two guards in front, one either side of me, and two behind, all with weapons up and ready, as Golubev led us deeper into the labyrinth.

The corridor beyond the steel door was not the gateway to Hell, unless Hell really was a derelict Seventies hotel. It looked identical in décor to those we'd come through, though as I was prodded along I could see exposure to the elements had taken its toll. The further we went, the worse it got. Wallpaper had peeled in huge sheets in some places, leaving dark cracked walls. It may never rain here, but that didn't mean it was dry. The ceiling sparkled with frost, somewhere in the distance the wind moaned, a cold breeze tickled through my hair.

The heavy door closed behind us with another solid thunk from the lock, with Anya on the warmer side.

We marched round corners and along dark corridors, torches flashing as we weaved around the fallen masonry of collapsed sections of floors above, as well as rotten doors hanging from their hinges.

Golubev dropped back and took my arm, leading me through the dark interior with his torch on the floor. The howling wind tore through the cracks and windows above us. There was an odour in the cold air, difficult for me to distinguish with a near-frozen nose, but like the faint scent of cooking.

'I said there was an incident,' Golubev said. 'As you have no doubt guessed, this side of the hotel suffered a terrible accident some time ago.'

'A fire?' I asked. The smell of burning was stronger now, as if it was seared into the walls.

He stopped and nodded. The sound of the wind rushing above had increased. I realised there were no walls here, but it was somehow more claustrophobic with the black surrounding us, dancing torch beams of the guards heading off in all directions.

One of the guards set a box down on the ground and knelt by it. Suddenly, a bright white light filled the space, forcing me to squint. A large, battery-powered work-lamp. I turned away to let my eyes adjust, taking in what had been a large room.

Dust and snow danced in the beam, blown around by the misty breath of the troops lurking uneasily in the gloom. The far edges of the room were still in shadow but the empty windows nearby were decorated with elaborate plasterwork. Some of the red and white paint remained, but mostly the walls were blackened with age and, I presumed, the results of that fire. Smelled like bacon, weirdly.

As my eyes adjusted, I could see there was none of the rot associated with ruins in milder climates, no moss or lichen or slimy mould. I realised now why there had been such a thick steel door separating what would have been one building at one time, with various inter-connecting rooms and corridors. Now that door would seal out these ruins, this cold.

A couple of Golubev's security guys were talking excitedly to each other in Russian. I turned to them and stopped.

Several metres away, on the ground in the middle of the pool of harsh bright light, was a steaming pile of clothes. I held up a hand and realised the dust and snow dancing in the light was not dust and snow at all, but tiny charred flakes. My nose wrinkled. All of a sudden the stench of burnt bacon made sense.

'My head of security,' said Golubev, putting a hand over his mouth.

I took a deep breath and moved closer. A burned face grinned at me, lips and skin and hair all gone, the white eyes and teeth shining brightly. He was looking at me, into me, accusingly. The top of his suit was so mangled and burned, it was difficult to tell where it ended and skin began. Wisps of smoke and steam still drifted from the remains of his clothes.

I looked at Golubev and frowned.

'My men extinguished the fire before it claimed the body entirely.' He took his hand away from his mouth. 'This is Mr Volkov.'

I looked across the corpse, putting my own hand to my mouth. 'I don't want to seem insensitive, but how do you know it's him?'

'His clothes, his shoes. And this.' He gestured to one of the other men, who rolled up the smouldering corpse's trouser leg. On the side of his shin was a tattoo of a star sliced through with Russian script. 'A gang symbol,' Golubev said.

He spoke with one of his men, who went on for a while in Russian, pointing to the windows and back outside. Golubev listened carefully, nodding, but the only phrase I caught was *Belyy bies*, 'white demon'. Something flashed in my brain, but it faded as I tried to focus on it. A memory, or possibly an old story I'd heard.

Whatever had burned Volkov hadn't reached any further than his chest.

'Strange way to murder someone,' I said. 'Or are you suggesting this was an accident, too?'

Golubev narrowed his eyes. 'In the disused ruins of an Arctic hotel with no sources of ignition, I would suggest it is an even stranger way to have an accident.'

'Which suggests Burton's death was no accident either.' As if anyone had really believed it.

He nodded grimly and looked at the leader of the team, who was casting his head around nervously. 'This is Gregori, who as of ten minutes ago is my acting head of security. He saw the man who did this.'

I cocked my head. 'Saw him?'

Golubev said something to Gregori, who lifted his ski goggles onto his head to reply, and shook his head.

'He didn't see his face. He and another man were patrolling outside,' he pointed to the windows behind us, 'they saw the flames.' He paused to consider something, and asked Gregori another question. When the answer was received, he nodded, then started speaking English to me again. 'My men jumped through the windows and ran to see what was on fire. As they did they saw the killer. They lost him in the ruins.'

'What did the killer look like?'

Golubev didn't have to ask Gregori; evidently he'd already been told. 'Old clothes. Cold-weather gear, Soviet military style.'

'How does he know?'

'Mr Chambers, you are English and not entirely unfamiliar with your nation's military dress, so I presume you would know what an English soldier during the Cold War would look like. Gregori was in the special forces in the Arctic for over ten years. If he says the killer was wearing old Soviet-style gear, then he was.'

'You misunderstand. I meant, how does he know this other man was the killer?'

Golubev paused to consider this. 'I suppose this is not certain.'

'Hmm.' I nodded.

'But who else would be out here with the body at such a time?'

'Who indeed?' I muttered.

'What do you think?'

'About what?'

'Well, this.' He waved his arm around.

'I think I'm bloody freezing my nuts off.'

'Mr Chambers. Clearly, I am asking for your help.'

I looked from Golubev to the troops standing around, all nervously looking behind them, fingers still not straying far from triggers. I looked down at Volkov's perma-grin.

'I'm afraid he's beyond help, Mr Golubev.'

'Don't be stupid.'

'You seem to think I'm a detective.'

Golubev looked round his men and leaned in closer. 'You are in a unique position, Mr Chambers. You arrived this evening, *after* these strange events began. Also, Mr Volkov was killed while I was with you.

'All of this means you are one of the only people in the Barensky Hotel who I can be *sure* is innocent of Mr Volkov's murder. Your predecessor was also probably killed by the same person, so you have an interest in this crime. So you will help me, yes?'

The irony would have warmed my soul were it not approaching minus thirty. 'I won't help you, no. I'm here to look after Dr Carr and right now I'm not doing that. There's a killer on the loose and I'm out here. I should be in there.'

His voice took on a new tone. 'Mr Chambers, do not mistake this as a request.'

'I'm telling you, I have no experience in this…'

'Let me put it another way. You will do this, or,' he looked me up and down and smirked, 'without trousers, I suspect it will not be long before frostbite takes hold in your extremities.'

I smiled. 'General Kayembe told me you could be persuasive. Well, let's see what we have then.' I crouched, muttering a string of obscenities as my frozen nostrils got within more effective range of the charred flesh. 'Has anyone moved him?'

'No one has touched the body, except to confirm his identity. When they found him they sought help, then stood guard. They are not idiots.'

'Uh huh,' I nodded, looking along the ground at the scuffled boot prints in the dirt. 'I don't suppose you can identify any tracks?'

'Gregori looked but found nothing identifiable.'

'No tracks in the snow outside?'

'*Pozharnyy*,' said Gregori.

Golubev gave Gregori a look which cut him off. He asked a question, waited for the reply, then shook his head. 'The killer just… vanished.'

'Which means the killer is still here. He didn't run off into the snow so he's either in these ruins or the hotel.'

'This is my thoughts also. But since this is a labyrinth it does not help us.'

Half of every breath crystallised in the air right in front of me; the rest clung to my moustache and instantly froze. It created an accumulation I had to wipe from my mouth and face every thirty seconds, which the others took as a sign of squeamishness on my part.

I heard a scuff in the dirt behind me as one of the security guards shuffled closer. '*Pozharnyy,*' the man muttered. '*Belyy Bies.*'

I looked up into Golubev's eyes. 'How much credence do you give these ghost stories?'

Chapter Fifteen

Severnaya Zemlya, Siberia

Present day

Golubev narrowed his eyes, fog swirling and hanging in the air as he breathed deeply. Finally, he cleared his throat. 'I didn't take you for a superstitious man, Mr Chambers.'

'I'm not, but someone else might be.'

'It certainly seems we have awoken *something* these last few days, whether that is a ghost or...' He held up his hands.

I waved to Gregori, the nearest security guard, gesturing for his torch. He passed it over. I clamped it between my teeth while patting Volkov's body down. As I panned over him, though, I made the mistake of looking at his face. His teeth glinted in the light, still grinning at me, steaming eye sockets following me. I gipped, dropped the torch, and pulled away.

I took a deep breath, suppressing the urge to cough, and picked up the torch. 'Was he armed?'

'Yes. Try the inside waistband.'

I opened his jacket and felt around for what I knew wasn't there, because I could feel it pressing at the base of my spine. 'Looks like the killer took his gun. Never heard of a ghost that needs a gun.' I put the torch between my teeth again and forced myself to bend closer to Volkov, then took it out and rocked back on my legs. 'He has an injury.' I pointed the torch at the bit of head where I'd clouted him with the ashtray. 'Looks like he was smashed over the head with something heavy. I'd say he was killed right here.'

'Why not elsewhere? There are marks in the dirt. It looks like he has been dragged?'

'I don't think so.' I flicked the torch beam around in the scuff marks, put on my most authoritative voice, and did a great impression of every Home Office pathologist I've seen, while spouting absolute bullshit. 'The wound is deep – it would have bled a lot. If he'd been killed elsewhere there'd be a blood trail.' I pulled on his suit to turn him over, making a show of looking at the floor under him. 'I think he was hit over the head and then quickly set on fire before it got the chance to bleed a lot. What blood there was, evaporated in the heat.'

'What is that?' asked Golubev.

One of the scrappy paper notes I'd seen earlier had fallen out of his pocket. I moved them and his phone clear. Gregori stepped forward with his glove out, so I handed them to him and looked around. Obviously I knew Volkov wasn't killed here, because he was killed in my room. Someone – singular or multiple – had carried him out here then set fire to him. Why?

Behind me, Golubev swore and launched into a heated discussion with Gregori. I looked up at them both as they excitedly pawed over the scraps of paper.

'Does it tell us who the killer is?' I asked, already wishing I didn't have a bulky jacket covering my gun. It felt like I might need it at any second.

'In a way, yes.' He turned one of the scraps of paper round to show me, which was pointless as it was in Russian. 'It says that someone has travelled to the Barensky Hotel with the objective of killing Professor Balakin.'

Volkov's questions and demeanour in my room made sense now: obviously, he quite rightly suspected the assassin was me. 'Balakin?' I put on a good puzzled Columbo face. 'Your bioweapons expert, right?'

He nodded. 'I'm not sure why someone would want him dead, but obviously this is the reason Volkov was killed.'

I rocked back onto my feet, squatting next to the body. 'So Volkov got a tip-off from someone. He worked out who's been sent to kill Balakin, probably confronted them. He was lured out here, possibly to meet them? Or maybe he lured the killer out here? Either way, when confronted, the killer struck.'

It was a pretty good theory because it was almost correct. Golubev liked it, he was nodding like a Churchill Dog on a speedbump.

'Why is Balakin so important?'

'He is crucial to the sale of some of my products.'

'Any other reason?'

'He is an important man for lots of reasons, but no, I cannot think of anything in particular.'

'Well, someone is going to great lengths to get to him. I'll need to see him.'

'Of course. Tell me, why did the killer burn the body?'

'I think if your men hadn't intervened it would have made identification impossible.'

'But there was only one man missing from the hotel. It could only be Volkov.'

'Only one missing *so far*…' I was almost enjoying myself in my new role. 'Mr Volkov here makes three burned-up corpses.' I looked Golubev square in the eyes. 'Maybe the killer is planning on more.'

'Come!' He shouted something to his guards, who started moving all at once. 'There is no more to be done out here, not tonight.'

No arguments from me; I could no longer feel my fingers or toes. We made it out through the demolished rooms with the help of a couple of Golubev's men and their torches. It was interesting to see what remained – not just debris, but relics from years gone. Some were fairly innocuous, like the upturned mustard-coloured office phone, a room filled with soot-blackened melamine coffee tables and chairs, and another with a fatback TV half-melted to its cracked, smoked-glass stand.

Others were more ominous reminders of the past. An Ushanka hat with a hammer and sickle hiding under a frozen pile of old military parkas, all bearing CCCP logos. A portrait of Brezhnev hanging askew on a half-collapsed wall. An empty concrete staircase ending at a void, littered with an avalanche of pamphlets that looked like nuclear safety information, judging by the mushroom cloud on the cover. Urbexers or eBay profiteers would have a field day with the kitsch.

I held my hood as the wind increased, realising we were heading outside, rather than retracing our steps through the ruins. I shoved my bare hands deeper into my pockets and squinted as snow was whipped into our faces.

'We are unlucky with this weather,' Golubev shouted.

'I guess, don't build hotels in the Arctic if you don't like snow?'

'It doesn't normally snow, it is unseasonably warm.'

I sniffed. My nose was freezing up. 'Remind me not to visit when it's really cold.'

'You should go inland, where it gets down to minus forty. You don't take a piss outside, I tell you that.' Golubev smiled and pulled his hood tighter. 'Here at the coast it is quite tropical. Still, it is not good to spend too long outside.'

We turned a corner only to be assaulted full-on by the wind and snow, making further discussion impossible. We trudged on through the drifts. Above me, the whirling snow obscured the top of the building, where dark concrete stretched away to meet black sky. The concrete was entombed in thick ice, punctuated by black openings like the ruins of some ancient castle. Accumulated rime ice framed glassless windows in the yawning void and rounded everything off like insects trapped in clear amber. Every time a torch beam flashed across the building it sparkled back, turning everything into a mirror. In contrast to the wing I'd woken up in, which was frozen only in time, this side of the hotel was actually frozen, derelict and slowly decaying.

Golubev had lied about not being out here long enough to feel the cold. I gritted my teeth to stop them chattering, and wondered how long it took for hypothermia to set in up here without the gloves and hat and everything else the others had. Even the Arctic-hardened security guys had pulled their hoods in tighter, turning their heads away and leaning forward until we reached the lights of the main entrance.

The snow wasn't as bad under the huge porte-cochere, with its thick concrete pillars supporting a slab way overhead, big enough for a coach or truck to pull up under to drop guests in relative shelter next to the doors. But the uncovered front and sides did nothing to stop the wind gnashing at my uncovered face and digging through my trousers.

Bright headlights swung across the building. I shivered as I watched as a canvas-backed truck rumbled across the car park. It shuddered to a halt outside a brightly lit garage filled with a couple of Lada 4X4s and a Land Rover.

Golubev shouted to a man who snapped off a salute and jogged over to the truck. The tailgate dropped, disgorging more heavily armed Arctic commandoes.

'Wait here,' Golubev shouted above the wind. He stamped across the icy parking area, gesturing at his men, who formed up in front of the truck.

I stomped up and down to stop my legs seizing up and counted guns. Ten new guys plus six of Golubev's existing men, including the leader shouting to his boss above the wind, were waving at different points around the building.

There was a shout behind me, I looked round. Anya was holding the main door open, gesturing to me, before retreating through the inner doors back to the lobby.

Again, I didn't need telling twice, running inside and closing it behind me. The wind died down, I blew into my hands, watching Golubev and his team stamp back through the blizzard as the new guys unloaded equipment from the truck. Behind me, just inside the inner doors, Anya was speaking into a radio. Next to her was a concerned-looking Abi.

A blast of frozen air flooded the lobby as Golubev pulled open the doors. I shoved my hands back into my pockets and breathed slowly, watching the glass on the inner door fog.

'My reinforcements,' Golubev said. 'I told you I had this in hand.'

'Lucky they were ready to come up here.'

The corner of his mouth twitched upwards. 'I have friends in many places.'

He opened the inner doors. The lobby felt like a sauna. Our escorts peeled off their masks and unzipped their parkas. As Golubev spoke a few words to Anya, I grabbed Abi and steered her away from the herd.

'Christ, it's happened again, hasn't it?' she said.

I nodded. 'Someone's running round torching people. You need to be straight with me. What's going on?'

She looked past me, at Golubev. 'Later, I'll tell you what I know.'

'Mr Chambers?' I turned to see Golubev was waiting for me, arm extended to shepherd me away. Eyes darting, he hustled me into a room off the lobby, a small office stacked with shelves of old stationery.

He sat on a desk and waved at me to close the door. I did, leaning back against it and unzipping my jacket, too hot while my legs simultaneously felt frozen solid.

'Mr Chambers, what do you know of...' he paused as if waiting for a word to materialise, '...spontaneous human combustion?'

Chapter Sixteen

The Peoples' Democratic Republic of Nambutu / French Equatorial Africa

1999

People always said we were alike, Justin and me. The truth was, I'd always just copied him. He wore an A-Team T-shirt, I wanted an A-Team T-shirt. He got a Nintendo, I wanted my own Nintendo. He started playing guitar, I started learning the drums. As a result, by the time I was eleven, I was the only first year in high school with long hair and Nirvana in my Walkman.

That all changed when I hit fourteen. He disappeared, joining the Paras at just the right age for me to start getting my own life. And for years I forged that life, until he reappeared. It started with trips home on leave to see us, instead of the usual holidays he'd take to avoid us. And he'd tell me all about what he was doing, *who* he was doing. All very exotic and adventurous, but five years after he'd gone, I'd put in an application of my own. I didn't fancy jumping out of planes. I wanted to fly them.

And now, in the late spring of 1999, I was six months away from joining the Fleet Air Arm of the Royal Navy. Of course, he'd taken the piss, to the point where I'd genuinely considered following him – just like I always had. That was when he'd asked for a hand with something. Easy money, he'd said. Low risk. I needed the money, and I'm naive.

The man walking over to me as I climbed down from the sticky brown vinyl seats of the Chevy was not the boy I'd grown up with. Dimmed by a cloud of mosquitoes, the yellowy light on the wall of the brightly painted building shone off his shaved head, showing up a moustache just like Walshe's, his arms thicker than my legs squeezed into a Hawaiian shirt as tight as it was bright. I realised for the first time what an idiot I'd been to come; we inhabited different worlds now. I still got the skateboard out on a weekend while he was away on another continent, stripping his rifle.

He grinned and opened his arms to embrace me, and I felt some of that familiarity. Out here in the jungle, it was good.

'You get the guns okay?' asked Walshe.

'No problem with them,' Justin replied. 'Is the road out again? I thought you'd be back ages ago.' He pulled away, saw the blood matting my hair and frowned. 'Johnny?'

'Truck's making funny noises still, and it's pulling more.' Walshe slammed the door and walked round the truck.

Justin pushed my head down and started brushing my parting around.

'Everything went fine,' continued Walshe, 'except, oh yeah, the silly prick got in the wrong car, didn't he? Had to follow him for miles.'

'Get off, I've had worse down the skatepark.' I shoved Justin away and looked past him at the lights of the street heading down into the city. We'd pulled into a rough parking area behind what looked like a bar on the edge of town.

'Hey,' Justin punched me on the arm. 'Tell me what happened.'

'The headhunter is what happened,' said Walshe, leaning his rifle on his shoulder.

'Oh Jesus.' Justin wiped blood off his hands onto his trousers and grabbed my rucksack. 'Get inside, we'll put you on the first plane back tomorrow.'

'Back to mommy,' said Walshe.

'Who's the headhunter?' I asked.

I followed them into the breeze-block shack and through a doorway into a dark, musty room. Tables and chairs were stacked at one side of the room beneath a papered-over window. One had been pulled out with a few candles jammed into beer bottles giving off the only light. It stank of stale weed and even staler beer.

'Who's the headhunter?' I repeated.

He ignored me. 'Your hotel was bombed this morning,' said Justin, 'so we're dossing down here.'

I looked around at the dingy room. 'Yeah, I heard. What is this place?'

'Bar. Brothel. Closed down a while ago.'

'Can we go to a real bar?'

'No.'

'Take him to Dexter's' said Walshe. 'Dexter's is full of expats.'

'Anything more... local?'

'No,' said Justin again. 'Dexter's is for journos and spooks.'

'And birds,' added Walshe.

'I don't wanna go somewhere filled with journos and spooks, I wanna go somewhere for real people.'

'We're on a bloody job,' said Justin.

'You a couple of fucking benders or what?' said Walshe. 'We'll get some beers, get some birds.'

'Shut up, both of you.' Justin kicked an empty beer crate across the room which shattered against the wall. 'We're not on holiday. We keep our heads down and travel at night. If the militia take an interest in us we're an easy target.'

'Target for what?' I asked.

'Europeans come to Nambutu for one reason: to exploit. Whether it's dealing arms, mining or farming, it only lines the pockets of a few. Anyone that doesn't have the right permits – and by permits, I mean lining the pockets of the Commissaire – is fair game. That means us.'

'What do they expect? They don't manage their shit properly, they get exploited.'

'Nice attitude,' I said, 'really nice.'

Walshe slapped me on the side of the head.

I walked to the wall to look at the huge map pinned up. 'It bloody stinks in here, is all.'

'You get used to it.'

I traced a finger along the roads on the map. 'This is where we're hitting them?'

'You're getting back on the plane, sunshine,' said Walshe. 'Alphas only.'

'Really? 'Cos Village People called, they want their 'taches back.'

Walshe grabbed me in a headlock and squeezed, slapping my cheek. 'Gob off again, you little dipshit.'

'All right, let him go,' said Justin.

Walshe threw me against the wall. I winced and ended up on the floor.

'Do you really call him Triple-F?'

'No one does.' Justin chucked a bottle of beer to Walshe and cracked his own open on the bar. 'I was wrong, you're not ready.'

I massaged my neck and pointed at Walshe. 'If Triple-H had been on time to pick me up I'd have been here hours ago.'

Justin shrugged. 'Excuses won't help once the shit hits the fan.'

'I saved your life, you prick,' said Walshe. 'You speak to me like that again I'll knock ten bells of shit out of you.'

'How much is a bell of shit?'

'What?'

'I mean, it's knock seven bells out of me, or knock the shit out of me. Either, or.'

'You dickhead.' He made to stand, but Justin put his arm out.

'Leave him.'

'You could knock triple-shits out of me if you like.'

'Look at him, the skinny runt. Thinks he's in *Pulp Fiction*, long hair and cheap suit in the middle of Nambutu.' He pointed at my Italian shoes. 'Bet those did well in the jungle. Where's your gear?'

'My suitcase was taken at the airport.'

'Taken? By who?'

'The guards, they…'

'We don't need a brew bitch.' Walshe grabbed my rucksack and opened it, emptying it on the grimy floor. 'Just look. What the fuck's this, Acqua Di Parma?' He threw the bottle over the bar behind him where it smashed on the floor. 'You want to smell like a bitch when you're upwind of two hundred rebels in the jungle? And what's this for?' He held up my Discman. 'Going for a jog in the rainforest listening to Boyzone? And what on God's bloody Earth is this?' He opened a plastic wallet. 'Your fucking PADI certificate! Where do you think you're going to go scuba diving here?'

I shrugged. 'I thought I'd better be prepared.'

'Dib dib dob, I bet you were in the scouts. And it's in your own name too, Muppet.' He tapped it against the top of my head. 'We need a proper driver for this job, and Kurt fucking Cobain here can't even get off an aeroplane without help.'

'None of that matters, I can drive.'

'How long you been driving? A few months?'

'I've been driving on the farm since I was ten. I've been racing since I was fifteen.'

'Go-karts are a bit different to driving dirt roads through the jungle under machine gun fire.'

I walked over to the bar. 'Well, I know the front right brake calliper is sticking on that '81 Chevy Suburban outside. You could hear it grinding.'

'Bollocks.'

'I could feel the heat when we got out. Also feels like the centre bearing's giving up too, or maybe the diff. You push it much more and you'll lose four wheel drive, probably when you need it most.' I shrugged and picked up a warm bottle of beer. 'But you know that.'

Justin looked at Walshe, raising his eyebrows in a *told-you-so* way.

'We don't need a mechanic, we need a driver,' spat Walshe.

'You could have Colin bloody McRae, but if your car doesn't work, you're not going anywhere.'

'Fine, smart guy. Go out there and fix it.'

'How many other Chevy Suburbans are there in the city?'

'It's a fucking boss truck,' said Walshe.

'Fucking aye, it's rad, but you got it cheap because it's about to die and the owner couldn't get the parts. Some GI will have brought it over back in the day. The 350 V8 is a great engine but where you gonna get parts from if that shits?'

'You telling us it's BLR?'

'Beyond Local Repair,' Justin translated the Army jargon.

I nodded. 'If you want something reliable, you look at what everyone else is driving.'

'Old French cars.'

'Ignore those. I'll tell you what I saw, a few Landys but mostly Japanese 4X4s. Nissan Patrol, Toyota Landcruiser, Mitsubishi Pajero. That's what we need.'

'We?' Justin had a smirk on his face.

'Well, he can't drive for shit,' I said, pointing at Walshe, 'and I know I'm better than you. You need a driver if you're gonna pull this off.'

'And a car.'

'I've got one in mind.'

Chapter Seventeen

Severnaya Zemlya, Siberia
Present day

Golubev shuffled forward on the desk, waiting for me to speak. He'd asked about *spontaneous human combustion*, what the hell did he expect me to say?

My face broke into a smile. 'It's in the same box as Bigfoot and poltergeists.' His own face remained blank; this was clearly not a source of amusement for him. 'Okay, I've seen pictures of upturned zimmer frames and legs sticking out from piles of ash.'

'I'm not sure I believe in ghosts, Mr Chambers, but there are other phenomena… Things are going on which are unexplainable.'

'Fire is only inexplicable to a primitive brain, Mr Golubev.'

'This is all a joke to you?'

'No, I'm deadly serious. People are dying horribly; we need to find out why. And that means you filling me in on some history.'

Predictably, he skirted it. 'You believe there is a killer somewhere here now amongst us?'

I smiled. 'You're hosting an arms deal, I presume they're not all Cubs.'

'Cubs?' He furrowed his brow then shook his head. 'Ah, you are being sarcastic again. This is not helpful.'

'Most of the people here are killers, so you've created this situation.' I shrugged. 'It's your guy that's been murdered, I just don't see how I can help.'

'As I said out there, you are the only person here I can trust. You arrived after things started going wrong, and you were with me in

99

the ballroom when Volkov was killed. You are the only person in the building who can say this. Yes, you may think this has nothing to do with you, yes, yes. But if one of these people here is responsible, catching them is in both our interests.'

'There's nothing to suggest I'm next, and really that's all that matters to me.'

'Mr Chambers,' he growled, 'my patience and my hospitality have a limit.'

'Then explain it with crayons.'

He sighed. 'Well, apart from incurring my displeasure – which will not be inconsiderable – you are here as a representative of General Kayembe, who has assigned you to look after his representative, Dr Carr.'

I nodded.

'And Dr Carr is here to purchase goods, for which she needs my representative, Professor Balakin.'

I nodded again.

'Mr Chambers, you are being deliberately obtuse. Mr Burton came here to keep Dr Carr safe and he is now dead. Volkov discovered Professor Balakin's life is in danger, and then woosh, he is dead also. It seems someone wants to prevent this transaction. If Balakin dies next, there is no deal. If there is no deal, you and Dr Carr serve no purpose. If you serve no purpose, then why am I tolerating your presence?'

'If I help you, will you see Dr Carr is safe?'

'Of course.'

'And Abi?'

'She just needs to recover from her wounds, she will be fine.'

'Not if you believe in this ghost. She saw something. You should post guards on her room.'

'Do not mistake this for a negotiation. You will help, or you will not leave here.'

I massaged my nose between my fingers, inhaling deeply. I'd been sent here simply to collect information from a man. I now found myself in the middle of someone else's story, and not a very fun one at that. But there was a way to turn this to my advantage.

All the way here I'd been wondering how to get to Professor Balakin, but here was that opportunity being handed to me on a plate. Looking after Professor Balakin would give me ample opportunity to speak to him, without arousing suspicion.

'If I'm going to help you, I need a gun, some trainers, and some biscuits – not necessarily in that order.'

-

Like much of the Barensky Hotel, time had abandoned the dining room decades ago. It was as if the decorator had somehow managed to buy everything from a fifty-year-old IKEA catalogue, all spindly legged, square-looking chairs and angled, polished wood upholstered in all the colours of the vomit rainbow. I looked around the velour and corduroy opulence and wondered how best to play Golubev's game.

We'd arrived at an uneasy deal, a fairly one-sided bargain whereby I'd find the person responsible for Volkov's murder in exchange for getting out of here alive. Seemed fair, but there was an obvious catch. There was a high probability the person responsible for Volkov's death would be killed in a nasty way, and since that person was me, it was somewhat limiting my enjoyment of the excellent steak the kitchens had rustled up.

Essentially, I had twelve hours to find someone terrible enough to frame for Volkov's murder. I had no qualms about this; the hotel was full of some of the worst people on Earth, and I included myself in that. The terrorists in the ballroom, Mr Abid or Redneck, could fit the bill nicely, plus I'd be doing the planet a favour.

But my worry was finding someone to frame who didn't have an alibi. Someone who could feasibly have done it and, importantly, someone I could invent a motive for.

Of course, there was one person I could pin it on, if I could identify them: the person who'd dragged the body out of my wardrobe to the other side of the hotel, and set it on fire. But somehow catching that person and handing them over to Golubev didn't seem like a sensible option, since they may let slip where they'd got his body from.

But I still needed to find them, if only to understand why they'd done it, why they'd attacked me and Abi on the ice, why they'd presumably killed the security guard in the Jeep, and let's not forget they'd killed my predecessor. To put it mildly, there was definitely something going on, and I wasn't sure if I wanted to find out what.

Maybe the best option was to find this person and put a bullet in them before they could do any more damage or – most importantly – spill any incriminating information on me.

These were the thoughts pulsing through my brain as I swept potatoes through peppercorn sauce, but even they kept being jostled out by an even bigger problem.

Professor Balakin was a target, but I needed him alive for two reasons. Firstly, for the information. More importantly, if he died, it would be very bad for me.

I decided the best course of action would be to stick close to Balakin, just like Golubev wanted. And as agreed, I'd keep him alive in exchange for information. This white demon, the Cold War relic stalking the dilapidated corridors, would have to come through me. Two birds, one stone, hopefully keeping Golubev happy enough for me to leave unscathed.

Speak of the Devil, in he strode.

Golubev looked around, eyes landing on me. 'It is ready.'

I pushed the chair back from the table and stood. 'Good steak.'

He walked over to me and took my hand, looking me square in the eyes. 'You will keep my man safe, yes?'

'I give you my word.'

'Do you get claustrophobic?'

'Depends on the box, but not generally.'

'We are going to somewhere no one will be able to get to you.' He barked a command at a man by the door who promptly disappeared. 'Come, we will go now.'

'I'm not going anywhere without Dr Carr.'

'Dr Carr cannot come, I'm afraid.'

'She could be in danger, too.'

'She could also be the killer.'

I pictured her shooting Eric Gambetta in X-Base two years ago, not to mention the snarl on her face as she pulled the trigger on me. 'I can vouch for her.'

Golubev didn't look convinced. 'We need to move fast.'

I sat back down. 'I'm not going anywhere without Carr. She's my responsibility. First and foremost, my job here is to protect her. Besides, if someone wants to prevent the transaction as you said, she's in as much danger as Balakin.'

Golubev's eyes creased as he weighed it up. 'This makes sense. As you say, she is your responsibility.' He looked at Anya and spoke in Russian, then turned back to me. 'Very few people know of this. I will accompany the professor now, before anyone knows he has moved. Dr Carr is being brought here, Anya will show you the way.'

I nodded and sliced another piece of steak.

It only took five minutes before one of Golubev's guards came through the double doors and nodded to Anya, held out a carrier bag. She shot me a look before dismissing the man.

Anya opened the bag and looked in, then walked over to me.

'English woman is coming, enough food.' She placed the bag on the table with a thud. 'We go now.'

I shovelled another potato and pushed the plate away, dragging the bag across the table. First thing out was a small packet with a cartoon cow on the front. I opened it to reveal biscuits. A pair of trainers were next. Size 11, which was good. Garish neon running trainers, which was not so good. I'd rather go outside barefoot. I shook my head at Anya and put them back in the bag. Last out was my HK pistol, loaded, and a spare magazine, returned to me.

I shoved the pistol into my pocket and grabbed the cow biscuits and the parka they'd given me. 'Come on then.'

She held the door and we crossed back into the lobby to music and low-level chatter still spilling from the ballroom, suggesting Golubev's clients didn't have the foggiest that people were burning to death in the shadows around them. The lift pinged and Alice appeared, flanked by two body-armoured and combat-ready commandos. One had a nervous grip on his submachine gun, the other on what I presumed was her suitcase.

'What's going on?' she asked. 'Why am I being moved? No one's told me anything.'

'We both need to start sharing information,' I said, as the security team led us towards the staircase.

One of the guests came out of the ballroom over the other side of the lobby and was swiftly intercepted by a well-suited member of Golubev's security team. The guest turned towards us as he was shepherded in the direction of the toilets. It was Redneck. I glared at him. He looked me up and down and sneered before I was steered away.

Anya slammed through the same door Golubev had taken me through earlier.

Alice did a double-take at the faded, peeling wallpaper as she swept a dangling wire out of her way. 'Where are we going?'

'Third-class accommodation, I suspect.' I raised my voice so Anya could hear. 'Does she need cold-weather gear?'

Anya looked back at Alice and grunted. 'We go quick.'

She flicked on a torch. The two troops behind us did the same as the door squealed closed.

Alice shivered and hustled up closer to me, our breaths fogging in the cold air. I tried to hand her my parka, but she thrust it back into my arms and scowled. 'I've come undercover all the way to an arms deal in Siberia,' she hissed. 'I am not some damsel in fucking distress.'

I slung it over my shoulder. 'We're going to have to work together if you want to get out of here alive.'

'Work together? With the man who—'

I dug an elbow into her ribs as Anya pushed open the second door, waiting for us. As soon as we stepped through, she locked the door then jogged forward.

The walls and ceiling shimmered in the flickering torch beams.

'This place is a timewarp,' said Alice, running a finger along the wallpaper, scraping the light frost with a fingernail. 'You've lost weight. Being dead obviously agrees with you.'

'Well, I've developed a phobia of drive-thrus,' I whispered. 'You're looking well, prison was obviously good to you.'

'I heard you were gunned down in a dirty car park. Couldn't happen to a nicer guy.'

'Nothing to do with you, I suppose? I mean, you already tried to shoot me once.'

'What's with the long hair? Mid-life crisis?' she countered.

The massive iron door loomed from the darkness. Anya slowed and signalled to the two commandos behind us. I heard a rustle as one of them shunted past, gun into his shoulder, the underslung torch directing a powerful beam right onto the lock mechanism. Just as before, Anya produced the substantial key and slid it into the lock. There was the same solid *thunk* as multiple latches disengaged.

'John, I don't want to go in there,' whispered Alice.

'Who the fuck's *John*?' I hissed. 'Get your shit together.'

The guy with the gun went through first, striding forward after the beam of his torch.

Anya gestured down with her own torch. 'Watch feet.'

'It's freezing,' said Alice, through chattering teeth. 'This is the destroyed side of the hotel?'

Anya grunted.

'Are we going back outside?' I asked, trying to work out where the bobbing light up ahead was going.

Anya shook her head and pointed at a junction in the dim light. 'Different place.'

'It's a bloody maze,' said Alice through clouds of condensing breath. 'How do you find your way?'

Anya started walking, turning to hustle us along. 'I do not come out here. Security, they know ruins better.'

'Does everyone have a key?' I asked, wondering how someone had carried Volkov into this side of the hotel past the guards.

'Only I have keys.'

'Not even Golubev?'

'Only I have keys.' She put an arm across my chest to stop me, I grabbed Alice and waited.

The lead guy was holding up a fist in the light of Anya's torch. He whispered something, and the second guard put down Alice's case and brought up his rifle.

I pulled out my pistol, aiming down the corridor.

'What's going on?' Alice whispered.

I elbowed her in the ribs. 'Sshh.'

Anya clicked off her torch as the men in front did the same. Darkness was almost absolute, but a tiny glow crept from somewhere way up in front. I pulled my pistol in, holding it close and looking behind and in front, surrounded by blackness.

No one moved. The glow up ahead briefly flickered, as if something had moved across it. Another whisper came from in front.

I could feel Anya move in close to my head. 'Ilya has seen something,' she whispered.

A rustle in front indicated that the guy she'd called Ilya was moving away from us, along the hallway. The briefest glow from him told me he was using the night-sight on his rifle.

'He is checking is safe,' Anya continued.

We sat completely still for a minute, listening intently, hardly daring to breathe. The wind howled. Alice squeezed my arm and pulled in tight. Her teeth chattered in the bitter cold. I looped my jacket around her back, and this time she relented.

Gradually I picked up a soft sound coming from in front. I felt Anya tense from a metre or so away, and held my gun up to the nothingness, but a call out confirmed it was Ilya. He spoke Russian for a few seconds then turned on his torch, pointing it down the corridor away from us. I squinted as my eyes adjusted. The glow lit up Alice next to me, her face set like cast iron.

Anya stood and flicked on her own torch, pointing it behind her. Way back down the corridor the enormous door stood as locked as it had been. One of the troops shouldered his weapon, jogging back to grab Alice's case. His face was white, and he seemed in a hurry.

'Ilya thought he saw somebody in corridor ahead,' whispered Anya, pointing her torch forward again and motioning for us all to keep walking, 'but no one is there.'

I gave Alice a nod and followed Anya. 'So there's no way anyone else could be here?'

She shrugged. 'I think a trick of light.'

'Or of the dark.'

We reached the junction where a section of scorch-marked wall had fallen in, half collapsing the wall on the other side. The corridor was blocked by masonry, bent ceiling lights, electrical wiring and wooden beams.

Anya spoke to the troops, who replied and carried on walking down the other branch of the corridor, an even more decrepit space, no wallpaper left and huge cracks everywhere, wires hanging down from the ceiling. The corridor had doors along it like those in the other side of the hotel, though these must surely have been service areas or function rooms. Most of the doors were open, hanging from their hinges, or missing entirely, ominous windows onto black holes. One mercy was the temperature and latitude meant the place wasn't filled with the cobwebs and bugs you'd normally find in a building in such a state.

It was freezing now. We were essentially outside and while we were out of the wind, it didn't help the temperature. The concrete surrounding us had been in deep freeze for decades. How long before hypothermia began to set in, ten minutes or so at these temperatures? It felt like ages, but we'd only stepped over the threshold of that big metal door a couple of minutes ago.

'How much further?' I asked, shivering, acutely aware that, as Golubev had suggested earlier, Anya did indeed seem impervious to the temperature.

She stopped outside one of the more upright-looking doors and pulled it open. 'Inside.'

I took Alice's arm and pulled her through into the darkness. The two commandos came next, their torches lighting a small empty room with another door on the opposite wall. The first guy put Alice's bag down next to me, then both flanked the door, rifles ready.

Anya took one last look up and down the corridor, then stepped into the room, pulling the door shut. She nodded to the commandos. The first reached out and rapped the back of his hand against the door, then stepped back. A dull thud echoed around the space. This was not a wooden door.

A second later there was a clunk, a thud, and it opened without a creak, spilling light into the room. I blinked as a figure stepped out, another of Golubev's security team. He beckoned to me and Alice. I picked up her case and took her arm.

The fake wooden door was attached to another door behind it, three times thicker, solid steel with thick rubber seals around the edge like a bank vault. As we stepped over the raised threshold, the man moved aside and said something in Russian, pointing the way down narrow dusty concrete steps that descended in a straight run at least a couple of storeys, mercifully lit by bare bulbs hanging from the sloping ceiling. I looked back at the guys we'd left. Anya nodded to me, then disappeared as the guard closed the steel door behind us. He swung a lever and spun a wheel in the centre of the door to lock and seal it.

'It's an underground bunker,' whispered Alice grimly.

Chapter Eighteen

Severnaya Zemlya, Siberia

Present day

'A nuclear bunker from the Cold War.' I nodded and started down the stairs. 'Real VIP treatment.'

'I don't like this, feels like a trap,' said Alice. 'Why are we going down here?'

'I'll explain soon. First let's see what Golubev has in mind.'

'Not me,' came a voice from below. At the bottom of the stairs Golubev appeared around the corner. 'This is Professor Balakin's idea, though I do agree it is a good one.

When we reached the bottom he took Alice's case from me. 'Please, follow me.'

He led the way along a bare corridor, under buzzing, flickering lights.

'Is there a lift to get back out again?' Alice asked.

Golubev turned to walk backwards. 'If a nuclear bomb lands above us, you would not be in a rush to get out. The heaters are running, so it is really quite lovely down here.'

The ominous-looking steel door at the end of the corridor begged to differ.

'As long as it has a shower and a bed, I'll be happy,' said Alice.

'Oh yes. These are the bunkers beneath the old hotel, set up to live in for an extended period of time.'

'Hopefully I won't be down here for an extended period,' Alice said, hugging her arms about herself.

'How many entrances?' I asked.

'Two. The door you have just come through, and another on the far side of the bunker which leads to the coast behind the building. The second serves as an escape route if the building collapses above us, you understand.'

'How many rooms?'

He thought about it for a couple of seconds. 'Nine or ten. You will see.'

'How many people can access…'

Golubev stopped. 'You will *see*. Please.'

He swung the groaning door open, the warmth hitting as I followed him in. The room was military utilitarian chic, dusty and faded from decades of abandonment, but still in a surprisingly good state. Desks lined one wall, covered in old stationery, packs of paper, boxes of pamphlets and sagging notepads, typewriters, and a row of old telephones. A huge map hung on the wall with little magnetic dots stuck all over it. Each wall had one door.

Golubev walked across the room to the door opposite. 'Being twenty metres underground, is well insulated. As long as the doors are closed, of course.' He opened it and another rise in temperature was noticeable immediately. 'Heats up fast,' he explained. 'But cools just as quickly.'

A man was already waiting for us, another of Golubev's security team, I presumed from the generic suit, the bulge under the left armpit, and the way his eyes tracked me as we came in.

Golubev smiled at him and said something in Russian. The man replied, impossible to follow what was being said.

'So where's the prof?' I said to Alice.

She looked at me warily. 'Surely we're not sleeping down here?'

I kept it breezy. 'Looks cosy enough. Warmer than my room, as well.'

It wasn't a lie, either. This was a sort of lounge area with a few brown floral print sofas and discoloured melamine coffee tables. The whitewashed walls were hung with prints of Russian cities and rural scenes in an attempt to bring some normality into the concrete box. Next to the door hung the obligatory portrait of Brezhnev with his chest full of medals, looking down either in smug self-satisfaction, or possibly in the knowledge he was about to have us shipped off to a gulag.

'I can't breathe in here,' Alice said.

'Not much different to the place we met.'

She scowled. I smiled back, trying to inject some warmth into it. No denying it, here in Siberia we needed each other. We may have ended up deadly enemies a couple of years ago, but there were worse things to worry about.

She seemed to thaw a little. 'At least we could go outside there.'

'And it had sea views.'

Now, despite herself, her smile looked genuine.

The security guard made his way out, Golubev stopped him in the doorway and began murmuring quietly, glancing back at us every couple of seconds.

'Drink?' I reached for a bottle of Stoly on a sideboard and looked at Alice.

She snatched the bottle; I gave her a raised eyebrow chaser.

'I've been here longer, I think I need it more,' she snapped, sitting on one of the sofas and looking remarkably unfazed now.

Alice downed a swig straight from the bottle then held it out for me.

'Not tonight, I don't think.'

'Mr Chambers.' Golubev was ushering his guard through the door and holding it for me. 'As you have gathered, this is the most secure part of the hotel.' He tapped on the door. 'The stairs we came down lead only to the blast door, which is fifteen centimetres of tungsten-reinforced steel set in two metres of reinforced concrete. You saw there is no handle on the outside. The doors can only be opened from within.'

'It's a coffin down here.'

'There are bedrooms, a kitchen, stores. This is not a coffin.'

'So it's a fancy coffin. Where's Balakin?'

'Safe. You see, he is important not just to me, not just to this auction – but to other people. Important people. I do not have to spell it out.'

'I could be a killer for all you know.'

'Mr Chambers, I am quite sure you are a killer, or General Kayembe would not have sent you.'

He proceeded to give me the grand tour while Alice slumped on the sofa drinking Stoly. Storerooms, bare shelving but for a few dusty bits of obsolete equipment, mouldy boxes of filters and parts and tools. A kitchen with nothing in the cupboards but snacks and bottled water, various bedrooms lined with empty metal bunk frames. Nowhere anyone could hide. Each bare concrete box held not a single item bigger than a microwave. Despite the labyrinth of tunnels a spider would struggle to hide in here, not that there were many around.

Alice had been designated a single made-up bed in one of the old barrack dorms, whereas I would be in a separate part of the bunker, with Balakin.

'Through here.' He led me through yet another doorway in the rabbit warren and flicked on the light. This time it was a long corridor with buzzing strip lights that stretched all the way to a single steel door at the end.

'The most secure part of an already secure bunker,' said Golubev, footsteps echoing as he strode along the passageway. At the end he swung a heavy lever and opened the door with a groan. 'The old offices, but we have put you in here.'

The small room had a double bed made up, drawers, a desk, and a shelf holding drooping box files and dusty radio equipment.

'This is original command station. Bathroom there.' He pointed at a door with a large grubby old mirror propped against the wall next to it, then at another door on the opposite wall. 'Here's the second exit.'

He opened a door into a musty box room with a metal ladder embedded in the far wall. I poked my head in and looked up. The ladder went way up a concrete tube into darkness.

Golubev joined me in the doorway and looked up, too. 'The bunker is designed to withstand a two megaton nuclear strike nearby, but unfortunately such a weapon would obliterate everything above ground on island. This could leave people trapped under tons of collapsed hotel. But here we are well away from building.'

'What's up there?'

'Another door like the one you came through. It comes out disguised as a small boathouse.'

'What's stopping someone coming down it?'

'Apart from several centimetres of tungsten steel? Again, the door can only be opened from inside.'

'And this one?' I rested my hand on a small steel door set deep into the wall.

He gave me a wry smile. 'We do not go in there.'

'I'm not sleeping anywhere I can't check.'

'It is locked.' He pulled the handle.

I folded my arms. 'Show me every room.'

'Mr Chambers…' He sighed, making a decision. 'Very well, since you are helping me, I am trusting you.'

He fished out a key and inserted it into a metal box on the wall, unlocking it and pulling it open. A keypad glowed, he gestured for me to turn around. A couple of seconds later there was a metallic thunk as locks disengaged.

I turned back. Golubev pointed at the door handle and stepped aside. It was stiff but after a little effort I was looking into a dark void. 'What is it?'

He smiled and reached past me, turning on a light. 'This is why we don't go in here.'

The lights buzzed on, revealing a simple, small, concrete-walled storeroom. Equally simple metal shelving racks ran along two walls. The contents of the shelves were anything but simple.

Gold bullion was racked along one shelf, and cardboard boxes piled with velvet bags, the contents of which I could only guess at. Bricks of dollars were stacked like a drug-dealer's lair.

'My business is lucrative,' Golubev explained. 'Given some of my clients' unusual currency, the problem is what to do with the proceeds. Of course I spread it around. Physically, in the usual places: deposit boxes and vaults. Digitally, with banks around the world. But there comes a point when you are taking it in so quickly you need somewhere to put it. Given our location, this is one of the most secure places on Earth.'

I've guarded CIA dollar deliveries in Iraq, and watched pallets of hundreds being loaded onto pickup trucks in the Green Zone, so it wasn't nearly the biggest haul I'd seen by any stretch. Still, I had to work hard to keep it nonchalant.

'No way in or out, no hiding places?'

'Look for yourself.'

And I did, but there was nothing bigger than a duffel bag and not so much as an air vent.

He flicked off the lights and closed the door, giving the handle a test. He led me back into the warmth of my bedroom and pointed to one final door. 'Professor Balakin is in his room. One way in, one way out, through your room. He will only open the door to you.'

We made our way back. Golubev's security agent was waiting for him at the foot of the stairs.

'Follow and seal the door behind us,' Golubev said, starting up the stairs.

Halfway up, I wished Alice's hope of a lift had been realised. Our steps echoed around the lonely space. At the top, Golubev stepped through the door and turned.

'I return to my guests in the knowledge that my scientist is safe. Because if anything happens to him…' All the friendliness of the last hour or so vanished entirely. His face was as impassive as the concrete behind him as the door swung closed.

The metallic thud echoed around the bunker with a finality that sent shivers up my spine. I spun the lock, gave it a test, then walked back down the stairs, pondering my next move.

I could hear Alice clinking bottles as I neared the lounge. She looked up from her suitcase as I came in. 'Is Golubev gone?'

'All locked up.'

She pulled out a handheld radio. 'Then we can dispense with this charade.'

I held up a hand and crossed to the desk at the side of the room. She watched me with a strange expression as I grabbed a marker pen and scrawled across a post-it note. I walked back and held it out. *Quiet. Bugs.*

Alice burst out laughing. 'So fucking serious.' She twiddled the dial on the radio but got only static through the speaker.

'Radios won't work down here,' I said.

'What do you mean?' she asked, more concerned than I'd expected.

'It's a nuclear bunker,' I said. 'The lead shielding that protects against fallout also prevents any signals getting in or out.'

She started chelping but I ignored her, making my way back through to my room to stop at Balakin's door. I knocked, there was no reply. I knocked again, harder, then tried the handle.

It opened onto a short grey corridor of naked bulbs and pipework, ending in yet another door.

I walked along it and knocked on the next door. This time there was a scuffle on the other side. 'Who is it?'

'Professor Balakin, it's Mr Chambers.'

The door opened a crack.

When people say 'professor' I picture a studious little grey-haired nutter, maybe wearing a knitted jumper and a bowtie, wire-rimmed glasses and sensible trousers. I realise I need to work on my prejudices, because this could not have been further from Professor Yaroslav Balakin's appearance.

He opened the door further. I knew Balakin was fifty but he looked younger, and obviously took care of himself. Sporting more grey in both his closely cropped hair and carefully trimmed beard than Golubev, he was wearing jeans and Adidas trainers below a shirt and jacket. But the most striking feature was straight out of Golubev's rogueish style catalogue, and made him a contender for best suave, rugged seafarer of Severnaya Zemlya. As he stepped out from behind the door, I saw he wore a black leather eyepatch over his left eye, while the ice-blue right eye regarded me with a mixture of amusement and curiosity.

I stood and shook his hand, firm and rough. 'Professor Balakin, the man everyone wants to meet.'

His bright eye lit up in the fluorescent lights. 'Mr John Tyler, the man many wish they hadn't met.'

I held a finger to my lips. He guessed why, face cracking.

'There are no bugs. Moving into this bunker was my idea.'

'But, still?'

'The walls are two-metre thick, lead-lined concrete. Have they gone?'

'All except Dr Carr, who's staying down here with us.'

'No.' He made to shut the door, but I shoved my foot in the gap. 'No, only us,' he said. 'Someone is here to kill me…'

'Calm down, she's not going to kill anyone,' I said, hoping he didn't know about Alice's past.

The door to the corridor behind me opened.

'Speak of the Devil…'

'We need to get out,' Alice said, shaking the radio, still spewing static.

Balakin tried to shut the door, but I kept my foot in it, pointing back at Alice. 'My job is to keep her alive. That means she stays in my eyesight. I've come down here to keep you safe, so the three of us are stuck like glue from now on, understand?'

'Do you trust her?' he asked.

I looked at Alice, who nodded.

'With my life,' I replied.

He let the door open, though all I could see of the gloomy room was a picture on the wall behind him.

'Good evening, Alice,' Balakin said.

'Why didn't you tell me you'd asked for Tyler?' she said.

'You know each other?' Balakin looked between us, confused.

'What's the point in aliases if no one uses them?' I said. 'Here I'm Chambers, she's Dr Carr.'

Alice held the radio in front of my face. 'Look, we need to get outside,' she repeated.

I ignored her, pushing Balakin's door further open. 'You wanted to talk to me. First, how do you know me, why did you ask me to come?'

'No,' said Alice, stepping in between us. '*First* we need to go topside, and I mean right fucking now.'

'I'm not leaving this room until tomorrow,' said Balakin.

'If we don't get outside now, you might not be leaving at all.' Alice looked at her watch, then me. 'At ten p.m. we receive instructions from Mason. That's in fifteen minutes.'

'Instructions on what?' asked Balakin, looking either perplexed or alarmed.

'Jesus Christ!' Alice held up the radio again. 'Our route out of here!' She looked at me for support.

'Mason never gave me the details,' I said.

'Why would he? I'm in charge, you're just hired help.'

'John Tyler is more than hired help,' said Balakin, looking into my eyes. 'He is the man on whom both our fates rest.'

'Yes, he's a hero, we all love him.' She rolled her eyes. 'Right now, we need to think about how we're going to get our instructions if we can't get a signal, because otherwise we're stuck here.'

'What happens if we miss ten p.m.?' I asked. 'Will he message again?'

'The signal repeats at ten a.m., then ten p.m., every twelve hours until we check-in or until Tuesday, whichever comes first.'

'Ten a.m. is too late,' said Balakin, worry creasing his brow. 'Most of the guards will be at breakfast at six, I thought we should aim for that.' Balakin was looking more worried by the second.

Alice tapped the radio. 'Then we have just over ten minutes to figure out how to get this to work.'

'Risky going back upstairs, with Golubev's men patrolling,' I said. 'Give me the radio, I'll go.'

Alice pulled the radio in to her chest. 'I need to decode the message.'

'Tell me how.'

'No.' She turned away, hugging the radio tight. 'My job is to do the thinking, your job is to keep me safe.'

'I'm not staying down here on my own,' said Balakin.

'Fine. How are you both with ladders?'

117

Chapter Nineteen

Severnaya Zemlya, Siberia

Present day

I left Professor Balakin and Alice down in the bunker and climbed the ladder up to the escape door. All the way up, all I'd been thinking was, *I hope the door isn't seized.*

I reached the top and took a breather on a platform next to the huge steel door, then leaned over the ladder and shouted down to the others.

Balakin appeared first, then Alice. The heat didn't seem to have made it this far. We shivered, even though we'd kitted out in parkas from the stores.

Just as with the other door, I swung the latches and then spun the wheel in the middle. It was tough at first but then gave; I reasoned it was more the result of decent maintenance than Seventies engineering.

'Torches off,' I said. 'And don't fall back down, for fuck's sake.'

I pulled out my pistol and held it down low. With the door unlocked and the seal broken, I gently pulled. It swung without a sound. I held my gun out in one hand and felt my way through. Fresh grease slid between my fingers on the frame, confirming my hunch. Recently serviced.

There was no light at all, which told me we weren't out yet. I briefly clicked my torch on and off. In the flash I'd taken stock: a tiny space with a few steps up to a wooden hatch in the ceiling – probably a trapdoor in the floor of the boathouse Golubev had mentioned. I walked slowly up, hand above my head until I felt the wood. Fresh, like pine. Above, I could hear that constant low moan of the wind over the sea ice. I gave the wood a prod and felt a centimetre of give.

'Four minutes,' Alice hissed somewhere in the darkness.

'You wanna come out in the middle of Golubev's party?' I whispered back.

I tipped the hatch up a little more, a soft glow appeared around the edges. An inch more and the glow was enough to see wooden tread boards and tools stacked around. The sound of the wind increased but only a slight draught made it to me. I turned through 360 degrees. Spades, a chainsaw, some pick axes, and further away, a couple of small dinghies on trailers. Definitely inside the boathouse.

I pushed the hatch fully open and stood up straight on the steps, just my head through the floor, gun ready. Nothing moved, no sounds above the wind. I gently lowered the hatch onto the floor and crawled up.

The light was coming through large windows in the sides. I crouched and moved closer to them, feeling colder as I slowly lifted my head and saw the ice-encrusted windows and snow piled on the ledges.

The black shape of the hotel was just about visible through the rimed glass and whirling snow, with some lights shining from windows on the left. A few smaller lights moved around near the ground, which I guessed were the extra guards Golubev had liberally sprinkled around. I crossed to the other window but there was nothing but black.

'Okay,' I whispered down the hatch. 'Looks clear.'

Alice appeared first.

'Keep low,' I said, pointing to the windows.

She nodded and scuttled into the far corner. Then Balakin appeared, crouching next to me.

'This is an adventure,' he said.

I rolled my eyes. 'Give me strength.'

The more Balakin spoke, the more there was something familiar about him. The way his eye creased when he talked, the way he held himself, there was something I couldn't put my finger on. Then I remembered he'd asked for me. Clearly our paths had crossed somewhere before, but *where*?

He looked out of the window for a minute or so in silence before turning back to me. 'You want to ask about my eyepatch.'

'I had a friend, she lost her eye.' I made a little weighing motion. 'Best driver I knew, but couldn't shoot straight for shit. What happened?'

'An old war wound. Much like this, I imagine.' He pointed at the jagged scar bisecting my eyebrow.

'How does a professor get a war wound?'

'By working for the military.' He smiled. 'When you work in a lab, the signs telling you to wear eye protection are there for a reason.'

'Health and safety gone mad,' I said sarcastically. 'It's not your eyes I was wondering about. Why did you ask for me? How do you know me?'

'It is simple enough, I have heard of you from a friend in the security services.'

'Which friend?'

'It doesn't matter. I know you are the man to get me out of here.'

'I need information first.'

'Ah, no,' he said. 'That's not how it works.'

'Shut up,' hissed Alice. Static burst from the radio, so she hurriedly turned it down.

'Christ,' I said, looking out of the window at the torches. 'Why don't you get some tunes on, we can have a party.'

'Shhhh.' She shuffled cross-legged and turned the static up slightly. It combined with the howling wind to give the shed an uneasy vibe.

'You get me out,' whispered Balakin, 'I give you the information you need.'

'And what if it's not worth it?'

'Then I definitely wouldn't want to tell you before I'm out.' He grinned in the moonlight. 'It is worth it, trust me. And you—'

A tune cut through the static, a short repeating creepy ditty played on an electronic keyboard, which increased the otherworldly atmosphere. Alice turned it down.

'What is that music?' Balakin asked.

'The Lincolnshire Poacher,' I replied. 'Retro, I didn't think it was used any more.'

Balakin frowned. 'What is a… Link…'

'It's an English folk song,' I said.

The tune kept repeating.

'Shush,' said Alice, pencil poised above a pad of paper.

'Tell me, why are we sat in a freezing shed listening to English folk music?' Balakin whispered.

'It's a numbers station,' I replied. 'Transmits at a specific time on a specific frequency.'

The tune stopped, replaced by a couple of beeps that repeated several times.

'But why?'

I held a finger to my lips and looked back out of the window.

'Three, nine, seven, one, five,' said a crackling woman in a clipped English RP accent.

'Coded messages, one-way comms only, but it can be picked up by anyone with a radio, pretty much anywhere on Earth.'

'Three, nine, seven, one, five,' repeated the robotic woman on the radio.

'Instructions from our friend, Mr Mason,' Alice added.

The torches outside seemed to be grouping together near the derelict side of the hotel.

The radio repeated the code as I watched the torches. Then a bright light swung around the corner of the hotel just as the woman changed her numbers.

'Six, six, four, seven, five,' said the radio, then repeated it.

The bright lights stopped. It was a truck that'd pulled round the side. The driver seemed to be talking with the guards.

'One, nine, two, seven, four. One, nine, two, seven, four. Seven, eight, four, nine, four. Seven, eight, four, nine, four.'

The torches swung onto the shed. We ducked low as the beams swept across the interior.

I risked another look up. The torches were weaving around. Could have been an accident.

'Two, four, one, four, six. Two, four, one, four, six. Six, eight, five, four, two. Six, eight, five, four, two.'

Several torch beams fell on the shed, so we ducked again. This time they held the shed in their beam, lighting up the interior. No accident.

'Alice, we gotta go,' I whispered.

The radio kept repeating lines of numbers, with Alice hastily scribbling them down on her pad.

The lights intensified, the inside of the shed was lit up like day. I chanced one last look and saw the truck barrelling towards us.

'Alice!' I shouted, shoving Balakin towards the hatch. He scrambled down into the darkness.

'Now!' I hissed.

'It's nearly finished,' she said, scribbling before she slid across the floor towards the hatch.

The truck was louder than the wind now.

'We're out of time.' I grabbed the radio from her hands and dragged her into the hatch. She carried on scrawling the numbers as I swung the hatch closed, clicking on my torch.

'Inside!'

She jumped through the steel doorway to join Balakin. The radio crackled as the signal broke. I held it up while she leaned against the wall to keep scribbling strings of numbers.

Voices came from outside, shouting commands. I turned the radio down and crept towards the steel doorway.

Two beeps came through the radio, repeating, followed by the creepy tune again.

'That's it!' she said.

The shed door above opened with a rush of wind as I stepped through the blast door. I switched down the volume and thrust the radio into Alice's arms, then swung the door closed behind me, spinning the wheel to seal it shut.

The sound of the trapdoor slamming back above us was muffled by the thick steel, but I could still hear the shouting troops making their way down the stairs. We held our breath, listening.

Scuffles came from the other side of the door. The sound of scraping as one of them ran something across the door. More shouts, then the boots thudded away and the hatch slammed shut.

'They're leaving,' said Alice.

Balakin let out a breath. 'We did it!' he whispered.

'Maybe.' I pointed at Alice. 'Turn around.'

She did; her arse was covered in white.

'The dust,' I said. 'We shouldn't have gone up into the shed.'

'Then they know?' said Balakin.

'They might suspect.' I thought about it for a second. 'But more likely they might think someone's been trying to get in the bunker.'

'We got what we needed though,' said Alice. 'I need to decode this.'

I listened carefully, but couldn't hear a sound. 'Go quietly,' I said, ushering them towards the ladder.

Chapter Twenty

Severnaya Zemlya, Siberia

Present day

Balakin had disappeared back into his room as soon as we'd descended. I was slouched on a sofa scanning a map while Alice thumbed through her paperback at the other side of the room.

I threw the map on the table and rubbed my eyes. 'How's it looking?' I asked.

'I've decoded the message,' she said.

I stood and stretched, then walked over to her. She looked up and quickly tore the page of her notebook, stuffing half into her pocket.

'What does it say?'

Alice spun the other half of the paper round on the table.

Position compromised Stop Phoenix to interrogate and terminate Owl Stop

With proper full stops inserted, it read much better.

Position compromised. Phoenix to interrogate and terminate Owl.

'Compromised,' I muttered. 'Nice way of putting it.'

'It's the last bit that got my attention.'

I gave her a hard look. 'I'm not an assassin.'

'Oh, really? You're *Phoenix*, you have your orders. And I know for a fact you've—'

I cut her off. 'I kill when necessary, *not* on orders. There's a big difference.'

'So never for revenge, no?'

I gritted my teeth. 'I need to know why Balakin asked for me specifically. That means no terminating, at least not yet.'

'Maybe he's a fan. The enigmatic John Tyler, your reputation precedes you.'

'You're missing the point. How the hell does he even know I'm alive?'

She shrugged. 'Okay, but after you have the information, you'll kill him? My neck's on the line here.'

'Your neck'll be slit wide open if we kill Balakin now.'

'So find a way. Isn't that what you're paid to do?'

'I'm paid to take the action on the ground *I* think is necessary. Me, not you.'

'Wrong, I'm in charge here.'

'Is that why you kept the rest of the transmission from me?'

She pretended to look confused, then saw it was futile and patted her pocket. 'I'm not stupid. You play your cards close to your chest, I will, too.'

'Give me the other note.'

'It's the details of the evac, our route home. You're not leaving me behind.'

She turned to leave but I grabbed her arm. 'Then I need to know so I can work up a plan to get us out of this place.'

She wrenched free. 'Then you'll just have to keep me alive, won't you?' Reaching into her pocket, she quickly shoved the paper in her mouth and started chewing.

I picked up a piece of Alice's notepad. 'Gimme that pencil.' I scrawled on the paper, coordinates, a couple of meaningless names and towns and the name of a ship, a small drilling outpost in Alaska I've been through a few times. I folded it and put it in my pocket.

Alice nodded, she understood. She swallowed and showed me her empty mouth. 'You share, I'll share.' She gave a brief impression of a smile, picked up her notepad and left the room.

There's a bloody good reason I prefer to work alone.

I found the Professor cramming his cold-weather gear back into a big plastic suitcase. His room was small and spartan, more like a jail cell than a bedroom. A no-frills armchair and bed, but the prison look was underscored by a stainless-steel toilet and sink fastened to the wall opposite the door. Above the taps, the large omnipresent frowning portrait of Brezhnev and his medals stared down, presumably to check everyone was washing their hands.

'Where does that go?' I pointed at a vent high up on the wall.

'The vents circulate air around bunker,' said Balakin.

'How big is the vent?'

Balakin sighed. 'If the vents were large enough for anyone to get through, it would not make a very good defensive bunker.'

Balakin opened the drawers and started rifling through his clothes. 'So, I will give you information you want, but first I need to know how we're getting out.'

I opened the door to the wardrobe and poked my head in. It was empty but for the stink of old wood and mould. 'We steal transport and make our way to Severnaya, where we'll be picked up by the Tiburon.'

'Tiburon, Spanish for Shark, yes?'

I handed him the note I'd just written. 'A Canadian icebreaker.' The lies came thick and fast. 'Polar research vessel. Their helicopter will take us the final leg.' I pointed at the coordinates on the paper. 'Next stop, Athabasca, in Alaska.'

'Good.' Balakin nodded. 'I don't believe in ghost stories but I do believe there is danger here. The sooner we are gone, the better.'

'No arguments from me there.' I finished checking over his room; there was nowhere to hide. I sat in a musty armchair facing the toilet. 'It's getting late.'

'I will give you the information you have come for, but I want your word that you will get me out.'

'The word of a mercenary, a man who by definition does bad shit for money, and who you don't know, means that much to you?'

'It does, because I do know a little about you. There is a reason I asked for you to come here.'

'Obviously.'

'It is because you, and you alone, will see why my information is important.'

'Go on, then.'

He slid the suitcase across to the chair and sat on the bed. 'You said I seemed familiar. We met once.'

'Really?' I propped my feet on the suitcase and leaned back.

'Very briefly. Despite what you may think, I am not a terrorist, a traitor, or a bloodthirsty mad scientist.'

'I'm sure everyone in this place thinks they're in the right, I don't judge.'

Of course I did.

'I teach molecular biology at Novosibirsk University. I have a house in the suburbs, a car, and a girl in a local café who I have been on two dates with. I go to the gym four times a week, I cycle, I play football and I wrestle. I am not a monster, I do not kill kittens or load bombs with anthrax. I am a normal man. But then sometimes I get a phone call, it says, "A car is coming, be ready." I am booked on holiday from university and whoosh, I end up here talking to people from every corner of the world about biological weapons.

'As you know, I show that I am a good man by passing information to the American embassy, I do this through another man at the university. They pay me a small amount but that isn't why I do it. I do it because these are bad people. You know what happens if I say no to them? This is not a choice for me. This is not a life that I want, and I will do anything to get a better life.'

I nodded. 'That, I do understand.'

'It is important to me that you do. Anyway, a few years ago I was in London for a summit. I always stay at The Grimaud in Bloomsbury, which is never the best for location but is close to the British Museum. Well, this time the summit was being held in the museum itself. Imagine my excitement! You can really feel fog of old London seeping out of cobbles there.'

'I nearly bought a place round the corner once.'

'I envy you. Perhaps I should have approached the British instead, and asked for a house in Bloomsbury.'

'I doubt whatever information you have is worth a place there.'

'Well, there is a reason I did not approach the British. We will come to that. I was crossing the road and suddenly my FSB minder shouted out to someone across street. I thought it was strange, as normally they keep a low profile, but then you came and gave him a hug.'

'Doesn't sound like me. Wait, it wasn't Nikko, was it?'

'Nikko, yes! I told you.'

'How is he? I've probably not seen him since then.'

'Well, the last time I saw him he was fine, but we are not close friends.'

'I'm sorry, I don't remember meeting you.'

'It was very brief. I was waiting to go in the museum while you two talked. Later I asked who you were and he told me.'

'He never could keep his mouth shut.'

'Oh, he didn't tell me anything interesting, just alluded to things. But he did say you were a good man, a moral man. A man to have on your side.'

'Not sure any of those are true!'

'Your name came up again recently, and suddenly it flashed a lightbulb in my mind. As I said, Golubev uses me occasionally. There is a man who I have met here several times. A British man. He holds a senior position in military intelligence, and in NATO. This man is an agent, working for the Russians.'

'Okay,' I nodded. 'Carry on.'

'This information is my ticket out of here. I have told you part of it, but not the whole truth. I have more information, personal information which will be of value to you and you alone.'

'Such as?'

'As I said, your name came up in a conversation recently. Not here, it was at a dinner in Moscow. It was only a fleeting comment but I put two and two together. I did some digging and it is true. You see, my information is valuable, enough to get me to America, but how do I know they will keep their end of the bargain? How do I know they will get me out, and not just leave me here? And this is the reason I asked for you in particular.'

'I'm no more trustworthy than anyone else.'

'A long time ago you were in Afghanistan with your brother.'

I sat up straight, ears on stalks even though you could see where it was headed a mile off.

'You were on the trail of one of Bin Laden's commanders, and were close. You were going to capture him and take him to the Americans for a tidy sum. You'd planned to grab him at an appointment in town, and had been given intel on a safe route through hostile territory. But on the way, you hit an IED.

'For years you'd believed it was bad luck, until you heard rumours that it wasn't an IED at all, at least it wasn't planted by Al Qaeda or insurgents. It had been planted by a rival team of security contractors. But why?'

'How the hell do you know all this?'

'What you didn't know at the time was the man you were tracking, the man you were on your way to abduct, had been dealing with a Western agent for quite a while. He couldn't be allowed to talk to the Americans. If he had, he'd have revealed secrets about a corrupt British intelligence officer that had led to the deaths of lots of Westerners: soldiers, journalists, civilian workers. If you'd caught up with him and brought him to the Americans, it'd all be over for that British officer. And so you had to be stopped.'

'Look, I don't know where you've got all this from, but you're too late. The last of the men responsible for that bomb died yesterday.'

'I did not know that.'

'How could you?'

'In any case, you are wrong: there is one other. Since your attempted murder two years ago, you have systematically hunted down and killed the members of that team. But not the top man responsible, who ordered your deaths, and ultimately killed your brother. The man who left you dying on a roadside in Afghanistan and, when you survived the blast, kept you on a short lead until you were no longer useful to him.

'And two years ago, when you started getting close to the truth about your brother's murder, that man sent an assassin to Yorkshire to kill you. The same man who right now sits in Whitehall passing NATO intelligence to Russia.'

'It can't be!'

'Yes. Colonel Holderness is your mole. Colonel Holderness is a cancer in British intelligence and NATO. Colonel Holderness is the man who ordered your death two years ago, and the man responsible for your brother's murder in Afghanistan.'

Chapter Twenty-one

The Peoples' Democratic Republic of Nambutu / French Equatorial Africa

1999

The buildings on the outskirts of the city were in darkness, but by the light of the full moon and stars the street was easily navigated. Even now, at three a.m., the heat in the Chevy was almost unbearable. The woolly hat didn't help. I'd left the tie and jacket back at our bar, and sat in the back of the truck in rolled-up shirtsleeves, peering between Justin and Walshe in the front seats as we rumbled slowly along the tree-lined avenue.

The city seemed to be a contrast between haves and have-nots, or rather, between the scumbags that benefitted from bribes and corruption, and those that were exploited by them. Sometimes that contrast was evident on the same street.

On the left we passed a crumbling breezeblock wall topped by a rusting chain-link fence, behind which stood several squat block houses, corrugated tin roofs and open windows. Coming up on the right was a three-storey, colonial French-style affair, the grandeur of which might be as faded as its pink stucco façade, but it was clear who was top dog in the street.

'It's this one,' I said. 'Stop here.'

Justin pulled up on the poorer side of the road and looked across at the house. 'How do you know?'

I looked at Walshe. 'We came down here and turned up that hill, right?' I pointed between them, out the windscreen, at a plain grey apartment complex a little further along.

'Yep, this is the way we came.'

'I remember Léon Gambetta.'

'Who?'

'French Prime Minister who...' I shrugged. 'The statue, over there.'

'You're sure?' asked Justin.

I looked at the house, in darkness. Three a.m., no human was stirring. In the distance, street dogs were competing for loudest howl, and somewhere beyond them the ever-chattering nocturnal jungle warned everyone to stay out.

I nodded and pulled down my ski mask.

Justin got out of the truck, pulled down his mask and started walking to the other side of the street, looking back for me. I got out, closed the door softly and followed, sticking to the shadows alongside the wall. We crept along until we reached a wrought-iron gate, twisted into the monogram of some long-dead colonial Frenchman who'd decided to make his name here. A shiny padlock hung from the centre. I pointed through the bars at a row of cars. An old Jag, a Merc estate, a couple of newish Honda Civics and, at the end, a small white 4X4, parked up close to the side door of the house.

Justin looked at the car then shook his head. 'Looks like a Power Ranger fucked a Land Rover.'

'Mitsubishi Pajero Evo. Limited edition. 300 horsepower, underbody protection, independent suspension, built to compete in the Dakar. It's perfect.'

'If you say so.'

He backed up along the wall and prepared to jump.

'Why do you put up with him?' I asked.

He leapt up, grabbing the top of the wall and slinging a leg over.

'With who?' He reached back down for me.

I grabbed his hand. 'Walshe. The dude's got the redeeming qualities of bin juice.'

'He saved your life.' He pulled me, scrambling, up and over into the patch of cracked dirt that passed for a garden.

We paused for breath, scanning the windows of the house. Nothing moved.

I started counting off on my fingers. 'He's racist, sexist—'

'He's an arsehole but it's his intel, so it's his job.'

'Plus I get, like, a rapey vibe from him.'

Justin held up his hand. 'I once saw him kill a man for—'

'And are these the qualities you look for when you're doing a job?'

'Maybe when the job is in Hell.'

'We don't need him.' I started to move but Justin grabbed my arm and dragged me back.

'I know he's a dick but we *do* need him. Three people, we need. Unless you've got friends in Nambutu who could join us?'

I shook my head and sighed. 'Come on,' I said, jogging for the car.

I slid down on the gravel, crouching by the oversized exhaust at the rear. Justin came up alongside me, going for the door.

'Locked,' he said. 'Can you hotwire it?'

'Yes, given long enough, but I'm worried about the alarm. I thought you said no one bothers locking them here?'

'Most don't. Follow me.'

He rounded the front of the car and climbed the steps leading to the side door of the house.

'Where are you going?'

'Why do you think we wore these?' he pointed at his ski mask.

I followed and stopped to look back. Over the wall, the roof of the Chevy was just visible, shining in the moonlight.

'Why are you crouching?' whispered Justin.

'I don't know,' I replied, straightening up.

'In and out, just like Robbie Key's house.'

'We weren't stealing his car, we were stealing crisps.'

Justin chuckled. 'I'm more scared of Robbie Key's mum than whoever lives here.'

I put my hand on the door handle. 'Ready?'

'Go.'

I turned the handle, the door opened. I breathed a sigh of relief at not having to break in, and stepped into a dim, dark painted hallway, ornate tiled floor lit by a single bare bulb dangling from a wire. I looked around for car keys but there was no furniture, nowhere you'd throw your keys down. Justin slipped past me and opened the door to the first room, so I pushed in alongside him.

The relief was short-lived.

The room was dimly lit by a lamp in the far corner, hazy like a fog, but it was bright enough to freeze us both in the doorway.

Six pairs of eyes swivelled, locking onto us immediately.

The moment stretched on for what seemed like minutes. The haze was thick with beer and weed, I felt stoned just standing there. One guy blew out a lungful of smoke, which curled and drifted, adding to the fog. There was no furniture, just piles of blankets over crates. Three of the men were leaning against them on the scuffed parquet floor, and a couple of women were sat on a box in the corner. The last guy was on all fours in the centre of the room. He'd frozen, a gold-bangled wrist hovering over a pile of playing cards and dollar bills in the centre of the floor. A record scratched and jumped on a player by the door as the needle hit the end.

Justin reached behind his back and pulled out a Glock. 'Nobody move.'

Nobody had been anyway, but now one guy's hand began creeping towards an AK on the crate nearest him. Another guy started giggling, which set the women in the corner off. All of them were high as giraffe balls.

'I said, don't fucking move,' shouted Justin. 'Anyone else in the house?' he asked.

The guy nearest held out a joint to us in a shaking hand.

Justin slapped it away. 'I said, anyone else in the house?'

The dude on his hands and knees in the middle of the floor shook his head. He still hadn't moved, like he'd bet everything he had on a game of Twister.

I edged further into the room and looked at a cardboard box next to the record player. A Beretta sat on top of it, I picked it up. Several of the men tensed, but still none of them spoke.

I pointed the gun at the nearest guy. 'Mitsubishi car keys.'

'You're making a big mistake,' said Twister.

It was only then, as my eyes adjusted to the fog, that I saw the cash under the shuttered window behind him. Piles of loose dollar bills of all denominations, and beneath the shutters of the other window, clear bin bags filled with green. The guy wasn't a government official or shady businessman. He was a drug dealer.

'Car keys,' I repeated. 'The Pajero.'

'I will find you,' Twister said.

I cocked the pistol and pointed it at his leg. 'Last chance.'

He grinned. 'I will find you, I will gut you, and I will hang you for the crows.'

I pointed at the pile of cards. 'Right hand, green.' I pulled the trigger.

Nothing happened. I tried again, but they were all laughing now. I looked at the gun, flipped the lever on the back of the slide, and pointed it back at the cards. There was an explosion of shattered wood and paper as I realised I'd accidentally pulled the trigger. I flinched back, inadvertently pulling the trigger again and blasting a hole in the ceiling. Plaster dust rained down as everyone ducked, hands in the air.

'Everybody freeze!' Justin shouted yet again, striding into the room and pointing his Glock at the guy near the AK.

The shouting stopped and everyone froze again, including Twister, who'd now shifted position. He stood slowly, hands first above his head, then he reached out to the side, down to his pocket, and pushed one hand into it.

'Who sent you?' he said, narrowing his bloodshot eyes. 'I'm protected. There'll be consequences.'

'I'm sure,' I said, pushing my ski mask up onto my head as I regained my bravado, though I was now pointing the pistol down at the floor, away from him.

Twister slowly pulled the keys from his pocket and tossed them onto the floor at my feet. I stooped to pick them up. 'And one bag of weed.'

'No,' said Justin. 'We're here for the car.'

'And a bag of weed,' I repeated.

Justin picked up the AK and reversed towards the door. 'Time to go.'

'The money, then,' I said.

Twister glared at me as I backtracked to the door.

'Get the car started,' Justin said.

I ran out of the room and stopped. Shoes were piled by the door, among them a pair of blue Converse All-Stars. I picked them up and looked at the label; they were my size. Taking them with me, I threw open the door and blipped the Pajero, running round the front to the driver's side, all Evos being right-hand drive. I slid the key in and twisted, the V6 burbled straight into life and revved nicely, loud in the night through the huge exhaust. I tossed the trainers on the back seat and ripped off the ski mask, pushing my hair behind my ears, giving the horn a blast, just as Justin appeared at the top of the steps.

He frantically pulled the door shut, scrabbling with it. I realised he'd taken the key from the inside and was locking it behind him. I clicked my seatbelt on and slipped the gearstick into reverse. A second later, he was bounding down the steps and into the passenger side, just as shutters flew open on an upstairs window. Gunshots ripped the night air. I gunned it, reversing straight down the drive, slamming backwards through the gates and out onto the street. As the gates clattered onto the pavement, I swerved, the car rocked up onto two wheels, screeching as we reversed down the road, howling at full throttle.

'What are you doing?' shouted Justin.

'Belt up!' I shouted back.

I heard the click, then spun the wheel hard left. The car lurched, heading straight for a parked truck. I stamped on the brakes, the front tyres squealing and locking up on the dusty road, then dropped the clutch into neutral. The front of the car broke traction and slid, spinning us round through 180 degrees. Now facing the right way, I took my foot off the brake and onto the accelerator, slipping the stick into second and screaming away up the hill before Walshe had even got the Chevy started behind us.

Chapter Twenty-two

Severnaya Zemlya, Siberia

Present day

I'd suspected Holderness, of course. In the list of people responsible for the holes in me, he ranked near the top. But then, it was a very long list, and with the trail long cold there'd been no way to narrow it down.

And now here, one day after killing the last of the team responsible, the end-of-level boss was handed to me on a plate. One and the same. It was very neat, and I don't normally like neat, but here we are. Even when you suspect something, hearing it confirmed aloud shocks you to the core, so I hadn't felt like chatting after that.

I'd left Balakin with the Glock I'd taken from Volkov, making sure he knew how to use it, in case anything happened to me. After that, he'd locked himself in for the night. I'd checked over my room, including another look up that creepy evacuation ladder with my torch, before locking my door and shoving my HK pistol under my pillow.

I'd been in bed five minutes before there was a soft tapping. Assuming that burned-up Cold-War soldier hadn't risen from his ashes, it could only be one person.

I opened the door to find Alice leaning on the frame in baggy shorts and a T-shirt. It looked like she'd redone her makeup, her tousled hair was still dented and awry from her earlier ponytail, but now her fringe was held back by a pink headband.

'Can I come in?'

'You're going to anyway.'

'So much has happened in the last couple of hours, we haven't had chance to talk.'

'About what?' I turned back into my room.

She followed me in and closed the door behind her. 'Erm, I don't know. About you ruining my life?'

'Remind me, because I'm getting on a bit. Was that around the time you tried to shoot me?'

She glared from under furrowed eyebrows. 'For a couple of months I constantly looked over my shoulder. I saw you behind me in every mirror, felt you every time I turned out the light.'

'Well, you either kill someone or you don't.'

'And you'd know.'

She was right. 'Look, you weren't even the first person to try to kill me that month, and I'm sure you won't be that last. If I kept score, I'd run out of pencils pretty quickly.'

'Well, I'm sorry, okay. It was a new experience for me.'

'Then I'd find a new job.' I gave a smile.

'If only. Thanks to you, it was whoosh, off to HMP Low Newton.'

I leaned against the wall, folding my arms. 'There's a saying about living by the sword.'

'Oh really? So you *didn't* go after the guy who killed your brother in Afghanistan?'

I narrowed my eyes. 'How do you know about that?'

'Mason told me, said that's how you wound up dead. Revenge, so don't go telling me about living by the fucking sword. Anyway, I didn't, I have a daughter, you know that? She's seven, I don't even know where she lives. I haven't seen her since that day. No trial, no press, whoosh, straight to prison, don't pass go.'

'Do you want me to feel sorry for you? Are you asking for forgiveness, or do you want me to apologise?'

'Amy was five. I just wanted her to have a better life than I'd had. A traitor, that's what they were told. Held under terrorism laws. Her dad never even came to see me. Used it as an excuse to shack up with some bitch from his office. Full custody and a fat pay-out from the government to keep schtum.' Tears had welled at the corners of her eyes. She wiped her nose with the back of her hand. 'And then they told me you were dead and it was weird. I should have been relieved but it was like… I don't know, like it brought home how mad it all was.' She held up her hand and ticked off her fingers. 'The people on that island in Scotland, dead, dead, dead, dead, dead, dead, prison. Then you dead. All that life gone, for nothing.'

She padded over, bare feet slapping the concrete. I noticed she'd done her toenails turquoise. Somehow the little things catch your eye and make you realise that normality exists even here, fucked in a Siberian bunker surrounded by people who wanted us dead and the rest who'd kill us if they found out why we were really here.

'How did you get out?' I asked.

She smiled. 'How did you survive so many holes?'

'You go first.'

She looked around the room nervously. 'Well, I guess if you're important to important people you don't really stay inside for long. Maybe I knew too much, or I could still be useful. I mean, technically, I was a CIA agent, if only by default, so a deal was done and I was transferred to the States, all hush-hush.'

'And the British were okay with that?' I knew only too well they'd be fine with anything if there'd been something in it for them.

'Your Colonel Holdensomething came to see me before I got out. He actually said since you were dead, no one gave a shit any more. Anyway, off to a new life in Maryland, and a new job. They own me now.'

'I know that feeling.'

'Oh, really?' She sat on the edge of the bed. 'So how did they get you here?'

'Long story.'

'We have all night.'

'I was done. Chris Rea, driving home for Christmas. Let this be a lesson to you, drive-thru fast food is bad for you.'

'I heard you were blown away in a car park in Yorkshire, is that right? Sorry, that sounds insensitive, it's just… a couple of hours ago you were dead as far as I knew.'

'It's okay, I mean, I survived, so...'

'It's clearly changed you, though. Where are the witty comebacks, the sarcasm, the cavalier attitude?'

I closed my eyes. 'More likely the intervening years that did it.'

'Why?'

'Settling old scores.'

'So Mason had it right. When you set out for revenge, first dig two graves. No wonder everyone's trying to kill you.'

'I'm already more than two graves deep, believe me.'

'But how did you survive, miles from anywhere?'

I smiled. 'They do have hospitals in Yorkshire now. Even in Skipton. But no, it was down to a friend of mine. Her and the 709th Military Intelligence Battalion.'

'And who are they when they're at home?'

I pushed off the wall. 'Aha, that's the point, they're not at home. You ever been to Skipton?'

She shook her head.

'Well, funny thing. If you have a fast enough car – and I did – a short drive from Skipton is a lovely big base full of CIA and NSA types.'

'In the middle of Yorkshire?'

'You seen the big golf balls on the moors outside Harrogate?'

She shook her head again and then her eyes went wide. 'The listening station?'

I nodded. 'It might be called RAF Menwith Hill, but it's run by the Americans. The person I was with is hooked in with some shady friends and took me straight there. It's a full-on US military base with all the hospital facilities you'd expect.'

'I get it. So everyone thinks you're dead, and bingo, the Americans have a ghost?'

'Got it in one. Only they're annoyed with me this time.'

'Well, I can't imagine *you* annoying *anyone*.' She leaned forward. 'So now we're both here to get information and take it back to our masters.'

'That about brings us up-to-date.'

'Almost. Do you want to know what really happened on Gruinard?'

'Do I want to know *your* version of events? Save it, I know enough.'

'That's just it, you don't. You only know what you saw, what you pieced together. And you were mostly right, but mostly doesn't justify what you did.'

'What *I* did?' I realised I couldn't reach my pistol. If she had one, I was fucked. It wouldn't be loaded with blanks this time.

'Why is it different when you kill someone?' she snapped. 'It could just as easily have been you in my position. You do this sort of thing day in, day out, and you don't question it.'

'You're wrong, all I do is question it.'

'Really? You just said you've killed several people in cold blood purely for revenge for killing your brother – and that's before we even get onto *why* they killed your brother. Doesn't sound like someone who questions their actions.'

I looked at the tiny cracks in the concrete floor, the scrapes from old boots and furniture.

'Go on then,' Alice pressed. 'If you're so good at questioning things, ask yourself what really happened on Gruinard Island two years ago.'

I looked up. 'I know what happened.'

'You're the big hero, right? Everyone's the hero of their own story. Well, you were the villain in that one.' She held a hand up before I could protest. 'Let me finish, I've gone over this so many times in my head. I thought if anyone could understand, it'd be you. I wanted to tell you so much, but I just couldn't. Then you worked it all out and… Well.

'I'd worked at Porton Down fifteen years, almost since university, and seen how little we're valued by the government. People like you, you have no loyalty, you sell your services to the highest bidder, why shouldn't I? Why was I wrong to make some money on the side?'

'You took money from a foreign government.'

'Says you.'

She had a shittiness in her voice now, so I injected some into mine. 'But never against my own country.'

'Don't treat me like I'm stupid. Besides, how do you know you haven't worked against your country? You wouldn't even know, so don't come at me.'

'Alice, you stole a biological weapon for money and killed people to cover it up. That's never the right side.'

She went quiet, fiddling at a stray thread on the hem of her shorts. 'Sounds exactly like the kind of mission you'd take on.'

I sighed and sat on the bed. 'Are you completely oblivious or stupid?'

'Easy money, they said. Low risk.' She shook her head. 'Maybe I *was* stupid, or naïve, but I needed the cash. The Americans approached me. They said there was a leak in British intelligence, that anything I turned in would find its way to Russia. I was to get the sample to them instead, and cover it up.'

'You believed them?'

'We both know you destroyed it. You don't trust them either.'

'Ah, but I don't trust anyone. That's your flaw.'

'Well, anyway, the Americans wanted it, and more importantly wanted the British not to have it. As a bonus they were willing to pay a lot, enough to pay off the mortgage, private school, blah blah. Then that horrible Frenchman got involved and took it on himself to test it out. Poor Andy Kyle. A sprinkle in his tea then he followed him around like a puppy until he dropped dead. I didn't know anything about it, Gambetta told me that night. Andy Kyle was clawing his way through the mud trying to get help while Gambetta stood over him, kicking him and laughing. Can you imagine? I cried myself to sleep that night, did you know that?'

'So you were part of a conspiracy that'd killed an innocent man?'

'Yes, but don't forget it was me who sabotaged the base, me who got you involved.'

'Because you thought I was incompetent and it'd get you off the hook.'

'No, because I wanted Gambetta *stopped*! Because I was in over my head. Gambetta was out of control, he was already planning to kill Demeter, to frame him for it all. What could I do? Me! Do you know how unstable Gambetta was?'

'You could have told me, I could have protected you.'

'But – and I was wrong, so wrong, John – once you arrived I did think you were incompetent. Swigging from that hip flask, wandering around like you were in a daze, how could you have protected me? I was terrified of him.'

'So you just let him kill Demeter?'

'I saved you, don't you see? So that you could end it. I saved your life that morning, John! And you never even knew it.'

It felt like the air was sucked out of the room, I couldn't breathe. My head felt hot. She was still talking but the sound was muffled under the weight of the words.

'He was getting rid of the evidence. I saw him throw it in the incinerator. Then I saw you go in after it. He watched you, I could see him. As soon as you went in, I knew I had to do something. I opened the door and shouted, so he knew there were witnesses around. If he'd known it was me he might not have stopped trying to burn you up, but he couldn't take the chance, so he ran away, all the way back to the base. I disconnected the gas pipe then ran back inside so you wouldn't see me. I waited by the window to watch, to make sure you were safe, and out you popped.'

'Why? Why do that and not tell me?'

'How could I tell you? I was in too deep, I didn't think you could help me. But that doesn't mean I could stand by while he killed you.'

'But you still went along with the plan.'

'No, after he tried to kill you, I *changed* his plan, don't you see? I found out what he was planning to do and *I* changed it, *I* killed Gambetta. I did it for me, for Kyle, for Demeter, for Ingrid, *for you…* I did it to be rid of him and that whole mess. I thought, he's already killed innocent people, he's set the whole thing up with poor Demeter as the bad guy, they're all dead. There was nothing I could do to change any of that, but I knew that if I killed *him,* it'd be over. One less psychopath, and nothing to connect me to any of it.'

'You nearly pulled off the perfect crime.'

She smiled and bumped against me, putting on a comical voice. 'And I would have got away with it, too, if it wasn't for you, ya meddling kid.' She sighed and leaned back. 'But don't you see? I only killed Gambetta. I didn't want a part in the rest of it. And then when you figured it all out, Brainiac, Gambetta was already dead. You killed Hurley, so there was no one else to back me up, no one to vouch for me, no one else to pin everything on. I was the only one left standing, so you, in your shiny white knight costume, pinned the whole thing on me.

'As soon as I saw you line up those guns on the ship, it hit me. My prints were all over that gun, and forensics would have a field day with my clothes. Can you honestly say you've never snapped when backed into a corner? In fact I know you have, I know more about you than you think. If the boot had been on your big foot, and you'd been in my position, you'd have resorted to self-preservation mode. You'd do *anything* if you were backed into a corner, and don't lie.'

I was quiet. There was a lot to process. A Russian mole in British intelligence, a reason the Americans wanted that anthrax sample destroyed – I'd have called her a mug at the time, but now, after what Professor Balakin had told me...

'Say something, then.'

I looked at her.

'John, I was honest with you because we need each other. We're in a vat of shit, and I need you to know we're on the same side.'

I couldn't speak. *Everyone's the hero of their own story.* By that token everyone is the villain in someone else's. I'd been the villain in hers. Who was the villain in this one?

I looked her in the eye. 'It's all about perspectives, I guess.'

'What is?'

'It's a strange life, this. Who'd want it?'

'Not me, that's for sure. I wish I could disappear like you did.'

'I didn't, not fully. The CIA own you for getting you out of prison; they own me for fixing some holes in me and keeping it quiet.'

'Show me.'

'Excuse me?'

She reached to my T-shirt. 'Show me the holes.' She reached a hand under, I flinched away. She tried again and I couldn't help but laugh at the absurdity of two enemies trapped together in a bunker beneath the Siberian wastes.

She sat back. 'What information did Balakin give you?'

'What did the rest of that transmission say?' I countered.

She pushed me down. In one fluid motion, her hand was under the pillow and out with my pistol. I lay back on the bed, staring down the barrel of my own gun.

'This is the same crappy old gun you had in Scotland.' She swung a leg over, straddling me, gun at my face. 'What did Balakin say? What's so important that we had to come thousands of miles to this dump?'

'You don't know why we're here, do you?' I asked. 'Mason's playing us off.'

'So tell me.'

'Balakin asked for me. He specifically said he'd only give me the information.'

'Seems no one tells me anything.'

'You're not going to shoot me.'

She held the gun out to the side, then leaned forward, grabbing my wrists, pressing it into my hand. 'Not with the safety on, no.'

'Only works in the right hands.'

'Your hands?' She pressed her weight into me and leaned closer, whispering, 'Tell me what Balakin told you.'

'We've got to be up extremely early.'

She leaned in, her breath tickling my ear. 'You'll have to be quick then, eh?'

Chapter Twenty-three

Severnaya Zemlya, Siberia
Present day

Something had stirred me from sleep. I turned over and threw an arm out that landed on the bed. Alice had long since retreated into her own room.

There was a noise somewhere, a scuffling in the darkness. I held my breath and let my eyes adjust to the dim glow of the light from the corridor under the door, wondering if Alice had come back. The noise was faint. There were no rats on the island as far as I knew and besides, if rats could infest a sealed nuclear bunker, then I didn't reckon it'd be up to much.

The noise came again, and I realised it was coming from the room behind me. Balakin was moving around in there.

I rolled onto my back and looked at the ceiling. Apparently, Alice had warmed to me enough for some things, but that hadn't extended to sharing details of how we were to rendezvous with our evac. Clearly, she didn't trust me, and was clinging to what was her indispensable knowledge to avoid being left behind. Good job I had my own plan which didn't need to involve her.

There was a bang next door, like something being thrown, then a shout.

'You!' Balakin was arguing with someone, either enraged or terrified. 'How did you… No!'

I leapt from the bed and threw on my trousers. I'd just fastened them when a gunshot rang out, muffled behind the concrete but clear enough to speed me up. Even so, by the time I'd snatched up my pistol and reached the door, another three gunshots had completely shattered the quiet of the bunker.

I slammed against the door.

A terrible scream rent the night, echoing through the bunker.

I turned on the lights and looked around the room for something heavy. I shoved my gun in my pocket and grabbed the bedside table, running to the door and not stopping. The table collapsed but the door bowed. I threw the smashed table away and pulled on my boots, not bothering to lace them up as I kicked.

An alarm started blaring somewhere in the bunker, the lights cut out, flashing on again a second later, violent red pulsing eerily in time with the wailing siren. I renewed my efforts, booting the door over and over, watching it bow in with each kick.

Finally the lock surround splintered. I pushed it open and ran down the short corridor to Balakin's room. His bedroom door was closed, but a yellow glow showed around the edges, reflecting off the walls.

I kicked it open and immediately recoiled, hands over my face. There was a blast of heat as air was sucked in, then thick acrid smoke spewed out along the ceiling. Fierce orange blazed as I ran inside, turning to the source of the fire where I stopped dead, the blood freezing in my veins despite the soaring temperature.

Through the thick chemical smoke I could see Balakin seated in the chair, back to the wall, mouth open in a soundless scream. I put a hand to my own mouth as my legs weakened.

The shrieking alarm and flashing red lights on the ceiling made the scene even worse. His head was a ball of flame, lipless mouth locked in a shining grin, empty eye sockets smoking. The rest a mess of steaming, spitting red. His entire body was ablaze, or the bits I could see anyway. Half of his torso had already burned down to bone, one arm had separated and dropped to the floor. Next to his smoking eyepatch, his charred left hand still clutched the Glock. I turned to look at the wall opposite: four bullet holes had punched through the tiles and stainless steel toilet. Who had he been shooting at?

I dashed to the sink, looked around frantically as I coughed smoke. I filled a glass tumbler with water and threw it but it was like pissing on a bonfire. Above the sink, Brezhnev grinned down at my attempts. There was nothing to be done.

I coughed again, violently, retching in the chemical-heavy air. The old armchair and molten plastic suitcase were spewing cancerous black smoke. I followed the rolling clouds to the vent high up on the wall. Death would come for anyone trapped down here, overcome by fumes, but the worst of it was being sucked away as part of the automatic fire system.

Above the alarm, another scream echoed through the concrete corridors. *Alice.*

I sprinted back into the corridor, pulling my gun, straight through my room, swinging open the door as the alarm grew louder. The passage to the main bunker was empty, the emergency lights flashing in time to my boots slapping the ground. I slammed through the door into the room beyond, skidding to a halt.

The alarm box was set high on the wall, shrieking, a strobe light flickering unnervingly. Beneath it, Alice lay face down on the ground, blood trickling from somewhere under her hair down onto her white T-shirt.

I crouched and felt her neck. She had a pulse and was breathing.

I jumped up and ran to the stairs, taking them two at a time. When I made it to the door at the top, I was panting, gun ready.

The huge metal door was still sealed from the inside, but I could smell something chemical, and not just the wisps of smoke I'd carried along with me.

There was a shout in Russian somewhere on the other side of the door. *Golubev's guards.*

A rushing sound came. I waited for a second, confused. It was a second too long as the odour got stronger. A tiny patch of paint on the door blistered and bubbled.

The guards were cutting through the door.

I ran back down the steps, leaping over the still-prone Alice, heading for my room. The vents were starting to struggle as black smoke, carrying the sickening stench of cooking meat, drifted in the fetid air of the bunker.

I skidded to a stop, looking back at Alice.

Leave her to the flames or Golubev? Or take her, and risk us both getting killed?

She got her hands beneath her. I sprinted back, sliding down onto my knees to pull her up.

She pushed me away. 'What happened?' she shouted, looking up at the strobe light.

'You tell me.' I ran into her room, grabbing a handful of outdoor clothes and her boots.

'What is that?'

'Fire alarm.' I put an arm around her and dragged her up. 'We need to get moving.'

'There was a man.'

'Who?' I started, pulling her along the corridor.

'He had no face. He...' She put a hand to her head, it came away sticky.

'We need to move fast, come on!'

I pulled her into my room, towards the smoke which was curling across the ceiling. I kicked the door shut behind us to dampen the nagging alarm, then dropped her on the bed and pulled Balakin's door shut, sending more smoke around the room.

I unzipped the bag of clothes Golubev had lent me, pulling everything out. 'Put these on!'

She sat on the bed, hands on knees, dazed. 'Why is the fire alarm going off?'

I picked up the cold-weather trousers and threw them on her lap. 'Get them on right now!'

'He had a parka on and his hood up. He'd come from outside. How did he come from outside?'

I threw on a T-shirt and grabbed her by the shoulders. 'Alice, look at me! Golubev's troops are cutting through the door right now, and when they get in here they're gonna find his favourite scientist burning alive in his bedroom and us sat here like fucking lemons.'

'Burning alive?'

'Figure of speech, we should leave.'

'Jesus Christ.' She finally clicked into gear and started pulling on her trousers. 'He's dead?'

'Very.'

She seemed to notice the stench and smoke for the first time, holding a hand up in the haze. 'But we didn't kill him.'

'You want to tell the angry men with guns that, be my guest. Me, I'm bugging the fuck out.'

She pulled on her boots and started to lace them up. I threw a few T-shirts and sweaters to her and grabbed a couple of parkas from the bed. 'Put everything on, we don't know how long we'll be outside for.'

I opened the door to the escape shaft, clamping a torch between my teeth and shrugging into my coat. The smell of burning had even made it this far, though it was dark and quiet. For now.

'Alice, I swear to God I'm gonna leave you here!'

She jumped up, pulling on a second jacket. I ushered her onto the ladder then followed her up. Shouts echoed through the bunker below us. It sounded like the guards had broken through the main door. Above me Alice picked up the pace, hand over hand flashing in the beam of my torch.

We made it to the top, I pushed past her to the door and put my ear to it. Silence. Another shout below prompted me to grab the wheel and turn. Alice pulled the latches back. The door swung open.

'It was locked,' she said.

'They both were.'

'So how the hell did he get in?'

'Come on.'

There were no rifles to greet us, so I crept up the steps to the hatch and switched off the torch. The only sound was the wind howling around the shed. I pushed up the wooden boards tentatively and the wind noise increased, but thankfully nothing else happened. I crawled up further and peered through the shed's window at the torches bobbing in the distance near the hotel.

I crouched back down by the trapdoor. 'Okay, go,' I said, pushing Alice up into the shed.

She swatted my hand away and crept upwards while I went back down, pulling the big steel door closed. There was a rush of wind above as Alice opened the boathouse door.

'Wait for me,' I hissed, moving up the stairs.

Snow was blowing in from the door. I cursed under my breath as it slammed in the wind. Another glance out of the window told me the torches over near the hotel hadn't noticed. I opened it and stepped outside, sticking close to the shadow of the wall.

Golubev stood off to the right, arms folded. Beside him was his security guy, Gregori, gripping Alice tightly.

My hand twitched at my pocket as I glanced around his team of commandos encircling us, each holding a rifle trained on me.

Golubev grinned and unzipped his fancy Canada Goose parka. 'Leaving us, Mr Chambers?' He reached inside and pulled out a pistol. 'But I thought we had an agreement?'

A rifle butt flashed in the corner of my eye, then nothing.

Chapter Twenty-four

Severnaya Zemlya, Siberia

Present day

Time had no meaning, my senses had no meaning. I knew it was early evening but only because that's what they'd told me. For the umpteenth time in the last 24 hours I woke with a splitting headache. The difference this time was there was no aversion to light, purely because there was none. Not a single reflection, nor the faintest glimmer of a match.

I was waking up bound again, which was getting really old. It was cold, freezing cold, but I couldn't wrap my seized arms about myself since they were hanging from ropes which barely let my naked toes brush the cold concrete. I blinked, feeling sticky blood clogging up my eyes, and breathed in lightly to avoid the pain in my ribs.

They hadn't asked me any questions, not a thing. I'd been dragged down that dark dingy corridor, all the time the security guy Gregori periodically clubbing me with a broken chair leg. Oak. Weird the details you focus on. Stripped naked and hung from the pipes across the ceiling while that bit of wood continued its work. Never hard enough to break anything more than skin. Finally Golubev himself had taken over, preferring to use his pistol as a club.

On and off, all day. I don't know how many times I'd lost consciousness, only to open my eyes for it to start again.

I knew the drill, that this was the softening before the questions. The reminder that I was entirely helpless, that soon I'd say or do anything to make it stop, even beg for it to end permanently. I knew that, but it didn't make it easier.

Then I'd woken up alone in the pitch black. Except for Balakin's still cooling corpse, if the stink was anything to go by.

I tested the ropes again. No chance. I swung up, wincing at the bruises forming everywhere, and pulled up my legs. The ropes bit deeply. I felt some give in the pipe but not enough for hope, and it certainly wasn't worth the fire it sent raging through my limbs.

'Mr Chambers.' A torch clicked on, burning into my eyes. It was Golubev's voice. 'This weekend's business is concluded. Sadly, we were not able to finalise the sale of any of our biological weapons for obvious reasons, but you'll be pleased to know I did complete orders for most of the small arms and trucks. Nearly all of my guests have now left, which means you have my full attention.'

I screwed my eyes shut. 'I'm less likely to talk now than when you brought me down here.'

A chair scraped across the floor. I opened my eyes but pain screwed them shut again.

'A man like you will be fine in a few hours, no doubt. There is no permanent damage... yet.'

'Where's Dr Carr?'

'Elsewhere.'

'You cowardly bastard, I'll—'

'You'll do nothing at all. Fact is, she has not been harmed. There is no need. You see, I already know she killed Professor Balakin.'

'She didn't kill him.'

'Oh, but she did. Now I need to ascertain whether you were party to it or not.'

'Someone got in. This place obviously isn't as safe as you thought.'

'Please, tell me again what happened. Take your time.'

'I've told you twenty times already. I woke up, Balakin was screaming at someone. He tried to shoot them, I broke his door down, found him on fire.'

'We have examined the professor, he was entirely consumed by fire. Do you know how long it takes for a human body to burn?'

'Just like your guy out on the ice, just like Volkov, just like Burton. She couldn't have done that.'

'I thought so, but now… We'll see.'

'Cut me down, tie me to a chair or something, I'm fucking freezing and I have long enough arms as it is, I don't want them stretching.'

'What happened after you found Professor Balakin burning alive?'

'I went to get Dr Carr.'

'And you escaped?'

'I went to the main door, which your men were cutting through.'

'Because it was locked.'

'Yes, so we went up the escape ladder.'

'Where I found you.' He started pacing. 'So, I will repeat it back to you. Three people are sealed into this bunker. You yourself check it from top to bottom, it is not a big space, there is nowhere anyone can possibly have hidden.'

'*Someone* got in.'

'One of the three is attacked. A disgusting, brutal attack, the most horrible death. I only have your word that you broke down his door and found him there.'

'It was someone in Soviet cold-weather gear.'

'And yet by your own admission both bunker doors were locked tight before you yourself opened one to escape. Indeed, you had to break down the door to get into his room. No one could have got in.'

'Tell me about Pozharnyy.'

'Ha, the white demon. Fairy stories to scare children.'

'Something happened in the past that has a bearing on what's happening now.'

'The first thing you have been right about.'

The bright torch went out. Boots scraped on concrete, the main lights buzzed on. I opened my eyes again and squinted at Golubev in front, arms folded across his chest. Three of his men stood by the exits, rifles in hand. The nearest was Gregori, glaring at me intently.

On the chair were my folded clothes, on top of them sat my pistol.

Golubev walked to the chair and placed his hand on it. 'Heckler and Koch VP70. A terrible gun.'

'It works.'

'Not very well. Don't get me wrong, it was a good gun in its day. Polymer frame which predated the Glock by what, fifteen years or so? Large capacity, simple, reliable. Yours has been modified to use a suppressor and also burst mode, even without the stock attached.' He pulled the trigger, the rapid cracks were deafening in the enclosed space, setting my ears ringing and plaster dust flying around the room long after the echo died down. 'I never liked burst mode on these.'

'You know a lot about guns,' I said, still wincing.

He held it to the light. 'I am an arms dealer.'

'Fair enough.'

'So I know this was a good gun, an interesting gun, in its day. Sadly its day was back in the 1970s, like this hotel.' He waved the gun around the room. 'A relic, just like its owner. Why do you keep it?'

'Sentimental value.'

'Yes, I believe you.' He walked over to me and tapped the barrel of the pistol against my ribs. I flinched. 'For a man who leaves no trace you are incredibly sentimental. No women to speak of, indeed no men, either. No real friends, little family left.' He ran the gun up my arm. 'But all these tattoos of the places you've been, those rusty old cars you keep, your scruffy jacket, your scratched watch.' He stepped back. 'But most of all this gun. This terrible, antiquated, outdated gun. As with the scars that cover your body, each of these items has left an indelible mark, isn't that so?'

I narrowed my eyes and breathed in deeply. 'Who are you?'

'They are signs of deep psychological trauma, you know. Fear. Anxiety. An inability to deal with an ever-changing world, even though you have more of a hand than most in its formation.'

'How do you know me?'

'You've done much to boast about, but these memories have become a crutch. Comfort food for your soul – if indeed you still have a soul; I know The Devil has owned it for twenty-four years now, since the first time you picked up a gun. I imagine when you relax – do you ever relax? If you do, I think you would watch the same films, read the same books over and over again in a bid to give your world the order it needs, because you know it is only ever one bullet away from anarchy.'

'You know a lot about me.'

'Much more than you think, *John Tyler*.'

Chapter Twenty-five

Severnaya Zemlya, Siberia
Present day

'Who *are* you?' I asked again.

'I am Viktor Golubev, former Spetsnaz officer, former agent of the GRU, now merely a salesman. It is my job to know the people who come here. No mystery.'

'Why didn't you say anything before?'

'What would it have achieved?' He shrugged. 'I thought I could trust a man such as you. I thought you could be the only man who could keep my scientist alive. It seems John Tyler is not infallible. He does not always complete the mission or get the job done, eh? Maybe you are slipping since you died.'

My mind raced. Why did he know so much?

'I can see you trying to add two and two, and you will likely make ten. Please stop. I am exactly who I said I am, nothing else. Which is more than can be said for you and your friend, Dr Alice String.

'It seems strange, does it not, that two people are sent here to my hotel, both under false identities, who already know each other, and who end up being the only people who could possibly have killed my man. It sounds very much like a conspiracy. Tell me, if you were in my position, what would you conclude?'

'If you knew we weren't—'

He held a hand up. 'Please, Mr Tyler. Half the people I do business with do so under an assumed name, and almost all the people I meet are killers, thieves, or otherwise scum. Why did you really come here?'

'I was sent to protect Dr Carr… Alice. To keep her safe and get her back.'

'Nothing more?'

I shook my head. 'Nothing more. I don't know anything else, I don't have any ulterior motives.'

'This is important, so take your time before answering. Sent by whom?'

'I think you know it was our friends at Langley.'

'Thank you for not insulting me. I gather you have no particular love for your current masters. What do they have over you, I wonder? No matter. Yes, the CIA, MI6, Mossad, the DGSI,' he sighed. 'They all like to visit now and again. Sometimes as allies, sometimes enemies, but always as friends, never nonsense like this. It is the game we all play.'

'I prefer Guess Who.'

'Aha! There it is! Alice said you like sarcasm. Perhaps this wit only makes an appearance when you're about to die?'

'Cut me down and I'll stop.'

'I think not. You see, Alice is lying to me. I *know* she is lying to me. Now I just need to know if you are as well.'

He reached inside his jacket pocket and pulled out a piece of paper. He unfolded it and walked closer.

'This was in her pocket. In her handwriting.'

Position compromised Stop Phoenix to interrogate and terminate Owl Stop

Stupid idiot, she'd kept the other bit of the note, the transcript of the decoded message.

Golubev dropped the paper at my toes, massaging the bridge of his nose as he spoke. 'She is *Phoenix*, I take it. And an *owl* is obviously a professor. Boy scouts and their little code-names, and you say it's not a game, ha! Of course it is. Our little *Phoenix* travelled here to steal information from Professor Balakin, or *Owl*, and then assassinate him. This is obvious, yes? So as I said, the only question is whether you played a part, or were an unwitting pawn in *her* game.'

For a second time. For fuck's sake, was that what this was? Another of her labyrinthine schemes, or even a twisted and macabre form of revenge? *No.* I had to remind myself, Alice had been nowhere near when Balakin had been torched.

Well, either way, Alice was in some deep shite, and it wouldn't serve either of us well for me to be neck-deep in the same.

'That scheming bitch.' I threw on my best confused face. 'I had nothing to do with it. And if you knew she wasn't who she said she was, then you're to blame. Setting me on the killer's trail without giving me all the facts… His blood's on your hands, too.'

'I think not. Not when you were here under an alias. We have both withheld information. But that is the nature of our business?'

'We're not in the same line of business.'

'Perhaps a different role, but ultimately the same industry. War. Death. Mayhem. Money.' He grinned, the light reflecting off his cold blue eyes to give him a menacing Terminator glare. 'What information?'

'What information?'

'Yes, that is what I asked. The note mentions information. Did you speak to Balakin before he died?'

'Briefly, before we went to bed. Small talk, Siberia, the weather…'

Gregori stepped into the light, flexing his fists. Golubev put an arm across him and shook his head. 'There is no need, Mr Tyler will not leave Barensky Island alive. If Balakin gave him any information… it will die with him.'

He gestured with his head, as one of the men stepped past Gregori and sliced the ropes above me. I dropped to my feet, then found they couldn't hold me and crumpled to the cold ground.

'You may have a long night ahead of you.'

'I'm not playing your game any more.'

'Though if you're lucky, a *warm* night.'

'If you've got your head screwed on, you'll let Alice go. You don't want to turn this into a personal grudge with the CIA.'

'The CIA, they do not care about Alice String. She is merely an errand girl, sent to pick up a bill.'

'The GRU won't like it either. The unwanted attention will make you unpopular.'

He shook his head. 'Again, you forget this is a game, Mr Tyler.' He swung a boot into my ribs, not with his full weight but just enough to punctuate his point. 'Neither you nor Alice will be leaving here alive.'

'So you don't believe me?'

'I think I do believe you. But that means you failed me. If, as you say, you did not kill Professor Balakin, then you did nothing to prevent his murder, despite knowing the risk, all the signs saying he was going to be killed. And killed by your own comrade, which you did not see coming. If you *didn't* kill him then you're *stupid*, which is even worse. Take him.'

Two of his guards grabbed me. I didn't have the energy to resist. It wouldn't have done much good anyway, not with Gregori pointing a gun at me, and Golubev holding my own pistol.

My vision swam as I was dragged into the next room. Lights flickered, faces leered. Before I knew what was happening, I was on my back in the centre of the floor, pressure on my arms and legs. It let up and I pulled, finding I was tied down to metal rings set into the concrete.

'I am obsessed with the idea of your witch trials,' Golubev said, pacing at the periphery of my vision. 'Ducking people in water in particular.' He pointed up as he spoke, smiling. 'This idea that if someone sinks and drowns, then they were innocent, but if they float and survive, well, they are a witch and they should be executed.'

'It's cold and I'm getting cramp, get to the point.'

I heard the clink of glass. Golubev appeared above me, holding the bottle of vodka. He took a swig and smiled.

'You've noticed it's cold in here. The air conditioning has been turned off for some time. The main door now has a large hole in it. You will be frozen solid by morning.'

'You've missed the point, you bastard.' I pulled on the ropes. One of the wrists had a bit of give. 'They didn't just kill the witches, they had a chance. Fucking twisted, but a kind of chance.'

'Oh, you have a chance to not freeze. You asked about Pozharnyy.'

'You bastard.'

'Have you ever heard of Psi Particles?' He saw how blank my face looked and continued. 'Pseudo scientific nonsense,' he laughed, taking a decent swig of vodka. 'ESP, astral projection, telekinesis, you name it, they tried to make it work for KGB. There is a lab in Siberia where kittens were taken away from their mother into another room and killed, just to see if the mother reacted.'

'Don't tell me, you worked there?'

'A team of Soviet scientists claimed to have perfected the use of ESP, but of course, it is all nonsense. The military had always run this hotel but after a few years they moved equipment in and slowly used it more and more as a safe place to test wild theories. Until the accident.' He took another swig of vodka. 'I'm sorry, would you like a last drink?'

'You'll forgive me if I don't get up.'

He poured the vodka on my face. Burning, spluttering, I blinked it from my eyes. It made me even colder.

'No one really knows for sure what happened.' He slung the vodka bottle away into a dark corner where it smashed. 'You asked me if I give these ghost stories any credence, and the answer is no. But the rumours are that KGB had perfected a way to control objects through the mind. Soldiers from Petrograd to Khabarovsk were tested and selected for their latent abilities. The story goes that they would use these bunkers beneath the hotel as a way to isolate objects; cards, chess pieces, that sort of thing. They would then try to control them with their mind remotely from the laboratory above, the room in which we found the body of Mr Volkov.

'After a while, the experiments moved on to the test subjects transporting themselves out of body, into the bunker to interact with objects directly.' Golubev laughed then paused to think. 'Pyrokinesis, I think they call it in English. They discovered that one of their best test subjects was able to start fires. There were several incidents, erm…' he thought for a moment. 'Spontaneous combustion. During these experiments, while sedated and under observation in the laboratory upstairs, he would appear briefly down here in the bunker. One day an officer challenged him, to ask what he was doing, and spontaneously burst into flames. The poor man was running around down here burning alive, nobody could douse the flames, and all while the subject was actually in the lab in a trance. Well, after that, the KGB knew they had a weapon, if only they could harness its power.'

'An assassin sitting in Moscow appearing in the Oval Office and killing Reagan?' I tried to put humour into my laugh, but I didn't like where this was heading.

'Exactly this.' Golubev was walking circles around me now. 'The downside is they couldn't get it to work over distance. A few hundred metres or so, but the potential was there. Sadly, the more they tried to control this man, the less they could. There were more incidents until they realised too late he had gone quite mad. He was imprisoned down here, in the bunker, sealed in.'

'Harsh.'

'As these legends always are. You are now, note, tied to iron rings set into concrete. In the stories this is where he is tied down, sealed into the cold bunker alone, while the scientists and officers eat their evening meal above.

'But as they dig into their *Pelmeni*, the captive soldier impossibly appears at the doorway. One by one the officers around the table burst into flames. Soon half the lab staff and garrison are running around on fire. The building goes up in flames.'

'I used to watch *X-Files* too,' I said, chuckling.

He stopped pacing and looked down at me. 'Yes, urban myth and fairy tale, I quite agree. But what is fact, is that around 1977 there was a fire. Something like twenty people died. The whole place was closed up and abandoned.'

'I see why the place was going cheap.'

'Well, after the fall of the Soviet Union these old military sites were sold off. Old stocks were big business, it's how most of today's oligarchs made their money, in that grey time. Last time I was in London, I watched a programme on television about people who buy old shipping containers, not knowing what is inside. It could be a container of mouldy business cards or it could be a Ferrari. Well, this is just the same, a container sale. And I got this,' he waved his hand around. 'Not much to look at but at the end of the day it is a safe and secure hotel with all the right facilities, in one of most isolated spots on planet. That in itself is very useful for people wanting to meet away from any prying eyes.'

'And comes with a good story for Halloween.'

'Ah, but I haven't got to the best part. When my men surveyed this section of hotel several years ago, they found rooms blocked with rubble. As they got through, they found the steel doors had been obviously bricked over. They broke through and found the door welded shut. When they finally got down here, they found a skeleton in middle of the room.'

'Bullshit,' I laughed.

'Not at all, I saw it with my own eyes. Still chained to the floor where you are now. Perhaps the man could project himself out of his body, but that is not the same as actually being somewhere else.' Golubev disappeared from my field of view. 'With the doors sealed and the hotel burning above him, it seems he set fire to himself.'

The lights flicked out. I could hear boots scraping on the cold concrete.

'I don't believe any of this, but, of course, there are more stories.' Golubev's voice was drifting from further away in the dark. 'Pozharnyy appears, someone dies. I learned quickly that many won't come here. Even most of my men refuse to enter the ruins. You would not believe the security personnel I have gone through. I thought it was all nonsense, but given the events of this weekend, who knows?

'So we come back to those witch trials. In several hours, you will be frozen solid. But, if you are telling the truth about how Professor Balakin was murdered, this ghost who can walk through walls and appear in this bunker undetected, then you may not freeze to death. You might instead burn alive.

'In which case you will have been right, and you were telling the truth about Balakin's death, and I will, of course, apologise profusely to you.'

'You son of a bitch.'

'Mr Tyler: *adieu.*'

The door slammed.

Chapter Twenty-six

The Peoples' Democratic Republic of Nambutu / French Equatorial Africa

1999

Contrary to what they'd told me, I was not getting used to the grime and the very particular aroma of our little bar.

'Let's go over the plan one last time.' Justin cracked a couple of beers open and handed me one.

I took a swig, not grimacing at the warm, out-of-date local brew this time. 'We know it,' I said. He'd always been so anal, planning and sketching and writing lists, even as far back as sorting Lego into colours and brick types. 'I can do this.'

'I bloody hope so,' said Walshe.

I pushed him out of the way and pressed play on the Discman. Hole blasted from the tinny speaker.

Walshe rolled his eyes. 'Why do you have to put this shit on every time?'

'It helps me concentrate and remember.'

'But why *this* shit?'

'Some twat smashed all my other CDs.'

'Knock it off. Johnny, turn it down and listen.' Justin pointed at the map, and a road junction. 'You'll be waiting with the car here.'

I nodded and put on an exasperated voice. 'On the old logging trail that leads off from the main road.'

'Where you hide the Mitsubishi.'

'She's called Yoshi.'

'She's not called Yoshi, it's a car, it's not even a bloody she.' He held his head in his hands. 'Can we just get through this, please?'

'Like from Mario.'

Justin shot me a look. 'I know this is boring to you, but we plan and go over and over so it goes smoothly.'

I took another swig and nodded. 'Proceed.'

'From the trail you can see all the way down the hill to the mines at Cherub Rock.'

'Where the deal goes down,' I said.

He nodded. 'So the Russians come in with the truck from the south, from Boande, right past you. They turn down the mine track…'

'How do you know all this detail again?'

'Like I said, I know someone who knows someone,' said Walshe. 'The intel's good.'

'It's a guy who was in our section in Kosovo,' said Justin. 'He's gone private, that's where the money is.'

'Can we get this done?' said Walshe, looking at his watch.

'Sorry,' I said. 'This is my first heist.'

Walshe sighed. 'So the DPAN will come in from the north, past us.'

Justin rubbed his eyes. 'I told you, it's not the DPAN,' he sighed. 'DPAN is the Democratic Peoples' Army of Nambutu, they don't exist any more since they hold power.'

I smirked. 'Yeah, it's not the bloody DPAN, jeez Walshe.'

'The fucking ALN then.'

'The Armée de la Libération du Nambutu are the leftist guerrillas,' said Justin.

'Leftist guerrillas,' I parroted.

'These guys are the PRVN,' said Justin. 'The Peoples' Republican Volunteer Army.'

'Too many acronyms,' muttered Walshe.

'Says the squaddie,' I said. 'And the PRVN are the militia, yeah?'

Justin nodded. 'The right-wing pro-government guys.'

'But why are the Russians supplying arms to a right-wing militia?'

'Because the main opposition are the ARN, the Armée de la République du Nambutu.'

'This is ridiculous, do we have a blackboard in this dump?' I looked around. 'I feel like we need a blackboard.'

'It's complicated.' He made a grabbing motion for a cigarette from the packet I'd just opened. 'The ARN are the slightly less right-wing Pro-French rule guys, basically the remnants of the pre-revolution government. The ARN don't recognise the current government of Nambutu, and since the UN haven't either and this is still officially French Equatorial Africa, the ARN think it gives them legitimacy.' He stuck a cig between his lips and flicked a lighter, inhaling deeply and blowing smoke up at the low ceiling. 'The fact they only control a handful of villages in the west and no major cities is neither here nor there.

'Anyway, the ARN are supported by the CIA. By supplying arms to the PRVN and other right-wing rebels, the Russians drain CIA resources and hold off a NATO foothold in the region.'

I lit my own cig and shook my head. 'So why don't the Russians support the left-wing guerrillas instead?'

'Catch 22, the ALN don't have the funds to mount serious opposition to the government, so they don't get the people behind them, so they don't get the funding, so they can't mount serious opposition. The Russians don't care who rules Nambutu as long as it's not the West.'

'And you honestly understand all of this?'

'I'm sure you got some of the groups the wrong way round,' said Walshe.

'Regardless,' shouted Justin, pointing then taking another drag. 'It doesn't matter if we understand it or not. We're on the right bloody side. All you need to do,' he said, blowing smoke and jabbing his cig towards me, 'is watch and wait. The militia come in from the north, past us. You signal when everyone is at the party.'

'And it's two pulls on the string?'

Walshe held up two fingers. 'Can you count that high?'

'I just got a Nokia 5110, you know. I could have brought it.'

'You'd probably have left it in your suitcase,' Walshe sneered.

I turned to Justin. 'It's got these different coloured covers you can change and there's this game called Snake and I swear to God it's more addictive than crack…'

'Mobiles are no good,' said Justin, slamming his bottle of beer on the bar. 'No phone masts.'

'Dickhead,' added Walshe.

I made a face at Walshe and earned a slap that knocked my cigarette onto the dirty floor.

Justin glared at me as I picked up the cig, rubbing my cheek. 'You'll be keeping watch. There'll be some checking of the goods, yadda yadda yadda, it'll go smoothly because even though this is a big one, these guys do business all the time, everyone's friendly. The Russians will take the money and leave, in out, fast as they can. They don't like it this deep. They come out and head south back to Boande. You don't even blink until those Russians have gone. They're bad news.'

'Bad like how?'

'One of 'em's a complete psychopath,' said Walshe. 'They smell anything out of order, they'll be all over our shit. So you don't fucking lift your little finger until they're well clear.'

'Bad news,' Justin repeated, nodding. 'The PRVN guys will drive the truck north the way they came. When they pass you, it's three pulls on the string, and we set the ambush.'

'And you're sure you can take them?'

'This is the militia, it's basically teenagers with old AKs. Intel says there'll only be four of them.'

'And if there are more?'

'We'll make the call. Regardless, then it's three pulls on the string, tree across the road. You bring the Pajero up behind…'

'Yoshi.'

'You bring the Mitsubishi up, the truck has nowhere to go.' He put his cig between his lips and made a pincer motion with his fingers. 'We come in from the sides, game over.'

'And explain "game over" to me again.'

He exhaled smoke. 'They'll fold, they always do. Imagine you're a nineteen-year-old with no combat experience, holding an AK-47 you know you can't hit anything with.'

167

'I don't have to imagine.'

'So you know how they'll feel when two big hard bastards tooled up to the neck come at them. Trust me, these militia guys, they're feckless idiots. The ARN, they're hard guys, they live out in the jungle, they're CIA funded. I mean, they're nothing up to us, but at least they're the real deal.' Justin dropped his cigarette and ground it into the floor with his boot. 'The PRVN live in the city, they walk about giving it all that, they don't have ideals, they're just out for themselves. They're not political, they just support the government because it's easy. Total pussies.'

'But still, no killing, right?'

'Not if we can help it.'

'Lions don't care about zebras.' Walshe laughed. 'You two need a good scrap and a fuck, that'll sort you out. Then you'll be killing these motherfuckers left, right and centre.' He picked up his sidearm and aimed at the window, miming shooting it.

I ignored him. 'Then it's a bridge too far?'

Justin nodded. 'When the truck doesn't show, the PRVN are gonna get suspect. And that's gonna happen really bloody quickly, and it's gonna be big, because when the Commissaire hears, the shit will hit the fan.'

'And why does the Commissaire care?'

'The Commissaire of the Democratic Peoples' Army of Nambutu is like the president, basically, but on the city streets he uses the PRVN as his secret police. Think of the brownshirts or the Hitler Youth.'

I pushed my cigarette into the tabletop, watching it crumple. 'Dude, this is nuts confusing.'

'None of it matters, you don't need to remember any of it. All you need to know is – truck stopped, weapons heisted. So you come around this older trail here and get down to the crossroads at Lusemba before the army come up the main road from the barracks. You'll have less than ten minutes to blow the bridge.'

'And the charges are set?'

'They will be,' said Walshe.

'It sounds fancier than it is, it's only a one-lane girder bridge, we're not talking Operation Market Garden here. You blow the bridge and head back. Meanwhile, we've driven the truck south-west to meet the ARN and do the deal. You come in and pick us up.'

I was still playing with the crumpled cig, flicking smoking ash around the tabletop. 'And the ARN will be cool, yeah?'

Justin looked at Walshe and raised his eyebrows.

'They're not gonna dare pull anything.'

'Sounds iffy to me.'

'They'll be fine.'

'So we've done the deal, got the cash, and are west over the border into Zangaro before anyone even knows anything's happened.'

'Clear?' asked Walshe.

I sucked air through my teeth and flicked the tab end across the room. 'There's just one thing I've been thinking of.'

Justin sighed. 'What is it?'

'I'm on my own in the jungle.'

'We'll be a couple of hundred metres down the road.'

'Okay, but basically, what if that guy comes?'

'What fucking guy?'

'What did you call him? The weirdo that picked me up at the airport.'

'The headhunter?' asked Walshe. 'Don't worry about him.'

'I feel like I *should* be worried about someone called Headhunter.'

'To be fair, he's never far away,' said Justin. 'Fucker can smell blood, the guy's a vulture, creaming off combat.'

'What do you mean?'

'They call him Le Démon Blanc,' he said. 'The White Demon, but no one really knows who he is. He appears whenever there's fighting and disappears again just as quickly. Takes the bodies. And the wounded.'

'There's no hunting like the hunting of man,' I said. 'Anyone who's hunted armed men long enough and liked it, never cares for owt else afterwards.'

'What film's that from?' asked Walshe.

'Hemingway, you nonce.'

'Not seen it.'

Justin picked up another bottle of beer from the crate. 'He gets paid by the Commissaire to hunt out rebels in the jungle, dollars per head.' He cracked the top on the bar and handed it to Walshe. 'He takes it literally.'

'He's just a scumbag mercenary,' Walshe spat, 'who's spent too long with the natives.'

'*Heart of Darkness*,' I muttered. 'So why did he want me?'

'A head is a head, he'll take people the easiest way he can. Usually that's after skirmishes in the jungle.'

'And sometimes it's waiting at the airport for morons,' added Walshe.

'Right, so I get a gun, yeah?'

'No,' said Justin. 'You get a gun, you're more likely to get shot. Just keep your head down and do what we said.'

Walshe laughed. 'Told you he was scared.'

I put on a defiant look to mask the fact I was scared shitless. 'Welcome to the Jungle.'

Chapter Twenty-seven

Severnaya Zemlya, Siberia
Present day

There was zero light in the bunker, and not much more heat. It must have been over an hour since Golubev had slammed the door, an hour of thrusting my arm back and forth over the rough concrete. Dead with exertion, I carried on regardless. Several times I'd slipped, my concentration dipping, or my muscles simply giving out and cramping up. Each time, my knuckles and wrist bones had scraped along the same patch of concrete, which I now pictured scuffed with skin and streaked with the blood that I could feel running across the back of my hand.

Ubiquitous blue plastic rope: 6mm, tensile strength five-hundred-odd kilograms, or more than five of me. Impossible for me to snap; my bones would give way before it did. On the plus side, it's not great with abrasion.

The rope had been getting noticeably looser for some time. Now I was scraping bare skin with every pass because the rope had almost rubbed through. I hurried up, gritting my teeth, and with a grunt and a pull, it finally gave way.

I let my arm flop to the ground, panting. But not for too long, as my muscles started up again, this time involuntarily as the cold crept in to fill the space determination and concentration had occupied.

I rolled onto one side and scrabbled at the rope on my left hand. The knot around my wrist was tight but I found I could just about get some wriggle room on the side tied through the iron ring on the floor. A few painful minutes later it was loose, and I was sat up massaging my wrists before setting about my ankles, with two hands this time.

I tried to orientate myself in the darkness, lying back down and imagining what I'd last seen.

Easier said than done when you're barely conscious, but I was sure the door out was over to my right, with the door into my bedroom over to my left. I'd had a torch on my bedside table.

I crawled, one arm outstretched, feeling my way across the freezing floor. I reached a wall, cold plaster and condensation-damp paint flaking beneath my fingers. I crawled up close to it and followed along until my hand brushed a corner. Creeping my fingers around it, I felt a wooden door frame. But which one?

I reached up to open the door: more darkness. Feeling my way with my hands, I felt around for a light switch. Took me a while as it wasn't where you'd normally think it was, but eventually I ran a hand along the metal conduit that carried the wire, and followed it to the metal box and toggle switch.

Nothing happened, which was as expected; the generator or supply had been shut off.

Turning to face the opposite wall, I got back down and crawled. Wasn't long before I hit the opposite wall. I turned left and followed it, which I reckoned would take me to the bed.

The wall went on for too long, so I decided to cross to the other wall. The empty space went on too long as well; I was disoriented in the tunnels and had got turned round somehow. I stopped, taking a breather. The air was fetid, either from the lack of air con or the fact someone had been cooked in here.

A scraping noise came from somewhere in the darkness. I froze, literally, listening intently. It came again. Something was moving somewhere in the bunker. I wasn't alone down here.

I had no idea how to find my room now but I wasn't going to do it by staying put.

I went straight forward, away from the sound, crawling for a while before I found what felt like a door frame. I went into the room and turned, following the wall, figuring I'd find some furniture sooner or later that might be useful.

It stank in here. I gipped as I moved forward. My hand touched something wet.

I recoiled, staying put. I'd somehow gone straight through my room, through the doorway, and followed the corridor into Balakin's room.

The noise came again from the darkness, a scuffling, scraping sound. Someone was moving through the tunnels. It was impossible to tell where it was, quiet and muffled through the walls but then amplified by the darkness and my tuned-in ears.

I moved forward, hands sliding on wet floor through what I can only describe as matter. The smell was awful. My fingers brushed something soft, then cold and metallic. It was a familiar shape. I grabbed it and hefted it. Volkov's Glock, plucked from near the remains of Professor Balakin's half-cremated arm.

Now I could orientate myself. I dropped the magazine out, ran a thumb over the round at the top, and slid it home. Racking the slide then holding the pistol out in front, I made my way back along the wall. Turning right at the door, I made my way down the corridor, still crawling. As I reached the doorway into my room, I stopped to listen.

The sounds had disappeared.

Had they gone? Or were they waiting?

I held my breath. Both the black and the silence were infinite.

I carefully stood, sidestepping until my leg touched the bed frame. I crouched and felt underneath, rejoicing as it brushed the bag of clothes Golubev's men had dug up for me. Whatever was down here with me, I felt a lot better about facing it with clothes on.

A minute later I had what I presumed by touch was the security team's black commando outfit: combats and a sweater with some clean socks. Even my watch was still sat where I'd left it, next to the torch on the bedside table. I didn't turn the light on for fear of dazzling myself and also shining a beacon for whoever – or whatever – was down here.

Clothed and with a gun in my hand, suddenly the dark bunker was less forbidding. I sidestepped and touched something else. There was a scrape, something moved against the wall. *The propped-up mirror!* I dropped to my knees and reached out, catching an arm under it just before it smashed across the floor. It rocked on my arm, tapping the floor gently. Hopefully, seven years bad luck averted. I picked it up and heaved it onto the bed, lying it down where it could do no damage.

With the torch still off, but held ready in my left hand, I moved towards the far corner, and the door into the main area of the bunker.

I moved slowly, fingers alert, and felt the door frame. I ran them across and felt the void. The door had been open earlier as I'd managed to crawl straight through. I slowly crept along the tunnel, making it to the next door without making a sound.

The scuffling sound came again in the dark. I stopped halfway through the doorway, inadvertently tapping the torch against the wood.

The noises stopped. It'd heard me.

I held my breath.

The faintest brush of fabric rustled against the wall. I reckoned it was on the other side of this room.

I held out the pistol, feeling like Pat Garrett aiming at Billy the Kid in that dark bedroom, waiting for another sound to give them away. When the sound came again, it was to my right, a scuff on the floor. Someone was creeping round the perimeter of the room, towards me.

I backtracked, hugging the wall, moving clockwise as I pictured someone opposite doing the same.

A loud scrape bounced around the walls as furniture moved. There was a grunt close by, a rush of air as something moved quickly. I spun, dropping down, trying to home in on the sounds but they were moving too fast, whirling first this way then the other, like a trapped rat. A door slammed against the wall.

A tiny orange spark erupted in the black, growing into a flame that dazzled my light-starved eyes. I turned the gun on the flame, looking for something to aim at, when it disappeared just as abruptly.

I quickly rolled to my left, blinking rapidly, trying to clear the glowing spots from my vision. Someone was banging around; I was disorientated, and not sure which room they'd gone into.

On the basis they had tried to scarper, I decided to go for it, jumping up and walking quickly into the black until I felt the touch of the wall. The door was alongside it, so I put my ear against it and listened. The faintest orange glow showed below the door from inside the room, as if there was a small fire starting on the other side. *The White Demon, the Fireman.*

I felt for the handle to open inwards. With one movement, I pushed it, crouched, swinging round the frame into the room and bringing my gun to bear on the flame. I clicked on the torch, brighter than the sun in the enclosed space, holding it alongside the pistol.

Details swum into focus rapidly, as my brain made sense of the scene even as my finger squeezed the trigger. Shelving, boxes, big old computers and files and papers. A figure crouched behind a desk, readying to pounce, knife in hand. I flicked my hand to the side as the Glock kicked.

The explosion was deafening in the enclosed space, setting my ears ringing. The figure was shouting, obscenities no doubt, due to her own ears ringing and the plaster fragments spraying from the bullet impact centimetres from her face.

Abi dropped her lighter and knife, throwing her hands up and dropping to the floor.

I rushed forward to catch her. 'Are you okay?'

'Fuck me sideways, is that how you greet a friend?'

Chapter Twenty-eight

Severnaya Zemlya, Siberia
Present day

'Why the hell are you creeping around down here?' I asked Abi.

'Because, Tyler, there's a bunch of really pissed off Russkies on a short fuse up there.'

'Fair enough. Wait, you called me Tyler.'

'Why do you think I'm down here?' She picked up her knife and dusted herself down. 'I overheard them talking about you. Your mate killed Balakin and you're taking the rap.'

'So what's it to you? You work for Golubev.'

'How long do you think it'll be before someone puts two and two together, eh?'

'On what?'

'Look, Alice killed Professor Balakin, and probably the others, for all I know. But she didn't kill Volkov, did she? She was in the party in full view of everyone.'

'We don't know who killed—'

'Shut up, you silly bastard. I know you killed him.'

People often say they were taken aback, but I fair jumped, shocked into silence.

'I waited outside,' she continued. 'I saw you come out.'

'So why didn't you say...'

'He was a sadistic son of a bitch. Kill you as soon as look at you, he got what he deserved as far as I'm concerned. I saved your arse, so you can get me out of here.'

'Listen up, and listen very carefully. I can rebuild a car, pretty much fly a plane, maybe not land it, but I can sail, dive, ski, snowboard, skateboard and play drums. I know how to lie, cheat and steal. I can pick most doors and forge most documents. Most of all, I know how to kill.

'What I have *never* been any good at is keeping people alive. I've tried, God knows, but unfortunately for you, today's probably not the day I'll start. Thank you very much for coming to help me, I would love to repay you someday, but right now I'm on my own.'

'And where would you be without me?'

I held up my hands. 'I'm grateful for the help but I was on my way out anyway.'

'You'd have been dead long ago,' she said, walking to the door. 'Golubev sent men to search your room. Fortunately for you, I'd already moved Volkov's body. Fucker wasn't light, I'll tell you that. Wasn't easy hauling him down the back stairs and round the hotel without being seen, but I couldn't let you get caught, don't you see? You're one of the good guys, so I don't give a fuck if you see yourself as some kind of brooding lone wolf action man, you're gonna repay me by getting me the fuck outta here.'

'Hang on, that's a shitload to unpack.'

'Well, unpack it fast because we've gotta get a move on.'

'You moved the body from my room?'

'Unpack faster.' She elbowed past me through the door. 'You coming or what? This is a rescue.' She beckoned me to follow up the stairs.

'I need my gear.'

'No time, come on.'

I followed her through the tunnels, snatching my HK pistol from where it still sat on the chair in the centre of the room. We ran up the stairs by the bouncing light of my torch. As we neared the top, she put a finger to her lips and motioned for me to switch it off.

A soft glow fell through the hole in the steel door. Abi pushed herself through it then waved back to me. I followed, immediately recoiling as I had to step over two bodies. One lay on his back, a pool of blood from his neck still glistening in the light of his dropped torch. The other had slumped against the wall next to him, beneath an artful arterial spray.

'You're not just an engineer, are you?' I asked, staring down at the bodies.

Abi waved me to be quiet, standing still like an animal sniffing the air. 'No one is *just* anything.'

The wind howled through the broken walls, cutting me to the bone. I shivered and looked for any movement, but there was none. At the end of the corridor was the corner that would take us along to that huge bulkhead door into the hotel, but Abi turned the other way, deeper into the ruins. She beckoned me to follow. 'We only have a short window.'

I padded after her, socked feet slapping against the tiles, then wincing as I crunched over sharp debris. Through a crack in a wall, I saw what I thought was the ballroom where Volkov's body had been found. Moonlight spilled through window frames but didn't make it far into the rooms. I paused as something flashed across a window, briefly flickering in the blue light.

I brought up my pistol, squinting into the darkness.

'Who else is out here?'

'No one,' said Abi, sliding alongside me. 'Not here, anyway. Just the guards patrolling inside the hotel.'

I crouched, eyes on stalks for any movement. 'Someone's in there.' I tried to stay still but I was shivering uncontrollably now.

She crouched and looked at the room for several long seconds. 'Come on,' she whispered. 'We don't have time.'

We turned a corner into the dark, she immediately pulled open a door into a room and dragged me inside. I looked back as the door closed. Something flashed in the rubble at the end of the corridor.

'We've got a tail,' I said.

'If someone was on our tail they'd have done something about it. Believe me, these guys aren't subtle.'

Her torch flicked on. We were in an office or storeroom. It was hard to say with any conviction as half the ceiling had come down against the far wall, leaving a yawning chasm above. The wind howled, finding its way down even here.

'If you had a torch, why didn't you use it in the bunker?' I asked.

'Lighter's better for the old night vision.'

'Where are we going?'

'Follow me.'

I eyed the door warily and pushed the Glock into my waistband as she ran to the collapsed masonry and started climbing hand-over-foot. Soon she was balancing on a beam like a monkey while I was still only halfway up. She shone the torch back down, pointing out the bits of jutting concrete and ice-encrusted wood to climb. From there it was a ladder up through a couple of floors, difficult to estimate in the darkness. The rungs of the ladder were frosted over, and several times I slipped. I looked back down, but there was nothing below my feet except certain death, impaled on whatever piece of smashed hotel was waiting.

A noise drifted up from below. The briefest flash of moonlight across the floor as the door below was opened then shut.

Above me Abi was calling down, barely audible above the screeching wind ripping through the window frames.

'Come on, man, hurry up.'

'I've been tied up in a bunker for ages, now I'm climbing a building in a T-shirt and it's, like, minus twenty.'

'That's why we need to move fast. You don't get up here now you'll freeze and fall off.'

I threw my hands over the top and pulled myself over the edge into a bedroom. Abi had turned off her torch.

In the glow from the moonlight outside, I could see half the floor was missing, leaving a bed teetering perilously over the ground floor way below. Shards of glass were entombed in the thick ice across the floor, blown from the window decades ago. I looked out over the back of the hotel, and could make out the boathouse in the distance which marked the bunker escape ladder. A glow escaped its windows, presumably from guards stationed above it. I wondered if they'd heard the gunshot, but then again if the door was sealed you'd be hard pressed to hear an explosion.

A truck was stationed behind it, and the exhaust smoke pluming in the red glow of its rear lights suggested more troops were huddled inside keeping warm.

'What's this ladder attached to?' I asked.

'Nothing,' she shrugged.

I crouched at the edge and grabbed the top rung, pulling. The ladder was heavy, too heavy. As I held on, it trembled.

'Someone's following us up.'

'No way,' she whispered, face white in the moonlight. She crouched next to me and tested it, together we succeeded in lifting it a few centimetres. There was a noise in the darkness below as something scuffed on the floor.

'Fuck me,' she said.

I pulled my gun, aiming down into the void.

Abi swatted my hand away. 'They'll hear,' she whispered, pointing to the window and those guards.

I sat on the floor, bracing my feet against the top rung. Abi got the gist and sat next to me, and together we shoved the ladder away from the beam it was resting against.

'Hold it there,' I said when the ladder was vertical. Abi strained her legs as I spun round to grab it. With a hard shove, the ladder was gone.

A second later, an almighty crash erupted through the space as the ladder bounced and slid along the wall.

Abi spun round and lay on the floor. She clicked her torch on, pointing it straight down. The ladder was lying at an angle against a nearby wall, caught against a piece of pipework.

Abi inhaled sharply. At the edge of the dim pool of light below, a white parka flashed then was gone into the shadows.

Chapter Twenty-nine

Severnaya Zemlya, Siberia

Present day

'Move,' Abi said simply, and she didn't have to say it twice.

We sprinted along the frozen corridor, Glock held alongside my torch. With my finger tensed, the beam danced across ice-packed carpet, past sagging doors and piles of wallpaper that'd peeled and were lying discarded like rotting leaves in a gutter.

'There's a door up here. Once we're through, we're in the warm wing. Torches off, quiet as a mouse, yeah?'

I gave a grim nod. A few seconds later, we rounded a corner to a solid-looking door that was probably reinforced and definitely well insulated, but not on a par with the huge bulkhead on the ground floor. Abi paused and pulled out a key, wiggling it for several seconds before it clicked. She switched off her torch and waited for me to do the same before slowly opening the door.

This one creaked so loudly I thought it'd wake the whole hotel. She stopped part-way and squeezed through. I followed. First the light hit, just dim night lighting but bright as day after navigating the darkness of the ruins. Then the warmth hit like a wall. Compared to the temperatures of the bunker and destroyed wing, it was positively equatorial.

We'd emerged behind the staircase on what seemed to be one of the middle floors, if the views out of the dirty window were anything to go by. Abi leaned over and looked down the stairwell. Way below, the tiled floor of the lobby shone. Voices drifted up as a couple of men called to each other in Russian.

'What are they saying?' I asked, running to the corner of the corridor to check the floor was safe.

'Don't worry. They're talking footie.'

'One of the guards was following us back there in the ruins, what happens when he raises the alarm?'

'That was no guard.'

'How do you know?'

'Did you catch that jacket? No one round here wears that old stuff. Come on.'

She grabbed my hand and led me down the stairs, sticking to the walls, onto the floor below. She stopped at the end and paused to look around the corner.

She just had time to utter 'Fuck,' before launching, whipping the knife up from her pocket.

There was a scuffle, a gurgle. By the time I'd stepped around the corner, she was lowering a twitching man to the floor with her knife sticking from his neck.

'There are always two,' she whispered.

As if on cue a door opened a few metres ahead, a second guard stepped out into the corridor. I started running before he realised what was happening. He fumbled with his holster as I leapt.

My foot caught him in the chest, knocking him back into the room. I followed him in with a left fist to his cheek, swinging my Glock round into his rebounding head. The effect was instantaneous: he crumpled to the floor, out cold.

I looked around. We were in a time capsule bathroom. I dragged him into the nearest green Formica cubicle and dropped him against the wall.

Abi pushed in past me and lunged at the prone man. There was a sickening crack and pop of cartilage and bone.

'Jesus Christ.'

'Grow some balls, mate,' she said, flexing her knuckles.

She shoved me out of the way and went back into the corridor. I stared at the misshapen lump in the man's throat, his head tilted unnaturally backwards towards the ceiling.

A few seconds later, Abi reappeared in the doorway.

'Little help,' she said, holding open the door with one hand, the other balled around the first guard's jumper.

I grabbed him under the arms and hauled him in. We dragged him head first into the same cubicle, then Abi leaned in and pulled her knife from the man's neck with a sucking sound. A spurt of blood leaped across the minty green tiles and pulsed out across the emerald toilet. She angled his head down into the bowl, wiped the knife on the back of his jumper, and shoved it back in her pocket.

The water turned a murky red.

'Snap out of it, man,' Abi said, at the door keeping watch. 'Next you'll be telling me you never killed anyone before.'

'Too many. He should have been out cold for long enough.'

'My skin's worth more than "should have". Come on.'

She burst from the door and sprinted along the corridor. I followed, noting the door numbers. They all started with three, so this was the floor below the one I'd started on yesterday.

'Wait.' I grabbed her arm and pulled her back. 'You said Burton was killed on the floor below me?'

'What?'

'Burton was killed in a room on this floor?'

'This is not the time for playing detectives, it's the time for running the fuck away.'

'Tell me the number.' I let go of her arm and backtracked. 'Or I'll try them all.'

She closed her eyes. 'Fuck's sake.' She ran back to me and pulled me along. '305.'

The smell hit way before we reached the door. It increased several-fold when Abi opened it. With another glance up and down the corridor, I followed her in.

The stench was unbelievable, like burnt bacon fat with hints of rotting meat. 'Jeez, they just left him in here?'

'Not the body, that's wrapped up in the garage downstairs. But they couldn't take all of him outside, if you know what I mean.'

She clicked on her torch, illuminating a burnt patch in the middle of the duvet. Black smears radiated out; the bed was sopping wet. I walked closer; my socks squelched in the saturated carpet, presumably from however they'd doused the flames.

'You didn't wanna tell me any of this in the van on the way in?'

'I didn't know you.'

I crouched, turning my nose up. 'He burned to death here, on the bed?'

'So I was told.'

'And yet the bed is hardly touched. The duvet has burnt through but that's nothing. Where's the damage? The blind panic?'

Abi pointed the torch up at the ceiling. Fat and smears of soot had stuck to the woodchip around the light fixture. 'He must have burned up pretty good. Greggy says he was like a torch when they found him, still screaming. *Pozharnyy, Pozharnyy.*'

'And yet he just lay there and burned.' I leaned in close to the bed and looked up at the ceiling. 'Who found him?'

'Guy next door, Abid. Got himself moved up to the fancy suites at the top.'

I stood and wiped my hands on my trousers. 'Golubev said it could have been an accident.'

'They reckoned he'd been smoking in bed.' She walked over to a sideboard and tapped the torch against something that clinked. 'While downing vodka.'

'Burton wouldn't have been drinking. Not much.' I opened the bedside drawer and felt around inside, then knelt and unzipped his suitcase, tipping it out on the floor. 'Where are the cigs?'

'Huh?'

'You said he was smoking in bed.'

She shone the torch around the room slowly. 'Can't see any smokes.'

'Or a lighter. He was the first?'

'I told you, there's been heaps of things happened over the years.'

'I don't care about urban legends, I mean this weekend. Burton was the first death?'

She nodded, still casting the torch around the room. 'Two of the guards said they saw someone in the corridor just before. Wearing an old-style parka.'

'Uh huh.' I ran a finger through the black tar on the bedframe and rubbed it against my thumb. A thin layer of grease had been deposited over everything in the room, with charred flakes of black soot adhering to them. 'Hang on, shine the torch back up.'

She moved the beam to what had caught the light. Yet another of those ridiculous Brezhnev portraits that seemed to hang everywhere, the great leader staring on while the occupant of the room burned alive. I thought back to that same portrait above the sink in Balakin's room in the bunker, smirking in the flickering orange light. Something was nagging me about it.

There was a noise in the corridor outside. Abi flicked off the torch; we both froze in the dim moonlight.

A floorboard somewhere creaked.

'Guard doing the rounds,' Abi whispered. 'He brought a load more in yesterday night.' Her breath hung in the cool air, fogging in the silver beams creeping round the soot-stained curtain.

I nodded. 'I saw them.'

We waited, not moving, for several minutes. I peeled off my cold, wet socks and threw them into the bathroom, then grabbed a couple of Burton's fresh pairs from the pile on the floor, stuffing them into my pocket, since he no longer needed them. Finally I crept to the door and put an ear to it. No sound. I looked through the peephole: it was empty.

'I'll go first,' Abi said, pressing against me. As I slid behind the door, she opened it and poked a head out. 'Clear,' she said, jerking her head.

Closing the door, we moved quickly and silently along the corridor, past the stairwell.

'In here,' said Abi, pushing a door open and darting in.

She kept the lights off, the room was dark with the curtains shut. With one last look up and down the corridor, I followed her inside and locked the door.

'Was it worth it?' she said. 'Did that help you figure this mess out?'

'Maybe.'

'Maybe? Make your mind up.'

'There's something that pulled at me…'

She did a slow clap. 'Wow.'

'Do you actually have a plan?' I asked.

'Why do you think I sprung you?' she asked, crossing to the window and peering around the curtains. 'I was kinda hoping you had a plan.'

I looked at my watch. Two a.m. 'It's quiet.'

'Most of the guests left this arvo.' She went into the bathroom, placing her torch in a glass in the shower, then pulled the door to, so there was just enough light to make out the furniture. 'There's a couple kicking around until tomorrow but mostly it's the big man and the staff.'

'We need to keep moving before they realise I'm missing.'

'We've got until six at the earliest,' Abi said. 'They're under strict instructions not to go near there.'

'What happens at six?'

'That's when the guards change and they find two corpses. So you've got time for a wash, then we're gonna take a look at those wrists, they look pretty nasty.'

Chapter Thirty

Severnaya Zemlya, Siberia
Present day

'So how did she do it then?' Abi closed the bathroom door to block the light. I heard the lighter flick as she sparked up a cig.

I shook my head. 'I just don't think she killed Balakin.'

'You said you guys have history. What kind of history?'

'Well… let's just say she's no stranger to this kind of thing.'

'So there you go then. Did she distract you in any way? Do anything to get you to take your eyes off that door?'

I sat on the floor to pull on the fresh socks. 'Not… really. I don't think so, no.'

Wafts of smoke blew round the bathroom door. 'I don't get why you're set on springing her. You don't owe her shit. I say we split now, while we still can.'

'I'm not leaving her behind to end up in a Russian prison.'

'She won't get anywhere near a prison, mate.'

I leaned back against the wall and put my hands on my head. 'Which is why I'm not leaving her.'

'Oh my fuckin' God.' She swung the door open and stared at me, the tip of her cig glowing as she took a drag before jabbing it towards me. 'You fuckin' banged her, didn't you?'

I didn't answer.

'Classic.' She flicked ash in the sink. 'You're a fuckin' idiot.'

'This has nothing to do—'

'You don't know how she killed Balakin? Chick goes from being your mortal enemy to fucking you in less than an hour, and you don't think she distracted you. Gimme a break.'

'Stress can—'

'Stress.' She rolled her eyes so hard I thought they'd get stuck backwards. 'Yeah, sure, and you're irresistible, too. Stress, my arse. Classic seduction and distraction.'

'I don't think that's what it is.' But out loud I didn't sound convincing.

'Righto, how about this, and hear me out. Three people locked in a concrete box: one is you and another ends up dead. Reinforced sides, floor and ceiling. That you checked every inch of, no way anyone coulda got in. The *only other* person locked in there, this chick, she'd just got orders to kill the dude. She hates you, but screws you anyway, you take your eye off the ball for a minute...'

'It was longer than a minute.'

'...For two minutes, and the dude dies soon after. Then you find her *apparently* knocked on the head and *apparently* fuzzy on what happened. Now you tell me – and be honest – you tell me what the most likely conclusion from all that is.'

'Okay, when you say it like that it does sound iffy.'

'Iffy? Jeez, did you hear they've taken gullible out of the dictionary?'

'All right. Doesn't change anything.' I closed my eyes and inhaled deeply. 'I was sent here to keep her safe. And to do that I either need to find Balakin's killer, or prove it was her.'

'I'd say *fine, your funeral*, but it'd be mine too.' She dropped her cig in the toilet and stood. 'So she stays here.'

I tried to stare her out but it was impossible. She'd saved my life and was about to do so again, even if it wasn't for entirely altruistic reasons. 'Have it your way.'

'I will. Now we need to put our energy into getting ourselves out of here.' She clicked off the torch and pocketed it, then grabbed a bag from the bed. 'Remember, give me fifteen to sort the gear then come meet me.'

I opened the door and looked out. All was quiet. 'Don't forget the biscuits.'

'Just be on time, okay?'

I watched her creep to the stairs, gave it a few seconds, then left the room, closing the door softly behind me. I padded in the other

188

direction, back along the corridor, past the silent doors to the end, and looked at the door into the emergency and/or staff stairwell, whatever the sign said. Abi had told me Alice had been taken to suite 620. Top floor. I pulled my HK from my pocket and wondered when I'd catch a break.

It gave as easily as the others. Pushing the broken door shut behind me as best I could, I went up the dark stairs two at a time, all the way, until I came to a fire door with a big crash bar which I assumed led onto the roof. I felt my way back down one level and tested the door. This one put up a little more fight and I couldn't put all my energy into breaking it for fear of waking everyone, but after thirty seconds or so I was standing in the open doorway, head round, looking along the dim corridor.

The top floor had been done out nicely to match the lobby, dark wood and grey carpet. Contemporary prints adorned the walls and the light fixtures were fancy brass wire affairs that wouldn't look out of place in a boutique European hotel. It was clear Golubev enjoyed the idea of his private escape up here, taking the lift past the dilapidated lower floors in between.

No one was on guard outside the rooms. There was no time like the present.

As I padded through the plush carpet, I noticed the doors were spaced further apart up here, which obviously meant larger suites. 620 came up almost immediately.

All was quiet. An ear to the door revealed nothing – either the occupants were asleep or resting quietly. Abi had told me Golubev's own suite was at the other end near the lift. I hoped at least he was sound asleep. A headless snake, if even for a short time, is much easier to deal with than a wide awake viper.

I backed up to the door on the opposite side of the corridor, gun held low, and knocked softly, hoping there'd be no reply.

My luck ran out as I raised my hand to tap again, and a soft light splashed from under the door.

A brief muttering preceded the door swinging open, then I was face-to-face with the redneck American I'd rescued Alice from the previous night. The interaction was brief and to the point as I swung my forehead directly into the bridge of his nose. He stumbled backward. I followed him into the room with a fist below his ribs before finally, as he doubled over hacking, a knee into his already smashed nose.

He crumpled to the floor. I swung the door closed behind me softly and pointed my gun at his head.

'You're not having much luck with your rooms, are you, mate?'

He curled up in a ball, whimpering, his hands at his face.

'Listen up, if you make a noise, I've got no reason to be quiet any more. You understand what that means?'

He whimpered again.

'For clarity, it means I'll shoot you in the face.'

The bed moved. I looked at the chair, the clothes on the floor, the holster, and put two and two together. I grabbed a corner of the duvet and pulled. One of Golubev's naked security guards quickly scuttled away to the edge of the bed. I waved the gun at him, and he put his hands up.

'You speak English?'

He nodded.

'Don't try anything and you'll live, you understand?'

He nodded again.

'We were just talking!' said Redneck as he finally found his voice.

'Didn't I tell you to be quiet?'

He pulled his head back down and began crying again.

'Open your mouth again and you'll know about it.'

He whimpered, a pool of piss spread dark on the carpet beneath him.

I moved forward, the guard on the bed flinched. Without taking my eyes off him, I unsnapped his holster and pulled out his Glock. I pushed it into my pocket then backed up to the door.

'Into the bathroom,' I said. 'Both of you.'

The guard moved warily, backing up to the wall as he skirted round me and into the small ensuite.

'Come on.'

The sobbing redneck crawled in to join him, leaving a trail of dark blood on the cream carpet.

'Any noise from either of you and I'll defenestrate your arses, get it?' Redneck tried to get up, so I rammed him back to the floor with my foot. 'That means I'll throw you both out the window, you inbred shit.'

I closed the bathroom door and flicked off the lights, then went to the main door.

I opened it slowly. The corridor was still in silence.

Holding the door open with one foot, I stepped into the corridor and leaned across, knocking on the door of suite 620.

I quickly backed into the room, closed the door quietly, and put my eye to the peephole.

No lights shone under the door. I presumed whoever was in the room was looking through their own peephole. A good twenty seconds later, the door opened cautiously. One guard, pistol in hand, poked his head out and looked both ways. He stepped out, holding his gun up in front, checking first down the corridor towards the main stairs and then back the other way. He whispered over his shoulder, and a second guard appeared in the shadows of the room. Like the guys we'd encountered a couple of floors below, they both looked like the rent-a-toughs that'd got off the truck.

The guard looked directly at me, and I forced myself not to flinch, not to move from the door in case he saw some kind of flash of light or movement. After a few more seconds he retreated back into the room.

I waited. The seconds ticked by. I slid the magazine from the security guard's Glock and flicked out each 9mm round, pocketing them, then ran the slide back to remove the round from the chamber.

As I was doing this, the door to room 620 slowly opened and the guard reappeared, no doubt hoping to catch someone creeping back. He reminded me of our neighbour when I was ten, hoping to catch us out at knock-a-door-run. Unfortunately for this guy, I was raised on the mean streets of Halifax. I knew all the tricks.

I opened the bathroom door and beckoned to Redneck, who was now sitting back against the bath, glaring.

'Go fuck yourself,' he lisped thickly through his broken nose.

'You've perked up,' I said. I pointed the gun at him. 'Come on.'

He relented and climbed to his feet. I stepped backwards towards the door and he flinched, then regained some bravado and lurched at me. I sidestepped and brought my arm up against his head, just knocking him off balance. He staggered, throwing his hands against the wall to stop himself going arse over tit.

'I told you, I'll throw you through that window naked,' I said.

He growled. 'Golubev's gonna have your balls.'

'Maybe, but yours will be frozen solid.'

Keeping one eye on him, I picked up his thong from the floor and a lighter from the bedside table.

I crept out again, lit the pants with the lighter, then tossed them down the hall. I knocked on the door opposite and retreated. Redneck looked puzzled. I pushed him against the wall, pistol pressed into his back as I put my eye to the peephole.

The door was wrenched open, the angry-looking guard filling it. He looked straight at my door, at my peephole, then left and right. Turning to mutter something back inside at the second man, he flicked the catch off his holster.

In the room, the second man waited in the shadows.

In the wide fish-eye lens of the peephole I watched the first guy stare at the burning pants, confused.

I took my gun out of the guy's back and gave him the now empty Glock.

'Do us a favour, hold this for a second,' I said, pressing it into his hand.

As the guard in the hall walked over to the pants, I silently opened the door and shoved Redneck out into the corridor.

As I walked across the hall, the guard in the room's eyes went wide. He scrabbled at his holster as I shoved Redneck aside and squeezed the trigger once.

I sidestepped into the room as he dropped, backing up behind the door. There was a shout in the corridor outside, cut off by a gunshot and the thud of Redneck dropping to the plush carpet.

Boots pounded. I could picture the first guard checking Redneck's naked body, the gun in his hand, then looking into this room and seeing his dead partner. As I pictured his actions in real time, he ran into the room.

I stepped out behind him, raising my gun to hit him on the back of the neck. He heard me and turned, bringing his pistol round. I brought my gun down as I moved to the right, we fired at the same time.

He staggered back and crumpled, dead by the time he landed on his partner. I swung the gun round and winced, feeling a burning stiffness in my shoulder. I held a hand to it and ran forward, gun first.

Alice was sat up on the bed, hands over her ears and knees pulled up under her chin. Her hair was a mess, still pushed back in her bloodstained headband but sticking out at odd angles. Her makeup was smudged, mascara trails from her eyes. I reached out as she recognised me and jumped to her feet.

'John!'

I pulled her off the bed then paused and looked back. A pair of Converse All-Stars were parked underneath the bed. I grabbed them.

'Get your gear,' I said to Alice, pointing at a chaise longue, and the pile of cold-weather gear she'd been wearing when we'd been captured.

Shouts were coming from all over the building. I slipped the trainers on as Alice bundled up her clothes, then dragged her out of the room, over Redneck's trembling corpse. The shouts from the main stairs were getting closer. Alice twisted to look back at Redneck, still processing the last ten seconds. I tugged her arm, slamming through the door into the service stairwell.

We were into the stairs before anyone arrived. I leaned back against the door to catch my breath. Alice started to speak but I held a finger to my lips.

It'd take them a few minutes to unravel the mess. I was hoping they'd assume a shootout between Redneck and the guards. Maybe until they found that poor naked guard still huddled in the bathroom.

Alice put a hand to my shoulder, I flinched.

'You're bleeding,' she whispered.

I rubbed my shoulder and felt a nick. 'He missed.' I looked at my watch. 'We have less than ten minutes.'

'What happens in ten minutes?'

I pushed off the door and pulled Alice down the stairs, still clutching her bundle of gear. Down we went, counting off turns in my head, until I held my hands out in front and stepped forward, feeling for the door.

'Why aren't we going all the way down?' asked Alice. 'Don't we need to get to Ground?'

I pulled open the door to the third floor and swung round the doorframe, gun first. It was quiet so far, the guards were all heading upstairs. I reached back in and dragged Alice out.

'Where are we going?' she asked, looking at the doors rushing past as we sprinted along the corridor. 'How we getting out?'

'One question at a time.' I slowed to stop by the main staircase.

It looked clear as I peered around the corner, but as I beckoned to Alice, a head appeared on the stairs. I ran forward as the guard carried on climbing. He did a double-take, then raised his AK-74, cocking it but not getting the chance to pull the trigger as I dropped a shoulder and broadsided him into the handrail. There was a thud and a grunt as he smashed into it, then a scream as he toppled over. He finally pulled the trigger, a clatter of bullets tore the stairwell. I ducked back as concrete and splinters ricocheted around. A sickening crump ended the fusillade. Shouts echoed up from the lobby.

'Come on.' I grabbed Alice, dragging her round the corner and behind the stairs as more noises erupted above.

Boots hit carpet as all the guards in the place converged on us. She shook off my arm and overtook me as we sprinted to the door that marked the way into the old destroyed section of hotel.

I slowed and turned at the doorway, pistol up and ready. Shadows danced across the far wall as men made their way down the staircase. I backed into the corridor and closed the door softly behind us, locking it with the key Abi had left in it, then ran to catch Alice.

Chapter Thirty-one

The Peoples' Democratic Republic of Nambutu / French Equatorial Africa

1999

It was late at night when I heard the Chevy truck pull into the dirt parking lot behind the bar.

Justin had turned in a long time ago, but stealing a car from a bunch of drug dealers had left too much adrenaline coursing through my veins for me to close my eyes.

The plastic chair was cutting off my circulation in the thin swimming shorts. I swatted at a mozzie and put my book down, drained the last of the rancid beer in the bottle and stood it on the floor. There was a crash outside as Walshe collided with the bins. I walked to the papered-over window, cracking a fresh warm beer from the crate, and looked through the tiny patch of glass where the paper had peeled away.

Walshe was staggering in the moonlight, one hand running along the wall to keep him upright. I opened the door and stuck my head out, inviting a whole new swarm of biting insects.

'It's Kurt Cobaaaaain,' he said, grabbing my face with both hands then slapping it hard. 'Come here.'

'Fuck!' I said, rubbing my cheeks and stepping back inside.

'You should... you should have come to... what?'

'What the hell are you doing?' I said.

'What did you call me?'

'You're bleeding.' I pointed at his shirt.

He grinned and wagged a finger. 'Not mine!'

'We have to be fresh tomorrow!'

'Stuck up bitch,' he muttered, pushing me out of the way and walking into the room.

'What the hell did you do?'

'What you reading?' He picked up my book and turned it over.

I snatched it back, then he grabbed my arm and twisted it up my back. I dropped the book but refused to make a sound. I could feel the ligaments stretching, I gasped then held my mouth shut tight.

He spun me round and shoved me across the room then picked my book up off the floor. 'Who's Joseph Conrad, you bent bastard?'

'Go to bed.'

'What did you say?' he asked.

I shook my head. 'Nothing.'

He tossed the book over his shoulder behind the bar. 'You're just like your brother.'

I ran at him, but he sidestepped and swung a fist into the side of my head so hard it spun me round and smashed me face first into the bar. I screwed my eyes shut, felt warmth radiating from my cheek.

I dropped to the floor, got back up, and turned to face him. He grinned, beckoning.

'Come on then,' he said. 'Come on, let's have ya.'

I put my fists up and stepped closer, but he swept my feet from under me. I crashed to the floor, then felt his hands on my shorts. He grabbed, pulling them, ripping one leg as he hoisted me into the air then slammed me into the bar again.

There was a smash, a crash, then everything was quiet.

I curled my fingers around an empty beer bottle then rolled over, leapt to my feet, smashing it against the bar in one movement and whipping it round.

Justin grabbed my arm.

'I'll fucking kill you,' I screamed.

Walshe couldn't hear; he was out cold in the middle of the stack of upturned beer crates.

'Get in there,' Justin said, pointing to my room.

'I'll kill him,' I said, still holding the broken bottle, panting.

'He'll tear you apart,' Justin said. 'Go sleep it off.'

'Sleep it off… I'm not the one that's pissed!'

'You're as bad as each other, get to bed.'

I took a step forward, but Justin grabbed my arm, took the bottle, and swept my feet away. I landed painfully on my arse.

'Get cleaned up and get to bed,' Justin growled.

Chapter Thirty-two

Severnaya Zemlya, Siberia

Present day

The wind howled through the shattered windows of the ruined bedroom. Almost total darkness enveloped us except for a silver moonbeam illuminating a stripe across the ice-entombed carpet and up the crumbling plasterwork of the far wall. In between the two was a yawning chasm of black which enhanced the feeling of cold. A fresh gust shrieked.

'Stay here,' I said to Alice.

She nodded, still zipping up her parka in the shadows by the wall.

It wouldn't be long before our pursuers decided to break through that door. And that was assuming they weren't already swarming the ruins below us, though a lack of lights and noise suggested so far they were concentrating their efforts on the indoor spaces.

Now I looked at the black chasm, the wall opposite, and inhaled deeply. I tucked the pistol tightly into my pocket and gave Alice a grim smile. To my surprise, she threw her arms around me.

'Thank you,' she whispered in my ear, her warm breath tickling my hair. It took everything I had to tear myself away from that slim warmth in the moonlight by the freezing window.

I pulled away, pushed off the window ledge, and ran full tilt. The chasm came up fast, my trainers skidded and I leapt into the darkness.

It seemed like forever before I could feel I wasn't moving forward any more, only dropping. Then time sped up as my arms hit, I grabbed, slipped, grabbed again and locked on. The ladder shuddered as it took my weight but it held, leaning where I'd left it against the far wall. I gave myself a second, took a better grip, then kicked away from the wall.

The ladder leaned drunkenly, hung in the air for a moment, then teetered the other way. As it dropped, I wrapped my arms through the rungs. There was a clang, a reverberation throughout my entire body as the top of the ladder caught against the edge of the bedroom floor. It slipped with a grating tearing noise, as the feet slid across the ground below before being wedged against the debris.

'Okay,' I said, working my way around to the other side of the ladder. 'Seems solid.'

'Seems?'

'Get down here.'

Alice appeared above as I started climbing down. The cold metal bit into my fingers and slipped against my trainers as I scuttled into the enveloping black hole. I looked up at Alice, slipping and sliding as she looked over her shoulder at me.

'Hurry up,' she said. 'How far is it?'

'A few storeys.'

'In metric.'

'Just don't look down.'

'Don't project; you're the one who's scared of heights.'

'I'm scared of falling. Isn't everyone?'

'I've bungee-jumped that big dam in Switzerland.'

I grunted. 'Fine, you get us out of here then.'

'I'm not entirely useless, you know. So I don't like the cold, we each have our fortes.' She put on a mocking tone. 'You can't be good at everything.'

The ladder was bouncing less, and in the dimmest of light that fell this far I thought I could see reflections off the ice. I slowed and eased down, feeling with my foot.

Once both feet were on solid ground, I whipped the pistol back out and looked round. The wind sliced through the cracks. I shivered. Alice slid down beside me, huddling up close.

'It's cold,' she said, both understated and unnecessary.

'You just realised we're in the Arctic?'

'But you have no outdoor clothes.'

'Sshhh.' I waved her back as a sound came from somewhere in the ruins.

I crept forward, one arm outstretched and pistol in my other hand ready, tapping the floor ahead with each step to avoid dislodging noisy rubble. I felt something behind me. Alice grabbed my jumper to steady herself.

'Get off,' I said.

'I can't see.'

'Neither of us can.'

My hand brushed something. I felt cold rough wall and a hard ice flow where melting snow had run down sometime past. I shuffled to the right, still groping the wall, when it changed. The wooden doorframe was hard as iron in the permanent deep-freeze.

I shook Alice off and crouched, running my hand down the frame and along the ground until it touched something soft. Feeling further, I grabbed a handle and slid a bag across the ground.

'What's that,' asked Alice.

'A lifeline.'

I unzipped it and found a torch at the top. Holding it inside the bag, I flicked it on, cupping the end to reduce the glare as I scanned the rest of the contents. I pulled out a pair of Arctic overtrousers, a parka and a hat, which I tossed across to Alice.

'You must have been planning this escape.'

'I had help.'

She pulled on the hat, and in the dim light of the torch I could see her standing with one hand on her hip. 'Don't tell me, that Aussie bitch?'

I unravelled my overtrousers. 'Beggars can't be choosers.'

'I mean it, I don't trust her.'

I took out several chemical warming packs from the bag. 'Neither do I, but we're shit out of options.' I tore open a couple of the packs to activate them, throwing them to her. 'Besides, once we're away there's two of us and only one of her.'

'And you trust me, right?'

200

I grunted. 'I don't trust anyone. Did you bring your boots?'

'I dropped them way back.'

I looked at her hi-top trainers. 'Better than nothing, I suppose. Put those packs in your shoes.'

'John, you do trust me?'

'And put your gloves on.' I ignored her glare, zipping up my parka. I was still cold but it kept off the worst of the wind. My left hand was thankful for the thick glove but I shoved the right glove in my pocket, keeping it off to grip my pistol. I kicked the bag aside and flicked the torch off.

'Wait for our eyes to adjust.'

'Hmmm.'

'You can't be pissed off at me. I don't even trust myself.'

'Maybe Abi and I should ditch *you.*'

'You'd probably do better. Come on.'

I gripped the handle and turned. The door creaked as it opened into the ruins beyond. Left would take us back past the bunker and on into the hotel. Abi had told me to turn right.

I tapped Alice and shuffled forward. The warm chemical packs in the suit were working their magic, but now the enemy was the wind screeching through the ruins, stinging our faces. I pulled my hood up and squinted through the dim moonlight. There was an opening up ahead. I bent and looked at the ground. The fine snow which had been driven inside was kicked up where someone had gone before.

I turned to wave to Alice, pointing at the light spilling through the windows. She nodded. I held a finger to my lips then gestured for her to stay put.

I crept forward over a section of collapsed wall which marked the doorway into a large room. I shuffled down onto the crumbling parquet floor and looked around. The room was brighter than the corridors thanks to its broken windows facing into the moonlight. Decaying sofas and chairs were scattered around, blackened by age and alternating damp and freezing. I skirted the shadows along the inside of the room, squeezing my eyes shut against the flakes whipped by the gale, then quickly moved to the other side, hitting the wall next to one of the smashed windows. Back in the corridor Alice huddled down behind the piles of rubble.

I held the hood strings tight and peered round the window.

In the distance, the security truck's headlights cut a path through the swirling snow. I pulled my head back in and beckoned to Alice.

She ran over and crouched next to me, her face pale. 'Now what?'

'There's a bunch of security straight forward, by the boathouse. We're going to climb out that window over there,' I said, pointing further along the room, 'and come out behind the parked trucks.'

'And then?'

'Then we hitch a ride.'

Chapter Thirty-three

Severnaya Zemlya, Siberia
Present day

I crouched and ran, sticking close to the wall along the room, stopping in the middle where the shadows deepened. Here, a huge shape blocked the moonlight which was spilling through the other windows. As Alice ran to join me, I peered around the frame to look out.

'Okay, go,' I said, kneeling down to give her a foot up.

She jumped straight up and over the frame. Her trainers disappeared, followed by a bump and a hissed curse. I jumped and hauled myself over, avoiding decades-worn glass embedded in the old aluminium frames.

A huge six-wheel drive Zil flatbed truck was pulled up close to the building. I looked along the wall, another three were parked behind it, one with a missile launcher in place of the canvas cover on the back, another painted up in orange and sporting oversize balloon tyres for paddling.

Alice had scurried out of the way. I swung over and dropped to the snow.

With another glance at Alice, I rolled under the truck and looked out the other side. A row of old UAZ vans in various states of repair were pulled up close to each other. I could see the lights from the truck over by the boathouse.

I crawled to the front wheel and looked both ways before rolling out from under the truck and climbing onto the step.

The truck was encased in a layer of ice but the door handle and edges had been melted. Easing the door open, I checked inside.

'You're late,' said Abi from where she was huddled in the footwell.

'I had to stop off to collect someone.'

'You're fucking joking, right?' Abi slid up into the driver's seat, fury on her face.

Alice popped up beside me, I climbed into the cab and pulled her after me as Abi lit a cig.

A fire alarm started blaring from inside the hotel. A second later an alarm started wailing outside too, like an old air raid siren.

'You couldn't slip out quietly, could you?' shouted Abi out of the side of her mouth. She blew smoke across the windscreen. 'Oh no, that would be too easy.' She flicked a bank of switches on the dash, the fuel pump whirred into life along with the heater vents.

'Will it start?' I asked.

Abi looked at me from under arched eyebrows. 'Mate, I'm the fucking *mechanic*.' She saw the scepticism on my face. 'I've had the engine heater going.'

'Head down,' I said to Alice. 'Once we start rolling, it's gonna get hairy pretty fast.'

Abi punched a button on the dash, impressively the big V8 engine roared into life first time. She slicked the gearstick home and lurched forward, crawling out from behind the other trucks and gathering pace.

Across the ice, torches were weaving as the security guards in the boathouse ran out, responding first to the alarms, then to the truck now barrelling along the rear of the hotel. Abi flicked up through the gears. The speedo only said 50 kph but it felt much faster with the huge wall rushing past on one side and ice mounds flashing by on the other.

'Hold on to something,' Abi said.

I braced my feet against the dash. Alice gripped my arm like a monkey. The truck ploughed into a drift, slowing as it dug in, sending us flying forward and spraying snow across the windscreen.

'Send it!' Abi shouted, keeping the accelerator planted as she dropped a gear.

The chassis shuddered, we tipped back, windscreen pointing at the stars briefly, before lurching forward again as the truck jumped the low outer wall at the edge of the hotel.

I caught a glimpse of more torches coming round as the security guards ran, snow and metal flew across the windscreen as we tore straight through a chain-link fence, then the truck settled and picked up speed across the open ice.

'How long before the rest of the trucks heat up?' I asked.

'They're gonna heat up real quick.'

She'd barely finished speaking when a bright orange flash reflected off the ice in front. A couple of seconds later, the crump of a huge explosion rolled past, blowing snow along with us. I leaned past Alice and looked in the wing mirror. A fireball was rolling up into the night sky.

'You're my new favourite person,' I said to Abi.

Alice groaned beside me.

'I couldn't get the cars in the heated garage, but they'll probably take a while to get on our arse.'

'Still got this fella to shake though.' I pointed out of her window at the headlights in the distance, the security truck racing to catch up.

'Zil, same model as this. We're heavy, and carrying all this shit in the back they'll eventually catch us, but it won't be anytime soon.'

'Turn west,' I said.

'But east it's only fifteen miles to the mainland.'

'That's where they'll expect us to go.'

'West just takes us further out to sea.'

I tapped the GPS box stuck to the dash. 'Stick on 77 North, west to 103.'

'I hope you know what you're doing.'

I settled back in my seat. Alice finally let go of my arm and looked out of the window.

'You okay?' I asked.

'Fine,' she snapped. 'So this is your big plan? Blow everything up and drive out to sea? Genius.'

'Hey, the blowing up bit was my plan, love,' Abi said.

'If you had a better one you should have said something,' I said.

'And where are we driving to, exactly?'

'Abi, pull over,' I said. 'I think she wants to walk.'

'Long walk back,' Abi shouted. 'We're already on the sea ice.'

'You can't take criticism, can you?' said Alice. 'Do you always have to be right?'

'Sorry to break it up guys,' said Abi. She wound the window down a touch and flicked her cig out. 'But they're catching quicker than I thought.'

A second pair of headlamps had joined the first, growing every second.

As if on cue the radio on the dash crackled, Golubev's voice cut through the static. 'Where do you think you're going? Surely you don't think you can get away?'

Abi flicked the radio off and glanced in the mirror. 'There's a few of them now. Golubev's Landy and a couple of Ladas from the garage. Fuck, I shoulda taken more time to disable them.'

'We didn't have more time. More guards, more risk. Where are the rifles?'

'In back.'

'Lot of use they are there.' I leaned forward and pulled Alice's arm. 'Shuffle over.'

She squeezed past as I climbed over to the door. With one hand on the seatbelt, I opened the passenger door and climbed down onto the step. The cold wind blasted into the cab. I huddled down and swung a foot up onto the fuel tank, grabbing the chunky treads of the spare tyre behind the cab.

'Keep it nailed,' I shouted.

'Well, I wasn't gonna stop!'

I pulled myself up onto the rear, half-crouching by the spare wheel. I tried to unhook one of the loops of rope holding down the canvas side, but it didn't move, it was hard as iron. The canvas itself was tough as a sheet of plywood. I pulled out my knife and stabbed it through, far more difficult than it should have been, and sawed at the frozen material until I'd cut a slot. The canvas bent as I pushed through onto the rear truck bed.

The wind followed me in, swirling around the freezing interior as the truck lurched and bobbed over the rough ice. I pulled out my torch and scanned the back. A long row of Jerry cans was strapped along one side. A couple of boxes and a green wooden crate had slid back across the wooden bed as we'd accelerated, and were jammed against the tailgate.

I dropped to my knees and scooted over to the crate. The stamp said it was the property of the Izhmash factory. I lifted the lid and pulled out packing material to reveal several shiny new AK-203 assault rifles.

I took one out, hefted it, and grabbed a box of ammunition from the bottom of the container. I clamped the torch in my teeth and slid out the rifle's magazine. It didn't take me long to load the rifle. I put it down and sliced open a section of the rear canvas flap. I pulled at it, almost snapping the frozen material before it finally bent. I could see the lead headlights were close now, maybe 100 metres behind, with more beyond them.

Sitting on the cold wooden bed of the truck, feet braced against the rear tailgate, rifle at my shoulder, it was easy to take a bead on the pursuing lights. I charged the rifle, flicked the fire selector to full auto and waited, squinting along the fixed sights at the lights. Finally I breathed out and squeezed the trigger. The stock thumped into my shoulder as a hailstorm of lead burst out of the back of the truck. Almost immediately, the lights swerved. I pulled the trigger again, straight into the lights behind. They swerved too, but weren't as fortunate. I followed them, punching holes through the canvas as I emptied the magazine. The headlights flicked one way, then the other, before spinning crazily, casting white beams into the air randomly like a laser show at a festival.

One down, several to go.

I reloaded and settled in again, following another set of headlights and squeezing again. A short burst forced them to slow and turn the other way, and now all the pursuing lights had backed off.

I put the rifle down and walked back to the front, leaning out of the flap I'd cut. In the rush of freezing air, the night sky was pitch dark, but the headlights were bouncing off an increasingly bumpy ice field. I settled back down, pulling my hood tighter. The lights behind looked to be keeping their distance now. They had no need to push us; they knew we couldn't escape.

I wiped the ice from my goggles and held my gloves over my face in an attempt to stave off the frostbite I could feel gnawing at me. The wind had eaten through the down of my coat and burrowed deeply into my thermal layer, but though my fingers felt solid, anything beneath my knees had long since stopped responding. I hunkered lower and looked out over the tailgate at the unending night and unyielding ice.

Chapter Thirty-four

Severnaya Zemlya, Siberia

Present day

I opened my eyes with a sudden intake of breath. Alice jumped beside me.

'Ssshhh,' she said, smoothing my hair down. 'You were dreaming again.'

'How long was I asleep?' I asked, blinking to clear the fog and rubbing my eyes.

'Only a few minutes.'

I glanced at the mirrors. 'Are they still following?'

Abi snorted. 'Yeah, they're still back there.'

I pulled out the cow biscuits from my pocket, spraying crumbs across the seat. 'Do you want one? They're a bit crushed.'

Alice turned to look out of the window. I stuck several in my mouth and settled back into the seat. The ice was still rushing at the windscreen, the side mirrors and any area not swept by the constant wipers and heat were engulfed in a coating of rime-ice. I looked at the coordinates on the GPS unit and unfolded a military map Alice had fished from the glovebox. We were less than five miles from the mainland.

I folded the map up. 'Okay, it's time.'

'For what?' asked Abi.

'I'm going on the back again. After five minutes turn left, head north for a few hundred metres, then turn south-east and put us back on track for those coordinates.'

'We diverting for a hitcher or something?' asked Alice.

'Just make sure she makes those turns, okay?'

'You're the boss.'

'We're heading for this island, aren't we?' asked Alice, jabbing a finger at the map. 'Krasnovraisr...'

'Yes, and we've got to shake these bastards first,' I said, reaching for the door handle.

'There's nothing there!' shouted Abi as I swung out.

The blast of freezing air was unwelcome after a while in the warm cab. I swung back onto the spare tyre again as Alice slammed the door behind me, face pressed against the window.

I climbed up and over the wheel, through the canvas, and into the back. Out of the wind I took off my gloves and unzipped my parka.

The ice was relatively smooth here, and at about forty miles per hour, walking around in the back was easy enough. I dragged the crate of rifles to the front and took out another couple, plus all the boxes of ammo, and set them down at one side.

The boxes of clothes and supplies were heavy but dragged forward easily enough. I opened one and took out a packet of those same cow biscuits, placing it next to the rifles, and pulled out a sleeping bag.

Abi had stacked ten huge Jerry cans of petrol down the side, enough to get us hundreds of miles, strapped against the bench with webbing ties. I freed them and dragged them to the rear. Next I crouched to unfasten the tailgate but the latches wouldn't give. A few blows with the butt of the rifle smashed the frozen-brittle hasps. With some help from my boot the tailgate dropped, a clear path down onto the ice rushing past. Abi would be starting the turn soon.

I dragged four petrol cans over and stood them on the side, so the caps stuck out over the rushing ice. I didn't waste any time undoing the lid of the first. Sickly sweet fumes hit my nose as petrol sloshed out behind us. While it chugged away, I unscrewed the second and let that one pour.

The truck moved as Abi began to turn.

I dragged a full can over, unscrewed the lid, and kicked it off the back. It skittered along behind us, coming to rest sloshing out over the ice before it was lost in the darkness.

The headlights way behind turned to match us, following our sprint to the island.

The first petrol can ran dry, then I kicked it off the back and opened the third before the second ran out. When it did, I kicked it off and opened a fourth. In between, I opened the remaining cans and dropped them off the back, leaving pools of spreading petrol.

Finally there was only one can left glugging over the tailgate.

The truck lurched as Abi turned us back on track to the coordinates, facing diagonally to my trail.

I held the sleeping bag under the last can then moved it away, dangling it over the back, and lit it gingerly.

It went up with a whoomph, lighting the drips on my jacket and the fumes in the air. I dropped it, kicking the last can overboard, rolling back along the bed of the truck. I patted my sleeve and looked over the small flames dancing at the back of the truck.

A line of petrol snaked along behind us, following the last of the drips. At the same time it raced backwards, tracing a line the way we'd come.

The first can went up with a boom that shot orange flames straight up into the night sky. Almost immediately another went up, then another, periodic explosions along the burning line as the cans ignited like bombs.

There was a lurch, then the truck slid as the reverberations rocked the ice, rippling under our wheels. After just a few seconds the line of fire stretched for nearly a quarter of a mile, the pursuing headlights hidden from view by the wall of flames. The last of the blasts marked the first can I'd kicked over.

A different explosion rolled across the ice, louder and temporarily cutting over the constant moan of the wind and roar of the engine. Smaller cracks echoed like rifle shots. Some of the flames disappeared, doused by sprays of seawater as chunks of ice calved and sheared in the breaking sea ice.

Abi slowed the truck, I heard Alice shouting. I stuck my head out the flap at the front, keeping it down behind the cab. Alice was leaning out of the window.

'What the fuck have you done?' she shouted.

The truck slid, squealing to a halt. Abi was cranking her window down. 'You've just burned up all the bloody petty!'

'We can get far enough,' I shouted. 'Drive!'

'Far enough?' Abi leaned right out to shout at me. 'It's a long bloody walk to Dikson!'

'Just head for those coordinates.'

Alice opened the door and leaned out. 'They'll drive around the fire,' she shouted.

'Would you fancy driving across all those cracks? It'll be a hell of a long way around.'

'And you stink of petrol,' said Alice. 'You'd best hope Abi doesn't want a fag or you'll go up like Balakin.'

A sound came on the wind, distant, rhythmical pulsing. Alice heard it at the same time, looking back at me in horror.

'What is it?' asked Abi, but by the time she'd finished the sentence she could identify it too. The unmistakable thump of rotor blades, growing louder by the second.

'How far out are we?' I shouted.

Abi swung back into the driver's seat. 'Four miles, give or take.'

'Nail it.'

Alice jumped back in, slamming the door as the truck lurched forward again, picking up speed over the ice.

I ran to the back of the truck, grabbing the loaded rifle, then ducked under the charred canvas above the flapping tailgate to scan the fiery sky behind us.

The thudding rotors were maybe a couple of miles out but it was difficult to gauge in the clouds. I thought I saw a pinprick of light.

I slid over to the weapons crate and removed all the magazines from the rifles, ten in total, and started loading them all, jamming them into my pockets. I'd got as far as seven when the rush of blades swept overhead. The truck swerved as Abi instinctively spun the wheel, the chopper pitched up and banked in front.

I ducked out of the flap and looked up to see the underside flash in the headlights for a moment as the chopper almost flipped over on itself metres above the ice, coming to rest facing into us. It roared forward as we rushed towards it. Russian pilots are crazy but playing chicken with seven tons of truck would not end well for them. Abi didn't flinch and the pilot, mad as he clearly was, pulled up at the last second, the rotor wash nearly tearing the canvas from the truck. I ran to the open tailgate and watched the pilot take the nose up, transitioning into a more conventional sweeping turn high behind us, like a rollercoaster.

I slammed the first mag into the rifle by the tailgate and pulled the charging handle, then slid back a metre or so.

The chopper's landing lights blazed on, blinding me. I sat down, legs braced against the planks along the side of the truck's bed, and took aim.

The chopper roared forward then slowed to match our speed. I waited until it was almost on us then squeezed the trigger. A burst missed, I squeezed the trigger again, one of those huge spotlights exploded and disappeared. I squinted into the light and squeezed the trigger a third time as the helicopter banked, peeling off to the left.

Watching it recede into the distance, I noted with satisfaction it left no patches of light on the ice. I'd shot out both spotlights. I may not have disabled them, but I could still claim first blood.

The thump of the rotors announced the chopper's return. I leaned out of the back and scanned but no lights dotted the sky. Then I saw it, off to the right: a black shape discernible only by an absence of clouds.

I loaded a second rifle, cocked it, and held it out of the passenger side, tapping the butt on the glass. Alice cranked the window down and took it, then stuck her head out.

'I can't use this!'

'You've got plenty of experience with guns. Point and pull the trigger if he comes up on your side.'

He was coming up fast now, straight into the side of us. A burst of gunfire opened up from Alice's window. In a few seconds she'd emptied the mag.

'Too soon,' I yelled, leaning forward with a spare magazine.

Alice muttered and grabbed the spare mag from me as the chopper swung round on its axis, jinking side-on to us. A burst of gunfire exploded from the chopper. I ducked, rolling across the truck bed. I waited a few seconds then crawled to the rear and slid my legs over the back, down onto the bouncing tailgate.

Leaning out, I could just about get a bead on the tail rotor. I took aim and fired a burst, again, and a third time, but the truck was bouncing too much and the pilot was wary, swaying side to side now.

I rolled up onto the bed as more flashes came from the dark sky. I scrambled to the side and pulled out my knife, stabbing a jagged hole through the stiff canvas and peeling it back until I could see the helicopter. Its side door was open, close enough to see figures moving inside.

I stuck the rifle through and fired into the interior. The chopper peeled off, climbing rapidly into the distance. Abi mashed the accelerator.

'Stop,' I banged on the roof.

Abi hit the brakes, pumping them as the truck skimmed across the ice. I ran to the back and jumped off the tail before the truck stopped, running for the driver's door and up onto the step as it slid sideways.

'Lights off!' I said, pulling open the door and fumbling for the switch.

Abi swatted my hand away and hit the switch, killing the lights. Finally we came to rest, the engine chugging away as we all took a breath. In the distance, the rotors roared as the helicopter turned somewhere a couple of miles away.

'Out!' I shouted. 'Leave the engine running!'

I jumped down and ran for the back, scanning the sky. A red light winked in the clouds.

'What do we do?' Alice shouted, nearly running into me at the back of the truck.

'If you see a polar bear, throw out whatever is in your pockets.'

'What?'

I reached in and grabbed a rifle. 'They're curious, they can't help stopping to look.' I passed the rifle and two magazines to Abi.

'I mean, what do you want us to do, where do we go?' said Alice, pulling her hood up tight.

I gave Alice two magazines and pulled my scarf down. 'Run that way,' I shouted, pointing west. A dark outline loomed above the sea ice. 'Get behind cover and wait for me.'

Abi finished pulling on her gloves and loaded her rifle. 'What are you gonna do?'

'Keep their attention.'

'Like hell,' shouted Alice, slamming in a fresh mag.

'We need to deal with that chopper or we'll never make it.'

'That truck's a magnet,' she shouted.

'That's what I'm counting on.'

Chapter Thirty-five

The Peoples' Democratic Republic of Nambutu / French Equatorial Africa

1999

Sat in a bush in a hot, steaming rainforest, with nothing else to do but flick an endless variety of insects away from me, I visualised the plan again in my mind. Above the animal noises, thunder rumbled in the distance. The huge butterflies dancing between the low-hanging leaves in front of me gave up and headed home. Fresh, more insistent bird calls started up.

I couldn't see any clouds, just deep blue sky through the slim gap in the dense green canopy above. I looked at my Casio; it was well after one p.m. Right on cue. I sat up, checked the road was clear, and shook out an old Barbour waxed motorcycle jacket that Justin had nicked for me. Swiped from the back of a car on the way here, since I'd told them my own anorak had been in my suitcase. That'd been a lie, I hadn't packed an anorak.

I flicked a huge beetle off my knee and pulled the jacket on, fishing out my cigs. I'd used up all my Embassy and was on a local brand, Supermatch King Size. I'd chosen them simply because the packet was red, and it hadn't turned out too bad as it happens. My pink plastic lighter was still going strong. I sucked in the smoke and blew it up into the fat raindrops that started to fall, splatting across the lenses of my new Ray-Bans.

A month or so ago, if you'd told me I'd be sitting on a carrier bag behind a bush in a rainforest in a country in the midst of civil war, I'd have thought you were nuts. Yet here I was, international adventurer, scourge of the Nambutu drugs trade, car thief turned getaway driver.

It all sounded more glamorous than the reality of me huddled in a bush in a well-worn waxed jacket in the rain.

An engine sounded in the distance. I stubbed the cig out in the puddle growing between my trainers and listened. Sounded big. A truck.

A few had gone past in the last couple of hours but the arms deal was scheduled for one-thirty. This had to be the Russians.

By the time the truck appeared, the rain had stopped. I'd lain down in the mud, shrinking deeper into the undergrowth as the huge wheels rumbled past. Another smaller engine followed it, splashing through the puddles and braking, taking the corner towards the old mines.

I waited a minute then sat up and turned round. Through the wisps of steam drifting up, I could see the track, conspicuous by a gap in the trees snaking down towards the smoothly rounded Cherub Rock itself. A boulder outcrop jutting into the steep valley from the foothills, in its shadow was a dirt clearing, in the centre of which sat a silver Nissan 4x4. I shuffled, getting comfortable, removing my sunglasses. Lifting a pair of binoculars to my eyes, I winced as the eyepieces touched too close to my bruised cheek.

In the magnified image I could just about read the plate on the front of the Nissan. The driver got out, slamming his door soundlessly. He wore combat fatigues and a belt slung across his hip carrying a huge pistol.

I could almost hear the truck as it rumbled out into the clearing. A couple of other men climbed out of the Nissan, similarly dressed, one wearing a bright red beret, smiling as the truck pulled in a wide circle and squealed to a halt. I panned across, it shuddered as the engine cut out. A blue Toyota 4x4 pulled in next to it carrying what looked like two other men. The Russians, and I couldn't help wondering which one was the psycho.

The truck driver climbed down. He was dressed in civvies, dark hair, pale, clammy-looking face like an albino worm. He walked over and shook hands with the lead guy from the Nissan. The introductions were brief as all four men disappeared round the back of the truck. I put the binoculars down and rubbed my eyes. Down in the clearing the distant blobs talked business. I yawned and looked around the bushes, watching the steam rising from the leaves, listening to a hundred different animals competing for loudest call.

I picked up the binoculars and checked how things were going. One of the Russians, the clammy-looking driver from the truck, walked to the centre of the clearing. He scanned the treeline, watching carefully. After a few moments he seemed satisfied and walked to the Nissan, opened the rear and took out a few duffel bags. He carried each over to the Toyota. Two trips, four bags. As he put the last down in the dirt his face creased and he spun round.

I dropped the binoculars as I remembered the plan. I picked up a stick on the ground and gave it a pull. Nothing happened. I looked at the stick – I'd tied green string around it, which ran all the way down through the trees to where Walshe was waiting. I pulled again, but it was slack. I began to reel the string in, hand over hand, and pretty soon reached the end. It was frayed where it'd caught and snapped.

It was at that point the world tore apart.

An explosion rocked the trees, I looked at the clearing to see flames and smoke rolling up into the sky. Automatic gunfire opened up, I scrabbled for the binoculars and swung back onto the truck. The Russians were running, one dropping to the ground, writhing. I panned to the trees and saw two new dudes running out of them, towards the truck. Each fell on the ground in turn. I panned again onto the Nissan, which was burning furiously.

Something flashed past. It was the blue Toyota, reversing up the road. More gunfire, then it swerved into the trees and turned over on its side, wheels still spinning. Sparks jumped as bullets smacked into it, a tyre blew out. I panned across: the lead guy I'd seen getting out of the Nissan was stood on his own in the middle of the clearing, big pistol in his hand. A ball bounced up next to his leg; an instant later there was a flash. I took the binoculars away from my eyes and blinked. That had not been a ball. When I put them back all I could see was a crater in the dirt surrounded by what I can only describe as bits.

The gunfire stopped as quickly as it'd started. Everything was silent, not even the monkeys or birds made a sound, even the insects held their breath.

I watched in the binoculars as a woman limped into the clearing. Blood dripped down her leg from a rip in her combat trousers, but she hobbled with purpose, face set impassively as she pulled out the magazine from the AK-47 in her hands and slammed a fresh one home.

What the hell had just happened? Someone had got the jump on us. The ambush we'd planned had been swerved by someone directly ambushing the exchange.

No one else joined the woman, and I realised she must be the sole survivor of the brief carnage. She looked around, as if wondering what the hell to do next, when suddenly she froze. I focused on her face: her lips were moving, she was talking to someone I couldn't see. I zoomed out a little and panned around but all I could see were bodies and smoking debris.

A single gunshot rang out. The woman dropped her rifle and put her hands on her head. I scanned and saw at the edge of the treeline a face above the bushes, a rifle poking out. I squinted but it was impossible to see any more.

The woman walked into the undergrowth back the way she'd come, the face in the trees melted away, leaving the fires burning alone.

I waited, realised I was rocking, and forced myself to sit still. Where was Justin? Shit, I'd even take Walshe. I tried to steady my breathing.

I looked at my watch. It'd been a full five minutes since the shooting had stopped, and nothing had moved. I stood, massaged my legs and looked around. The birds had started singing again, the insects were creaking. As far as anyone knew, everything was back to normal.

Except it wasn't.

I made a decision and ran for the road through the orange mud and into the bushes at the other side. In thirty seconds, I was pulling branches off the Mitsubishi. I jumped up, shoved the keys in and twisted them. The V6 growled, I slid her into gear and pulled off the trail, onto the road, then over the other side and down the track to the mines. I picked up speed, jumping through the ruts and flying over boulders, sliding in the mud. I flicked the wipers on, skidding sideways around a corner, and then changed up as I accelerated past the upended Toyota and out into the clearing. Flames still licked from the Nissan, the acrid aroma of burning rubber and plastic hung in the air with the tiny black sooty flakes.

I swerved to avoid the crater and the worst of the gore and skidded to a halt, scanning the ground. Where were the duffel bags?

With one arm over the passenger seat, I reversed away again quickly, up the trail, until I was parallel to the underside of the Toyota 4x4, lying on its side in a ditch. I climbed out and ran round it, turning my head to look through the shattered windscreen. Blood spattered the glass and empty seats, no trace of the two occupants.

I went round the back, splashing into a stream, and looked through the boot. The duffel bags were heaped in a pile on the rear side window, which – given the Toyota was lying on its side – was now crushed against the muddy ground. The boot lid was well and truly embedded in the mud, with the stream swelling against it, so no way in there.

I climbed up the bank of the ditch and round to the underside of the car, grabbing the chassis like a ladder and climbing onto the uppermost side. I pulled myself over the top, onto the rear door, and looked down through the glass. The duffel bags were heaped below me. I stood on the front door and tried the rear handle but the body was twisted and the door wouldn't open. I looked back down to the clearing, but nothing moved. Up the road, nothing.

I slammed the heel of my trainers down into the window and almost slipped off the car as the glass gave way, dissolving into a million diamonds that dropped twinkling inside. I kicked away the pieces clinging to the frame then sat, dangling my feet inside. Standing on the side of the rear seats, I climbed down into the car, reaching over the headrest for the bags. I grabbed the first. It was heavy. I unzipped it and found dollar bills, wrapped around with little paper bands just like in films. Some were twenties, some fifties, I'd no idea how much there was. I zipped it back up and held it above me, pushing it through the window and outside. It fell to the ground with a wet thud.

The car rocked, glass crunched under my trainers. I grabbed the next bag, hoisting it up. In seconds I was sweating, and heaving the last bag up through the window, before climbing up the seats and pulling myself through the opening.

Twisted metal snagged at my shirt. I kicked and pulled myself free, jumping straight off the other side and scrambling to my feet. I threw open the boot door of the Mitsubishi and heaved each bag in, slamming it and jumping into the driver's seat.

I turned the car around quickly, facing back up towards the road. All my troubles were behind me, literally. Now I just had to find my brother and get the fuck out of this country.

I put the car in gear and looked in the mirror. Nothing moved in the clearing. Steaming puddles fringed with dense overhanging trees, chirping birds and insects. Parts of the Nissan were still burning.

The lone surviving rebel, the woman I'd seen limping into the clearing following the gunfight, had been taken. I was sure it'd been *him* in the bushes. Could I really leave her to whatever fate I'd escaped? I rested my head on the steering wheel and sighed, putting the car into reverse.

Chapter Thirty-six

Severnaya Zemlya, Siberia

Present day

Somewhere in the blank, featureless distance the rotors changed pitch and increased in ferocity. I didn't wait for Abi and Alice to start running, but instead charged to the driver's side and jumped up into the truck, tossing the rifle onto the passenger seat. I slammed the door and pushed it into first, turning the truck until the compass said I was heading north. Soon I was picking up speed parallel to the island, away from the other two. I flicked up through the gears, fumbling with the switches until I found the lights. I flicked them all on, headlights, spotlights and hazard flashers.

The helicopter's turbines grew louder than the truck's engine. I reached for the rifle, propped it on the dash, and prepared to joust with it.

Instead it swept round in a wide arc, opting to follow. I kept the truck in third gear and pulled the magazine out of the rifle, swinging it round and jamming it down onto the accelerator. By pushing the rifle's foresight under the seat, I managed to wedge the butt on the pedal just enough to hold the truck at a constant low speed.

With one last look at the flat sea ice ahead, I wrenched the GPS unit from its mount on the dash. Pocketing it, I opened the driver's door and climbed up onto the rear, through the canvas. Grabbing another rifle from the crate, I loaded it, cocked it, and slid across the planks to the back. With my boots hanging over the open tailgate, I aimed backwards and waited.

I was about to give it up, thinking the helicopter was playing safe out of range, but suddenly it accelerated, rushing forward. I waited until they got closer then opened up on full auto, most of the bullets going wide or high but achieving the objective – the helicopter backed off, banking high into the night sky, ready to turn for another pass.

I waited a few seconds then climbed down the tailgate until I was crouched above the rushing ice. Now that I was here, it seemed to be speeding beneath me a hell of a lot quicker. I dropped the rifle, it clattered and skittered away behind me. I lowered myself over the back, boots braced to hang behind the truck.

As predicted, it did no good on the rough sea ice, and as my boots caught, I lost my grip on the tailgate. I tucked and rolled, slamming onto the ice, spinning out of control. For a few seconds the rush of scraping material and my own panting breaths tumbled around my head. When I stopped, I was still in one piece and unscathed.

I jumped up, running in the opposite direction away from the truck as the rush of rotors came again. The rifle was a few metres away; I reached it as the helicopter appeared. With nowhere to hide out on the sea ice, I threw myself down on the rifle, hoping the Arctic camo parka and overtrousers would be enough to disguise me if they were focused on the truck.

It appeared they were, as the turbines roared overhead. They changed tactic, as automatic gunfire opened up almost immediately. I picked up the rifle and reloaded, running for the island.

A crash echoed across the ice. I felt the vibrations through my boots as metal screeched and tore. I looked back at the truck, now a good couple of hundred metres away, almost lost in the darkness and freezing mist. I could see its rear lights and flashers still going, but it took me a second to realise it was sliding on its side, slowly spinning as it careened away. I doubted the small arms on the chopper could have done it any real damage, more likely with no driver the truck had hit a mound of ice and overturned.

So much for the truck leading the chopper away. When they found it empty they'd come for us. I switched direction and ran for a large mound of ice that offered the best cover. There I took a breather and listened to the helicopter. Sounded like it was hovering.

Then the pitch changed again. I looked round the ice and saw the black shape coming towards me. Fortunately it levelled off, hovering about halfway between me and the truck, suspended for a few seconds before lowering. No trepidation about landing on the ice now, though the pilot did keep the power up as if ready to shoot back into the sky.

Against the flashing lights three passengers disembarked, the elongated bulky silhouettes showing they were kitted out, rifles up and ready. They split apart from each other and advanced on the truck from different angles. Three beams clicked on, sweeping side to side like mini lighthouses; from the way they moved I guessed at underslung rifle-mounted torches.

I brushed condensation from my face and beard and pulled up my mask. Time to go to work.

I set off across the rough sea ice at a jog, rifle firm against my shoulder, trigger finger ready. No need for stealth, the turbines were making that much racket they wouldn't have heard me on a motorbike.

Moving cautiously and covering all angles, the three shadows were still only halfway to the truck when I ducked under the chopper's tail boom, coming up on the open side door.

With one last glance at the truck and its converging attackers, I chanced a look inside. The passenger cabin looked empty, I stepped up onto the short metal ladder, reached and grabbed a handle and slowly climbed up. I was wrong, the compartment wasn't empty.

I noticed the blood first, a dark trail creeping along the steel flooring and pooling around a discarded magazine.

I looked round and realised there were several holes in the fuselage and flooring. These military choppers were usually armoured against small arms fire, so I'd either got lucky or in its civilian life some of that plating had been removed to save weight in favour of enhanced range. I followed the blood trail back along the floor and saw a body slumped across the seats a couple of rows back.

A radio squawked up front. Through the open cockpit door, above the turbines, I could just about hear the pilot shouting something in Russian. I moved forward, rifle barrel leading the way through the bulkhead into the cockpit. Up one short step and I could see both pilots' helmets bobbing, lit up in the Christmas tree glow from the instruments. Something sparked through the windows in front, flashed, then red smoke plumed upwards as one of the soldiers lit a flare. Others burst into life, bouncing around, lighting up the truck. I could see the three of them properly now, scanning the darkness, and wondering where I'd escaped to.

I crept forward then paused as the pilot spoke rapidly into his headset. He laughed and turned to the co-pilot, then jumped a mile as he saw me out of the corner of his eye. I stepped forward, swinging the rifle into his helmet then spinning it round and slamming the butt into the other pilot. The first guy fumbled down by his feet, I twisted the rifle and swung it like a bat. He slumped in his seat, out cold.

The second got his belt off and jumped up. I saw a pistol in the corner of my eye. I manged to get my arm across, pushing his hand back.

He somehow produced a huge knife in his left hand and brought his helmet down to headbutt me. I stepped back and ducked away, with the downside that I lost my leverage on his arm. As he brought the pistol down to put a bullet through me, I slammed the butt of my rifle up into his chin with a sickening crunch. His head snapped back, helmet cracking the side window, before he slid onto the cockpit floor.

The three soldiers in front were still scanning the darkness, oblivious to what was going on in the noisy chopper.

I picked up the pilot's knife from the seat and started slicing and hacking through anything I could. Several lights winked out, others started flashing angrily. Something started beeping an incessant warning. I crouched, finding a hydraulic line, but sawing got me nowhere on the steel braided cover.

Outside the windscreen the beams casting around on the ice started to move back towards the chopper.

I reversed through into the passenger compartment, out the door, and down the steps. The nearest torch beam was sweeping side to side, lighting up millions of swirling diamonds kicked around in the rotor downwash. I pulled up the rifle, knelt, took aim. As the beam swept one way, I pulled the trigger twice.

I was already dropping under the helicopter before the sound rolled away across the frozen sea. Both remaining beams swung onto their dead comrade, bouncing as they ran. I launched sideways away from the helicopter for a few seconds, then slid back onto my knees, taking aim at the nearest beam of light. I traced it backwards to the owner of the rifle and squeezed twice again.

The beam pointed skyward, a scream cut across the ice. I was already running towards the truck, the only cover out here.

The last torch beam switched off, so his brain had finally kicked in, though not quite as he didn't start moving quickly enough. And thanks to the angle, he was now silhouetted in the running lights of the helicopter.

I took aim one last time and squeezed. Three down and one disabled helicopter.

It had come at the expense of our truck – but the alternative would have been to let them kill us anyway, so I still chalked it up as a win.

After the exertion I suddenly realised how cold I was, sweating on the sea ice. Sweat that would freeze me even faster. I ran back to the chopper and climbed up, out of the wind.

I peeled off my gloves and held my hands over the air vents, cranking the cabin heating right up. The out-cold pilot groaned, so I took his pistol from under his seat, threw it out the door, and pulled my gloves back on. It's a shame I couldn't cut through something more serious. Even more of a shame I didn't have any explosives on me. I could rig something but I was cold, the chopper was disabled, and now my priority was to get moving.

I looked at the GPS unit I'd taken from the truck. Just two miles to go to the coordinates I'd set, and at least this time I was wearing decent cold-weather gear. I set off across the ice.

Chapter Thirty-seven

Severnaya Zemlya, Siberia
Present day

It didn't take long before the sound of the helicopter's turbines were drowned out by the moaning, creaking ice. With the rifle strapped across my back and my hood down tight, I shoved my gloved hands deep into my pockets and walked at double pace. Not easy going sideways to the wind, but in the thermals and proper military gear, it was a hell of a lot easier than the previous evening, when I'd tried and failed to make it to the hotel.

It was probably colder, but without it dumping snow on me, visibility was clearer and the going better.

I pulled out the GPS to check it again, figuring this was approximately where I'd dropped Abi and Alice. I turned west, looking at the looming cliffs through the freezing mist. Less than half a mile away, in similar gear to me, they should have made it okay.

I pushed the GPS back into the big pockets and hunkered down, plodding forward, the wind now at my back. But I spoke too soon, as the island was washed from view by increasing gusts, pulling more drift ice up and throwing it against the low cliffs. I knew they were out there somewhere. I know how easy it was to get turned around, even with a steady wind, so I checked the GPS regularly as I trudged on.

Soon the ice rose. It became apparent I was walking up a slope of a beach, even if the ice encasing it stretched the usual definition. I adjusted so the bluffs were to my right and carried on up the slope, looking for shelter.

I found it in the shape of a rock formation that'd been drifted over a long time ago. I pulled out my torch and flicked it on, not improving visibility by much as the swirling ice reflected a good percentage of it straight back in my face.

I almost rounded the corner then placed the torch on the ground, backpedalling then turning to walk around the rocks from the other direction.

I chanced a look round and found I was right. Silhouetted in the glow reflected from the snow were Alice and Abi, crouched on the ground sheltering from the wind. Both had their rifles pointing the other way.

'Bang,' I shouted. They both jumped.

'Jesus fucking Christ,' shouted Alice. Abi shouted something similar but it was more muffled since she had her hood right up over her face. 'We could have shot you.'

'Might have hit me if you'd been pointing the right way. Come on, we need to keep moving. It's not far.'

'What's not far? What happened?'

'The helicopter's not going anywhere any time soon, but we need to crack on before the others catch up.'

Abi pulled her hood open and stood, brushing ice off her jacket. 'And the first question?'

'Where are we going? That'll be answered in about five minutes.' I pulled the GPS out, looking at the coordinates, orientating myself, and put a hand up to shelter my face as I scanned the rocky island.

'Where's the equipment?' asked Abi.

'Gone,' I said simply.

I gave Alice a hand up, then signalled for them to get moving. Out of the shelter of the rocks the wind buffeted us again but the going wasn't too bad. The enemy now was the sheer cold – we'd been out of the truck for half an hour or so, which wasn't lethal dressed like this, not immediately, but it would be at some point. It was bitter, I was shivering, trying to focus on that horizon. Not far, I kept telling myself. Not far.

The next time I checked the GPS, Alice had fallen behind. I waved for Abi to wait then shuffled back, difficult straight into the wind

– I had to pull my hood completely shut and angle my head down; even then I could practically feel it slamming the top of my head and wicking away my body heat.

'Keep moving.' I grabbed Alice by the arm and pulled.

She didn't answer, or offer any resistance, but I could feel her waning. I put an arm round her and looked up at Abi on the ridge.

'It's not far,' I shouted to Alice. 'Just up here.'

She stumbled and dropped her rifle. I caught her and dragged her onwards. She was heavy, slipping from my grip, and I realised her boots had stopped moving and were dragging twin furrows through the snow. I put my other arm around her and dragged her up the slope. Abi came to help, putting one arm around the other side.

'If this is it I'm gonna be real pissed off,' Abi shouted.

'What do you mean?' I replied as we reached the top of the slope.

'This!' she said, pointing.

Several metres away sat what at first appeared to be a rock forma-tion, half buried in drifts that covered the windward sides and rounded over the top. The giveaway was the corrugated sheeting exposed along the ridge where the fine snow was continually being pulled away by the wind, telling us it was man-made. If that wasn't enough, a large antenna stuck up behind it a good thirty metres or so into the sky, though it was ice-rimed to twice its size and leaning so drunkenly to one side you'd be forgiven for not knowing what it was. The wind screeched across the antenna, an unearthly sound halfway between a dying fox and a deranged crow, which added to the general sense of unease about the whole place.

'Told you it wasn't far.'

'This? This!' Abi let go of Alice and wrapped her arms around herself. 'This fucking… shed?'

I hauled Alice onward, hands under both her arms. We were actu-ally heading for what looked like a series of sheds, though in reality they were more than that, and mostly built of preformed concrete. Abi caught up and took Alice's other arm again, and together we carried her around the far side, sheltered from the wind.

I sat Alice on the ice and pulled down my mask. The door was set into a wooden extension from the main building, crusted with rime and edged with snow, the tiny windows shuttered securely. I walked up the ice slope which represented the few steps to the door, and tried the handle.

It didn't give immediately but there was no lock – theft isn't really a consideration this far north of humans. I turned and gave it a shoulder. The ice creaked, the door gave a little. Holding the handle down, I leaned back then slammed it full force. This time it gave, swinging open into the dark interior. I flicked a light switch. As expected, nothing happened.

'Let's get her inside,' I shouted into the gale.

We grabbed an arm each and lifted Alice, carrying her sideways through the narrow doorway. Once inside I swung the door shut behind us, plunging us into pitch black but stopping the worst of the wind. I sat Alice on the floor and pulled down my hood.

'It's warm,' Abi said. 'Who the hell lives here?'

'No one,' I said, fishing out my torch and lighting up the porch area. 'At least, not at the moment. They left a couple of months ago.'

'What is this place?'

I shone the torch on the interior door. This one was sturdier, but protected from the weather it swung open easily, its draught-strips rubbing the wooden floor. It was warmer still inside the main room.

I half-carried Alice inside and sat her on the floor, back against the far wall.

Abi stamped her boots and followed me in. 'How is it so warm if no one's here? It's not just the lack of wind.'

'It's not really warm – not unless you've come in from minus thirty.'

'But there's power.' She pointed to a glowing green sign above the door.

'Thermoelectric generators.' I shrugged off my outer jacket and hung it on a peg on the wall. 'They work off a temperature difference and generate enough to run low power electronics. Sensors and data updates to the cloud.'

'So what is this place?' asked Alice.

'You're still with us!' I said. 'Welcome to Meteorological Station Zulu. Take off your gloves. Check your fingers.'

'For what?' asked Alice, struggling to bend to reach her boots.

'Well, that you've got ten attached. Same for your toes, assuming you had ten in the first place.'

'You didn't count them last night?' Abi asked.

I gave her a hard look. 'You, too. Frostbite comes on quickly.'

'Inbred bitch could stand to lose a few toes,' muttered Alice.

'You got a fucking problem?' shouted Abi. 'I wasn't the one needed carrying in here!'

'All right, shut the fuck up!' I said. 'We need to stick together if we all wanna get out of Siberia, get it?'

'Sure, side with your new fuck-buddy over the woman who saved your arse.'

I shook my head and opened another internal door to the left.

'Where are you going?' asked Alice.

I ignored her, shining my torch across a long desk with a couple of computers and other electronic equipment. A door at the far end was marked with an electric sign.

Inside the next room was a small diesel generator on a pallet against the wall, next to several fuel drums and cannisters of what I presumed was water.

I unscrewed the lid of the tank on the generator and gave it a sniff: it was full. After priming it and giving a few pulls on the cord, it sputtered into life, to cheers from the other room.

'Lights!' shouted Abi.

I listened to the generator for a minute, satisfied it was purring nicely, then turned a dial on the wall and left the room.

Now flicking the switch on the wall lit up a room packed with electronics. I understood almost none of them, except for the computers. They'd have internet via the sat connection, and be capable of making VOIP calls as well as email – but would be password protected. I switched one on and after a few seconds the familiar start-up screen confirmed it.

Back to old-school methods, then. An HF radio set at the end of the desk. I flicked on the power, the screen lit up.

I left it for now and went back into the main room.

Abi and Alice were both sat on a small sofa, still pulling their boots off.

'Should be toasty soon,' I said.

'Don't suppose you've got a Sunday dinner stashed about the place?' asked Alice.

'It's Monday morning.' I fished in the pocket of my jacket hanging on the wall, pulling out the crumpled pack of biscuits and tossing them to Alice. 'Leave some for me.'

'I'm not hungry actually,' she said, crinkling her nose.

'Seriously, eat some. You lose a few hundred calories an hour just existing out here.'

'Sounds good to me.'

'Don't bite them, they'll be like rocks. Hold them in your hands for a bit first to warm them up.'

I crossed to the other side of the room to explore the last door. It opened into a windowless bedroom and storage area, racks of equipment along one wall and bunks along the other.

'So what is this place then?' asked Abi.

'Weather station run by Durham University. It was set up a few years ago to study climate change, but it's only occupied in summer. The sensors tick over themselves and automatically transmit data back to the university.'

'And you know all this because…'

'Because it's in my interest to know.' I pulled off my mask and unzipped my second jacket. 'Shall I get a brew on?'

Chapter Thirty-eight

Severnaya Zemlya, Siberia

Present day

The thermostat on the wall said it was 19 degrees, which was the warmest I'd been for over 48 hours. The clock suggested it was now daytime, not that you'd know it from the tiny window by the door. I sat up in the chair and rubbed my eyes to clear the last of the nightmarish visions, yawning wide.

I stretched and looked into the bedroom at the two snoring bunks then closed the door softly. I dressed quickly, not relishing the thought of going back outside, but at least my clothes were warm and dry after spending a few hours by the heater in the corner.

Last night while I'd got on the radio, Abi had rustled up some chilli from the freeze-dried packets in the storeroom, which had done wonders for the three of us. Alice had been just as useful collecting all our ammo and refilling every magazine we had, stacking them by the door.

I grabbed two and pushed them into my pockets, then picked up a rifle and loaded it with a third. Pulling on my hat and gloves, and some goggles I'd found in the supplies, I tugged up my hood and opened the door.

The blast of cold slapped me around the face, and I wasn't even outside yet. I pulled my mask up over my nose and opened the outer door.

The day hadn't got started; the grey dawn – or what passed for it up here – wouldn't arrive for some time. The island was just as cold, dark and windy as I'd left it.

I cocked the rifle and set off round the side of the building, scanning the surroundings. Nothing moved. I could feel the depression kicking back in; all the joy brought on by eating and sleeping in warmth over the past couple of hours was evaporating with the breath that clouded in front of me. So was the warmth; the cold was already creeping in.

Depressed and frozen, at least I had some energy now. I set off down the slope to the sea ice, scanning the flat horizon all around. There were no sounds save the low moaning wind and the grating, creaking ice.

I did a couple of circuits, patrolling a long perimeter around the base. I was conscious of keeping it in view on one side of me at all times, as if the weather closed in it'd be rough trying to find it again.

After twenty minutes or so, I'd had enough and went back inside.

Laughter greeted me as I unlaced my boots in the entrance way. I shoved through the door into the room. Alice went red, putting her mug of coffee down and turning away to rustle through pans in a cupboard. Abi was rummaging around the shelves in the store behind.

'Hey, we got time for some food?' she shouted.

The kettle was warm, I flicked it back on then unlaced my boots and pulled them off, looking at the clock. 'No, we need to be outside when the evac arrives. Once they come in it'll be a beacon for Golubev.'

'He can't still be out there,' said Alice, fishing some cutlery from a drawer. 'They'll have frozen.'

I peeled off my outer layers and hung them over a chair then took a mug from a cupboard. 'Not as long as their engines are running, or if they made a decent camp – we don't know what equipment they've got. We've got to assume they're out there somewhere, and not too far.'

'Okay, I found powdered eggs and powdered milk,' shouted Abi from next door. 'I reckon we can get some brekkie on the go.'

I dropped a teabag in the mug and poured the bubbling water. 'I told you, we don't have long.'

Abi came back into the room loaded up with several boxes and packets. 'So anyway, you didn't tell me Alice tried to kill you when she met you.'

'It wasn't when I met him,' Alice said. 'It was a few hours later.'

'She's gone up in my estimation,' Abi said to me. 'I've only known you a few hours and I can already empathise.'

Over her shoulder, Alice smiled.

'Feel free to go your own way at any time,' I said.

I left them to it, going through to the research room and sitting in the chair. I wheeled across to the radio set and flicked it on, then paused. The LED screen winked back at me. A few hours ago I'd used a couple of different frequencies before successfully making contact. The first two had skipped, bouncing off the ionosphere right over my target before I got third time lucky. The problem was, the radio was now tuned in to one of those frequencies I'd been unsuccessful with.

I looked at the paper scrawled with five frequencies. The third down had worked for me, but the radio was tuned to the second down on the list, a mistake made in haste.

The implication was clear. One of the women had not been asleep when I'd left the station.

'Got some dodgy-looking porridge,' shouted Alice. 'Your tea's brewed.'

I flicked the set off and went back into the main room. 'Hardly worth having, with this,' I said, holding up a tub of powdered milk that looked like it had survived since the weather station was built.

'I'll pop out to the Co-op for some,' said Alice, giving me a wink.

I stirred the powder into the tea and gave it a sip. The sludge was undrinkable. I poured it down the sink and went back into the room next door, sitting back at the radio with my head in my hands.

'Penny for them?' said Alice, nudging me and taking a sip of coffee.

'I'd be a millionaire.'

She kicked the door to behind her. 'You see them, don't you?'

'Who?'

'I've only ever killed one person. I know that's more than most people but... anyway.' She moved a keyboard and sat up on the desk. 'Sometimes I see Gambetta's face, that split second between me pulling the trigger and him dropping. It's like slow motion, but it's strange, it's like I can see right into him in that moment, the utter hopelessness in his eyes when he knows there's nothing more he can do, he's finished, end. I see that face in my dreams. My nightmares. Sometimes when I'm awake, I just close my eyes and there he is. It's crippling sometimes.' She took a sip of coffee and stared out of the window at the grey tundra, where dawn was trying to break. 'And like I said, I've only killed one person.'

A tear was beginning to form in the corner of her eye. She sniffed and gave it a wipe.

'I used to see them,' I said. I took out my pistol and stared at it. 'I haven't for a while.'

'Surely that's worse?'

'Maybe.' I ran my finger over the slide, feeling the scratches beneath my thumb.

'It is.' She put her hand on mine. 'You're like a frog in a pan, you haven't noticed you're boiling.'

I pulled back the slide and pushed the gun into my pocket, clearing my throat. 'Dark sky in the morning.'

'Tyler take warning.'

Abi leaned around the door. 'Guys, I'm starting to feel like a third wheel here.'

'Oh, that ring is amazing, where did you get it?' Alice said, wiping her eyes, pointing at Abi's hand and leading her out of the room.

I put my feet on the desk and looked out of the window at the charcoal landscape. The sky was churning, roiling clouds sitting low across the rocky peaks just visible through the black blizzard. A tiny pinprick of red light hovered in the distance. As I watched, it grew.

'Guys, gear up,' I shouted. 'It's time to go home.'

Chapter Thirty-nine

I pulled the Mitsubishi into the bushes behind the big Russian truck and killed the ignition, looking across at the rocks and dark trees beyond. In the shadows was a flattened area of vegetation, another trail leading into the forest.

I climbed down, closed the door softly, and skirted the rocks to get closer to the trail. Tyre tracks headed off the road, pulling mud up into the ferns. I grabbed a branch and pulled; it came away easily, revealing more tyre tracks heading into the trees. Looked like another overgrown logging trail. The jungle here was full of them.

I slowly followed the track as it snaked through the dense foliage. After thirty seconds or so it widened out. I gasped and knelt in the bushes. At the far end, facing me, was the beige Citroën that'd collected me from the airport.

I pictured the face in the trees. It *had* been him. Le Démon Blanc. The headhunter.

I watched the Citroën carefully. There was no one inside, no movement. The birds were silent, as if the jungle knew he was here, and had gone into hiding from him. I looked round through the steam rising from the damp ground into the humid air.

I could get back in my car, I thought. I *should* get back in my car. But I couldn't shake that woman's face from my mind.

I skirted the clearing, coming round, eyes alert and scanning for any movement. As I approached the Citroën I could see a small track behind it, a foot trail through the trees. With one eye on it, I walked out into the clearing to the car. Still no movement.

I cupped my hands on the glass and looked inside. It was just as it had been when he'd picked me up. The car was unlocked. I opened the passenger door slowly and recoiled as a fog of flies sprang from the seat, buzzing around my head. I swished my hands, brushing my hair back, and crouched behind the door.

The inside stank more than I remembered. I put one hand over my mouth as I opened the glovebox. His pistol was still there. I took it out and held it, turning it over. The letters stamped into the slide said it was a SIG Sauer P220, which meant little to me. Holding it firm, I pressed the button in the grip behind the trigger. The magazine dropped out into my hand, brass rounds glinted in the light. I put the magazine on the car seat and pulled the slide back on the gun, releasing it with a satisfying click. The hammer stayed back. I looked for a safety but there wasn't one so I pulled the trigger. It was tough but resulted in a satisfying click, which told me I now knew how to operate it.

I pushed the magazine home and pulled the slide back again. I wouldn't be caught short this time.

I stood and quietly closed the car door, disturbing more flies. As I walked back around it, I noticed the boot was slightly open. Without thinking, I hooked my fingers under the lid and pulled it up, then immediately backtracked. My hand went to my mouth again but it didn't stop me vomiting all over the car's rear bumper. I dropped to my knees and retched again, struggling to breathe. I sat on the ground for a moment, wheezing. When I finally had nothing left to throw up, I scuttered back on my arse, reversing into the trees.

A couple of those involved in the arms deal had been folded into the boot, along with the more recognisable pieces of the guy who'd been hit with the grenade. Clouds of flies swarmed, seemingly every insect in the jungle was headed this way.

Wiping my mouth with the back of my hand, I stood and closed the boot.

I held the pistol down low as I moved into the darkness of the trees. Instead of following the track, I stuck to the ferns, pushing through vines and branches. I paused at a puddle that hadn't completely dried up and splashed water into my face, brushing my hair back, then started worrying about bacteria and parasites. A problem for another day.

A smell drifted in the steamy air. Burning, which could have come from that Nissan, but there was another underlying scent, almost sweet. I started pushing through the ferns again.

The track ended and I found myself on the other side of the rocky outcrop, looking at a dirt clearing full of rusting machinery, ending at a smooth, rounded cliff face jutting into the sky.

I crouched and listened. A noisy group of birds took flight from a tree, something hissed nearby. As I played the game of snake or insect in my mind, I spotted rusty metal beneath the undergrowth. An overgrown railway track. I crept to it, hunched over, and placed a hand on it, tracing its path. It led across the clearing and towards the rocks themselves, heading into a black hole. The old mines.

Another scan of the bushes told me I was still alone, so I ran straight across the clearing, gun ready, hitting the rocks with my back. Pressing in, I sidestepped, head going ten to the dozen as I spun at every sound. The stink was drifting from the mouth of the cave, or tunnel.

I took a breath, steadied myself, checked that the hammer was still back on the pistol, and started hyperventilating.

I spun around the tunnel entrance, gun pointing into the darkness. A breeze from inside wafted smoke out towards me. I took a few steps forward, feet on the old wooden sleepers of the tracks, letting my eyes adjust to the gloom.

Spider webs fluttered in the breeze. I could hear something now, a soft sound carried along in the warm smoky wind. Singing.

I shuddered, moving forward, deeper and deeper into the heart of darkness. The rough stone walls echoed and amplified the sounds. I picked up the pace towards a corner, and a glow. As I reached the turn I pressed against the wall and peered around. It wasn't nearly as dim, heading deeper into the hill but somehow flooded with light and what looked like an opening into a bright cave. I turned and crept forward on the edges of the wooden sleepers.

I paused when I realised the singing had stopped, but other sounds came. I sidestepped along the tunnel, ears alert. It was lighter now, I could see the far wall of the bright cave clearly. Water dripped somewhere, echoing as it hit wet rock, mixing with the constant hum of wind and occasional pop of burning wood.

The light spilling into the end of the tunnel was bright as day, which didn't make sense. I edged closer to the mouth, so bright it hurt my eyes. I blinked, after a few seconds the scene swam into focus. It was another clearing, this one surrounded by rock, fringed with grass and vines. A natural sinkhole that'd eaten down through the middle of the hill, creating a wide, flat area several storeys deep.

Smoke wisped along the ceiling of the tunnel from a campfire. With the gun outstretched before me, I crept to the end. The rock face stretched above, I ducked to see the top way overhead, birds circling in a small patch of sky. The cliff sides were sheer, there didn't seem to be anywhere else to go. This had to be it.

I braced myself, took a deep breath and prepared to take the last step. The gun was slick in my hand, I switched it, rubbed my right hand on my trousers, then gripped it again tightly. In my head I counted down, 3, 2, 1, go. And still I was stood with my back against the cold rock.

The singing started up again. I almost jumped out of my skin. It was close, too close. Singing in a language I didn't understand, more noises, scraping, banging around, then something much worse. A drawn-out, bloodcurdling scream, both terrified and terrifying.

It didn't last long, choked off almost as quickly as it'd started. The singing drifted away. I breathed deeply again, holding it in my lungs, forcing it as I tensed everything. I brought the pistol up and swung around the corner.

I swept the gun across the scene, taking it in piece by piece. First was a wooden shack, an old lean-to shanty with a tin roof and rotten sides, all moss and algae. A system of open gutters drained rain into a big iron trough, spilling across the dirt floor.

It wasn't the shack that grabbed my attention. On the mud in front of it were four people.

The two closest were lying face down on the dirt, hands tied behind their backs, unconscious. Both wore camouflage clothing and from what I could see through the mud and blood, they looked to be the Russians from the overturned Toyota.

Behind them were two more captives, knees pulled up under their chins, ankles tied. Their arms were stretched round behind their backs, tied to one of the shack's timber support legs. Strips of dirty cloth had been forced into their mouths, held in place by tape.

The one on the left was a man dressed in completely incongruous sports gear, a basketball top with shorts and high-top trainers, all completely covered in the same orange mud that clung to every surface, other than the lines down his cheeks left by tears.

Next to him was the woman I recognised from the gunfight earlier, the lone survivor. Beneath her short braids her face was streaked with mud, but no tears here. Blood had soaked into her combat pants and her boots from a wound on her thigh, but she stared at the rocks opposite defiantly.

Both saw me at the same time and mumbled into the gags. I held a hand up and crouched, hands on my knees, as I retched again. Because it wasn't the captives that had grabbed my attention.

At the far edge, away from the shack, was the source of the cooking stink. Three charred bodies smouldered on the dirt, wisps of steam and smoke drifting up in fat rays of afternoon sun. A washing line had been erected between hooks set into the rock wall, from it hung strips of charred meat, sliced thinly like long ribbons of biltong.

A short distance away was the source of the scream I'd heard. Flames licked up from a small fire, from which a pair of naked legs stuck out, still twitching. The torso was a mess of blackened flesh and pale ribs, arms clawing upward. As I watched, the head, little more than a skull, turned and rested sideways, staring at me from black sockets, still screaming soundlessly.

Nearby were several jerry cans, next to a pair of blackened skulls.

The man was nowhere to be seen.

I ran forward, the two conscious captives bounced up and down, shouting into their gags and flicking their heads. I followed the motion and saw another tunnel cutting off into darkness.

I slid to the ground next to the woman and ripped the tape from her face. She swore under her breath and started a long tirade in French. I followed as best I could but then held up my hand.

'*Je ne parle pas… Parlez lentement…*'

'English?'

'Yes. Where is he?'

'Getting more petrol. He will be back soon.'

I pulled at the rope on her ankles but it was tied tight and my fingers didn't seem to want to respond. The guy next to her was shouting at me through his gag. I leaned over and tore it off.

'You!' he said.

I sat back on my feet and stared at him.

'You stole my car! *Bâtard*!'

'I'm sorry,' I panted, reaching for his ropes. 'I'm sorry, I'm sorry,' was all I could get out of my mouth.

A bang echoed along the tunnel.

'Hurry,' the woman said. 'Find a knife quickly, man.'

I stood and looked around, letting out a squeak as I saw the burning corpse again.

'Your friend?' the man asked.

'What?'

'A white man, dressed in combat gear,' said the woman.

I looked at the legs again and felt my own begin to buckle. My brother...

Singing echoed into the clearing, my eyes swivelled onto the tunnel. I saw with horror that the light of a torch was bouncing across the wall inside. I started breathing quickly, my vision swam, a ringing in my ears started up. My knees were about to give way.

I stood there, glued to the spot, looking at the two of them, over at the burning corpse, and back at the tunnel I'd come down. The singing came closer.

'I'm sorry,' I said. 'I'm sorry, I'm sorry, I'm sorry,' was all I could say as I ran back the way I'd come, into the tunnel.

I threw myself against the cold rock, panting, tears streaming down my cheeks, retching with every other burning breath. The singing grew louder, more banging. I looked down at the gun in my hand, shaking. The hammer was still back.

I looked round the corner.

The man – for it was just a man, not a demon at all – set a couple of plastic cans down on the ground and unscrewed the lid of one.

He picked it up again and poured fuel onto the naked legs, which danced with fresh vigour as the flames leapt high. As they blackened, I noticed with relief a tattoo, which meant it wasn't Justin's leg. That lasted a few seconds until shame kicked in; I was happy someone else had been burned alive.

He turned, still singing, looked at his next victims, then paused. He stopped singing and shouted something in a language I didn't understand, then roared.

The gags. He'd seen that I'd removed them.

He spun his head quickly, casting his eyes around the clearing and then landing squarely on me, still peering from behind the rocks. His eyes glowed with anger. He panted with fury, then a grin split his face.

'I told you I'd get you, boy.'

He started running.

It's only a man, I told myself. Flesh and bone, no more than a man.

I came around the corner, bringing the pistol up, and pulled the trigger. No impotent feeling this time, no dead weight, this time it kicked like a punch to the wrist, loosing a bullet towards him. I pulled the trigger again; it was easier the second time, the third, the fourth. I ran forward, squeezing the trigger again and again, flinching as each explosion tugged on my arm, forcing it back and the barrel up. I tensed my arm and carried on pulling the trigger as I ran forward.

The gun clicked, I skidded to a halt. He was already on me, tackling me about the waist at full pelt, slamming me backwards onto the ground and driving the wind from my lungs. He laughed, grabbing my head in both hands and smashing it backwards on the ground. My vision swam, the sunlight dimmed as if dusk had arrived early. I felt his hands on my head, everything was dark, he was pressing his fingers into my eyes. I brought a knee up, connecting with something, the pressure on my eyes fell away.

I curled up, slapping at the ground as I willed air back into my lungs. The moment stretched on for an age until finally I took a breath, filling my lungs and rolling away.

The man towered above, following me across the dirt floor. He kicked out, catching me under the chin and lifting my head off the ground. I screamed out in pain as the tied-up dealer on the other side of the clearing screamed, too.

He backed away, grinning. 'I told you, didn't I, eh boy? Told you he'd pay more for your head.'

I rocked back onto my feet and stood shakily. He grunted, head down like a bull about to charge. I realised not every bullet had missed him. A patch of red at his side gave him away. He ran at me again, this time I was ready, and as he approached I kicked out, using his momentum to drive the sole of my trainers into his ribs. It knocked me flying onto the dirt again but it momentarily paused him, as he clutched his side and probably realised for the first time that he'd been grazed. He snarled, running again. I scrambled on all fours and up to my feet, running for the still-burning corpse.

Something hit my chest, my feet left the ground. I'd run into the washing line of drying meat. He slammed into me as I spun, I grabbed him, taking him to the ground with me. We slammed into the dirt side by side, sliding through the jerry cans, tangled in rope and sliced meat. I scrambled away, knocking the full can over with my elbow, sending petrol sloshing across the ground.

The fumes stung my eyes. I jumped to my feet at the same time as he did. We faced each other, him snarling like a caged tiger, me watching for the tell-tale sign he was about to strike. His arm went behind his back and reappeared holding a large knife. That was a game-changer; he was bigger and stronger than me, and the next time he grabbed me would be the last.

I shuffled backwards. His eyes were focused, intent, boring into me.

I thrust a leg backwards, kicking the burning corpse. Instantly the petrol on my shoe caught fire, and before he understood what was happening, I ran and kicked the jerry can at him with all the force I could.

The puddle of petrol ignited with a whumph that seemed to suck the air from the hollow. I was already running as the flames raced up my leg. I jumped for the old water trough, putting my foot through the bottom and sending a cloud of steam rolling upwards. A pile of skulls tumbled onto the dirt.

I turned to see an inferno behind me, a tornado of flames spiralling upwards from the pool of petrol, caught in the draught from the mines. On the edge of the bonfire the man was swatting at himself and losing; a second later he was lost in a ball of flames. He ran towards me, for the water trough. I reached down and pushed it over, sending the last of the water spilling across the hard-packed dirt.

The man dropped to the ground and rolled, but the ground was hard and the water did nothing to stop the flames. He jumped up, running across the hollow, leaving shreds of burning clothes in his wake. He flailed, never once making a sound. I couldn't tell what was burning any more, clothes or flesh. At the far end of the clearing he turned, running into the tunnel, leaving a glow as he rounded the corner and disappeared.

I ran to the flames and dropped to my knees, pulling the sleeve of my jacket over my hand and grabbing the burning knife he'd dropped. My sleeve lit on fire, I threw the knife across the ground and slapped the flames out. Fortunately the waxed jacket had repelled most of the petrol.

I picked up the hot knife and crouched in front of the woman, slicing up through the rope at her ankles and her wrists behind her back.

'Cut him loose,' I said, handing her the knife and running to look down the tunnel. There was no sign of the man, no sounds and no glow.

'Come on,' the man shouted behind me, massaging his wrists.

I ran to help him, and between us we looped the woman's arms over our shoulders and half dragged her.

'What about them?' she asked. 'Are they dead?'

'The Russians?' I asked. 'No.' I stared at them for a moment then ducked out from the woman's arm. 'Give me the knife.'

She pulled it from her belt, I ran back and sliced the bonds on the Russians' wrists then rejoined them.

'We can't just leave them here,' the woman said.

'Twenty minutes ago you were trying to kill them. We need to get out of here, fast.'

'You think he is dead?' asked the woman.

'He cannot come back,' said the man. 'Not now.'

'It's not him I'm worried about.'

'Thank you,' she said. 'I thought you would leave us.'

'Me too.'

We emerged into the sunlight, I shrugged the woman's arm off and turned to face them.

'I presume you're ALN?'

She nodded. 'Captain Elonga Ntumba,' she said.

'Benjamin Kayembe,' the man said.

'You were hijacking that arms shipment?'

'No, I was looking for you,' he said. 'Someone saw my car up here this morning. One minute I'm having a piss at the side of the road, the next minute, oosh, I wake up tied.'

'That's great, but I was talking to Elonga.'

She narrowed her eyes. 'Why are you here?'

'He is a car thief,' said the man, turning to me. 'And if you hadn't just saved me I'd kill you right now. I still might.'

I took the woman's arm again, leading them both across the clearing towards the truck. 'Your car's fine, but we've got bigger problems right now.'

'And you stole my shoes!' he said, pointing at my charred Converse.

'But why are you *here*?' asked Elonga again.

'I'm not with the… the government forces or anything. I'm here for the same reason as you.' We stopped by the truck, I looked up at the crates stacked in the back and rested my hand on the open tailgate. 'Listen, this arms shipment should have turned up by now, which means we're about to be visited by some angry people.'

She nodded. 'The PRVN have a division stationed on the far side of Lusemba. We staged a crash to block the road, which should buy us some time.'

'How long?'

She shrugged. 'They will probably be here soon. We cannot take the truck, we need to stay off the roads.'

'Not necessarily. I think we can buy a little more time, but we need to work together.'

Chapter Forty

Severnaya Zemlya, Siberia
Present day

Getting outdoor gear on is so much easier when it's warm and so are you, but the wall of cold hits all the harder. What passed for dawn had brought a little light but no more colour; the jagged landscape was as monochromatic as ever.

Both women staggered as the wind took their breath away. Alice immediately hunched over, coughing and spluttering through the mask, dropping her rifle. Abi was more used to it; she simply pulled her hood a little tighter and looked up to the sky.

'Where is it?' she asked.

I pointed but didn't have to; an engine could be heard now in the distance. I picked up Alice's rifle and slung it across my back then took her arm and leaned in. 'Not long now.'

She nodded, gripping on to me as the three of us struggled down the slope of icy beach into the wind. Abi cocked her rifle and held it up ready, but visibility had dropped again in the whirling ice. My exposed cheeks stung. It seemed the entire frozen surface was being eroded and flung at us now. I shifted my goggles and pulled my mask up higher. The engine was close, throttling up, a turbo-prop roaring loudly above the moaning wind.

I balanced Alice next to a snow-covered rock and motioned for both of them to stay put, then unslung my rifle and cocked it. I followed the engine noise out onto the sea ice, scanning all around as the sound grew. The blown ice had whipped up a blizzard, reducing visibility down to mere metres. Trusting my ears, I followed the sound into the whiteout.

A welcome sight materialised from the whirling ice, the most welcome sight anyone who'd been through the last 48 hours could hope for. I wiped the ice from my goggles and smiled under the mask at one of Britain's most useful contributions to civil aviation – a little Britten-Norman BN-2 Islander, its rugged design and chunky fixed landing gear meaning the Land Rover of the skies could fly and land almost anywhere. This example carried the orange stripes and tailfin penguin of Utforske Luft, a small Tromsø-based charter airline. I didn't give two shits that penguins live at the opposite side of the planet, I was only interested in getting on board.

The door beneath the wing opened. A figure stepped down, spotted me and waved. I slung my rifle, returned the wave, then walked back to the others.

Abi was still standing sentry with the rifle, while Alice was hunched over trying to breathe. I took her arm and steadied her, lifting her face.

'The plane is just over there.'

'How far?'

I cocked my head 'Do you need me to carry you?'

'No, I fucking don't!'

She shoved me aside and did her best to follow Abi onto the sea, staggering in the onslaught. I caught an arm and led her through the worsening wind.

I could feel Alice speed up once the plane emerged. The door opened again as we got up next to it, just a crack to keep the worst of the cold out. It was next to impossible, as the wind took the door and nearly pulled it off its hinges, buffeting the tiny plane. I quickly heaved Alice up into the cabin and turned to help Abi.

A metallic dink came from behind me. It didn't register until a second later the crack of a gunshot sliced through the wind. I turned and saw a shape moving on the edge of visibility.

Another bullet ricocheted off the plane, the gunshot cracking briefly before it was torn away in the wind. I grabbed Abi but she didn't need telling, jumping on board.

'Go!' I shouted.

The engine throttled up as it started rolling. I jumped on board too, turning in the cramped cabin, slinging my rifle round and lying facing out of the doorway. A Lada 4X4 accelerated from the snow. I snapped off a couple of shots, it veered back into the whiteout.

'Get us up!' I shouted, squeezing the trigger again.

Another phantom in the snow took shape, this one a Land Rover Defender with a fully geared-up man hanging half out one of the back windows. He opened up with a volley, I turned to fire back, but the plane suddenly lurched, steering into the wind for take-off.

The ice raced by below me. I rolled to the side, up onto my knees, throwing the rifle onto my back and grabbing the door handle, trying to pull it shut as the engines reached full power. A line of holes stitched itself across the fuselage as Abi threw herself on the floor, a bullet punching into one of the seats behind me.

The Land Rover was coming again, spouting flame as we accelerated away. With a roar the wheels lifted, the ice dropped away from us rapidly. The pilot immediately pulled on the yoke. I held on tight to the seats as the plane rolled over on its side, giving me a view straight down: nothing beneath my boots. Below us the Lada and a couple of Land Rovers raced after us, still firing into the air. I managed to stand on the windows and grab the door pull. With some effort I got it shut, the rushing sound immediately quietened.

The plane tilted back, still climbing, I leaned over and let go of the door strap. I finally turned and got a look around the small cabin, just a couple of rows of simple seats covered in melting snow. Alice was slumped down in the single seat facing the door, gripping the seat belt, panting. Abi was at the back with the plane's occupant, stuffing clothes into the small bullet holes and covering them over with strips of gaffer tape from a toolbox.

I looked to the front. Through the door the pilot was still pulling hard, looking out of the side window. We were well out of range of small arms now. Let's hope Golubev didn't have any of those Verba surface-to-air missiles to hand.

The plane dipped a little, throttling back, climbing slower.

I propped the rifle on the front seat and unzipped my coat as Abi slouched in one of the chairs. The plane's occupant pulled off her ski mask and shook her long dark hair out.

'Abi, Alice, meet Anna Martinez, the woman who saved my life a couple of years ago.'

She walked forward and gave me a tight hug. 'Just saved your ass again, but who's counting, right?'

'Marty, this is Alice,' I pointed, 'who it turns out also saved my life a couple of years ago, and Abi, who has recently joined that club.'

'I'm getting a theme here,' said Marty, crouching to help Alice out of her cold-weather gear.

'Do you have women stashed all around the world who've saved your arse?' asked Abi.

'Surprisingly, just the one, until today.'

Marty pulled off one of Alice's boots and turned. 'Easy pickup, you said.'

I shrugged. 'Would you have come if I'd told you we'd be shot at by some angry Russians?'

'You know I would.'

'He might not.' I jerked a thumb over my shoulder at the pilot. 'Though to be fair he seems pretty calm considering his plane's shot up.'

'He's an ex-Royal Norwegian Air Force, and he doesn't care because it's your plane now, you bought it.'

'Great.' I looked at Abi. 'You think Golubev will want to buy a plane off me? One careful owner.'

I sat down and pulled off my boots, then grabbed a rucksack from one of the seats. I opened it, fishing around for a minute, then pulled out some clean clothes and a well-worn Barbour motorcycle jacket.

Alice was watching me, eagle-eyed. 'So you had this planned all along?'

'Always good to have a backup.'

The plane levelled off, engines settling into a drone. Most of my troubles were behind me, literally, now that we were getting the fuck away from this place.

I looked through the streaked window at the thick clouds rushing past, and thought about the last act. The assassination of Colonel Rupert Holderness.

Chapter Forty-one

Severnaya Zemlya, Siberia
Present day

The comforting drone of the turboprops couldn't smother the sound of the three women snoring. I threw my battered waxed jacket on the seat next to me and stood, stretching. My watch said we'd been in the air an hour or so. I yawned and squeezed between the seats into the cockpit, climbing over into the empty navigator seat next to the pilot.

'How long until Dikson?' I asked.

'Two hours,' the pilot replied. 'The wind has shifted.'

'John.' I held out my hand. 'Sorry about the plane.'

'Jan.' He grinned and shook my hand, warm and firm and slightly sheened from holding the yoke for hours. 'For thirty years I have flown supplies all over the Arctic circle. First in the Air Force, then for polar research teams, but this is the first time I've been shot at here.'

'It gets tiring.'

'You look like a man who'd know.'

'That rough, huh?'

'About as rough as me. I only said I hadn't been shot at in the Arctic.' He adjusted the heading slightly. 'First job I had when I left the Air Force was flying guns in and out of Central Africa.'

'Gotta be better money than flying students up to the North Pole?'

'It was, but I couldn't stand the heat.'

'Literally or figuratively?'

He thought for a second then nodded back over his shoulder at me and smiled. 'You've got a guardian angel there, you know.'

'She saved my life a couple of years ago and still goes on about it. I'll not live this down.'

'We sat on the runway at Dikson with her in that seat,' he pointed at where I was sat. 'For forty-eight hours waiting for you to call. I arranged refuelling, I got food, I slept, all the time she sat there waiting.'

I watched the snow and ice assaulting the windscreen, and the shades of charcoal beyond.

'If you're not sleeping, make yourself useful,' said Jan.

'Anything.'

He thumbed over his shoulder. 'There's a flask of coffee in the crates at the back.'

I nodded and climbed back over the seat, pushing between the chairs and snoring women in the cabin to reach the back. A plastic crate was racked with sandwiches, bottles of water, chocolate, crisps and flasks. I picked one up and shook it.

'Pass me that chocolate,' said Abi, peering out from under a blanket.

I threw her a bar of Cadbury's from the stash. 'Get some sleep.'

She opened the wrapper quietly. 'And you?' she whispered. 'What are your plans?'

'First I'm going to take this sludge to the chap up front, then I'm going to sit and pretend to sleep until we land in Dikson.'

'I mean, when you get back to England?'

'I have an appointment with a guy I've not seen for a while.' I made to squeeze between the seats but Abi leaned across and put a hand on my arm.

'Alice told me what happened. To you, to your brother.'

'What?'

'When you were out patrolling the ice, she told me everything.'

'I thought you were both asleep.'

She took a bite of chocolate and chewed. 'You try sleeping with that elephant plodding around the place doing God knows what. Sorry about your brother. And then that bastard tried to kill you as well. If I had a chance to kill the guy responsible I'd be all over it too. Count me in.'

'I can't ask you to help me. I have to do the next bit alone.'

'I was joking about saving your arse. You saved my life on the ice, and you got me out of there. I totally get that vendettas work better on your own, but realistically you need all the help you can get. We're gonna get this bastard together whether you like it or not.'

'I appreciate it, but you need to lie low. Go back to Oz, keep your head down. I've got enough with this one.' I nodded at Alice's gaping mouth as she snorted and mumbled something.

'She's a liability, mate. Cut her loose.'

'She's a lot more capable than you think.'

'Yeah, I know. Capable of killing. She murdered Balakin and was happy for you to take the rap.'

Alice grunted and turned over against the window.

'She didn't kill him, and I don't think she had much choice in the rest.'

'Oh really?' Abi shifted in her seat and looked over at Alice to check she was asleep. 'You're covered in bruises. Where are hers?'

'Maybe Golubev is squeamish?'

'He's not, trust me. If he wanted to know what information Balakin gave you before he died, he'd have beaten it out of her.'

I looked at Alice, sleeping serenely now. Her headband was askew, hair tumbling around her face, soft in the dim morning. Images of the previous night flashed through my mind, the two of us intertwined in a cold bed in a nuclear bunker. Then I pictured a couple of years ago, metres from her when she'd gunned down a French Secret Service agent in cold blood.

She mumbled something in her sleep and smiled.

Chapter Forty-two

Helsinki, Finland
Present day

The shiny modern airport contrasted sharply in every conceivable way with Dikson and the other places we'd stopped in at. It was heaving with tourists from all over Europe, some heading straight out into the city for early Christmas shopping, others jumping onto connecting flights up to Lapland. We jostled through and sat on a bench away from the crowds. I unslung my big rucksack and took out a smaller laptop bag, placing it on the floor beside it.

'Why don't you grab us a couple of drinks?' I said, pulling a bunch of credit cards from my pocket and thumbing through until I found one with an appropriate name that I hadn't used for a while.

'You're sure Abi will be okay?' she asked.

'She'll be fine, it was much safer for us to split up.'

'Should *we*? I mean, should I get on a later flight?'

'My job is to keep you safe.' I pulled her in close. 'And get you back to England in one piece.'

She pressed into my shoulder. 'How do you do this?'

'It's tough, but I promise airports aren't so bad when you get used to them.'

She pulled away and smiled. 'I mean this job. Why do you stick with it?'

I put on a voice and cleared my throat. 'I don't like work, no one does. But I like what is in the work – the chance to find yourself.'

Alice made a face. 'What fucking meme did you pull that from?' she scoffed.

'*Heart of Darkness*.' I shook my head and smiled. 'I sort of fell into it when I was young.'

'You were never young. You were moulded by Mars in a volcano or something.' She took the card. 'Coffee, yeah?'

'Don't you dare.'

'Two sugars?'

'You want to be stranded in Finland for Christmas, be my guest.'

'We both know there are worse places,' she said as she skipped away.

She'd mostly slept as we'd skirted 2,000 miles of northern Russian coast, hopping between tiny airfields to refuel. The sun had finally made a brief appearance as we'd made our way south, before disappearing again to leave us to fly through the night.

Our pilot seemed to be powered by dried meats and coffee, both of which he'd restocked at each airfield, before spreading out across the back seats and shutting his eyes for half an hour, then jumping up to do it all again. We'd finally crossed into Finnish airspace to land quietly and discreetly at Joensuu, then said our goodbyes.

I'd left Marty to sort out the plane with Jan, and left Abi to go on by train into Sweden. We'd taken a train south to Helsinki, eager to see the sun properly. Now late afternoon sunlight poured through the ornate curved wooden ceiling, lifting our spirits. Outside was crisp and cold and clear, and where there's sun, there's hope.

Alice walked over carrying two takeaway cups gingerly.

'I don't know what the tea's like, looks dodgy.'

'Can't wait to get back to Yorkshire. Proper tea. Long as it's not poisoned.' She looked uncomfortable; I smiled. 'Cheers.'

She tapped her cardboard cup against mine and frowned. 'Where's your bag?'

'Huh?'

'Your laptop bag, it was just there.' She put her coffee down and looked round frantically. I grabbed her arm.

'Sit down, shush.'

'Shush? Someone's stolen your bag!'

'It's okay. Did you see the guy in the green jacket?'

'No?'

'Good. He'd be shit at his job if you did. A friend of mine is taking something for us.'

'I don't understand.'

I gave the tea a stir with the wooden stick and curled up my nose. 'Did you put milk in first?' I took a sip, it wasn't as bad as I'd expected. 'We'd look pretty stupid trying to get through security with a gun in my bag, wouldn't we?'

'So how…'

'Guy I know who works at the French embassy. Diplomatic pouch, I'll collect it from someone at the other end.'

'That's very neat.'

'It's very bloody expensive.' I stood, pulled the rucksack onto my back, and picked up a carrier bag from the floor.

'You haven't told me how we're going to actually get on the plane.'

'My friend traded me these.' I rummaged in the carrier bag and pulled out a French passport. 'Bonjour *Michelle*.'

She snatched it from me and turned to the photo. 'But this is me, how… what…'

I pulled out my new passport and smiled. 'It's good to have people who owe you. Come on.'

Check-in was easy with no baggage, security was no problem with our genuine passports, and a short while later we were sat in the departure lounge of Helsinki Airport waiting for the screens to tell us to board our flight to Manchester. A second cup of tea from the 'Kaffet' round the corner was going down a treat despite not being Yorkshire Tea, and the people-watching was good. Families heading north to see reindeer and northern lights and ice hotels, business people nattering on phones as they hurried to close deals before the Christmas rush. Throngs heading into the book store opposite to buy something to read on the bus or flight home. The bright covers shouted at me. I couldn't take my eyes off one particular shelf.

'How long?' asked Alice.

'You're like a child. It's quarter to five.'

'We've got *ages*. There's a Burger King down the end.'

I winced. 'I told you, no drive-thrus.'

'It's not a… We're in an airport, no one's going to shoot you here.'

'Are you always this blunt?'

'It's over two hours 'til they call it.'

'I just like to sit near the gate, okay?'

'Plus, they call it an hour before the flight.'

'Fine, as long as we can sit down and see the screens.' I pointed at a nearby monitor showing our flight, still on time. *Quarter to five*, I reconfirmed. The screen begged for attention.

'Come on, then,' she said, practically skipping along the concourse. 'Noodles? There's a deli with veggie stuff further on.'

I sighed and set off after her then paused. The book store was still calling me.

'Get a table, I'll catch you up.'

She walked back to me, hand outstretched. 'I need your card.'

'Get some clothes too, but don't go crazy with it. We don't want to draw any attention.' I handed her the credit card and looked at my watch. 'I'll see you in there at half past.'

She walked back off again then darted sideways into the Luhta clothing store while I went the other way into the Suomalainen book shop. I paused at the entrance, feeling the hairs on the back of my neck stand on end. An odour crept up my nostrils, faint but there beneath the coffee and food. The smell of soot, petrol, cooking.

I turned casually, looking at one of the magazine stands while glancing in a window and taking in the reflections behind me. Nothing was amiss until I saw it. A white parka bobbing among the throng of tourists heading towards one of the gates.

I picked up a magazine and turned. The white parka's hood was pulled up, visible above a group of young women standing around their cases. I started to walk sideways, back towards the bench, eyes on the parka, when suddenly it ducked down.

It came up holding a laughing toddler in its arms, who pushed the hood down revealing a middle-aged man's greying hair and blown-out cheeks as he zoomed the toddler around in the air.

I realised I'd been holding my breath. I let it out in one go, blinking to clear the visions, and turned back to the book shop. Past the racks of magazines, I headed for the English books and onto the crime shelf, skipping various bestsellers and Scandi noir thrillers, landing on a familiar cover I'd been subconsciously staring at the whole time.

I picked up *The River Man*, the latest bestseller by a guy I'd never read but whose name I'd seen on book stands in airports around the world for years. Which was the whole point.

After buying the book, a pen and a little notebook, I walked quickly past the clothes shop where Alice was still raking through the rails, and onward to the travel electronics shop. I bought a small radio and a pair of earphones then looked back at Alice. She hadn't seen me, diverting instead into the Duty Free. With Bulgari and Burberry between us and the noodle place, she'd be a while.

I glanced at a departures sign to confirm it was almost five, and made my way quickly back down to the working area. It was full of suited people on laptops and phones. I took a seat at the far end next to the window overlooking the white landscape and ploughed runways, with their lights glimmering now the sun had dropped. The only person nearby was a young woman talking to herself while doing her makeup. Moving a vase onto a table to shield me, I turned on the radio and stuck the earphones in.

I tuned the radio to a shortwave frequency long committed to memory, and leaned back in the chair with my eyes shut. With my hand on the tuning button, I set it scanning up and down, sitting quietly for a while.

It took a couple of minutes but finally I found it. I held the button down to save the frequency and listened carefully.

The electronic tune played over and over again, the Lincolnshire Poacher bringing some creepy folky Englishness to this ice-bound far northern airport. My pen hovered above the blank first page of the notebook. Ten a.m. and ten p.m., Alice had said when deciphering the message in the bunker. That had been in Severnaya, seven hours ahead of GMT. Helsinki was only five hours ahead, which put the broadcast time right about now.

Finally the transmission beeped and the sampled woman's RP voice came across, loud and clear, repeating her groups of numbers over and

258

over. As I scribbled down the numbers I pictured Alice in the freezing boathouse, scrawling in her pad.

I waited until it'd finished then put the notepad on my knees and opened the paperback. A bestseller that was currently on a shelf in every bookshop across England, but more importantly an international bestseller, with the same English-language edition gracing every stand of every bookshop in every major airport around the world, not to mention readily available from various other places. And a book that wouldn't look out of place or suspicious in the suitcase of any agent around the world.

The perfect key to an Ottendorf cipher.

A simple code replaces a word or letter in the message with the location of that word or letter in the book, which is chosen specifically for being one easy enough for the sender, and more importantly, the receiver, to find. In the event an agent loses the book or has it taken from them, they have a good chance of being able to pick up another copy to receive their messages through the one-way transmissions of the numbers station. And now I held in my hand the same edition of that same paperback that Alice had left in the bunker.

Not foolproof, but very difficult to crack unless you have the key. Impossible for someone like me. But then again, I did have the key.

I wrote the original message as I remembered it, at the top of a new page.

Position compromised Stop Phoenix to interrogate and terminate Owl Stop

I was pretty sure on it; I'd held the scrap of paper and had it shoved in my face by Golubev. He'd been wrong about *Phoenix*. Alice had been designated *Magpie*, stealer of secret things, by Mason. He loved his little games, Golubev had been right about that. Games are fun when you're behind a desk, not so much on the ground. Professor Balakin was the wise *Owl*, and I was *Phoenix*, risen from the ashes – again, a fun little reference for him but far less fun for me.

I knew the first bunch of numbers in the transmission would likely be a header with meaningless information, with the actual message starting at some pre-determined point in the sequence. I had the key, but it wasn't the whole puzzle.

With nothing else to go on, I looked at the numbers. Grouped into five digits, it could possibly be page number, paragraph, line number, word number, and letter number?

I worked through various permutations for a while, thumbing through the book. The message started with 'Position'. A couple of times I got a 'P' but never 'position', and whenever I tried the same permutation on the next sequence there was no 'o' to spell the whole word.

I rubbed my eyes and looked out of the window. The snow had started up again, soft fat flakes that floated in the bright runway lights, rather than the glass-hard shards fired across the ice at Severnaya. I checked my watch. I'd been at it twenty minutes already.

I tried the next sequence and blinked. Three-quarters of the way through the book, in the middle of the page, a word jumped out at me before I ran the numbers. *Position*. I double checked, it was correct.

I tried the same permutation and the next sequence of numbers gave me *Compromised*.

I'd been half right. It was page number, paragraph, line number, word number — but in reverse order, with a seemingly random digit added to the end.

I had it.

With the full key, copying out the rest of the message — including the second part which Alice had kept from me — took me just a couple of minutes. I was back among the throngs of passengers in no time, and standing outside *Two Tigers Sushi and Noodles*. Alice was nowhere to be seen. I looked at my watch. I was late, but she'd been shopping.

Or had she?

I looked all around. Still a while until boarding was called. She wasn't in the watch and jewellery shop opposite, or looking at handbags in the boutique on the corner. She had her own ticket and boarding pass, and with that passport and my credit card she could go anywhere. Meet anyone.

My mind raced. Its brakes were slammed on as I passed *Ajisen Ramen* and spotted her huddled in a booth at the back. She looked up from a bowl and smiled as I weaved through the tables. I noticed she was wearing all new clothes, jeans and a sweater, and had somehow managed to wash, buy new makeup and apply it, and make her hair immaculate, all in the time it'd taken me to decode the message. I felt distinctly in need of a shower and some new clothes at the very least.

'You've been *ages*,' she said. 'I didn't know what to get you, but I thought you could just order when you got here. How long to go?'

'Still a while. You've been busy.' I pointed at her bags.

She coughed and took a drink of her water. 'Just some clothes, I've got nothing!'

'And you managed to get engaged, too.' I pointed at her hand clasping her glass, and the turquoise ring on her ring finger. 'Or have you got a husband stashed away that you've not told me about? Do I need to watch my back when we get to England?'

'Oh, Abi gave me that to look after. I did get some earrings to match, though.' She fished in a bag.

I held up my hand. 'Whatever you need, we're going to be lying low for a while.'

'Oh, I got you a present.' She leaned to the other side, reaching into a brand-new colourful Fjallraven rucksack. 'This is what you use, right?' She slid a round orange box across the table. Acqua Di Parma.

'It is, thank you, I need it. I got you something, too.' I sat down opposite her and pulled out the paperback, pushing it across the table to her. Her face went white.

'This is what you were reading, isn't it?'

She touched the book with a fingertip and flinched as if it was hot.

'You left yours in the bunker, I figured you could finish it on the plane.'

Her bottom lip was trembling.

'I'll go and order something.' I pushed the chair back and stood, her reaction had confirmed everything.

I'd binned the notebook. The full message written in it had been clear enough.

Position compromised. Phoenix to interrogate and terminate Owl.

Magpie eyes only

Obtain intelligence from Phoenix using any and all methods.

Terminate Phoenix.

Chapter Forty-three

The Peoples' Democratic Republic of Nambutu / French Equatorial Africa

1999

Benjamin drove the Mitsubishi along the jungle roads quickly and confidently. Perhaps not as quickly as I would have, but that was countered by the confidence. We rounded the corner, Benjamin flicked up into third, hitting 70mph as we bounced through the potholes and puddles. The Mitsubishi skidded, sliding sideways for several seconds before the wheels caught in a rut and shunted us back the other way. Benjamin nailed the accelerator again and settled back into his seat.

The tall trees flashed by, then we were heading down a winding hill with a steep drop through the forest on one side and a cliff face on the right, punctuated by waterfalls tumbling down. Sometimes the streams went under the road, carried below small bridges that spanned gorges; sometimes they cascaded across the road, spraying into the hot air as we raced through.

I turned round to check Elonga on the back seat. Her combats were cut off at the knee, with a makeshift bandage around her thigh. The wound had stopped bleeding but needed attention to stave off infection.

'You okay?'

She smiled a weary smile and went back to concentrating on filling magazines with rounds from a cardboard box on the seat next to her. In the footwell gleamed three new AK-74Ms, the latest upgraded and modernised version of a design classic, pilfered from the arms truck.

'Lusemba,' Benjamin said, pointing through the windscreen.

The outskirts of the town were marked by rough wooden and concrete shacks and low palms, tall grasses and the odd taller trees standing alone. Outside a low tin-roofed building, children in brightly coloured clothes ran in circles laughing, and a group were playing football on a field of brown grass. We passed a lake or reservoir fringed with palms, sparkling in the afternoon sun. I wound the window down to feel the breeze, slapping my pockets for my cigarettes. I pulled out the pack but they were completely crushed.

'Down,' Benjamin shouted.

'Huh?'

I looked round, he grabbed my arm and pointed. 'Police.'

I slid down as low as I could, into the footwell.

'Stay down,' he said. 'You are not inconspicuous.'

'Almost there,' Elonga said. 'No sign of militia yet.'

Benjamin pulled the car to a stop. 'Okay, you go, I'll hide the car,' he said.

I climbed out, stretching, and looked around. We were pulled onto a patch of gravel slowly being reclaimed by the forest. A wide river flowed quickly past in front; on the other bank a few low buildings flanked the road. Spanning the water was a rusty brown girder bridge.

Elonga climbed down, handing me a rifle and turning back to pick up the box of full magazines. 'We stop them at the bridge.'

I winked. 'Even better. We've got the bridge rigged to blow.'

'What? No!'

'Yup. It'll take them an hour to get further upstream to the next crossing.'

'No!' she shouted again, taking a rifle for herself and slamming the door shut. 'This is the only bridge for miles.'

'That's the point!'

'So how will the children get to school?'

I shrugged.

'How will the people on this bank get to the shops?'

I shrugged again. 'Don't you want to strike back at them?'

'At who? At the people who live here? Don't you think their lives are made hard enough by this war, without having to walk for a whole day just to see their family on the other side?'

'But... won't it be worth it for the struggle?'

'This *is* the struggle. Ordinary people don't care about Russians or Americans, they care about getting an education, getting to the shop, being with family and friends. You have exactly the same mentality as everyone else here, you are just the same. It doesn't matter what happens to these people because of the greater cause. These people *are* the cause!'

An engine sounded on the other side of the river. From round the corner of a building a Soviet army truck rumbled down the highway, then another, and another.

'Oh shit,' I said under my breath.

'Move!' said Elonga, limping towards a stack of logs near the entrance to the bridge.

I ran round to the back of the Pajero and opened the boot, grabbing the RPG launcher we'd brought from the back of the arms truck.

'Shift your arse,' I shouted to Benjamin.

I ran and slid down, back against the logs.

'Do you know how this works?' I asked, placing the RPG on the ground.

Elonga put the box of magazines down between us and nodded.

'What if we disable the first truck when it's on the middle of the bridge?'

'It will destroy the bridge.'

'Not if you hit the front of the truck. It'll burn it out and they won't be able to move it for a while, but that bridge is made of steel girders, the fire won't be big enough to damage it.'

'Are you sure?'

'Pretty sure. You disable the first truck to block the bridge, then we jump in the Pajero and head back up to Cherub Rock. If the bridge is blocked even for half an hour, we're home free. They can't follow us on foot.'

I looked back at Benjamin in the Pajero, giving him a thumbs-up. He looked nervous.

Elonga was already loading the RPG. I looked over the top of the logs, there were three trucks full of troops. I picked up the rifle.

'Give it me,' said Elonga, resting the launcher against the logs.

I handed the rifle to her. She cocked it for me and pushed the safety off. 'Don't close your eyes this time, you might hit something.'

I leaned down low, rifle resting across the top of the logs, squinting along the fixed sights. It made a tapping noise on the wood as my hands trembled.

'Ready?' said Elonga.

'Ready.'

I could hear her scuffling in the dirt beside me, in the corner of my eye I could see her moving into position. I kept my attention focused on the opposite side of the bridge.

'Steady,' she said.

The first truck rumbled up onto the far end of the bridge, picking up speed. In the corner of my eye something flashed. There was a bang and a loud hiss, a puff of smoke, and a split-second later the front of the truck evaporated in a cloud of black and yellow. Smoke belched out in every direction, flames leaping skyward.

We both ducked down as the cloud of smoke rolled back over us, raining hot debris.

My ear was blasted by the crack of Elonga's rifle next to my head; she was already up and firing. I put my hands over my ears. Elonga glanced down then squinted back along the sights of her rifle and continued pulling the trigger, emptying her magazine.

They were quick to reply. The ground to the side of me tore open as bullets smacked into the dirt, spraying my face. I pulled in my legs, curling up.

She ejected the magazine and grabbed another from the pile between us, reloaded, and fired again. I rolled away, ears ringing, eyes stinging, head pounding. The bushes next to me shook with the onslaught of bullets from the other side of the river.

Behind us, Benjamin started the car. I watched as all four wheels spun, and the Mitsubishi turned to accelerate away back along the road.

'Go!' shouted Elonga.

The logs reverberated with the impact of bullets.

'Go where?' I shouted.

Elonga dropped down beside me and saw the Mitsubishi speeding away. '*Bâtard*!' she screamed, spinning back around and opening back up on full auto.

'Run, John,' she shouted. 'They are coming.'

I looked above the logs to see the truck through the smoke, still burning in the centre of the bridge, as soldiers climbed around the girders at either side in the haze.

'Run!' she shouted again, reloading.

I picked up my rifle and got to my knees. Elonga squeezed the trigger again and again, screaming endlessly at the attackers. I looked over the logs to see people falling off the bridge, and through the heat haze, more troops disembarking from the trucks on the far side. An explosion ripped the air, water showered down on us. Another explosion came from the bushes to the right, throwing clods of dirt high into the sky.

'Mortar!' she shouted.

I dropped the rifle and curled up behind the logs again, hands over my ears.

Elonga was grabbing another magazine, screaming at me.

'Shoot! Shoot now or we will die!'

She knelt back up and fired again, pouring lead into the bridge as I lay curled up next to her on the dirt. The road behind us lifted into the air like a ball of mud. My breath was torn from me, I was blind, could hear nothing. I rolled around on the ground, blinking tears away. My ears rang, drowning out everything else. Metres away from us a steaming crater had opened up in the road. I looked round at Elonga. Blood streamed from her mouth but it hadn't slowed her down, she was still firing back onto the troops trying to cross the bridge.

The world was strangely silent. I was watching it like a movie, detached. My head felt hot; I put a hand to it and brought it away red. My jacket was torn, and more blood was running down my arm, but strangely there was no pain, everything was distant, like ships on the horizon. I wiped my face, picked up the rifle and squatted next to Elonga, aiming along the barrel.

I squeezed the trigger, the rifle thumped into my shoulder. I couldn't hear the shot, the ringing in my ears drowned out everything else. I squeezed again, aiming at a shape in the haze climbing along the outside of the bridge. I wiped my face, steadied my arm and squeezed again.

I aimed for the green trucks on the other side, squeezing over and over again until the sensation changed and the rifle clicked under my finger. There was no thump on the shoulder. I tried again but this time the trigger just pulled loosely.

Gunfire rose as someone turned the volume back up on the world. I wiped my face and dropped down behind the logs. I looked at Elonga who was reloading again. She rested her rifle against the logs and grabbed mine, pushing a lever in front of the trigger to release the magazine. She dropped it, rammed another in, then flipped the gun over and checked to see I was watching. She pointed at the bolt and pulled it back, released, then pushed the safety lever down. She pressed it back into my arms then picked up her rifle again.

There were just a couple of full magazines left on the ground.

I turned on all fours and fired around the side of the logs at the trucks on the far bank. A soldier was wading into the river, I fired at him a couple of times, forcing him to run back up and take cover behind a bridge support. More soldiers poured out of the back of the truck furthest from the bridge. I pulled the trigger for what seemed like just a few times but it clicked empty.

I dropped back behind the logs and realised Elonga was no longer with me. I looked round frantically; she'd relocated to behind a concrete block to my left, at the end of the bridge. She turned and dropped down behind it, reloading. I looked at the ground.

'Last magazine,' I shouted.

'Go!' she said, pushing off the block and limping back along the road. Blood stung my eyes. I wiped them and peered around the logs. Soldiers were running in all directions on the other bank but had stopped crossing the bridge for now.

I changed the magazine like she'd shown me then jumped up and ran, catching up with her and putting an arm around her shoulders to help her along.

'Head for the wall,' she said, pointing her rifle at a low breeze block wall running at ninety degrees from the road, the remains of a yard for a crumbling shack behind it.

I dragged her along, pushing her down into the weeds behind the wall. She cocked her rifle and pushed down the safety lever.

'That *métis* has left us to die,' she spat.

I wiped my eyes and tried to smile. 'Never trust a dealer.'

'You go. Follow the stream through the trees for three kilometres,' she pointed to a low waterfall tumbling over the rocks behind us, feeding the river. 'The stream will lead you back to the road.'

'And what will you do?'

'I will hold them.'

I knelt up behind the wall and looked back to the bridge. The troops were lining up on the far side, and a couple of them had started wading into the fast-flowing waters with a rope. I lifted my rifle and rested it on the wall.

'I think I'll stay here with you.'

'You have been no use so far,' she said.

I looked at her and frowned. 'This is my first battle.'

The frown cracked into a smile as she rubbed my forehead, wiping blood on her trousers. 'If you don't go now, it will be too late.'

'It's already too late.'

She pulled out a small knife and cut the other leg off her trousers, slicing it into a long strip. 'Turn around.'

She looped the strip of material around my head and pulled it tight, tying it off at the back.

I turned back to the bridge, squinting along the barrel. 'Do I look cool now? Like Rambo?'

'What?'

The two soldiers had reached our river bank, where one was tying the rope off on a tree. I squeezed the trigger twice, the rope went slack as he jumped behind a bush. Elonga fired beside me. The second soldier dropped face down into the mud.

'The material is holding your skin on,' she said. 'I can see your skull.'

'My…' I put a hand up to the bloodsoaked material. 'I can't feel it.'

'You will.' Elonga fired a burst as more troops started to cross the bridge. 'This is it.'

I swung the rifle onto the bridge, hands shaking. I fired a couple of bursts, the troops retreated.

A group were swimming across, I fired again. They scattered, swimming in all directions, making for our bank. Elonga fired into them and a couple flailed as they stopped swimming and were swept downstream. I turned the rifle onto a group on the bridge and fired another burst. As I fired again at the trucks, the rifle clicked.

'I'm out.'

Elonga dropped her rifle. 'I have been out for a while.'

The straggling swimmers had reached our bank. They tied the rope off on the tree and signalled to their comrades. A group of soldiers by the truck carried something down to the water's edge, a piece of billboard or something, and climbed on, hauling themselves hand over hand along the rope to the other side.

As the first group fanned out along the bushes at the river bank, a second group started to cross. Seeing the resistance had stopped, men started to shuffle along the outside of the girders, crossing the bridge. Soon there were twenty or so men along the bank.

I sat back down behind the wall. 'I'm John, by the way.'

'John what?'

'John Tyler.'

'Well, thank you, John Tyler. You extended my life by half an hour.'

I shrugged. 'Better than nowt.'

'It was good to fight alongside you.' She picked up her knife and held it to her wrist.

'Whoah, what are you doing?'

'As soon as I do this, take the knife and do yourself.' She pushed the blade into her arm, her skin creased along it. 'There are worse things than death, do not let them take you alive.'

'Hang on.' I reached into my jacket pocket and pulled out the headhunter's knife. 'Together.'

I pressed the blade into the soft flesh of my left forearm.

She nodded.

The sound of an engine came from behind us.

Elonga pulled the knife, but I knocked her arm away, slicing across the back of her arm rather than her wrist.

'What are you doing?' she asked.

I pressed down on the cut on her arm. 'That's a V6 with a fat exhaust.'

The Pajero roared from the trees as it rounded the corner, driving straight for the bridge. I could see Benjamin half hanging out of the window as he steered. There was a burst of automatic gunfire. We looked over the wall to see soldiers scattering in the middle of the road as the Mitsubishi bore down on them. A group by the end of the bridge dropped in unison as Benjamin turned his rifle on them, steering away with his other hand. Several explosions thumped, mud sprayed into the sky, as he skidded the car round and raced back towards us, tossing grenades out behind him.

More dirt fountained into the air as he skidded to a stop. I ran, hunched over, opening the rear door and reaching back for Elonga. She limped forward, I helped her up onto the back seat and followed even as Benjamin started driving up the road.

I slammed the door shut and lay across the back seat with Elonga, panting. She pushed me off and sat up to look out of the window as I slid down half in the footwell, caught somewhere simultaneously breathing, laughing and sobbing.

'You realise I cannot go back to my house now,' said Benjamin.

Chapter Forty-four

North Yorkshire, England

Present Day

The flight from Finland had been uneventful, but Alice hadn't read the paperback, leaving it untouched on the pull-down table in front of her all the way back to the UK. She'd hardly said a word on the plane, trains and automobiles. I had to wonder whether that was because she was still considering the contents of the message I'd decoded, or wondering whether I knew or not.

Only now, in the darkness near the end of our journey, had she seemed to perk up. The taxi dropped us outside a small brick building with a steel shutter. Its sign said it was a tractor engine specialist. I grabbed our bags from the boot and pulled my jacket on, breath fogging in the cold evening air. Alice was looking around with her nose turned up.

'I did not have you pegged for living somewhere like this.'

I followed her eyeline to the corrugated buildings and timbered cattle sheds. 'Alice, this is an industrial estate.'

'Smells iffy.'

I tapped the taxi's roof and turned to the building as it drove away. 'They're all farm supply places. Come on.'

I put a code into a padlock and swung open a cabinet which housed a more sophisticated alarm. Several beeps later, the steel shutter was rolling up. With one last glance round, I grabbed her arm and pulled her inside.

'What is this place?'

'Just a lockup.' I flicked a switch, the strip lights buzzed on.

The building was no bigger than a double garage. There were no tractor engines, no tools, no parts. The only inhabitant of the garage was a battered-looking long-wheelbase Series III Land Rover, rust and dents in the faded brown paint easily showing in the lights' harsh glare. I opened the door and popped the bonnet.

Alice turned up her nose. 'Is this yours?'

'No, in Yorkshire we just take each other's Landys. Obviously it's mine.' I opened the bonnet and slipped the earth lead onto the battery terminal, tightening the quick-release nut, then dropped the bonnet. 'Get in.'

'Does it work?'

I threw the bags in the back and twisted the key that was already in the ignition. The starter spun a couple of times before the diesel coughed and roared. A nice modern – and importantly, reliable – Ford powerstroke engine.

Alice pulled the passenger door shut, curling her nose up again at the hollow clang. I pushed it into gear and pulled out of the garage, jumping out to lock the shutters.

When I climbed back in, Alice was holding her hands up to the heater vents, shivering.

I tapped the thermometer on the dash. 'It's two degrees, practically tropical.'

'Why does it reek of mould?'

I put her into gear and wove around a trailer, out onto the main road. I indicated and immediately pulled into the farm shop next door.

'Stay here while I get some supplies.'

'Can you leave it running, it's freezing.'

'You've been living in the States too long.'

I was as quick as I could be. When I got back into the Landy, it was noticeably warmer, and yet Alice was still moaning.

'I was led to believe your line of work was lucrative?'

'It can be.'

'And yet you drive this.'

I gave her a look then indicated to pull out onto the bypass. 'If you don't have anything constructive to say then just stay quiet.'

Amazingly she managed it for almost twenty miles, staring out of the window and commenting only on the frost-laden fields and distant peaks, the occasional black sheep on the rolling white patchwork.

'It's quite pretty, isn't it?'

'You never been?'

'I've probably flown over it. Is it all like this?'

I gave her some side-eye.

'Where are we now?'

I indicated and turned right. 'Ingleton.'

'I've heard of that. Ing-gul-tunn.' She repeated it over and over like a toddler.

'Are you high?'

'What?' She drew a face on the condensation on the window.

'Are you high?' I repeated. 'How did you manage to score drugs while on the run, and why did you not share?'

'You don't have to be an arsehole.'

'I'm being serious, what's with you?'

She exhaled loudly and irritably. 'I just flew to Siberia, which is not my first choice of holiday destination. The guy I flew in with got burned to death in his room that night, then you turned up, the man who ruined my life, but is also, hello, back from the dead. That's all bad enough, but then I had to sleep in a dusty old bunker full of ghosts and the guy we were supposed to be bringing back with us also burned to death in the room next door. Oh, and he was killed by a fucking GHOST FROM THE COLD WAR. Then said Seventies ghost attacked me, we ran into the Arctic in minus fucking thirty, got caught, beaten up, escaped, got in the most uncomfortable old truck ever, got chased by a helicopter. Hello, a fucking HELICOPTER shot at us, I slept in a nasty little shed on the ice.' She screwed her face up and started punctuating her sentences by jabbing a finger at me. 'We barely escaped with our lives on the tiniest loudest most awful plane I've ever had the misfortune to climb aboard. I don't know what happens next, I don't know if I'll be hunted down and killed first by either Russian gangsters or the CI-fucking-A. I don't even know what day it is, but it feels like we've been on the move for most of my life, I need a bath and I haven't slept for, like, a week. This was not my ideal weekend getaway, and maybe, just maybe I'm trying to take my mind off it, okay?'

'Well, you did sleep on the plane.'

The rest of the journey was undertaken in silence.

I climbed through the gears and up the hill, a dry stone wall beckoning us onward in the yellow glow of the headlamps. Past solid-looking stone farmhouses that looked like they'd grown from the land itself, ancient cottages clinging to steep hillsides, inns that'd served locals warm beer for centuries. A string of lights passed above our heads and flew out into the darkness as a train made its way over a long viaduct.

Alice coughed and pulled herself away from the window. 'How far away from the world do you live?'

'We're here.'

A string of white painted rocks marked the entrance to a farm on the right. I turned left opposite, onto a gravel track that wound its way up the fell, following it for a minute, then shut off the lights and pulled on the handbrake.

'Why are we stopping?'

I watched the rear-view mirror. An ocean of black surrounded us, deeper than the endless night of the Arctic. From here I could see both ways along the main road – which was in itself a fairly small B-road. 'No tails.'

The heather and tall grass flanking the gravel track leaned over in the gusts, whipping this way and that. As I watched, a patch seemed to grow brighter, I could imagine the colours and contrast turning up until the grass was flaring orange and yellow. Flames leapt up, behind them a silhouette rose, face shielded by the long hood of a parka.

'This is creepy,' said Alice, breaking the spell.

I blinked, then closed my eyes and breathed deeply, gripping the steering wheel tightly. Alice put her hand over mine.

After a full two minutes, buffeted by the wind and feeling the temperature in the Landy plummet, I turned the key and flicked on the lights. Another flick of a switch on the dash and the LED spotlights on the roof rack lit up the expanse of damp moorland either side of the gravel. We climbed up the snaking track for a minute, and as we turned a corner the lights bounced off a derelict farmhouse slowly sinking into the hillside.

'No,' said Alice. 'Absolutely not.'

I looked across at her and steered the old Landy past the crumbling pile. The lights swept across a larger building and onto an attached cottage. I killed the engine and opened the door.

'Well, I've got to give it to you,' said Alice, wrapping her arms about herself. 'It's certainly hard to find.'

I grabbed the bags and a chunky plastic envelope from the back seat and slammed the door, leaving the keys in the ignition. 'Nearest place is the farm, and then it's the pub a mile back.'

'I presume the solitude is on purpose?'

'Necessary.' I unlatched the gate and held it open for Alice. 'A last resort.'

'Does it have electricity?'

Putting the bags down, I leaned over to a wooden birdbox screwed to the wall. I swung it to the right, over the window. 'We even have running water now.' Reaching my fingers round the back, into a cut-out, I fished out a key.

I unlocked the door and stepped into the darkness, taking a torch from a side table, lighting up a hallway, open wooden stairs and a huge antique sideboard.

Alice followed me in and flicked the light switch, which did nothing. 'I thought you said it had electricity?'

'Once the generator's going.'

In the reflected light from a big mirror on the wall I could see her curl her nose.

'It's off the grid,' I said, leading her through the hall, down a step into the lounge.

She walked straight to a bookcase in the flashing light, running her finger over the spines. 'You have enough books?'

'I might not have a lot to do in retirement.'

'Do assassins get to retire?'

I handed her the carrier bag and the torch. 'I'll get the generator going. Got a lot of work to do.'

'I thought we were here to lie low.'

'You are. I have an appointment in London tomorrow.'

'Like hell, I'm coming too.'

'Then you can walk.' I pointed through the lounge window. 'It's 250 miles in that direction. But there's a bus stop four miles away.'

I left her in the lounge and took a key from the drawer in the sideboard, making my way back outside. I shifted our bags into the hall, taking the plastic envelope with me. The clouds prevented even the faintest moonlight escaping, but I knew every stone and walked straight to the garage next door. I ignored the front door and the wooden main door, instead heading round the side to a tiny side door. Inside was even darker, but on familiar ground I moved quickly and confidently along the back wall. I keep my generator fuelled up and well-maintained. A few quick pulls on the starter and we had lights.

I opened what looked like an old electrical junction box on the wall to reveal a grimy keypad. I tapped in nine digits, an interior door thunked as a magnetic lock was released. An electrical whirr started up from the room next door as lights powered on and doors unlocked.

It was a crude alarm system but without the code it'd take someone a long time to get through the steel-reinforced doors, and without power there was no hope of inputting the code.

I carried the envelope through into the main garage and turned on the lights. They fizzed for a moment then pinged on, lighting up several cars, some covered by sheets.

'What the hell's this, you some kind of hoarder?'

Alice was leaning in the doorway behind me, hand at her hip.

'Everyone needs a hobby.'

'It's like a car museum, but for really shit old cars.'

'That hurts more than when you tried to kill me.' I pointed to an angular white sports car in the far corner. 'That over there is a Mitsubishi Starion Turbo. There are only, like, twenty left on the road.'

'Well, I hope you're not counting that one, doesn't look like it'll see a road anytime soon. What's that wreck?' She'd turned to point at a mangled old blue Ford Capri hunkered against the wall at the back, all rusted creases, front end crushed to half its size and no glass left in it.

'You're responsible for the state of that one. Hold this.'

I passed her the heavy envelope and walked to a car-shaped tarp, whipping it off. A dirty grey Audi RS4 estate stared back at us, the first time it'd seen light in over eighteen months.

'Are these... bullet holes?' asked Alice.

I realised I'd been staring at the car for a while. I blinked and shook my head to clear the images.

'I need something fast, reliable and under the radar.'

'Will it run?'

'She needs new brakes, fluids, an oil change and some TLC before morning. How handy are you with a spanner?'

She frowned and put the envelope on the bonnet with a heavy thud. 'Do you think I'm useless? It needs a number-plate too. Do you know how many automatic number-plate cameras there are these days? I presume it's not road legal?'

I pointed to the workbench at the side, and a stack of blank plates. 'We'll make our own.'

'I can do that. Tell me what to do.'

'You know what, you can do that. Listen carefully, there's a laptop in the study. Image search *grey 2007 Audi RS4 car show* and write down as many plates from the pictures as you can.'

'Can you write that down for me?'

'You know what, I'll just do it.'

'No, come on, I'm listening. 2007 Audi RS4 number plates.'

'Then get on the DVLA car tax checker and put those plates in.' I slapped my hand on the bonnet. 'Find cars the same as this one that are currently taxed and MOT'd. Then put *those* in the DVLA MOT checker, it'll give you the mileage between the last and most recent MOTs.'

'You want number plates of cars that have mileages same as this one?'

'The opposite: find cars with low mileages between tests, the ones that look like they're hardly used. No more than a couple of thousand miles a year, chances are they're show queens that get hibernated in garages for the winter. We clone those plates, so there's less risk of that same car being on the road somewhere else at the same time. Boom, every ANPR camera from here to London will register a perfectly legal car.'

'You're wasted in this mercenary business, you know. You should have gone into bank heists or something.'

'I've knocked over a few banks.'

She cocked her head. 'You're serious, aren't you?'

'They're easy, they don't usually shoot back.'

'And you had the nerve to say I was wrong for wanting to make a little money.'

'You just picked the wrong side.'

'Let's agree to disagree on that.' She shook her head as she made her way out of the garage. 'I guess I'll go and start some car fraud.'

I picked up the envelope and walked round the Audi to the Ford Capri. Like all good Seventies cars it was now more rust than steel. I opened its boot and ripped apart the plastic envelope, pulling out my HK VP70 pistol, kindly carried through customs in a French diplomatic pouch and couriered to my hotel at Manchester Airport by a novice French agent. I placed it on the Capri's roof and whipped a sheet out of the boot.

Several weapons were lined up on a piece of old carpet. An SA80 assault rifle, a submachine gun, a couple of bolt-action rifles, a shotgun. All gleamed dully in the garage lights, kept in good order and nicely oiled. Several boxes of varying types of ammunition were stacked along one side of the boot, as well as spare magazines for each gun. I took the submachine gun, an HK MP5SD, and cocked it, pulling the trigger with a satisfying click. I attached the collapsible buttstock and clipped on the sling, then took three magazines and slowly loaded each with Speer Gold Dot 9mm 115 grain hollow point cartridges.

I leaned over the other guns to pull away a snowboarding jacket, revealing a box of grenades and a crate of claymore mines. I dragged the box out of the way. Behind them was a rifle. A Heckler & Koch G28 Marksman, sprayed up white and grey, scratched and worn, hung with torn strips of white material, camouflage against a snowy backdrop. A weapon I'd used on a job a couple of years ago, and that I'd not picked up since. With the Schmidt & Bender scope next to it, it would be perfect for what I had in mind.

I attached the scope and cocked the rifle, holding it up snug to my shoulder, panning across the garage.

'Sweet fucking Christ,' exclaimed Alice.

I lowered the rifle to see her standing in the doorway holding some printouts of number-plates.

'You said you were meeting someone in London, not going hunting!'

I shrugged. 'Why not both?'

Chapter Forty-five

The Peoples' Democratic Republic of Nambutu / French Equatorial Africa

1999

The clearing at Cherub Rock was just as we'd left it. No army, no rebels, no flaming White Demon.

'I think that should hold,' I said, giving Elonga's leg bandage one final pull. 'You need to get going.'

Elonga winced, settling back into the passenger seat of the truck.

'Take this,' said Benjamin, pushing a joint into my hand before walking around the other side of the truck.

'Not sure that's a good idea.'

'For the pain,' he said, tapping his forehead.

'Doesn't hurt.'

'It will.' He swung up into the driver's seat. 'You take good care of my car.'

'Hang on.'

I walked round the back and opened the Pajero's boot, grabbing one of the duffel bags of cash. I carried it to the truck and pushed it into the footwell at Elonga's boots.

'My contribution to the cause.'

She held a fist up and smiled. I did the same then slammed her door. She leaned her arm on the open window and gestured for me to go.

I started walking back to the Mitsubishi, turning to wave.

Benjamin started the truck and wound the window down. 'Hey, John Tyler,' he shouted. 'You are English?'

'Yes, Benjamin Kayembe, why?'

'You can get the new Mitsubishi Evo VI Tommi Makinen edition in England.'

'We need to get going,' said Elonga. 'We have a long drive.'

'It comes out at the end of this year.'

'Drive!' Elonga shouted.

Benjamin put the truck in gear. 'The embargoes make it difficult but you can buy one and drive it down, yes? On the Trans Sahara Highway, I will pay.'

'Listen,' I shouted, 'the next time I come to Nambutu you two will be in charge and you won't have embargoes any more.'

Benjamin pulled the truck round in a wide circle.

Elonga hung out of her window and shouted, 'When you get back to England, do not forget about Nambutu.'

'I'll get a tattoo.'

Elonga smiled. '*Vive la mort*, John Tyler!'

'*Vive la guerre!*' I said, climbing into the Mitsubishi and slamming the door.

I pressed play on my one and only Hole CD, sparked up the joint, then followed the truck up the track and out onto the road. Cranking the window down, I blew smoke out and coughed.

After ten minutes or so, we reached a junction with a highway. The truck's hazards flashed, the horn beeped, they turned down to the left. I flicked the remains of the joint into the bushes and turned right, following a sign west for Zangaro, arm out of the window in a final wave.

I changed up and pressed the accelerator, heading towards the lowering sun over the distant peaks. The trees flanking the road grew thicker, the road grew dustier. I kept the speed down, following the road lost in thought. Several minutes after joining the highway, as I came round a corner, I saw several people in the road ahead. It looked like a crash. I slowed, glancing at the rifle propped in the passenger footwell, and changed down the gears, hoping there were no police.

The group turned as they heard me approaching, then two men detached themselves and came running towards me. My heart skipped as the first looked up and shouted.

'Johnny!'

I pulled on the handbrake and jumped out. My brother ran and lifted me off my feet.

'Where the hell did you go?' he pulled away and looked me up and down. 'What the hell happened, what…'

'Good job you decided to turn up,' said Walshe, taking a swig of beer from a bottle. 'Selfish fuckers wouldn't sell us their car. Jesus Christ, what the fuck shit happened to you?'

'What happened to you, more like,' I said, grabbing the hand hold and swinging up into the driver's seat. 'Get in.'

'We heard shit going down so came to find you,' said Justin, climbing into the passenger seat. 'You'd gone.' He picked up the AK-74M and looked at it, puzzled.

'So you just left me there?'

Walshe climbed in. 'Mate, you'd gone, the car had gone, everyone had gone, we had to fuckin' bug out through the forest before the MVPD arrived.'

'It's the PRVN, you fucking moron,' I said, putting the car in gear and lurching off.

'Whatever. Hey, you don't look so good,' said Walshe. 'Maybe I should drive.'

'Go fuck yourself.'

'There was another team, they ambushed the deal,' said Justin. 'Probably either the ALN or the ARN, it's all gone FUBAR.' He pointed at a road sign. 'The Zangaro border is only ten miles away. Where did you go, what happened to your head?'

'Shit,' I said, one eye on the rear view mirror.

Justin turned and saw what I'd seen. An Army Land Rover was accelerating up behind us.

'Probably not for us. We run, they'll follow.'

'We can lose him easily,' I said.

'Him maybe, but they have radios.'

'This is why we got this car,' I said, squinting into the distance. Another green Land Rover was pulled up on the gravel alongside the road ahead. 'Belts on.'

Walshe turned to look behind and buckled up. I dipped the clutch and dropped it down a gear, ready to accelerate.

'Stay cool,' said Justin. 'Turn down here.' He gripped the rifle with one hand and pointed to a side road marked with a town name. I indicated, slowed, and nonchalantly turned, driving slowly so as not to attract attention. The road curved past a large building. I kept it slow, glancing in my mirror. Nothing.

'Johnny!'

I looked back at the road and anchored on the brakes. A very sunburned man in a white short-sleeved shirt and khaki shorts stood in the centre of the road with his hand up. I noticed several soldiers kneeling in the bushes alongside us, rifles up and ready. Justin's hand twitched on the AK. I knocked it away and took the car out of gear.

'We're fucked,' said Walshe.

In the rear view mirror, the Land Rover came up behind us.

'We're fucked,' said Justin.

I put my hands up above the wheel. 'We're fucked.'

From behind the building strode a man, tall, purposeful, dressed in a well-fitting light grey suit. The pale, sunburned skin sticking out from it matched that of the man's in the road. The corner of his mouth curled upwards as he looked across at us, then muttered something to the first guy, who jogged to the verge. Another dark green Land Rover pulled out from behind the building, the soldiers in the bushes climbed on board.

The suit walked slowly to our Mitsubishi, stopping by my window. I wound it down.

'Good afternoon, gentlemen,' he said in pitch-perfect public schoolboy. 'Would you mind awfully if I cadged a lift?'

'We don't pick up hitchhikers,' said Justin. 'All sorts of trouble.'

Suit glanced at the rifle in the footwell and smiled. 'Yes, well, I gather you gentlemen have had a large dose already this afternoon. Could you move into the back so I can sit up front with young John here?'

'How do you...' I started, but he held up his hand and walked round to the passenger side.

The Land Rover pulled onto the road in front of us, boxing us in. Justin climbed out, Walshe shuffled over as he joined him in the back.

'Now then, if you'll just follow my colleagues,' the man said, climbing into the passenger seat and closing the door behind him. 'You smell terrible, by the way,' he clicked his seatbelt on and turned to me. 'The sky turns a wonderfully dusky shade at sunset, if we hurry we'll catch it over the foothills.'

'We're in a bit of a rush, pal,' said Walshe.

The man in the passenger seat ignored him and looked at me. His eyes flashed the way a shark's do. 'Drive,' he said firmly.

The Land Rover in front started to move, I put it in gear and followed. In my mirror the second Landy behind kept pace with us.

'Well, now, the Tyler brothers and Mr Walshe.' The man turned to look at Walshe. 'Nobody calls you Triple-F.'

'Who the fuck are you?' I asked.

'Just follow the Land Rover.'

'But you're English.'

'I'm Scottish, but for the sake of polite conversation, my name is Major Rupert Holderness.' He turned to Walshe. 'Everybody calls me The Major.' He turned back to the front and looked at me. 'And you, sunshine, are in an inordinate volume of shit.'

Chapter Forty-six

London, England
Present Day

Midweek, Charterhouse Street was busier than I'd have liked, even at this early hour. The sun, dusty through thick clouds, was still sitting below the towers of the Barbican estate. Beeping trucks reversed into the huge bays of Smithfield Market, while crowds of hi-vis jackets shouted up at cherry-pickers fastening premature Christmas lights to streetlamps.

My burner phone buzzed in my pocket. I switched my cardboard cuppa into my other hand to fish it out. A single text message from an unknown number, which I knew was Abi.

In position

I typed a reply, We're on, then pushed it down into my pocket.

The early go-getters were bustling for their offices, wrapped in scarves, steaming takeaway cups clasped in cold hands. The only thing marking me out as any different was the lack of an overcoat over my suit jacket; five degrees centigrade in a shirt and tie is pretty comfortable compared to where I'd been.

Amongst the bankers and lawyers one man stood out, not difficult since he stood taller than most and had a large head, like a sniper's wet dream. I took a sip of tea through the lid, fixating on the back of his huge bald head poking up from a camel coat as he bobbed through the crowds.

The hairs on the back of my neck prickled. I turned but nothing stood out. Nothing except the one guy in the dark suit who'd turned at the same time and was now looking at a restaurant menu. I couldn't make out his face, and chalked it up to paranoia.

Into the narrow canyon between shops and offices, past Charterhouse Square and the Christmas Fair being constructed beneath its skeletal trees, the bald man turned right. I followed and watched him enter a small supermarket, then turned to scan the street again, senses on fire. The man in the dark suit was nowhere to be seen.

I retraced my steps into a narrow gated alleyway next to a shop. Taking one last swig of lukewarm, malbrewed tea, I tipped it into the gutter and took off my rucksack, pulling out a blanket. I sat down, pulling the excess blanket over my suit and head, leaving only my face gazing down. I stood the empty cup in front of me and waited, all the time watching the crowds carefully.

I'd accrued fifty pence by the time my mark reappeared, which was fifty pence more than I'd expected. As he approached, he didn't give me a glance.

'Spare change, mate?' I said, in my very best Van-Dyke Cockney.

'Fuck off, smackhead,' he replied without breaking stride.

'Arsehole,' I muttered.

His shiny patent leather-soled shoes skidded on the paving stones. 'What the fuck did you say?'

I kept my head down as he backed up, head already glowing brighter than the Belisha beacons on the crossing behind it.

He kicked the cup over, scattering coins across the pavement. 'Don't you fucking talk to me, dirty little bastard.'

'Or what?'

He stamped on the cup and swept a ten pence piece off into the gutter.

'Or what,' I repeated, 'Jim Walshe?'

His eyes went wide: first, as he saw the grim hollow of a suppressor poking out from the blanket; second, as he realised who he was talking to.

'You!' was all he could splutter.

'Yes. So you know I'll pull this trigger if you move.'

The blood drained back out of his face just as quickly.

'That centrally heated office is too good for you, you've got fat.'

His lip trembled as he spoke. 'What... what do you want?'

I pulled the gun back under the blanket but left the tell-tale bulge of its barrel pointing at him. 'First, I want you to understand I won't hesitate to put this whole magazine into you and leave you here in the street. How long have we known each other?'

'About twenty years?'

'Twenty-four years, so you know I'll do it. And you know nobody will do fuck-all about it, since I'm dead.'

A couple elbowed past him, tutting. His hands trembled at his sides. He dropped his Tesco bag on the ground as his fingers involuntarily opened and closed.

'We're gonna go for a quick chat. If you do, you'll enjoy Christmas.'

'You gonna kill me?' His voice wavered as he said it.

'Walshe, I could have killed you at any point in the last twenty years, neatly and without fuss. What makes you think I've chosen today to do it?'

'I don't know. But...'

'But nothing. I just want to talk, come with me and I give you my word I won't harm you.'

I stood carefully, letting the blanket drape across my shoulders as I slid the pistol into the shoulder holster under my suit jacket. 'Listen, you're old and fat, with your fucking croissants and your giant festive Dairy Milk that you pretend is a present but really you're just gonna stuff your face before dinner time. I could sit you on your arse before you knew what was happening. You've got like, what, five or six stone on me? I bet you can't run fifty metres any more without sweating and falling over. Doesn't matter anyway, you can't outrun a bullet. Step back.'

He did.

'And pick up your bag, you're blocking the pavement.'

He picked up the Tesco bag like a zombie. I could see a tear reflecting the grey light as it forced itself up the corner of his eye.

I stuffed the blanket into my rucksack without taking my eyes off him then picked up the crumpled takeaway cup.

I handed it to him. 'Don't litter.'

I led him back along the street, past the square, past the loading bays of the market, left along East Poultry Avenue, through the middle of the market itself.

He regained some of his bravado as we headed back out onto West Smithfield, turning towards Farringdon Street.

'Wish it'd been me that shot you,' he said.

'I'm sure.'

'Only I'd have put you down for good.'

'Turn here.' I prodded him into an alleyway that dipped underground. Access to the original markets, more recently to Crossrail workers excavating the new Tube station, and now for construction of the new Museum of London.

'Heard your bird got it same time, too.'

'Stop here.' I reached to a keypad next to a door without taking my eyes off him, and tapped in a code.

'That kraut cyclops was found in a car crash in the Alps. She was a bit of alright from behind, but that face, fuck! Did she take her eyepatch off at night?'

I pulled the door open and jabbed him in the spine, making him cry out in pain. We were into a building site inside the old Victorian general market.

'Still, I always thought you were a woofter like your brother.'

I punched him in the side, he doubled up, wheezing. I had to stand over him for a full five minutes before he could walk again.

Pushing through plastic sheeting, traversing old floorboards and up an echoing staircase, soon we were in a corridor that reeked of decay and manky carpets, still hung with bright but forgettable prints.

'Stand there, face the wall.' I pointed to a particularly uninspiring picture opposite a numbered door and pulled out a key.

'I saved your life,' he said. 'I saved your fucking life, you ungrateful twat.'

'You've been dining out on that for years now.'

I held the door open and waved Walshe into a derelict apartment, shoving him roughly in the back along the scuffed floor tiles. Through a short, grubby hallway, I shoved him again, as he lost his balance and fell into an empty lounge, staggering towards a swivel chair I'd placed in the centre of the floor. Before he could steady himself, I lashed out with my shoe, sweeping his foot and sending him crashing face first into the back of it.

As he was still crying out in shock and pain, I spun him round, locking a wrist onto the arm of the chair with the thick cable ties I had ready. He realised what was happening and put up a half-hearted struggle, but a few slaps later he was tied to the chair.

His head was red and sweaty. 'Fuck me, you are a woofter, aren't you,' he spat when he'd regained his breath.

I walked to the table behind him, picking up a roll of duct tape and a small cylinder.

'Is that what you were doing out there on the streets, wanking off old men for—'

I jammed the cylinder in his mouth and stuck a strip of duct tape across it.

'I am so *fucking* tired of your incessant shit babbling,' I said, tapping him on the head. 'I said I wanted to chat but since I've taped up your mouth, you know that was a lie.' I walked round and stood in front of him. 'We've never had anything to talk about.'

He tried a muffled shout.

'Really, we can make as much noise as we like. These old apartments will be offices for the new museum, there'll be no one working here for a while.'

I removed my jacket and hung it over an old sofa, not wanting to get anything untoward on the immaculate grey Prince of Wales check of my second-favourite suit. I looked at him, adjusted my tie, and reached into the inside pocket of his camel coat to pull out a smartphone. I tapped the screen to wake it up, but the icon spun and denied me entry. It was old-school, no facial recognition here, so I held it on his thumb. I didn't give it much hope, and again it denied me entry. I tried all his fingers, confirming that the only way in was a passcode.

I tossed it on the floor at his feet, walking to the dusty window and looking down onto the road a storey below. The blurred view was of Charterhouse Street again, looking up the way I'd walked. It was even busier now, more hi-vis and suits. Londoners definitely felt the weather had turned, judging by the hunched shoulders, upturned collars, and hands stuffed deep into pockets. I looked at the building just down the street on the opposite side of the road and inhaled deeply.

'You're a racist sexist ableist homophobic xenophobic transphobic fucking I-don't-know-what-else sack of shite. You know this, you know *I* know this, but I want you to understand that I don't like you, okay? I've never liked you, the world will be better without you. Agreed?'

He just stared.

'Nod your head.'

He nodded.

'So you understand that I don't mind if you never leave this room. I have zero vested interest in you using up oxygen on this planet, and in fact since we're having this conversation, it actually works in my favour to kill you. I won't if you do what I say, because I promised, and because of our history. Okay?'

He nodded again.

'Do you know what that is in your mouth?'

Walshe made a noise normally reserved for the less work-safe corners of the internet, mouth full and taped over as it was.

'Yep, it's like a flashbang. I don't need to tell you this, but let's set the scene. A little time now will speed things along later.' I walked round the back of him, tapping him on the head again as I spoke. 'You've been around, you've used them, Christ we've used them together. A flashbang is a less-lethal helping hand to enter a room, but less-lethal doesn't mean non-lethal. This thing goes off, it'll make a real mess of your head. Remember that time in Iraq when Jules dropped one? I saw it roll against his boot. It was the last thing I saw for a while, to be fair, but next time I saw Jules he was missing a foot. Anyway, this is a training flashbang called the M12 Distraction Device. It's cardboard, and a heck of a lot less powerful than the real deal. Think of it as a giant banger.'

I came round in front of him and knelt down.

'You played with bangers when you were a kid, right? You always knew someone whose best friend's sister's boyfriend's brother's girlfriend heard from this guy who knows this kid whose fingers got blown off by one. Never happened to me, but I threw one too late once and fuck me, I couldn't close my hand properly for a week.'

I picked up his Tesco bag and opened the packet of croissants, taking a bite of one.

'If that goes off in your mouth it could kill you,' I said between chewing. 'But to be honest, it'll probably just obliterate your teeth and tear up the soft tissues of your mouth. Permanently deafen you too, I honestly don't know. What I *do* know is that *if* you survive, you'll never eat a croissant again.' I took another bite and wagged the pastry in his face. 'So, I will only ask once, okay?'

He made another gagging sound and nodded.

I placed the croissant on a box and picked up his phone, holding it to his hand. 'Put the passcode in.'

He screwed his eyes shut and flicked his fingers out, knocking the phone away.

I sighed as he whimpered, shrinking back into his chair.

'Listen, you tubby fucker, I said I'd only ask once. Your phone will make things easier, but it's not the be-all. I hope that little act of defiance was worth it.'

I pulled the pin on the flashbang sticking out from the tape, he bucked and screamed as best he could. A soft pattering sound on the laminate flooring announced he'd just let himself go. I dropped the pin onto the spreading wet patch on his lap and walked to the other side of the room with my hands over my ears.

Nothing happened, other than the fat tears rolling down Walshe's face as he sobbed.

'It's in your hands now. Well, your mouth. It has a 2.5 second delay but you're holding the spoon in with your teeth. You let go or let up the pressure and boom.' I shrugged. 'Fuck all I can do.'

He moaned, low and drawn out, as much as he could while making damn sure he was clamped down hard on that lever.

'Since you didn't want to play, I'm leaving now. I don't know how long you'll stay awake for but after a few days it'll literally be painful to be alive. Either you'll fall asleep or the muscles in your jaw will simply fail, and 2.5 seconds after that happens you'll find out what kind of mess it makes.' I reached for the door handle. 'Once it happens – and it will – if you do survive, you'll then have a long wait for someone to find you, tied to a chair with the lower part of your face missing.'

He shook his head gently, afraid of waking the explosive, and made some kind of weird gargling noise in his throat.

'I've seen you play hardball with people,' I said. 'You're a stone-cold bastard who never gave anyone a second chance, why do you deserve one?'

He gargled again and stared into me.

I rolled my eyes. 'Go on then, bring it up again, you did save my life once.' I walked back to him and held the phone to his hand. 'Last chance.'

He looked down at it and tapped the digits. It rejected it but he screamed and tried again, and this time he hit the right numbers and the phone unlocked.

'Good, that's good. Maybe we can still be friends.'

There was a creak in the hallway outside the door. I tensed, hand going for my gun in the shoulder holster. No one was working inside these buildings today, there shouldn't be anyone here. Could always be a foreman, or someone looking for something, but there were no more sounds, which was a hell of a lot more suspicious.

Walshe had heard it too, and was right now praying it was friend rather than foe.

I placed the phone on the kitchen counter, slid out my gun and cocked it, creeping to the door. I slowly moved to the peephole and looked out, recoiling almost immediately with shock.

Chapter Forty-seven

London, England
Present Day

The grubby peephole gave me a cloudy fish-eye view of the corridor, but there was no mistaking who was outside. On the other side of the door, pressed in against the wall, was Gregori, Golubev's head of security, dressed in a good, navy blue suit. The navy blue suit I'd clocked in the street below. My senses hadn't lied, he'd been my tail. Even smartened up and with his hair slicked to one side, the craggy features were instantly recognisable. A thousand thoughts blasted through my head at high revs. *Is he alone, where is his backup? How many of them are there? In a car, or downstairs? How has he found me? Was he staking out Holderness, did he stumble onto me?*

I bundled up all the thoughts and concentrated on the now. His presence would derail everything. He had to be dealt with.

As if reading my mind through the door, Gregori glanced back down the corridor nervously, one hand hovering ominously close to his jacket. He was deciding whether to retreat or continue.

I held my nerve, watching him through the peephole, holding my breath, not daring to blink. After a minute he seemed to relax but made a decision, turning away from the door and creeping slowly in the opposite direction.

I twisted the door handle. Out into the corridor, I jammed the pistol into his back before he even registered the sound.

'Hands out, against the wall...'

Something hit me from behind like a steam train, lifting me off my feet. I cursed myself, I'd been stupid and lax. There'd been a second team member on the other side of the door, out of sight.

I thrust an elbow out and slammed my head back, breaking their hold at the expense of covering Gregori. He turned; I swept a leg up and caught him under the ribs with the toe of my expensive Italian shoes, then turned to face the second man behind me.

A punch knocked me sideways before I did. I reeled and spun, managing to keep hold of my gun. To my surprise, there was no second man behind me. It was Anya, Golubev's bodyguard.

She rushed forward, narrowing the gap before I could bring up my gun. We crashed through the doorway and into the apartment, sliding back onto the laminate in front of a terrified Walshe, still crying into his duct tape. Anya grabbed for my hands, pushing them down. She had gravity on her side, and helped it along by bringing her head down into my face, narrowly missing pulping my nose only by me turning my head at the last second. As it was, she damn near broke my cheekbone.

I bucked, managing to bring up a knee into her stomach. She let out a strangled wheeze as the air was blasted from her lungs, but somehow clung on. I rolled just as a shadow crossed the threshold: Gregori staggering through, clutching what was probably a broken rib.

I used Anya's struggling weight to roll back the other way, dragging my pistol up and firing twice. The suppressed shots sputted into the doorway, blood fanning across the beige wall as Gregori cried out in pain. Anya was recovering, pressing down on me. She growled and tried to nut me again, but this time I pulled my head in, chin at my chest, and instead she smashed her own nose into my head.

There was a rapid phut phut phut of more suppressed shots. Anya screamed and went limp, her breath cutting short. She rolled away to the side, panting, as Gregori loomed over us, gun in his left hand, the other grasping his bloody shoulder. I rolled the other way, sweeping out a foot at him, trying to pull my own gun round to point at him.

My shoe connected with his shin. He staggered, shots going wide and punching neat little holes through an empty bookcase behind me. I rolled onto all fours, pushing up onto my feet, but Gregori came again, tackling me, knocking me flying backwards straight into Walshe.

We tipped over, Walshe tied to his chair landing sideways on the floor with a grunt, me rolling away towards the window, and Gregori going the other way.

I got to my feet a second before Gregori, but unfortunately he still had his gun in his hand, and I did not. Next to him, a wounded Anya pushed herself up onto hands and knees, reaching in her jacket for her gun.

The faint curve of a smile curled Gregori's lip as he moved the pistol down, aiming between my legs. Halfway between us, my pistol sat impotent on the rug.

Gregori squeezed the trigger.

I screwed my eyes shut and looked away.

A blinding flash filled the room. I was suddenly hot, ears ringing. I opened my eyes; between the dancing spots Gregori was flailing around, firing blindly. I dived onto the floor and grabbed my gun, firing twice.

I didn't hear the shot. It was suppressed, so I didn't hear Gregori and Anya's bodies slumping to the floor either. The ringing in my ears carried on, I stretched my jaw, put my hands over my ears, and screwed my eyes shut again.

The pain in my head subsided gradually, but the ringing persisted. I opened my eyes and crawled round to Anya. She was dead. Gregori had taken his round into the head so I knew he was, too.

I stood and looked round the apartment. Red ran from every wall, dripping from the ceiling, pooling on the floor alongside the upturned chair. I looked at Walshe, legs still twitching on the floor as the bottom of his face gaped open. Well, I guess that answers that question. You do die with one of those in your mouth.

Chapter Forty-eight

London, England
Present day

A cold shower works wonders for the soul as well as the body, even one in a derelict old apartment that smells of rot and rat piss. My suit was a write-off; a shame as it'd been my second favourite, but no amount of dry-cleaning would get that much Jim Walshe out. Nevertheless, showered and checked over for holes, and finding none where there shouldn't be any, I felt back on top of things.

Obviously no one had heard the suppressed gunshots or my struggling with Golubev's lackeys, and the short, sharp flashbang would have sounded like little more than a firework down on the street below. There'd have been no indication of where it'd come from, or why, and with the constant construction work going on, I doubted anyone would have batted an eyelid.

Now dressed in work trousers and a hoody, finished with steel toecap boots and a hi-vis vest, I was sitting on the floor at the open bedroom window. I snapped off a piece of Walshe's giant bar of Dairy Milk and looked out the window at the people on the pavement opposite. As I chewed, I glanced down at Walshe's unlocked phone, and the message string.

Walshe Need you at the office

Holderness In a meeting soon

Fifteen minutes had already passed.

I shifted and got comfortable, scanning the faces walking below. Something flashed in the corner of my eye. I looked into the shadows on my side of the street, down by the wooden hoardings across an alleyway. A flicker of white, a parka. The chemical scent of burning tickled my nose. I tensed, the shape moved, almost waving up at me.

I blinked. It was a white plastic rubbish bag, trapped in the wood and flapping in the breeze. There was no burning smell, no white demon, nothing but commuters and shift workers.

I stood and stretched, taking a swig of water from a bottle on the side. I poured some onto my hands and ran it over my face then sat down, lifting a small pair of binoculars to my eyes. Twenty minutes had passed. I picked up the phone to type a message when my senses tingled again. I raised the binoculars and smiled, snapping off another piece of chocolate.

I hadn't seen the man for almost exactly two years, since a parting argument on a destroyer off Scotland, but even in his civvies Colonel Rupert James Algernon Holderness, MBE, RVM, CMG was unmistakable. I'd seen him out of uniform so infrequently that I'd have put money on him sleeping in it, were it not for the creases you'd cut your thumb on. Now, in a tweed suit, brown mac, and close-cropped grey hair under a flat cap, he'd look more at home at the Windsor horse show than central London. But while most other post-rush-hour bodies in the street were strolling, he was striding purposefully like a dressage prize-winner. Holderness never strolled anywhere, and today he was positively racing.

I looked across to the opposite side of the road, a short distance along, at the old Port of London Authority building. Its pale stonework gleamed in the crisp cold, the blue lettering across the front glittered as the sun finally hauled itself over the rooftops.

The dates beneath the circular windows on each side of the building said 1914, but I knew the frontage hid a modern interior, I'd been inside plenty of times. The port building and old cold meat storage now housed power generators in tunnels four storeys underground, but above ground was offices. On the top floor was Holderness's department office where work could be undertaken away from Whitehall. A place to meet less desirable employees and contractors. Undesirables like me. The place where so many times I'd been summoned to embark on another job for him and this bloody country, or so I'd thought. How many had really been for the British government? Had I unwittingly been a Russian pawn? It didn't bear thinking about.

A silhouette flitted past a window on the top floor. Down on the street, among the columns fronting the adjoining cold store, a group of workers were enjoying a cig break. I leaned closer to the window and looked down, directly opposite them, at my side of the road. Pulled in against the wooden hoardings blocking in the construction site was a shiny new Mercedes saloon.

I waited until the back of Holderness's head bobbed in front of the big glass windows, his arm reaching for the door.

I dropped the binoculars, typed a messaged on Walshe's phone, and pressed send.

Walshe In the Merc across the road.

Holderness pulled the door open and disappeared inside. A couple of seconds later, he reappeared wearing a pair of glasses. He looked down at his phone, then took the glasses off and looked across the street.

I dropped the phone and shuffled behind an upturned dining room chair, picking up my rifle. I rested it on the chair, business end of the barrel just inside the open window, then leaned forward to look down the scope. In the corner of my eye, on the floor beneath the window, Walshe's chocolate begged for my attention. Something shouted out from behind the purple wrapper. I breathed deeply and tried to push it from my mind but it refused to budge, like a hangover from a nightmare.

I blinked and put my eye to the scope, panning across the big windows of the building next door until I hit light grey stone, a wooden door, and then Holderness himself, still wagging his reading glasses as he looked at the car.

Every feature was crystal clear in the magnified scope, every crease of his face, the glint of winter sun in his cold blue eyes, the hint of condensation on his moustache.

Cadbury's.

I blinked and stared at the chocolate. With the gun balanced on the chair, I removed my plastic gloves, dropping them on the carpet. I shook my head and settled back in behind the rifle. The illuminated reticle danced around Holderness's head as I flicked off the safety.

Confusion still showed on his face as he looked across at the Merc opposite. He put his glasses on and looked at his phone again, then back at the street.

I gently took up the pressure on the trigger.

Gradually the faintest smile cracked his face, washing confusion away. He took the glasses off and pushed them into an inside pocket, looking up at the buildings, scanning the windows, landing on mine.

Gotcha.

I squeezed the last tension out of the trigger, feeling the release as the rifle shunted back into my shoulder. Holderness dropped as I dropped the rifle; I was slinging on my rucksack and pushing through the door while the sound of the shot still echoed between the tall buildings.

Chapter Forty-nine

London, England
Present day

A short jog through the construction site, and I was back out into the bustle of West Smithfield in time to hear the first sirens. I moved quickly along the side of the market, cutting back through East Poultry Street, to end up back on the road only a stone's throw from the shouting crowds swarming outside the Port of London Authority building. I didn't look to the side, didn't need to; blue lights pulsed across every window in the street as police converged on the area.

Instead I walked straight across the road to a modern yellow stone wall joining two much older buildings either side. The wall was decorative, the steel fencing extending two storeys behind it was not. A glance to my right revealed flashing cars were closing the street off, a revving engine pulling up sharply belonged to a police van. Firearms unit, backup for the armed first responders in the Volvo down the other end of the street. People were being ushered towards hastily erected cordons.

I pushed through several workmen standing around not knowing which way to go, and headed for a black wooden door set into the wall. A few taps on the access keypad and I was through to the other side, closing it behind me.

I walked across scaffolding, down flights of metal steps, pulling a fake ID from my pocket and looping the lanyard around my neck. I took off my rucksack, and as I stepped off the bottom, I took a hard hat from it and put it on my head.

The railway tracks extended towards Barbican to my right, but I headed left under the new Farringdon station. On careful lookout on this busy stretch of track, ducking back alongside the high walls to dodge trains, I made it through into the older part of the station. Sticking to the walls, I went straight through, barely eliciting a glance from commuters and station staff alike in the ubiquitous hi-vis and hard-hat combo. Out the other side, still sticking to the high brick wall, I took a metal staircase two steps at a time and emerged on a quieter lane off the main road.

Pulled up on double yellows a few metres away sat a silver-grey Audi RS4, burbling away to itself. I took off the hat and hi-vis, opening the passenger door.

'Any problems?' Abi asked.

I tossed the jacket and hat on the back seat. 'None.'

'And it's done?'

I nodded grimly. 'Drive.'

She slipped the car into gear and pulled into the continuous traffic jam as more sirens wailed behind. We headed south down Farringdon Street, over the river via Blackfriars Bridge, past more oncoming police, between gleaming towers, picking up speed towards Clapham. At Wimbledon, we diverted through the centre of town, past an optician and a bookshop, full of people living normal lives, untouched by spontaneous combustion in Siberia, or even a shooting in Farringdon.

We pulled off the A3 and swapped places near Guildford, picking up speed, rapidly putting more distance between us and the city.

We were on a route I knew well, a run I'd done countless times. I turned north on the A331 within shooting distance of Aldershot, home of the British Army. At the imaginatively named town of North Camp, I pulled off the highway, heading straight into an industrial park, all steel fencing and high-stacked timber yards. Rather than follow the road, I pulled onto a rough gravel lane past a prefab concrete structure that spoke of its military origins. I jumped out, leaving the engine running, to remove a padlock and swing open wide gates in the high steel fence, then burbled the Audi through and round the side of the building.

A barrack block, dirty beige partially clothed in ivy, and where the walls were visible, they were cracked and peeling. The windows were opaque, thick with decades of grime and frames rotted with mould. The asbestos panels up top were so thickly covered in moss it could count as a living green roof.

'What the hell is this place?' asked Abi.

I killed the ignition. 'A sort of safe-house. We need to get the car off the road for a while, give her a makeover before we move on.'

'A makeover?'

I climbed out and beckoned for her to join me. 'Chance to get some food and rest. The shit's gonna hit the fan, they'll throw everything at trying to find us.'

'At *you*.'

'Yes, *me*.' I tapped a code into a keypad and retrieved a key for the door. 'But if you want to make a clean exit, you'll do well listening to me.'

I opened the door and turned, but she just stood next to the car, staring.

'Excuse me, I don't do as I'm told. I do as I'm asked, *if* I'm in the mood and *if* we're friends.'

'Sorry, I'm not in the best of moods right now.' I nodded inside. 'But I can offer you a brew and a biscuit.'

'Good enough.'

She followed me inside, I turned on the lights on a small entrance hall, the modernity of which jarred with the exterior. Tiled walls and laminate flooring were dusty but not dirty. Doors led right and left – the barrack block had been split into two units.

'They're like tiny apartments, for accommodating people outside the city,' I explained. 'Excellent transport links, good access to London and the south coast, and an Army camp on the doorstep, should you need it.'

'You trying to sell me one or what? No chance someone's home?'

'They hardly get used, to be honest. Plus, the gates were locked when we came in.'

I opened the door on the right into a musty apartment. The lack of opening windows meant the place was reliant on the air con for moving air around, and a lack of occupants for what could have been months meant it was pretty stuffy. I turned on the heating and the lights.

'Bathroom is straight on, there's a kitchen to the left. You get the kettle on, I'll move the car under cover.'

'Roger.'

I went back out and pulled the car forward under a tarp and next to several strategically placed scrap cars slowly being consumed by weeds and the elements, and took a suit bag and the HK MP5 from the boot. A helicopter swept overhead towards the Army base, I looked up at the sky and cocked the submachine gun.

When I went back in, the kettle was bubbling away nicely and the bathroom door was closed. I put my pistol on a side table and sat in a chair, closing my eyes and losing myself going over everything in my head. I hoped to hell my hunch had been right.

'I said, I presume you want a tea?'

Abi had reappeared, damp hair slicked back and fresh clothes on. She started doing her makeup in the lounge mirror.

'Please.'

I went into a bedroom and stripped off the work gear, had a quick wash, and ten minutes later I was in my new favourite suit, bumped up from third position following the other two being lost at the bottom of the Kara Sea and covered in Jim Walshe respectively.

Abi was back at the mirror with her makeup when I returned.

'You scrub up well,' she said, nodding to a mug of tea on the coffee table.

'Likewise.'

'I think I prefer the rugged version. Although this model doesn't smell like oil and blood. Drink your tea quickly before it goes cold.'

I held up my hand, she looked puzzled. I put a finger to my lips.

A scraping sound came from the hallway.

Abi put the makeup down and crouched behind the sofa. I picked up the submachine gun and pointed to my pistol on the side table. Abi picked it up and crouched back down.

I looked through the doorway, into the hall, and at the door handle for the apartment. It began moving down.

I sidestepped to the wall and waited.

The door creaked open, a pair of shoes tapped the laminate as someone walked cautiously into the apartment. Single pair of shoes, no more. Abi glanced over at me, eyes narrowed, face set. The shoes stopped right outside the lounge doorway.

Chapter Fifty

I looked at the door as boots echoed closer along the corridor beyond it. My tiny sick bay wasn't exactly the standard of hospital I was used to, but it was clean and tidy and stank of antiseptic, which was everything I needed. I put a hand up to stroke the padded dressing taped across the front of my head, carrying it on across the top of my fresh buzz-cut. I couldn't get used to the feel of a shaved head. Finally the boots in the corridor stopped and the door swung open.

'Chop chop, sonny.' The burly Glaswegian in the tight, short-sleeved shirt, who I'd learned was actually a Royal Marine, flicked a thumb over his shoulder as he held the door open. 'Tyler, is it? That a first or a last name?'

I sat up on the bed. 'It's the only name you need. Now fuck off, I'm injured.'

He stormed into the room and grabbed my arm. 'The Major isn't, and it's his time you're on now.'

I winced. 'Okay, okay.'

I shook his arm off and swung my bare feet down onto the tiled floor. They'd sorted me out with some new clothes but I'd kept hold of the waxed jacket. I pulled on a pair of too-big combats and khaki T-shirt and looked at myself in the mirror. I couldn't tell if I'd aged in the last few days, or it was bruising and ingrained dirt.

I picked up my new lucky jacket and padded after the Marine. Like Benjamin Kayembe's place where we'd stolen his car, this country house was in the French colonial style, but unlike his drug den was immaculately maintained. I was led along a pale blue corridor hung with paintings that seemed weirdly out of place: portraits of Victorian colonial overlords, Belle Époque Parisian scenes, sailing ships. I could only conclude the ARN had a serious hard-on for the Second Empire.

Wide fans spun across the ceiling that did nothing to assuage the evening heat. Holderness had described this place as a rebel encampment, but it was not the camp fires and tents strung between trees I'd had in my mind. The ARN were considerably better equipped than rival rebel groups, and we were deep into their territory, almost straddling the border with neighbouring Zangaro.

We stopped, the Marine knocked on a minty green door.

'Come.'

He opened the door and stood aside.

'Thank you, Bates,' said Holderness. 'Now then, Tyler.'

I stepped through and looked around the room. Holderness was sat behind an expensively old-looking mahogany desk, which obviously wasn't his, judging by the pictures on it. Likely the commanding officer of the rebels. Behind Holderness, the wall was decorated with newspaper clippings and a huge map of Nambutu with little stickers stuck all over it.

Dust danced in the last deep golden rays of evening sun streaming through the wooden blind. The window gave a slatted view out into a wide grassy area where several soldiers milled around laughing, smoking, sharing a joke.

Holderness had stripped down to his shirt, his suit jacket hung on a stand by the door.

'This damned heat,' he said, loosening his tweed tie. 'Well, close the door, then.'

I shut the door and stood in front of his desk, rigid with my arms behind my back.

'Please don't stand like that, Tyler. You're a civilian.'

I relaxed a little. 'Where's my brother?'

'Where's my brother, *Sir*. You may be a civilian but I am your better, Tyler, and you should not forget that. Do not mistake hospitality for amity.'

'Where's my brother, *Sir*?'

307

'The Chuckle Brothers are currently eating the finest *Poulet Moambe* north of Angola.' He pulled at his tie again. 'You will be joining them soon, provided your answers satisfy me.'

'Thank you, *Sir*.'

He looked up at me from under his eyebrows, trying to decide if I was being sarcastic or not. 'How's the head?'

'They glued it up pretty well.'

'You have the indestructibility of youth on your side, and heads always bleed more than they have any right to. No ill effects?'

A thousand cuts, burns and bruises. 'I'll mend.'

'That depends very much on whether you know anyone who can calm down these soldiers. They're out for blood.' He nodded at the window. 'Do you see that man out there?'

I looked outside, past the soldiers, at a man talking furiously into a huge satphone with a whip antenna as long as his body.

'The suit?'

'Bravo. That is Mr Mason. Mr Mason represents our cousins across the pond. They have very deep pockets. Mr Mason has come here with several rather neat little bags filled with bank notes. I had promised him he could exchange those bags for a truck containing lots of shiny machine guns and rocket-propelled grenades and explosives, which he would then gift to his friends out there in the Army of the Republic of Nambutu.' He picked up a stained mug and lifted it to take a drink, turning up his nose as he saw it was empty. 'I know you're not a military man so I'm keeping it simple for you, are you following so far?'

'Maybe draw me a picture, too.'

He stood and slammed the mug on the desk, breaking off the handle. 'Are you simple, lad? Did that shrapnel carry off some of your brain?'

I wasn't sure of the better answer, so kept my mouth shut.

Holderness tossed the broken mug handle onto the desk. 'How exactly are they supposed to fight the good fight if they do not have the means to do so?'

'The deal went wrong, they were ambushed.'

'You were supposed to ambush *them*.'

'There was another team there, they got in first.'

'I don't care about another team, I don't care if the deal went wrong. I hired you to provide a service, and provide it you have not.'

'You hired us?'

'Sweet Lord.' He waved in the air. 'A word in someone's ear here, a little suggestion there. The point is, I've been following your little jaunt with interest. So where is that truck?'

I shrugged.

'Do you want to go outside and explain it to these men? They only speak French, mind.'

'*Oui, je serais heureux de leur parler.*'

Holderness came around the desk and grabbed my arm. He dragged me to the door and opened it, storming into the corridor and through the mansion's front door, outside into the dirt parking area and onto the patchy grass. The foothills wrapped around the camp like a tiny bowl-shaped valley, the damp leaves of the trees surrounding us sparkling gold in the setting sun.

A couple of the soldiers turned to watch us then quickly looked away again.

Holderness beckoned to the guy in the suit, Mr Mason, who started walking towards us. He handed the satphone to a soldier and pulled out a pack of Lucky Strike cigarettes.

'Can I have a cig?' I asked.

Mason flicked a Zippo and sparked up, breathing in deeply. He ignored me entirely and looked at Holderness. 'This the little dipshit who took my guns?'

Holderness nodded. 'Take him round the back of the building and shoot him.'

The Major started walking back inside. Mason called to a couple of soldiers. I looked at him but he avoided my eyes. He spoke rapidly in French to them, one unshouldered his weapon and pointed it at me, wagging it to the side.

'Hang on, woah, hang on,' I said.

309

Holderness turned. 'I do not play games. Over one hundred thousand people go missing in England alone each year. Do you really think anyone on this entire continent will give one solitary shit if a scruffy oik of an English teenager ends his evening face down in a ditch?'

I tried to reply but my voice had dried up.

'Major!' One of the soldiers shouted from the far side of the grass. I turned to see a group huddled at the back of our diminutive Mitsubishi 4X4, and died a little more inside.

'Come with me, boy,' said Holderness.

I followed him across the cracked dirt to the mud-spattered car. One of the duffel bags sat open on the ground, its contents plain to see.

'Well now, what is this, young Tyler?'

I cleared my throat and did my best to stop my voice cracking. 'My money.'

'Your money, is it?' He waved the soldiers away, then leaned back against the car. 'So you lied to me. You actually pulled the job and then sold my truck?'

'I didn't lie. And I didn't exactly sell it.'

'Explain it to me. With *pictures*.'

'I gave the weapons to the ALN.' I looked down at my feet.

'And why would you go and do something like that?'

'Because they care about the people.'

'Oh, he has morals...' He burst out laughing. 'My sweet summer child, no one gives a tin shit about these people.'

I looked up. 'You're wrong. I do.'

'You're naive.' He kicked the bag and looked at the other two sat in the boot. 'How did the ALN cobble together this kind of money?'

'This is the Russians' money.'

He cocked his head. 'You heisted the entire arms deal? Three of you?'

'Nope. Just me.'

He stroked his chin and looked at the bags again. 'Well, now, I can't say I'm not impressed. But you see, this puts us in a delicate position.'

'Why so?'

'Never mind. You know, it strikes me that you could do with a friend about now. See these soldiers, and that nice man from the CIA over there, they were expecting you to turn up with that truck full of arms, so they don't like you very much at the moment.'

'They've still got their money, they can buy more.'

'I'm afraid it doesn't quite work like that.'

'Just let us go and we'll leave right now.'

'And go where?'

'Back home.'

'To do what? See, I've already made a few telephone calls. You're awaiting a date with the Admiralty Interview Board, eh? Fancy yourself a flyboy in the Fleet Air Arm?'

'That's right, Sir.'

'Your application has been terminated.'

'What?' I put an arm out to the car to steady myself as the ground tilted beneath my trainers. 'Why? But…'

'Even the Royal Navy do not employ outright thieves and murderers. I have already informed your brother and Mr Walshe that they have been dishonourably discharged, effective immediately.'

'You can't do that!'

'Oh, can I not? Here I am judge, jury, and I can also be executioner if I'm in the mood. So you tell me, what would you do with three young fools who have well and truly flushed several months of work by British Intelligence down the khazi?'

'I don't understand.'

'I have not yet decided whether we will instigate criminal proceedings against you.' He held up his fingers and ticked them off. 'Trade with a sanctioned country and breaking the foreign enlistment act for a start, then we have the charges here to consider. Arms dealing, profiteering, black market trading, numerous weapons violations, probably armed robbery and murder.' He waved at the foothills encircling us. 'It would be costly to the taxpayer to try you in England and then extradite you back to Nambutu. I may simply turn you over to the Commissaire.'

'But that's unfair, that's—'

'My boy, the dildo of consequences rarely comes lubed. I did tell you that you were in an *inordinate* amount of shit.'

'But you're doing just the same thing.'

'And this is why you need better friends.'

He let the silence continue for a full minute, before going on.

'Would you like better friends?'

'What do you mean?'

'You've put me well and truly in a pickle, a very large pickle, I can tell you. And you have ruined an operation. By my count, you owe me.'

'Owe you what?'

'It just so happens I have an opening. I may be willing to overlook certain things, if you do certain things for me in return.'

'What... kind of things?'

'My God boy, what is wrong with your brain? I want to employ you.'

'Doing what?'

'I'm always looking for people with talent. You're rough, insubordinate, definitely obnoxious. You'll need a lot of training but I believe there *may* be a grain of talent hidden beneath that.'

'So... you want me to work for British Intelligence?'

'No, my boy, I want you to work for *me*. I'll worry about the rest.'

'Doesn't sound like I have much choice.'

'Ah! You are as perceptive as your brother. You will find there are many benefits to being my friend.'

'Is one of them food?'

'Go and join your brother. We'll discuss what to do with you later.'

I pushed off the car and took a step across the dirt towards the building, knowing full well he'd just set me up and fleeced me good and proper.

'Tyler the younger, are you forgetting something?'

I turned.

He tapped the duffel bag with his shoe. 'Take my money into the office.'

'*My* money. I worked hard for that.'

'I have no doubt, but you work for me, which makes it mine.'

'I'll make you a deal. I'll work for you if we can keep the money.'

'I'll make you a counter deal. I will let you keep whatever notes you can pick up off the floor after I've had Bates break every one of your fingers.'

'I think I'll just take your money inside and get some food.'

'You're learning, but we need to work on your negotiation skills.'

Mason, the CIA man, had walked up behind me while we'd been talking.

'Major, you've got a visitor,' he said, nodding across the grass back towards the building.

'Who is it?' he asked.

'Some Russian.' Mason nodded.

I looked and saw Bates and a group of soldiers escorting a man across the grass. Bedraggled and filthy, I recognised him as one of the men from the arms deal, obviously now conscious, and livid.

Holderness raised his eyebrows at Mason. 'He's on his own, stay alert.' He glanced behind at the soldiers, nodding. 'Now then, my boy, get yourself out of sight.'

'Who is he?'

'Just some Russian agent, fancies himself a bit of a dealer but he's strictly Mickey Mouse. But this, my boy, is the pickle I spoke of.'

'Why is he a pickle?'

'Apparently his brother is a psychopath, and you've just stolen four million dollars from them.'

'*You* stole,' I said, backing away round the back of the Mitsubishi. 'It's your money.'

'Aha, you're a fast learner,' he said out of the corner of his mouth. 'Your problem has become my problem, I told you there'd be benefits if you stick with me.' He walked towards the man with his arm outstretched to shake hands. 'Good evening. Can I help?'

'My brother is dead.'

I couldn't see the Russian's expression from where I was hiding. I peered round the car to see he had his back to me. He shifted on the balls of his feet, tensing up.

'I'm sorry.' Holderness retracted his arm and lowered his voice. 'It had nothing to do with me.'

'You gave your word!' he spat.

Holderness growled low. 'Remember where you are.'

'Your word,' he said again, lower. 'You crossed me.'

'I gather your deal went south?'

'You were supposed to ambush truck after deal, not during! It was slaughter, I wake up tied in rebel camp where they're burning survivors alive, I barely escaped...'

Holderness shook his head. 'My team were ready and in position to lift the arms when you were clear. You were attacked by the ALN.'

'Then why did I see this car leaving?' The Russian slapped a hand on the Mitsubishi's bonnet.

Holderness tutted. 'It's a nasty business right enough. If you can't keep up then maybe arms dealing isn't for you.'

'I will take money or there will be consequences.'

'I'm sorry for your loss,' said Holderness, 'but you were a fool to come here. What did you think it would achieve?'

The Russian was silent for a moment.

'Revenge,' he said simply. Which was when the shit hit the fan.

Chapter Fifty-one

Hampshire, England
Present day

'Tyler, I'm coming in,' said a familiar voice from the hallway beyond the door. 'I trust you're not going to shoot me in the back.'

Abi stood, pistol outstretched, but her face dropped as she saw who opened the door, cycling through confusion, anger, bewilderment... It was a joy to watch.

I stepped out from round the corner, gun held down low. 'Colonel.' I nodded.

Abi looked from Holderness to me, then back again. 'I thought you were dead.'

'I know exactly how you feel, lassie,' said Holderness. 'I thought he was dead.' He nodded at me. 'You're looking remarkably well for it, Tyler.'

'Time away can do that, but you wouldn't know, would you? Work people into the ground, literally, then move on to the next. How many have you been through since I died?'

'There'll never be another John Tyler. There'll never be another Jim Walshe either, for that matter. I've seen some sights in my time but that will take some beating, so you'd better have a bloody good explanation.'

'That wasn't me.'

'I know you two have always been at loggerheads, and the man stuck around like a fart in a lift, but he worked for *me*.'

'You need a dirty job doing, get Tyler to do it. Need a downright fucking filthy job doing, send Walshe. Morals of a shark with none of the redeeming qualities.'

'And just as useful for it, so start talking before I have my men come in here and put you down on the spot.'

'I don't understand,' said Abi. 'How are you even here? I saw the police, we heard it on the radio. I even heard the shot, for Christ's sake.'

'The Russians killed Walshe,' I said. It was only a half-lie. 'I'll explain everything but right now there are more important things going on.'

'Yes, like you shooting at me! You've a bloody cheek, I'll tell you. You'd better have a damn good reason or you won't see the comfort of a prison cell, trust me.'

'I've broken a vow I made two years ago by doing this, so you better be bloody grateful.'

'What's going on?' asked Abi, more insistently.

Holderness didn't look at her, instead addressing me. 'It took us minutes to get to that old apartment in the building opposite. Your prints came back in even less time. You can imagine my surprise to learn a corpse was shooting at me. Worse, a corpse who *works for me.*'

His voice was rising now, in that way it did whenever he started losing his grip on one of his carefully prepared speeches, with his Doric Aberdonian accent creeping in under the RP. He inhaled deeply and took a second to regroup. When he had, the King's English was back in full effect.

'Of course, I never really believe anyone is dead unless I see a body, and you were always my Captain Scarlet. John Tyler doesn't miss, I thought, not from that distance, not that angle. It was an easy shot, the contents of old Algernon Holderness's favourite son should be painted across the door of that building. So I started thinking...'

'Always dangerous,' I said.

'The rifle was fully loaded but only one shot was fired. Stevie Wonder couldn't have missed, but let's say you've lost your touch – you could still have put several bullets into me on the ground. You removed your gloves just before pulling the trigger. You knew the apartment would be found, you knew your prints would flash up brighter than a Christmas tree. And then your car – the very same car you were last seen in on that fateful morning a couple of years ago – shows up on ANPR heading here. Oh, you switched the plates, but as soon as I saw that old grey Audi was in the area, I knew. Didn't take a genius to figure out you were heading here.'

'Well done.'

'So, you intended to send me a message. A very pointed message, and a very personal one, given the state of Walshe. Let's get to it before I lose my patience.'

I nodded, raised the submachine gun, and swung it onto Abi. 'Show me your leg.'

'What?' She swung the pistol onto me.

'Unbutton those jeans and show me your leg.'

'Get fucked.'

'Come on, we're not prudish and I think we're way past civility. Show me your right leg.'

'Tyler, if you've asked me here to see a young lady's legs, I must assure you, firstly that despite what you may think, I have seen such things before, and secondly, I do not think that ordering a young lady to undress at gunpoint is appropriate.'

'That slash on your leg, when I landed in Siberia. Chasing a phantom across the ice. That wound bled a fair bit, I imagine you don't heal that quickly.'

'When did you know?' she asked.

'I didn't, not until I was in the apartment. But something was nagging me. You said something on the plane, something about me killing the man responsible for my brother's death.'

'What are you talking about?'

'I can see it clear as day. You sat on that plane wrapped up in a blanket with half a bar of Cadbury's hanging out of your mouth. I don't know why but it stuck in my head. It wasn't until I was looking down that scope that I realised, you'd said Alice had told you. But Alice didn't know, I never told her the information Balakin had given me. So how the hell did you know my next stop was to try to kill the Colonel here, and why?'

'I don't mind finishing the job.' Her face turned into a sneer, she waved the pistol almost imperceptibly and flexed her fingers, squeezing the trigger slightly. 'I can finish the fucking job on both of you.'

'Oh, he does this.' Holderness smiled. 'It won't be loaded.'

'I'll do it,' she hissed.

'Trust me, lassie, he did it a couple of years ago with another stupid bloody cow.'

I flinched when I pictured Alice.

'Do it, pull the trigger, shoot.' Holderness seemed to be enjoying himself now.

The pistol clicked. Abi's eyes narrowed. She pulled the trigger again, another impotent click.

'Don't feel bad, it's a classic,' said Holderness, chuckling. 'It just means he didn't trust you.'

'This one's loaded though,' I said, waving the gun in my hands, 'and I won't hesitate to shoot both of you if you don't tell me what I need to know.'

Holderness's face turned from faint amusement back to annoyance in a split second. 'You don't give me orders.'

'I just saved your life.'

'Aiming an inch to the right does not constitute saving my life.'

'Tell me about Viktor Golubev.'

Holderness cocked his head. 'The arms dealer?'

'No, the landlord down the Fleece. Of course, the arms dealer.'

Holderness coughed. 'Not much is known about him. Former Spetsnaz, military intelligence, before going into business for himself. You mentioned Siberia a minute ago, they have their own little empire up there...'

'We'll get to that. Why would he want you dead?'

'Why does a Russian agent want a British intelligence officer dead?' Holderness was quiet for a moment. 'No, that's not the game they play. The Russians wouldn't dare.'

'It's very much the game they play, when they can get away with it. Isn't it, Abi?'

'I don't know what you're talking about. *You* don't know what you're talking about. I saved you, I got you out…'

'Convenient.'

Her eyes flitted between me and the door. 'No, you killed Golubev's new head of security. I hid his body to protect you. I killed his guards getting you out of there.'

'You *said* you moved Volkov's body. But you, carrying the body of a fully grown steroid-bodied man down several flights of stairs and into that derelict section of hotel – with one leg out of action? Come off it. And those guards? Please, they were expendable rent-a-thugs.'

Abi didn't answer, her eyes flitted back to the door behind Holderness.

'Golubev's security – his real security, not those late-comers – moved the body with you. You were all in on it, just like that carefully choreographed play on the ice when I landed. All to put the fear of God into me, set the scene, convince me a killer was running around that could strike anyone, anywhere. Was it one of Golubev's men dressed up in that old Soviet gear? Add a hapless corpse propped up against the ice, a dash of theatrics, a radio incendiary device – piss easy to rig up, especially for a cut-throat bastard like Viktor Golubev. Burning body right on cue for me to find, really drives up the menace, puts me on edge, starts me thinking about the threat to Professor Balakin.'

Holderness shook his head. 'What the Devil are you talking about, man?'

'Stay out of it for now.' I turned back to Abi. 'I remember that jacket I found on the ice, bloodstained. There was an empty water bottle stuffed in the sleeve. It'd been filled with fake blood, aye? To cover yourself in, then throw the lot into the wind before I found you. There was me thinking I'd shot someone, when really it was just his security team running around.

'So why? Why this elaborate setup to make me believe that Balakin's life was in danger?'

Abi's eyes went to the door again.

'Gregori and Anya are dead. You may as well start talking.'

'You don't understand, he'll kill me.'

'Who? Golubev? I'll kill you right now if you don't talk.'

'If the Colonel's alive,' she said, pointing at Holderness, 'I'm dead already.'

'I can protect you.'

'No one can.'

Holderness coughed. 'I can arrange for you to disappear. Somewhere Viktor Golubev will never find—'

'I'm not talking about *Viktor*, you idiot!' She glared at me, chin thrust out. 'He actually burned them alive, you know. He can find anyone, anywhere. There are worse things than dying, much worse. You think you're so fucking clever, don't you?'

'Not really. If I was clever, I'd have spotted that it was Gregori following me in Smithfield. If I was clever, I'd have realised he and Anya weren't there to kill me, they were there to keep tabs on me, to make sure I followed through with the plan. I'm sorry, Abi. By now someone in Colonel Holderness's department is firing off signals wondering why two Russians have been killed in a building site in London. Your only hope is to tell us everything. Who killed Professor Balakin?' I raised the submachine gun, she glared defiantly. The bolt shunted back as I pulled the trigger, three silenced bullets punched a neat little row of holes through the plasterboard a few centimetres from her head. 'Tell us now.'

Abi did a slow clap. 'So very clever. You've got it all figured out, eh? But there's one thing that you missed. One tiny thing.'

'Go on.'

'Yes, they were tracking me, but they were tracking you guys, too.'

'Bollocks,' I said. 'No way you got a tracker on me. I ditched everything in Helsinki, we bought new clothes, everything.'

'They weren't tracking you.' She held up her hand and pointed to her ring finger.

'Oh, Christ.'

'What is it?' asked Holderness.

I looked at him. 'The ring, Alice.'

'Who the heck is Alice...?'

320

Abi darted forward. I stepped back but she wasn't going for me, instead aiming for the coffee table. She snatched up the cup of tea before I realised what she was doing, and downed half the cup in one go.

Holderness looked confused, as I dropped the gun and ran to her, but she folded, smashing through the glass of the coffee table and convulsing on the floor. I dropped to my knees and grabbed her face, blood spilling from her mouth, I guess where she'd bitten off her tongue. Her back arched, head lashing each way. I let go and stood, looking away. Holderness was muttering, mostly rare obscenities.

'Shut up!' I shouted at Holderness. 'I need to think.'

He froze, staring at me as Abi made strange gurgling noises, still convulsing on the floor. 'I'll get a medical team…'

'Don't bother, she's dead.'

'You don't have much luck with poisoned tea, do you?'

'Probably the easiest way to kill me, to be fair. When she made that tea, she thought I'd killed you. She figured she was tying up loose ends.'

'Then she got what she deserved.' His mouth turned up as he tapped her still-twitching foot with his shoe, compassionate as ever. 'All of that went over my head. You need to come in, I need to—'

'We've no time. We need to get north, fast.'

'We?'

'You're coming, too.'

'This has been quite enough for me, thank you, I haven't been in the field since…'

'Look around you.' I pointed at Abi's upturned eyes. 'You're in the field right now.'

'Until a couple of hours ago I was enjoying a rather splendid breakfast with—'

'I don't give a shit, this was a plot to kill you, a plot which dragged me back from the dead, against my will. This is all your fault.'

'I haven't been this popular for some time. It would be nice to understand who wants me dead. But what's next?'

'We need to get to Yorkshire.'

'What's in Yorkshire?'

'They know where I live.'

'Who?'

'I don't know his name, the man behind all of this. The phantom, the ghost who can walk through walls.'

'Just when you start making sense you lose it again.'

I massaged my head then looked up at him. 'Did you fly in on that chopper?'

Chapter Fifty-two

North Yorkshire, England
Present day

The Wildcat Army helicopter made the two-hundred-mile journey north in a shade over an hour, about three hours quicker than I'd have done it in the Audi, for which I was grateful. We'd eaten into that advantage by hanging around in Aldershot to refuel, but I'd used the time to tell Holderness everything I knew.

He was conflicted – and rightly so. Here was I, back from the dead and until recently his would-be assassin. On the other hand, he couldn't deny I'd actually pulled his life out of the bag. Here was a plot to kill him, foiled by the assassin himself.

And, at the moment, we had the upper hand. According to the world, Holderness was dead, and Gregori, Anya and Abi were alive. Me, I was lying poisoned and dead, as far as they knew. Their operatives' silence might have sown confusion, but right now they didn't know anything was blown.

Holderness knew we had to press that slim advantage as far as we could. Because if we didn't – if they knew they'd failed – they'd try again. And this time I wouldn't be there to stop them.

The sun was dipping into the horizon as we came in to land at the cricket club in the centre of Ingleton, the flattest spot around. The police were keeping gawkers away, and had an unmarked car waiting to whisk us up the hillside. Another followed carrying Bates – Holderness's favourite grumpy Glaswegian corporal – and three of his Marines. We climbed out of the village, past the pubs and shops and up onto the moor, mirroring the journey Alice and I had undertaken a couple of days before. We sped along the high, wide valley, between the craggy grey masses of Whernside and Ingleborough, two of the three famous peaks. As the view widened still further we passed under the arches of the Ribblehead Viaduct. I pointed to a layby on the left, past a pub.

'Pull in here.'

The officer driving looked at Holderness, who looked at me.

'We walk from here.'

'He's in charge,' said Holderness.

The car pulled in. We climbed out as the second cop car pulled over.

Holderness went to speak to Bates. 'Move the firearms units up to the pub,' he said, pointing back down the road a short way. 'You and your men come with us.'

'No,' I said. 'They get wind of anything, they'll do one.'

'What do you suggest?'

'It's just under a mile to the house. Stay here and be ready.'

'A mile is a hell of a long way when someone's shooting at you,' sneered Bates. He turned back to Holderness. 'With respect, sir, we know Tyler can't be trusted.'

'We don't know where they are,' I said. 'They could be here already, waiting.'

'For what?'

'A signal. They'll be waiting to be sure the job's done, and I'm dead. Then it'll be time to clean up and bug out.'

'We go in now, take the house,' said Bates. 'Take them before they know what's hit 'em.'

'I'm sure that normally works in a warzone, but we go in guns blazing and we'll never see them again. And the next time *he* sees them,' I pointed at Holderness, 'is when he gets a sarnie full of Novichok. This may be the only chance we have. Don't fuck it up.'

Holderness shuddered. 'I'm inclined to side with Tyler on this. Hold here, Bates.'

Bates glared, breathed in, then turned to shout commands at his men.

'Leave the logistics to the meathead,' I said to Holderness. 'We need to get moving.'

We set off at a pace, just a couple of poorly dressed hikers in the drizzle. The weather joined in with the charade, turning into full-on rain by the time we'd got out of sight of the pub.

'Try calling her again,' said Holderness.

'Still nothing,' I said. 'But the signal's terrible there.'

We followed the road for a few hundred metres before I pointed to a layby on the left.

'We'll go over the moor, come up behind the house.'

'In these shoes?' Holderness asked, lifting up a polished, brogued Oxford.

I pointed down at mine, which were no better. 'And you were always telling me I was underdressed.'

He tutted and followed me onto the muddy track. Soon it turned upwards, a well-worn hiking trail up Whernside. Instead I kept going straight, plodding through the long grass as the mud soaked into my socks and up my trousers. The wax on my jacket only got me so far; soon my suit and shoulders were soaked. I could feel the water running down the inside of my shirt. The long grass became reeds, the mud became a million streams carrying fast-flowing water off the moorland and into the beck below.

The ground underfoot flattened beneath a black, rocky escarpment, churning rainwater tumbled around long-fallen boulders and cascaded on down the hillside.

'Step where I step,' I said. 'And *only* where I step.'

'We seem to be walking through a river. Are you sure you know where you're going?'

I signalled to the right, leading Holderness round the boggy ground and towards an easier route up. 'Try going a metre to the left and ask me again.'

'What happens a metre to the left?'

'At this time of year, in this weather, you don't wanna know.'

He grumbled and muttered.

We hit a dry patch of ground as the last of the light was finally doused behind the hill. Dusk brought a respite from the rain, as the clouds thinned and drizzle drifted across the moor. I took off my rucksack, brushed the rain from my face, and pulled out the HK submachine gun.

Holderness held his hand out. 'It's been a while since I've fired one of those, I can tell you.'

'And it won't be today either, this is mine.'

I cocked the gun, checked my pistol in my shoulder holster, then zipped my motorcycle jacket back up and pulled the straps of my rucksack tight on my shoulders.

Darkness pulled in around us quickly, but there was still enough twilight to navigate the familiar moorland. We waded through muddy pools that threatened to steal our shoes, climbed rocky outcrops slick with moss and algae, and skirted deep bogs fringed with thick reeds. Finally I gestured to Holderness.

'Down. Stay here.'

He knelt in the mud while I zipped up my jacket right to the top to cover the white shirt, then crawled forward. Over the crest of a mound I paused, looking down on the old cottage and barn.

Lights glowed on the grass blowing in the wind. The kitchen, lounge and upstairs windows blazed, but despite the lights the house looked still.

It was something else that really got my attention. Down to my right, in the hollow below the house, I watched a dim light carefully. A car, pulled up in the shadows behind the ruined cottage below mine. My combination of haste and caution had been justified. Down there, smoking a cigarette in the dim cold of a Yorkshire winter evening, the hunter had just become the hunted.

I shuffled backwards, working my way to Holderness, who was shivering in the mud and blowing into his hands.

He took off his flat cap and brushed his steel-grey hair flat. 'So how does it look?'

'Car, two occupants. Lights are on in the house but I don't think anyone's gone in yet. Looks like they're staking it out.'

Holderness pulled his cap back on and nodded. 'Waiting for you?'

'Or waiting for the signal that we're both dead, to go in and kill Alice.'

'Do you think she knows?'

'I doubt it.'

He pulled out a radio. 'We'll get Bates to handle them.'

I put my hand on his arm. 'We don't know enough yet.' I pulled a torch from my pocket and took off my rucksack, handing him both. 'Take these.'

'And do what, exactly?'

'Head straight down here. There's a track, you'll be fine. When you hit the road, turn left, and left again up the first turning, that's my drive. Walk straight up with the torch on, make as much noise as possible.'

'Be bait, you mean.'

'They're after me, not you. Besides, in that getup you almost look like a local.'

He shook his head and slung the rucksack onto his back. 'You just make sure you know what you're doing.'

I slung the submachine gun across my shoulder, wrapping the strap around my arm. 'Have I ever failed?'

He arched his eyebrows.

With a final nod to Holderness, I set off back over the moor. I went up further this time, crawling over the top, eyes on the house and the car. Nothing moved in either as I slithered through the mud down the other side, working my way into the scrubby bushes flanking the driveway. I paused to listen as a voice drifted on the wind.

Nothing moved. I gripped the gun tighter and slinked forward on my knees, sticking close to the bushes. Holderness's voice was clear now, singing about Loch Lomond. The interior light on the car went out.

I skulked across the cobbled path. The torch came into view around the corner as Holderness strolled up the centre of the lane. The swinging beam of light lit up the rain like an anti-aircraft spotlight. The car doors opened quietly as two shadows got out.

Holderness was halfway to the ruined cottage now. I squinted into the darkness, worsening by the second. One of the shadows detached itself from the car and moved silently across the grass verge towards Holderness.

Keeping hunched over, I moved out onto the lane, creeping forward towards the car. One of the occupants had waited behind, leaning back against the vehicle nonchalantly. The car, a big Jaguar saloon, was empty.

An argument broke out further down the lane as Holderness encountered the first man, doing his best impression of a drunk local and failing the accent terribly. In the flashing light of Holderness's torch, I could see the guy – it was one of Golubev's guards from the hotel.

I crept onward, coming up fast on the car. The man leaning on it just a couple of metres from me chuckled softly.

'Bring him,' he shouted to his comrade, and instantly I knew the voice.

I leapt onto the bonnet, crouching to jam the barrel of the gun into his back.

'Viktor Golubev, whatever are you doing in Yorkshire?'

'You!' was all he could manage, spluttering Russian expletives.

'You know the drill, hands on your head, fingers interlocked.'

Down the lane, his comrade turned. The torchlight flashed and went out. I raised the gun into the darkness and squinted.

'Holderness?'

'Got him,' he shouted back.

'Good man.' I prodded Golubev in the back. 'Move.'

We walked down to find Holderness crouching in a puddle beside the prone body of the second man.

'Well, that went smoothly,' he said, banging the torch to switch it back on.

'Too smoothly.' Motioning for Golubev to stand to one side, I knelt to feel for a pulse. There was none, my hand came away sticky. 'Do you think you could have hit him harder?' The stream of rainwater was already swirling blood across the gravel.

Holderness put the torch on the ground. 'Is he okay?'

'No, he is not *okay*.' I stood and pointed the gun at Golubev. 'Get him off the road.'

Golubev glared at me but bent and grabbed the man's legs, pulling him to the muddy verge.

'The man himself,' I said to Holderness. 'Viktor Golubev.'

'We meet at last,' said Holderness. 'You're an awfully long way from Siberia.'

'Pat him down,' I said to Holderness as I covered them both.

Holderness did as he was told and came out with a pistol. He pocketed it then stepped back, picking up the torch and pointing it into Golubev's face.

'I know this man,' he said, as Golubev put a hand up to shield his eyes.

'You probably know most Russian agents and arms dealers.'

'But not the elusive Viktor Golubev. And yet... I know your face.'

Golubev smirked, slicking his wet hair back. 'You will remember, soon enough.'

I nodded, gesturing at Golubev with the gun. 'Get walking, we can figure this out where it's warm.'

He started walking back up the lane, glancing around nervously.

'Expecting someone?'

'You're dead men.'

'So everyone keeps telling me – and yet, here I am.'

He looked at the Jag longingly as we passed, then we rounded the corner and walked the final stretch up to the house. Holderness was panting by the time we arrived at the gate.

'Sounds like you need to get out into the field a bit more,' I said.

'Not actual fields,' he muttered without humour.

I pushed Golubev through the gate and looked through the windows. Nothing in the house moved, it looked just as it had when I'd left.

'Are there any more?' I asked.

Golubev just scowled.

I tried the door handle, which to my horror was unlocked. I opened it quietly and stepped inside. The radio was on in the kitchen. I walked into the hall and beckoned for the others to follow. Holderness shoved Golubev roughly, then closed the door behind him.

There was a familiar smell in the hallway, petrol and soot, burning and cooking. *My imagination again or...?*

'Lock it,' I said, quickly scanning for anything amiss. 'Alice?' I shouted. 'Alice!'

Something crashed in the kitchen, followed by a fit of swearing which could only be her. I relaxed as she came into view, wearing a baggy pair of my shorts and an old Smashing Pumpkins T-shirt.

'Fuck, John, you could have called! And what the fuck happened to you, you're filthy!' She ran over and threw herself at me. 'I've got to tell you, I've been through your room, and I have *lots* of questions. Also, can I wear this shirt?' She pulled back and saw I wasn't alone. She did a double take, then stumbled backwards as she realised who they both were.

Chapter Fifty-three

North Yorkshire, England
Present day

Sat in a clean pair of jeans and a hoody, with a fire going and Golubev fuming on the sofa next to me, I'd filled Alice in as much as I could. Even then there were a fair number of gaps, but no amount of threats elicited a response from Golubev to fill them in. He hadn't said a single word since we'd got inside.

'Last chance,' I said. 'I actually said this to someone just this morning and he didn't believe me. It really did end up being his last chance.'

In the corner of my eye, Holderness shuffled forward, raising an eyebrow. Golubev just stared in silence.

'How was Professor Balakin killed?' asked Alice, raising her voice now. 'I know it wasn't me, and since we're sat here I'm pretty sure it wasn't John.'

'I'm less interested in how he was killed as I am in who killed him,' I said. 'And why. I know it wasn't you,' I said to Golubev. 'Tell me or I'll take you out back and shoot you.'

Nothing.

'I can do much worse than shoot him,' said Holderness. 'We have a prize fish here. Don't even need to rendition him, the elusive Viktor Golubev has very kindly dropped into our lap.'

'You hear that? I was going to tie you up and beat you with a wooden chair leg but the Colonel can do much better.'

'What I still don't understand,' said Alice, 'is why Professor Balakin asked for you specifically.'

'He knew Tyler and I had history,' said Holderness. 'And that he'd let that cloud his judgement because he's a bloody idiot. But did Balakin really believe the information he was passing on, or was he some unfortunate pawn in this game?'

Golubev smiled, barely perceptible in the light from the table lamp.

'A guy I've never spoken to,' I said. 'Before he died, Balakin said he met me once. I don't remember him. He is familiar though, I know him from somewhere. It's driving me crazy.'

Golubev smiled again, wider this time, and looked down at the rug.

'I know, right,' said Alice. 'He had one of those faces.'

'What do you mean?'

'One of those faces...'

'But... you knew Balakin?' I said, puzzled.

'Why would I?'

'I don't know, scientists move in the same circles, I suppose?'

'I know *of* him, lots of my colleagues have met him.'

'You mean you'd never met Professor Balakin before last week?'

She shook her head. 'I met him for the first time the day before you did.'

'But Burton knew him...' I took a few moments to digest the new information, moving pieces around and seeing where they fitted.

'John?' said Alice. 'What is it?'

'Of course Burton knew him! But still...' I went quiet again.

'Let us know when you have something better than babbling, 'cos I'm still as puzzled as I was two days ago,' said Alice, putting her mug of coffee down. 'Where do you keep the stronger stuff?'

'There's a cabinet in the lounge with a decent single malt for the Colonel.'

'I'll be right back.'

I watched her leave, still thinking about what she'd said and why it had triggered something.

'The portrait!' I said, making Holderness jump. 'In Balakin's room in the bunker, a portrait of Brezhnev above the sink. That's how they did it.'

332

'Sorry my boy, I'm with Alice. Perhaps something stronger than tea will help you share?'

I looked at Golubev and smiled. 'Clever, but not clever enough. Who was he?'

Golubev glared forward impassively while Holderness stared blankly, waiting for me to continue.

'I told you about the play on the ice, the stories, the atmosphere at the hotel. Everything was choreographed to put me on edge, make me believe Balakin was in imminent danger, I was in danger, anyone was at risk from this mysterious killer who could strike anywhere.'

'It's a lot of trouble to go to.'

'Not really, hardly any trouble at all. Just a little misdirection and suggestion, there was nothing difficult about anything they did.'

'They burned Professor Balakin alive, behind thick walls of solid concrete.'

'That was the easiest bit.'

'And the American agent, in his room. This Burton fellow, the chap you replaced.'

'I take it back, that was even easier.' I shrugged. 'They simply split him away from Alice and killed him. What was it, Golubev? A bullet, a knife, a noose? Doesn't matter anyway, because afterwards they burned his body. Abi was the one who showed me his room and fed me all that nonsense about spontaneous combustion. No one else heard or saw anything.'

'But to what end?'

I turned to face Golubev again. 'I thought we got away from there way too easily. A heavily guarded facility in the middle of nowhere, me tied up in a bunker underground. And helping me all the way was Abi.'

'Hang on,' said Holderness. 'I know Abi was working for Golubev but you're still going too quickly for me, you're going to have to back it up.'

'Sorry, Colonel, this is the bit where we get to the truth.'

'But you said you had to fight your way out of there?'

'They were hired mercenaries rather than Golubev's men, and I'm guessing not very expensive ones at that. It was amateur night, escaping

333

from that hotel. A punch here, a knife there, none of them got a shot off. In fact, a chopper couldn't even hit us in a truck.' I shook my head. 'I thought they were useless, but you'd probably told them to take it easy. They must have panicked when the truck overturned on the ice. They were cheap and they were shite, flown in to be expendable, to make it look right.' I looked at Golubev. 'I bet you were fuming when Volkov's body turned up, that wasn't part of the plan. Clever of Abi, though, using it to get onside with me.'

'But why?' asked Holderness.

'I was thinking about this on the chopper. If we follow the fact that Golubev was working a disinformation programme in which I was an unwitting pawn – why would he do all this?

'And in that question the whole house of cards collapses in front of your eyes. The whole scheme, this whole story of the phantom soldier, the spontaneous combustion. Why this seemingly elaborate setup to make me believe that Balakin's life was in danger?

'It's obvious now, isn't it? To impart false information about Holderness here in such a way that it's absolutely irrefutable. Here am I, sent all the way to Siberia for information. Summoned, no less, because Golubev knows I'll swallow anything if it gives me the answers I've been looking for. Rogue British agent that everyone thinks is dead, pops back up and kills his old handler. Why?' I shrugged. 'Any number of reasons, but the fact is none of them will be traced back to Viktor Golubev or the Russians. It's quite a coup for them.

'But to pull it off, to get me to kill you, I have to be on edge, unhinged, and absolutely swallow every word Professor Balakin is telling me. Obviously "Balakin" has to die as soon as he's passed on this information. It means he can't be questioned further but it also lends credibility to the information. And he has to die in my eyeline, so to speak. Put me on the back foot, move things along.'

'Why not simply put a bullet in him after he's given you the information?'

'Because they had to let me live, turn me loose to kill you. If I thought Golubev had killed Balakin, I'd have gone after him first! Too many variables. No, this was actually simple. Have Balakin give me the duff info, then die in such a way that the only target I had to aim at was you. Wind me up and watch me go, deal with me afterwards.'

Holderness was shaking his head. 'As a plan it is rather elegant, but it doesn't explain how he killed Balakin. You said yourself he was in a sealed room inside a bunker with only you for company.'

'And Alice.'

'But it can't have been her, surely?'

There was silence in the room but the inside of my head whirred at supersonic speed, fitting the missing pieces that Alice had supplied a minute ago into the puzzle and looking at it from various angles.

Finally I shuffled on the sofa, narrowing my eyes as I saw Golubev anew.

'Nambutu,' I said, almost to myself.

'Nambutu…' Holderness's voice trailed off as he stared at Golubev intensely.

'Twenty-four years, six months,' Golubev closed his eyes and sighed, 'and five days.'

'Shit,' I said, 'I've been stupid.'

The old floorboards outside the door creaked. I lunged, picking up my HK pistol and jamming it into Golubev's ribs so hard he squealed. Holderness shot out of his chair but was none the wiser. I concentrated on the door as an odour crept around the room. Acrid burning and the sickly sweet smell of petrol.

'What is it?' asked Holderness.

'The killer has been with us all along.' I ground the barrel deep into Golubev's side. He tried to squirm away but I held him firm.

The door swung open.

An arm appeared, filthy white material. The figure stepped out, covered in Arctic gear, smeared with soot and grime. The arm held Alice firmly around the neck, dragging her into view from round the door.

The hood of the parka appeared over Alice's shoulder, still gripping her tightly. The fur lining fringed a deep black, making it difficult to see the face beyond. Alice grimaced as the figure pushed a pistol deeper into her side, other arm tightening around her neck, bending her backwards. I could see she was struggling but refused to show fear.

Holderness squinted, furrowing his brow, then set his jaw. 'You,' he said simply, as he realised who it was.

Chapter Fifty-four

The Peoples' Democratic Republic of Nambutu / French Equatorial Africa

1999

'Revenge.'

I heard the Russian utter the word as I was crouched at the back of the Mitsubishi. In front of me, over in the trees on the slope of the hill, was a flash. I looked through the windows of the car and noticed the Russian had his hand in the air. I was processing the information when a metallic dink came from the front of the car. Flecks of paint millimetres from Holderness's head flew into the air.

The crack of the shot echoed across to us. Holderness was already reacting, dropping to the ground and rolling behind the car. I turned and sprinted away from him, into the nearby treeline.

I didn't stop running until the muddy ground started to rise beneath my feet, and I was dashing up a stream coming off the hillside. Several more shots echoed around the valley. I stopped, hands on my knees, and looked back. Through the leaves I could see the Mitsubishi, and just see Holderness lying behind it. It rocked as another bullet smacked through the door.

The Russian looked to have disappeared back into the jungle. The soldiers had either dashed round the side of the building or were taking cover behind one of the Land Rovers parked alongside it. I could already count three unfortunate men who'd not been quick enough. Two were still, one was working at the dirt with his fingers, trying to crawl, stopping every now and then to shout out in pain. No one dared pull him back into cover: the sniper had them pinned down.

In an upstairs window of the mansion I could just about see Justin with a rifle in his hands. He leaned out, a second later the glass in the window shattered with another gunshot, forcing him to duck back.

I took a bearing on the flash I'd seen from the trees, that first shot. It wasn't far. I had no weapons, nothing, but he'd been focused on Holderness – he probably hadn't seen me round the car. I was the only person not in his sights.

I reached down and picked up a handful of mud, smearing some across my face and arms. I crept forward, deeper into the steaming darkness, moving into the sodden undergrowth. My trainers sank in dead leaves, pushing through wet ferns and pale flowers growing up the trees. Insects hissed as I passed through their territory, mosquitoes buzzed angrily.

The gunfire continued as the sniper kept pressing them. I stopped to look back, but no one seemed to have been able to gain an advantage. Come nightfall it'd be a different story, but would Holderness make it that long?

I pressed on, forward and upwards, working my way round the slope, gauging that I was somewhere above the sniper. Now I crept slower, listening every few seconds.

The only sounds were the ever-present insects and the occasional shout drifting up from the house. I shuffled forward to look down through a gap in the trees and saw the Mitsubishi below me, only a couple of hundred metres away. Movement flashed somewhere by the building, a gunshot cracked. A second later the man dropped to the ground.

The shot had been close, below me.

I shuffled forward, peering into the darkness of the jungle floor. Evening was closing in, and among the trees the light was fading even faster. Another gunshot cracked, it nearly made me jump. It'd been not more than a few metres away, below and to my right.

With a bead on the sound, I moved at a snail's pace. More shouts came up from below as the soldiers tried to break out. I saw a flash of movement below, as the sniper's rifle cracked another couple of times in quick succession. They'd made it to the trees.

Glass smashed as the sniper turned his attention back to the Mitsubishi, trying to get Holderness. Another couple of rapid shots rang out. Now was my chance.

I crept forward slowly, using the gunshots to mask my movements, then froze. Not five metres away, behind a large fern, was the man. Combat trousers, boots, camo jacket, all covered in blood and mud. No prizes for guessing this was the second Russian from the Toyota, the brother Holderness had referred to as a psychopath.

He fired again and muttered beneath his breath, settling his eye back against the scope.

I moved forward carefully.

He fired, swore, and settled in again.

I moved forward, ready for the next shot.

He panned the rifle across to the right and squeezed the trigger, I shuffled forward quickly.

The man rolled onto one side to pull the magazine out, then saw me and froze. I did the same, staggering to a halt, then launching at him.

He thrust upward as I jumped, the barrel caught me on the ribs, spinning me over. I crashed to the ground beside him as he dropped the rifle and got to his feet.

I rolled onto my back and looked up. He reached into his waistband and pulled out a pistol. I kicked out, knocking his arm wide. A bullet exploded into the bushes to the left. I jumped onto my feet and ran at him, closing the distance as he pulled the pistol back onto me.

The gun barked again but I was too close, driving my head into his stomach and pushing him off balance. He gasped and fell, landing hard. I followed and leaned on top of him, fingers at his wrists as he pulled the trigger again.

I slammed his hand down, knocking the gun from his grasp as he brought a knee up. I flew off him painfully, ending up gasping on my back.

There was a shout from the bushes off somewhere to the side, another from below as the soldiers closed in.

The Russian was getting to his feet now. He bent to pick up his pistol.

I reached out to the side and curled my fingers around the hot barrel of his rifle, pulling it, grabbing it with both hands, rolling forward and swinging it hard into his knee.

He buckled, bringing the gun round as he fell. I jumped up, sidestepped, and swung the rifle again, catching him round the head. I dropped the rifle, nursing my burnt hand as he spun, landing on his back in the mud.

I stood on his wrist and reached down, grabbing the pistol and backing away.

He lay panting on the mud. I aimed the pistol at his head.

People were crashing through the bushes nearby.

I squeezed the trigger slowly. It was heavy, far heavier than any of the guns I'd used here.

He shouted something in Russian and threw his hands in front of his face.

I looked down at the man, his heaving chest, mud-and-blood encrusted face, filthy clothes.

I lowered my arm. 'Go home.' I staggered backwards and leaned against a trunk, breathing deeply, feeling the air filling my lungs. 'Go home!' I shouted.

The bushes shuddered. Justin appeared, looking at the man on his back, the gun in my hand, the rifle on the ground. He walked over and hugged me, holding me tight. I held him back.

'Give it me,' he said. I let the pistol slip through my fingers.

He turned and stepped back towards the man, raising it.

'Justin, no!'

He pulled the trigger. The man's head jumped and dropped in the dead leaves.

'Why?' I screamed. 'WHY?'

'He'd have killed you.'

I put my hands on my head as I sucked in air, looking up at the dark sky. 'Dad was right, we're nothing like each other, not any more.'

'Good.' He walked back to me. 'Go home, Johnny.' He dropped the pistol at my feet and shoved past, brushing leaves out of the way as he headed back down the hill.

I picked up the gun and followed him.

'Leave it,' said Justin.

HECKLER & KOCH GMBH it said, stamped into the slide. 9MM X 19 VP70Z

A few scratches had been gauged into the rear, like trophy victory marks. It looked futuristic, yet old and battered.

'It's my gun now,' I muttered. 'And every single time I pull the trigger, it'll remind me.'

Chapter Fifty-five

North Yorkshire, England
Present day

The figure in the doorway ground his pistol deeper into Alice's side, making her wince.

'Professor Balakin,' I said. 'Back from the dead. Again.'

'That makes three of us,' he said, hood nodding at Holderness and me. 'It's good to see you again, Colonel Holderness.'

'The Russian brothers,' Holderness said, with a heavy dose of venom.

'No prizes for guessing who took drama in school. You said "they" earlier. *They* have their own little empire up there...' I looked between the two Russians. 'You being the elder Golubev, I presume?'

'This is Ivan Golubev,' Holderness spat.

He tossed his head back to drop the hood. 'I'm impressed.' The leather eyepatch caught the reflection of the lamp. 'I knew Brezhnev would let me down.'

'It was you running around on the ice when I landed. While Abi was picking me up, you were staging the burning corpse. It was your jacket I found.'

'I had to give you *something* to help your imagination along.'

'I presume it was you following me in the ruins, too?'

'Had to make sure Abi got you to safety.'

'And what about the real Professor Balakin?'

Ivan smiled. 'We'd had our eyes on him for a long time. A prod here, a suggestion there. He got in touch with the US embassy just as we knew he would. The CIA were easy, so focused on getting that intelligence, they swallowed it all. The real Professor Balakin was killed as soon as he stepped foot on Barensky.'

'Hence why Burton had to die. He knew the real Balakin.'

'I don't know how, but yes. As soon as we were introduced, he was obviously suspicious.'

'An old war wound, you said.' I nodded at his eyepatch. 'You were telling the truth. You've got form for coming back from the dead.'

'My brother was wrong, that's not a terrible gun.' Ivan cocked his head, staring at the pistol jabbed under his brother's ribs. 'It only falls short in the hands of someone inexperienced with it, as well you know.'

'I saw you die.'

'I woke up with ants eating my eye, crawling inside my face, do you know how that feels? I had to drag myself through the jungle for a day before Viktor found me.'

'You knew so much about Afghanistan ten years ago. You knew everything about my brother's death, how I survived.'

'Ten years, ten painful years of reconstruction surgeries to repair the shattered bones. The bullet may have entered my eye, but it ricocheted and lodged inside my skull.'

'You're responsible for all of it! You hired the team in Afghanistan to plant the IED. You killed my brother. It wasn't anything to do with our mission, or Holderness, it was personal revenge, pure and simple.'

'So why have you come back now?' growled Holderness.

I answered for him. 'Because I started poking again.'

'An eye for an eye,' said Viktor, next to me. 'Your brother killed mine, I killed him, finished. But you couldn't leave it alone, could you?'

I narrowed my eyes at Ivan. 'It was you, two years ago in that car park. You heard I was on the trail.'

Ivan laughed. 'Not me personally, but we arranged it.' He nodded. 'It was a surprise to find you had survived the attempt. But when the team I'd hired ten years ago in Afghanistan recently started dying in rapid succession, I knew you were alive, and carrying on what you'd started.'

'What *you* started.'

A twitch of a smile flitted across his face. 'You started this, twenty-four years ago.'

'You chose *me* to assassinate Holderness,' I continued. 'Two for one. Revenge on Colonel Holderness for double-crossing you, and a way to get rid of me before I reached the end of the trail I was following.'

'You may have stumbled onto the plot, but that doesn't mean you hold any cards. They are all mine. Nothing has changed.'

'I'll kill him,' I growled, pushing the gun into Golubev junior.

'I'll kill her,' he replied with a smirk.

'Gentlemen, we seem to be at a bit of an impasse,' said Holderness.

'You're right.' Ivan moved quickly, the pistol cracked before I could react.

Before the shot had died away it was tucked back under Alice's ribs. Viktor Golubev spluttered, I moved away from him as he slumped back, getting blood all over my favourite Chesterfield, hands trying to move but failing. His mouth flapped, but the only sound was his breath escaping, through his bloody lips and also through the neat red hole in his neck.

'The impasse is solved,' said Ivan simply. 'No one can stop this.'

Alice's eyes looked right through me.

I brought the gun round slowly, Ivan grinned. 'Ah-ah-ah. You move that gun, she dies,' he said. 'I still hold the cards. And this one,' he jabbed the barrel, making Alice gasp and squirm against him, 'is an ace.'

'The bitch means nothing to me,' I said.

'Then move that gun, see what happens.'

Next to me, Viktor tipped sideways, the blood stopped pumping from his neck and soaked into the arm of my sofa. I kept my gun down low, pointing into the lifeless body.

'Shoot him,' said Holderness.

Alice's eye's begged me to, but there was no way I could bring my gun up in time, not without hitting Alice.

'Shoot them both,' Holderness continued.

Alice's eyes went wide. I flexed my fingers on the gun, weighing up my options.

Ivan narrowed my options down somewhat. 'Shoot Colonel Holderness right now, and I will let Alice go.'

I didn't reply.

His gun wavered. He may have had a better hand, but he'd played it and had nothing left. I was sure he wouldn't shoot Alice.

'Kill the Colonel,' Ivan growled.

I slowly swung the gun across towards Holderness.

'Ah, steady Tyler,' growled Ivan. 'Steady.'

I pointed it down at the carpet as I slowly swung in the Colonel's direction. 'You're responsible for all of this, Holderness,' I said. 'You always tell me actions have consequences, welcome to your own. You play games with people, it catches up with you.'

'So that's it, eh? I am either to be gunned down by a Russian psychopath or my own?'

'Colonel, long ago a wise man told me the dildo of consequences rarely comes lubed. High-ranking British spymaster executed by a rogue British agent, with no fingers pointing at Russia and a personal vendetta settled. Very neat.'

'Why do Russians always have to play three-dimensional chess?' asked Holderness.

'You'd play too if you were good at it,' said Ivan. 'But this changes nothing. Kill the Colonel or I kill Alice. I will count to three.'

'Shoot him,' said Alice, as he ground the pistol right up under her ribs, forcing a gasp from her.

I wasn't sure which of them she'd meant me to shoot, but I was now aiming at Holderness – because it was now a much tighter, easier angle to swing onto Ivan, though Alice was still in the way. I was positive he wouldn't shoot her.

'You think you hold all the cards?' I said to Ivan. 'What are you on? The mystery man I've been after for a decade willingly comes here, to my house, and is standing right in front of me.' I was fairly sure he wouldn't shoot her. 'You've played all your cards, and you've got twice fuck-all.'

'So be it.'

He moved the gun towards me and pulled the trigger. Alice bent forward, driving her elbow back into Ivan with her whole body. He stumbled, roaring. The gunshot was deafening, bouncing around the hallway. At the same time I jumped forward, pulling the trigger. Ivan darted behind the wall. Bullets stitched into the side of the staircase in the hallway as I continued to pull the trigger. Holderness threw himself backwards as Ivan's bullets replied, tearing into the lounge wall behind him, shredding picture frames and shattering the windows.

Alice slumped to the floor, gasping.

I leapt the coffee table, covering the distance in two steps, sliding down next to her. She had her hands over her ribs. I moved them, dark blood seeped out on to the carpet.

Somewhere in the house, glass smashed.

Alice reached for my hair with a bloody hand, trying to speak. My ears rang. I pressed a hand to her side, felt the warmth pulsing under the T-shirt. She'd thrown herself in front of his gun.

I looked at Holderness, he was already speaking into a radio.

A mile is a hell of a long way when someone's shooting at you.

Holderness crouched next to me, moving my hand and pushing his own in its place.

Alice stroked my cheek, her arm dropped, eyes rolling. Blood flecked her lips as she took her last gasps. Holderness brushed her hair, speaking softly. I touched her face.

He knocked my hand away and gave me a grim look. 'Get after him, man.'

Chapter Fifty-six

North Yorkshire, England
Present day

Winter darkness was almost complete on the moorland behind the house. In the distance sirens cut through the icy air, the sound of engines already tearing up the hill.

One of the windows behind me exploded. I crouched and listened as the shot echoed away up the hillside. In the pool of light from the house I could see the bushes at the edge of the garden had a person-shaped path pushed through them. I crawled forward as another gunshot rolled down from the hill but it wasn't close, nothing more than a parting shot to force my head down.

Staying low, I shoved through the bushes and looked up the hill. The sirens, the rain, the streams cascading off the hillside drowned out everything. The clouds raced overhead, dimming the moonlight.

I knelt low and looked at the mud, the boot prints heading straight up the moor. I decided to go for it, jumping up and following them at a pace.

Another gunshot cracked, and this time I saw the muzzle flash. I squinted, faint but definitely the pale parka was weaving across the hillside, far enough away to not get a decent shot at me. I held my gun firm, squinting along the slide, but there wasn't enough to aim for. I set off again, watching my footing as I dodged rocks and streams, splashing through mud as I worked my way up above him.

Down on the road, headlights swept past, with the growl of engines at high revs, more red and blue lights. Between us, silhouetted in the glow, was Ivan. I raised the gun and fired, the silhouette disappeared. I was doubtful I'd hit him, but the bullet must have been close enough to shit him up.

I kept going, working my way round, trying not to think about Alice. The police would be there now, had to be. The armed response units carried medical packs and gunshot wound training, and Bates's Marines would be useful.

A shot cracked. Something slapped the mud to my left. I spun and looked, just catching a flash of movement in the long grasses. I darted after it, down the slope.

I crouched as I neared the edge of a rocky outcrop, looking down the hillside. Halfway to the road was Ivan, glancing behind him. I stood and levelled the weapon.

'Give it up,' I shouted. 'There's nowhere to go.'

He turned and fired at the same time as I did, but with fifty or so metres between us, neither of our odds were good. I fired again, then the gun clicked empty. I kept it trained on him as he aimed at me, walking steadily towards him.

As I closed the distance, it hit me that he was still pointing his pistol at me, but not firing. He was out, too. This was confirmed a split second later when he threw the pistol and turned to run sideways across the hill.

I took off after him, panting as I struggled to keep up. He was faster, and gaining ground, when instead he stopped and spun round. I slid on the mud, looking at his hand and seeing he was clutching a knife. I held my gun ready like a club, circling him, waiting for him to move.

He lunged, I swung and dodged back. He lunged again, again I dodged easily. As we circled, I adjusted my grip on the gun.

He sprang a third time, I dodged to the side but one of my feet refused to move, caught in the mud. I swung for him and overbalanced, leaning forward.

He jumped to the side and came in with a kick under my ribs that caught me as I fell. I landed and rolled over to keep moving. Losing one of my shoes in the mud, I kept my momentum going as he stamped after me. I managed to swing my arm and smash him across the shin. He yowled, I grabbed a handful of mud and slung it up into his one good eye.

He roared and stumbled backwards, swiping at his face, giving me the time I needed to scramble to my feet.

He was still wiping his eye, so I didn't waste the chance, running towards him, tackling him about the middle and sending him sprawling into a stream on his back. I reached for the knife but his grip was iron, he swung a fist into my jaw that rocked me. I kept both hands locked around his wrist and brought my forehead down into his nose.

It gave way with a crunch that weakened him, his fingers relaxed. I wrestled the knife from his hand and pushed it up against his throat.

'Is this how you wanted it to end?' I snarled.

'It ends as it began,' he replied through the blood.

I pressed the steel into his throat, watching his flesh bunch up around it. A trickle of blood shone darkly in the dim moonlight as it ran along the blade.

'A Russian agent and arms dealer the world thinks is dead.' I rocked back off him and stood. 'I imagine the CIA would love to have a chat.'

He lay on his back, glowering at me.

I kicked his boot. 'Get up.'

He put his arms down, pushing up into a crouch, watching me carefully. I took another step back and gripped the knife tightly.

He launched a handful of mud at me, hoping to spring the same surprise I'd caught him with. Unfortunately for him I was ready, and simply ducked out of the way.

He scrambled to his feet and took off across the hillside. I took a deep breath and started after him, but with only one shoe I was losing ground. I watched the white parka disappear into the shadows.

I stopped with my hands on my knees, panting, when I heard a shout. It came from in front, I set off again through the long grass, carefully, holding the knife ready.

The wind blew down from the hill, pushing the reeds flat and rustling the heather. The rain grew heavier, bouncing off my head and shoulders. I swept my hair back and scanned the darkness, creeping forward. In the distance the steady thump of rotors echoed between the peaks as the Wildcat finally took off from Ingleton cricket ground.

The darkness spread out in front. I was on the edge of the low rocky ridge, looking down into the marshy hollow Holderness and I had crossed earlier, shining with cascading streams in the moonlight flashing between racing clouds.

Directly below me was a bright patch that could only be Ivan. He'd run straight off the edge and fallen. I backtracked, working my way down until I came up on him from the side.

He was struggling, clawing at the mud, panting heavily. I walked closer and saw both his legs were stuck up to his knees, probably both broken by the bog he'd landed in.

'Can't step off the paths round here,' I said. 'These moors can be deadly.'

He leaned away from me and grabbed a handful of grass, pulling it from the ground. He overbalanced, sinking deeper into the mud.

'There was a horse and rider had to be rescued from the mud a couple of years ago,' I said. 'By the time Mountain Rescue got to her she was up to her neck.'

He struggled and turned, panic in his eyes, fingers scrabbling at the mud.

'Takes a while, though. Hours.' I shrugged. 'Maybe less with all this water coming down from the hillside.'

'Please.' He stared at me, I could see the white of his eye.

One minute ago we'd have killed each other, but faced with a lingering death, sucked down into the mud, he was starting to lose his shit.

I watched him for a few seconds. He turned away and scrabbled at the grass again but succeeded only in sinking further. I thought about my brother, about all the people I'd taken my revenge on to get to this point. I thought about all those people dead because of this man. I thought about Alice taking her last breaths in my hallway.

Then I thought about what Alice had said. Everyone's the hero of their own story. Ivan had been the villain in mine, without me even knowing. By that same token I was the villain in his. I thought about that day in the jungle, the two brothers, about him lying there, double crossed and left for dead.

I took my pistol from my pocket and stared at the lettering stamped into the side. I carried it as a reminder of that day. All those faces, all the screams, the cycle never ends.

'Throw me your jacket,' I shouted.

He scrabbled at the mud for a few more seconds, sinking lower, then understood. He slipped his arms out and threw it across, I laid down and grabbed a sleeve.

He gripped the other sleeve and pulled, almost dragging me in. I turned to sit, digging my heels in, and heaved.

'Lie forward. You need to distribute your weight, your legs will float up.'

He leaned forward, still gripping the sleeve. I pulled again, and this time the mud gave up an inch of his legs. I gathered the jacket in and heaved again, he slid out a little more, leaning forward further into the mud to spread his weight. The elation on his face showed he'd temporarily forgotten what was happening, where he was, who I was. All that mattered in that moment was his thoughts of escape from a terrible, slow, painful fate.

Rapid gunshots convulsed his body, bouncing between the rocks and boulders and echoing on down the valley.

The smile slid, he dropped face down into the mud. Red sprayed across the filthy white parka.

'God damn it!' I screamed. 'Why?'

Holderness stood silhouetted on the ridge above me, submachine gun in his arms, still pointing down at us.

'I saved the man from a hideous death.'

'No one gets sucked under the mud in a bloody puddle in Yorkshire, you fool,' I shouted. 'He wasn't in any danger. We could have used him, think of the intelligence...'

'Normally you wouldn't hesitate to put a bullet in someone. Shoot first and ask no questions.'

'No.' I smacked the mud. 'Not like that, not in cold blood.' But I knew it was true. *Dig two graves.* 'You made this,' I shouted. 'Half my life spent running from people or chasing them, and why? Because Colonel fucking Holderness deems it so.'

'Why do you think I cut you so much slack?' His accent had entirely slipped, he was waving the submachine gun around like a man possessed. 'How much have I turned a blind eye to over the years?'

'Slack? You've cut me slack? Sending me off on suicide missions every other month? Maybe they were right, maybe it is you I should kill, not the Golubevs of this world.'

He just stared down.

'I'm done,' I said. 'Done.'

Holderness slung the submachine gun around his shoulder and adjusted his flat cap.

'There's no hunting like the hunting of men, Tyler,' he said. 'Remember, those who've hunted armed men long enough, and like it, don't care for much else afterwards.'

Above me Holderness turned away, disappearing below the crest of the hill.

I looked again at the pistol in my hands, and at the corpse of its previous owner. The faces came back all at once, drowning in the sea, hanging in a hotel room, clawing across a carpet, spluttering to death in the driver's seat of an ASBO-green '71 Plymouth 'Cuda.

I took a deep breath and stood, still rubbing my thumb across the lettering stamped into the pistol, the reminders scratched across its surface.

I tossed it into the mud. It slapped then sank.

Epilogue

I pulled the car up close to the doors on the double yellows and waited, much to the annoyance of someone waiting for a taxi and a couple having a fag under the shelter.

'Oi, dickhead, there's a car park over there,' said a morbidly obese middle-aged man intent on blowing smoke all over everyone who went in or out of the hospital. He scowled and flicked his tab end at the car windscreen. It showered sparks across the glass and disappeared into the gutter.

I wound the window down, pulled out my wallet, and flashed one of my more authoritative fake IDs. 'Get your fat arse down there and pick that up and we'll say no more, sunshine.'

He put his head down and picked up the smoking butt, muttering as he ground it into the ashtray bin and plodded back inside the Royal Lancaster Infirmary.

As he did, he passed Alice. She walked slowly, gingerly, one hand on her ribs. I got out and ran over to her, but she put a hand out to stop me. 'Don't touch me, I swear I'll tear in half if I move too fast. You didn't come to see me.'

'I can't stand hospitals, they knock me sick.'

'And you couldn't even call?'

'It's only been a couple of days. Holderness had me down in London.'

'Hmmm.'

'He's smoothed things with the Americans, just like we agreed. Officially we're both dead at Golubev's hands.'

'The second time you've died.'

'More like the fifth. Maybe sixth.'

'Well, anyway, that's good of Holderness.'

353

'He doesn't have an altruistic bone in his body. Mason sent CIA agents on a wild goose chase to Siberia as part of a conspiracy to assassinate a high-ranking British intelligence officer. Holderness will have him over a barrel for a while for cleaning his mess up. Besides, I did call!'

'You rang twice. In five days. And me, all shot up and left for dead.'

'I've been shot more times than that on a weekday before breakfast.'

'All right, Action Man, and look where it's got you. Have some sympathy.'

'Sympathy? Alice, when we met in Scotland I was shot at, stabbed, beaten, crashed, and do you know what you did?'

'This again.' She rolled her eyes.

'You shot me.'

'I didn't *actually* shoot you though, did I?'

'Look, are you getting in or what?'

'Don't tell me, it's a… Ford…'

'Mitsubishi Starion.'

She clicked her fingers. 'That's the one. Hey, did you know, there are only like five of these on the road or something.'

I opened the door and helped her into the seat, then reached over her to click the belt in.

'You smell nice,' she said.

'My mate bought me some nice perfume from a trip.'

I slammed her door and walked round to the driver's side. I climbed in and pulled the seatbelt on. 'I didn't want to ring too much. Thought I'd leave you alone to finish that book.'

Her face reddened. 'It wasn't for me, sorry.'

'I thought it had a good message.'

'You've read it?'

'The interesting parts. You don't think I'm stupid, do you?'

She inhaled deeply, winced, and stared straight ahead. 'I was never going to do it, you know.'

'Because you needed me to get you out of there?'

'Because I am not an assassin.' She turned and looked into my eyes. 'I told you why I killed Gambetta in Scotland. I don't just blindly follow orders, especially to kill. I'm not *you*.'

354

I clicked onto the defensive, considering a retort – but there wasn't one. A taxi beeped behind me.

'You should have told me.'

'I'd spent half an hour with you, after thinking you were dead for two years. Why would I tell you anything?'

'How can I trust you?' I asked.

'You think I trust you? Look, you know my main takeaway from prison? Revenge kills you. If I'd told you the truth, that they wanted you dead, you'd be off again, to America to kill someone else. It never ends, only when you're dead. Well, you are dead now, so forget about them and make the most of life.'

The taxi beeped again, the driver shouted something. I put the key in the ignition.

'It's not bumpy, is it?' She clutched her side. 'I have stitches.'

'I have stitches, too.' I twisted the key, the turbocharged two-litre engine roared and settled to a burble from the oversized exhaust.

'Why is it so loud? Is it broken?'

I rolled my eyes.

'Can't you drive a normal car?' she asked. 'Where are we going? I can't go back to yours, if that's okay?'

'I get it. Memories.' I put the car in gear and pulled out of the car park onto the main road.

'It's more the fact it's cold, damp, draughty and smells like books.'

'It's old.'

'So… are you ever gonna tell me?'

'Tell you what?'

'You know, how did Professor Balakin kill Professor Balakin? How did he resurrect himself after you found him burning?'

'You not worked it out?'

'Obviously not, don't be a dick about it.'

'Just keep thinking, you'll get it.'

She punched me in the side. 'Which side did he kick you on?'

The car lurched onto the wrong side of the road as I winced, before pulling it back. 'Jesus Christ.'

'Sorry, did that actually hurt?'

'What do you think? He broke my rib.'

'Sorry.' She stared out of the window at the trees. 'Look,' she said after a minute, 'just tell me how he did it or I'll punch you again.'

'It's really simple. I mean stupidly so. You'll kick yourself.'

'Go on.'

'We believed this man, Ivan Golubev, *was* Professor Balakin. We'd never met him before, had no reason to doubt it. So when we believed his life was at risk we went along with it, sleeping down in that bunker with him. In reality, we were playing a part in his plan to set up the perfect murder. Like I said before, it's that big portrait of Brezhnev in his room that swung it. It was set up above a sink. Who has a portrait above a sink? You have a mirror above a sink.'

'I'm still not getting it.'

'Do you remember when you came to my room?'

'Well, yes.'

'There was a big old mirror leaning against the wall.'

'Yes, I recall.' Her face went red.

'So the mirror had been taken down from his room, and a portrait had been hung in its place.' I looked across at Alice. 'And that was the key to it.'

'Why is the portrait important?' she asked.

'It isn't,' I said. 'But the mirror is. Why was it moved?'

'Go on?'

'Think about what I did when I woke. I heard the shots and the screams, I broke the door down, I knew Balakin was on fire. I could instantly see the glow and the smoke from his room at the end of that short corridor. So I ran straight into his room, and turned to find what I already knew, Balakin ablaze. But what would I have seen if that mirror had been on the wall?'

'Pass.'

'As I opened the door, I'd have seen the reflection of Ivan Golubev back along the corridor behind me, hiding round that first door I'd kicked open.'

'But... then who was burning?'

'Professor Balakin.'

'I'm lost.'

'The real Professor Balakin, who Golubev had killed before you arrived. Burton had met the real prof. He must have been suspicious, so he had to die straight away.'

'I'm just about following.'

'The real Balakin's body was burned. That's the weird thing about supposed spontaneous combustion victims. They're always burned up far too much while the room around them is relatively unscathed. The real Balakin was burned for hours, then sealed inside an airtight plastic bag like leftover food.'

'That's disgusting.'

'But necessary. Why burned? To disfigure the corpse, hide his features, so we wouldn't question his identity.'

'But we checked the entire bunker top to bottom.'

'And I had my bloody feet up on it while we talked, it was folded in that big plastic suitcase, easy enough. All Ivan had to do was wait until the early hours then prop it on a chair, bit of petrol from a bottle, whoomph. Scream and holler, fire a few gunshots at the wall, exit the room, hide behind that first door. In bursts me, and my attention is instantly grabbed by the very thing I fully expect to see by this point, which is a burning corpse. I don't notice Ivan Golubev slipping out behind me and running off.

'Now it's easy, he just hides in one of the other rooms while we make our escape. But out comes you, running like a mad woman to see what's going on, so he clonks you on the head from behind. You were lucky, he could have killed you, that would have really confused me.'

'What do you mean by that?'

'Well, you *were* the only other person in there.'

'You didn't seriously think I did it?'

I looked over at her and smiled. 'I mean, you've got form.'

'You're a bastard.'

'I've never hidden that. Anyway, both doors are sealed, he's hiding in one of the other rooms somewhere, we head out. They couldn't let us get away too easily. Golubev the younger threw in a couple of hints that he knew Balakin had given us information, make it known that I had a short window to kill Holderness. Send Abi along to help us "escape" and keep tabs on me. All wrapped up neatly.'

'You're right.'

'About what?'

'It is simple. Annoyingly so. I hate it.'

'That's the way it goes.'

Alice leaned her head on the window, staring out at the Victorian buildings zipping past, the battlements of the castle and old prison flashing between roofs. She was quiet for a couple of minutes as she processed everything. I let her stare at the river meandering past for a while, before breaking the silence.

'Any more thoughts on what you're doing for Christmas?'

She sighed and pulled her head off the window. 'Well, almost everyone on the planet thinks we're dead. There's no one left to come after you, and no one left for you to find. As long as your friend Colonel Holderness is good to his word then we can relax a bit.'

'And do what?'

'Well, I was thinking a holiday. Christmassy. You fancy coming to the Alps?'

I sucked in through my teeth. 'Not good for me, I'm afraid.'

I took the turn onto a dual carriageway, accelerating over a bridge with a roar from the exhaust.

Alice looked down at the wide shining river below. 'Germany?'

'Too many bad memories. How about Finland?' I said, with a grin.

'Absolutely never going there again. Denmark?'

'Used to know someone from Denmark.'

'Scotland?' we both said together, and laughed.

'Why don't you tell me where you haven't worked?' she said.

'Well, I was thinking. I've got this job planned, and I could do with a hand.'

'What? I thought you were done?'

'Just this one last thing.'

'No chance, no way. Turn around, take me to a hotel and fuck off on your merry way.'

'You don't even want to hear about it?'

'Is it dangerous?'

'Maybe.'

'Cold?'

'Definitely.'

'I'm out.'

'That's a shame. See, I know this place in Siberia. Private island, big old hotel on it. Grim place, lots of ghosts. But the thing is, no one lives there.'

'Any more.'

'Any more,' I nodded. 'And there's this big underground bunker that's full of approximately fifty million dollars' worth of diamonds and bullion and cold hard cash. Just sat there. Completely unguarded.'

She frowned. 'But...'

'But no one knows the Golubev brothers are dead. So no one is going to be heading there any time soon.'

I pressed the accelerator into the carpet, the turbo whined as we sped up the slip road of the M6 motorway.

'Maybe I *could* come out of retirement,' she said. 'Just for one last job.'

I winked. 'One last job.'

Acknowledgements

Books are a collaborative endeavour, and I owe a massive debt of gratitude to a huge number of people who've supported not just *77 North*, but this whole trilogy. Special thanks go to my editor, Craig Lye, who has helped me from the moment Tyler touched down in Scotland. These books are very different – and far better – thanks to his amendments, suggestions and guidance.

Everyone at Canelo, including but not limited to Iain Millar, Michael Bhaskar, Kate Shepherd, Thanhmai Bui-Van, Nicola Piggott and Claudine Sagoe. Enormous thanks to The Red Dress for taking the cover of this third book in a new direction, so good it led to their new covers for the rereleased *Anthrax Island* and *Black Run*. Thanks, too, to copy-editor Lesley McDowell and proof-reader Rachel Malig.

Thank you to the best agent on earth, the awesome Phil Patterson, who spots all the references and can always be guaranteed to roll out a movie quote or obscure anecdote. No other agent would have been able to steer and champion these books as enthusiastically. Thanks also to Sandra and Guy, and everyone at Marjacq.

Kate Simants, who I've learned a heck of a lot from, and applied it where I could. Likewise everyone at Noiser, especially Mac, Katrina and Pascal.

Jules, always my first reader and whose comments, feedback and enthusiasm over biscuits and films helped shape these books into the trilogy they became. Very sorry about the foot. Likewise Bob, always my second reader, whose feedback moulded these books into a state ready to press send on, ever a cheerleader and influencer. Sorry about the yachting incident.

Scragg, Parker, Vic, Effie, Roxie, Russ, Chris and Mik were there providing entertainment and support (and memes) throughout lock-down, before *Anthrax Island* was published, and have been here ever since. Sorry I've repaid that love by killing most of you.

Blood Brothers, Bloody Scotland, Theakston's Crime Fest, Newcastle Noir, Hull Noir, New Writing North and the Northern Writers' Awards all do incredible work supporting writers. All the writers, bloggers, reviewers, readers and booksellers that have supported me, with special shoutouts to Helen and James at Forum/The Bound, and Andreas (hope you were looking out of the window when Tyler drove past).

Everyone who read *Anthrax Island* and *Black Run*, which made it possible for me to complete the journey with *77 North*.

Finally, my family – Louby, who has been by my side right through Tyler's story, from the north-west Highlands of Scotland to north Lancashire, via the French Alps and La Rochelle, Salcombe in Devon, Skipton and Ingleton in North Yorkshire, San Anselmo in California, and London (and also to Siberia and Nambutu in my babblings). And my two little bookworms, who it sometimes seemed were trying their hardest to prevent these books from being written, but are nevertheless the biggest and best cheerleaders a dad could have.

Thank you.